IMPACT

MARK D. OWEN

ISBN: 978-1-09835-939-3 (printed)

ISBN: 978-1-09835-940-9 (eBook)

CONTENTS

PART 1:

MOONBASE VERITY

CHAPTER 1:

Conflict

"Conflict begins with miscommunication and often ends with calamity."
—*Journal of Kohlrabi Trust*

Commander Choi disregarded the Japanese astronaut's hand signals motioning him to slow his approach from the cupola windows on dock 7 of the International Space Station (ISS). After a thousand simulations, today he would become the first North Korean pilot to dock at the ISS. Uttering a racial slur under his breath, he mocked their waving arms. His decision to come in hot to make them a little scared caused them to motion him away frantically. Realizing his mistake too late, he heard the scream of his copilot as he fired his reverse thrusters. White hands gripped the throttle as his eyes opened wide with fear, then regret and resignation. The jolting impact against his restraints and the deafening crunch of metal told him he was still alive. He looked over at his copilot to see a bulkhead truss had pierced his suit, and he was writhing in pain. "I'm sorry," he said in Korean, the last words on the recording before the explosion ended all their lives, leaving the ISS module ripped and contorted.

* * *

Dr. Kohlrabi Trust awoke with a start, sure that something was wrong, sat up in his bed, and listened to the quiet hum of the air scrubbers and creaks in the ducting on Moonbase Verity space station. Nothing sounded out of the ordinary. Turning on the light panel beside his bed, he looked slowly around the room. Nothing seemed out of place. He walked across the floor out into his office near the top of the dome and peered down the two flights of stairs to the main galley; a whiff of olive cooking oil and garlic spices from the evening meal was still present.

He swiped his hand across his holodesk, activating the displays in the room. Images on the wall from the central domes and access ports were all devoid of action except for a few scientists playing a card game in the lounge. The system monitors showing air pressure, temperature, and dozens of other parameters were all nominal, but he couldn't shake the feeling that something was wrong.

He tapped his news feed, looking for alerts from any of the fourteen countries represented on Moonbase Verity. An urgent symbol rotated by the NASA feed labeled *Crash at ISS.*

That must be it, he thought. Tapping the symbol, he was given direct access to the video feed from the North Korean ship's cockpit as it crashed only moments earlier. He watched the different views, the frantic Japanese signals, the smug expression on Commander Choi's face changing to alarm, fear, regret, and finally, resignation. He wrote his observations carefully in his Journal. Finally, he sat up straight, looked up toward the ceiling, and breathed in and out in a practiced Zen breathing technique, the beginning of his morning meditation routine.

He arose and dressed, consciously aware of the unpleasant tasks of the day. As the governor coordinating the work of fourteen countries represented at Moonbase Verity, he managed the scientific and facility priorities, encouraging peaceful respect among the elite scientists. He loved the math and science, he enjoyed coaching people, but he hated the petty rivalries and jealousies, which always tagged along with those who excelled.

Two of the leaders from different research teams entered Kohlrabi's two by three meter office and took a seat across from his desk. All space was a premium on the Moonbase, with 224 people living and working under sixteen domes. In the crowded conditions, tempers flared.

"Dr. Nakahara, tell me what this is about." Kohlrabi requested details to slow emotions enough to work toward a solution.

"Thank you. As you know, the Japanese labs are developing robots for tasks in space. We loaned one to the French team. Now I found out they dismantled it, apparently to copy our design," the Japanese engineer began quietly in fluent English but ended loudly with an overtly strong accusation. Theft of intellectual property was the most severe crime at the base, next to murder, which so far had been avoided.

Dr. Leblanc could hardly restrain himself. Raising his hand to quiet them both, Kohlrabi asked softly, "Pierre, please tell us how you are using the robot and why you dismantled it."

"*Merci.* We are adapting household appliances for use in lower gravity environments like the Moonbase or on space vessels. The Japanese robot enables reliability testing, taking coffee out of the espresso machine, loading the dishwasher, etc. However, humans tend to lift things faster in the moon's gravity and hit the appliance's frame. Our minds take some time to overcome the information learned on Earth. The robot was so precise we introduced some randomness into the tests by printing some of its structural elements out of a flexible polymer. The flexibility introduced randomness. We dismantled and measured parts to 3D print these polymer components. While I can see how Dr. Nakahara could misunderstand our intent, we cannot allow such flagrant accusations to continue." The two leaders sneered at each other menacingly.

"Do you acknowledge, Dr. Leblanc, that dismantling another's tools without their permission is a violation of our agreement signed by all fourteen countries?" Kohlrabi looked at him until he shrugged, raised his hands, and nodded his head at least partially up and down. "Is that a yes?"

"Yes, I should have asked for permission." Dr. Leblanc stated flatly.

"Dr. Nakahara, your accusation of IP theft is a direct violation of the same agreement, which specifically states that all concerns or accusations will be brought first to the governor before being voiced publicly or to the perceived offending party. Do you also agree you violated these stipulations?" Kohlrabi's face was impassive and stern.

"Governor Trust, I had no intention..." Dr. Nakahara's face contorted in contrition, as only the Japanese can, genuinely surprised he had done something wrong.

"I'll take that as a yes. Based on my authority as governor of Moonbase Verity, both of you will be charged with a violation of the treaty and returned to Earth on the next transport ship." The two sat stunned at this announcement. Kohlrabi waited silently for some time for the impact of such a decision to be thoroughly contemplated. Each was a team leader, and such an outcome would damage their research, reputations, and countries.

Dr. Leblanc spoke first, "Dr. Trust, governor, if there is any other way to make this right, I, we, would be glad to consider it." Dr. Nakahara nodded his head rapidly, and then bowed his head low, almost to the table.

Kohlrabi waited a moment before replying while shaking his head. "You damaged trust within this facility and openly accused an esteemed colleague of a crime, breaking the treaty I am tasked with enforcing to maintain the fragile peace we enjoy here. What could you possibly propose to make this right?"

Dr. Leblanc, thinking fast, proposed, "How about if I pay for the materials for another entire robot. I will delete all related photos and records. I will request that Dr. Nakahara help us solve the randomizing problem, and we will sit together at dinner and show everyone we are now cooperating?" The Japanese engineer nodded affirmation to each proposal, and they looked expectantly at Kohlrabi.

The governor continued to shake his head. "Friendly cooperation was the right way to begin and would be useful now, but it is insufficient.

I think I must make an example to maintain justice, order, and peace." He stood to signal that the meeting was done.

Both researchers spoke simultaneously, uttering accusations and pointing at each other. The governor waited a moment and then slapped the table loudly and again signaled the meeting was complete. No one moved for a long, pregnant moment, but slowly their shoulders rounded, their understanding of their predicament sinking in.

Finally, Dr. Nakahara stood and motioned for Kohlrabi to please sit down. "I responded arrogantly and with unjustified indignation without sufficient information. I will stand at dinner tonight and apologize to all teams for violating the agreement and accusing my respected colleague unjustly. Only one of us needs to pay for my offense; I will resign and take the next transport to Earth." The contrition on his face was total, looking like he would cry in humiliation. He sat back down slowly, shoulders slumped, head bowed.

The humble apology seemed to break the scientist's resolve; the lines on his face visibly softened. The Frenchman stood and put his hand on the other man's shoulder and spoke facing Kohlrabi. "No, he's right; only one of us should pay for my mistake. I will apologize to everyone and resign." Then turning to the engineer, "Nakahara-san, please forgive me."

Still standing, Kohlrabi did not delay this time, not wanting to keep them in their pain any longer than necessary. "If you proceed as proposed with friendly cooperation and publicly apologize to each other at dinner tonight, I will suspend your sentence indefinitely."

The two men shook hands with each other and began walking toward the door. Kohlrabi said, "Dr. Nakahara, please stay for a moment."

Once the door closed, he said, "Tokai, I was informed that there was an incident on the ISS, and three astronauts from Japan died. They were your colleagues and perhaps your friends. I'll let you know when their names are released. I'm sorry for your loss."

Dr. Nakahara exhaled deeply and squeezed his eyes tight for a minute. Then he looked up and said, "I knew them all well. We trained together, and I spent time on the ISS before coming to Verity. This puts my earlier foolishness in perspective," he said with self-disgust in his voice.

Feeling compassion for his grief, Kohlrabi said, "There will be a full investigation, and we must not allow the incident to color the peaceful respect we enjoy here. I will need your leadership here. May I suggest that you spend time embracing your pain, allowing it to make you mindful of the value of your life and thankful for your many blessings?"

* * *

Tamarind Chase sat alone in his office at DroneTech, unaware the ISS explosion would trigger a series of events that would change his life direction. At 28 years old, he was healthy, his company was thriving, and his future was bright. The VP of Business Development's walls and holodesk were adorned with product images, patents, and scrolling images of adventures with friends.

One image showed the groundbreaking of DroneTech, the eager and excited faces of his two friends and himself proud in their accomplishment. He remembered that day—three orphans, graduates of the Pan-National Leadership Institute (PNLI), starting a bold, new company to develop a new generation of drones that would solve world problems. It felt different now—they weren't just three friends anymore.

Tamarind had a reputation for finding creative solutions to impossible problems. He had not, however, solved this problem. Though distracted and agitated, he kept the scheduled call with Moonbase Verity. The connection from the crisp display on his office desk in Colorado to the moon was not real-time, requiring him to use short phrases and wait for responses due to the two-second time delay. Speak. Pause. Speak.

"Good morning, Kohlrabi," Tamarind said. His friend was rubbing the pink skin on his cheek, still visible on his dark skin, a scar from last month's airlock failure. In the backdrop of Verity's white offices and labs, his face was almost the only color in the room. "Your injury is healing well." Pause.

Tamarind and Kohlrabi had grown up together with the other orphans trained at the PNLI.

"Good evening, Tamarind. Yes, it is getting better, but it itches inexplicably. How was the wedding last week? Did many of the Pan-Nationals make it?

"Yes, in addition to Flax and Almond, of course, Mace, Lavender, and Jasmine were able to make it. It was good to see everyone again. Taro came late—you know how busy he can get looking for aliens." They both laughed at Taro's chronic habit of showing up late and blaming his work at the Search for Extraterrestrial Intelligence (SETI).

"Sounds like a veritable stir-fry of Pan-Nationals," joked Kohlrabi. "So sorry I missed it. When you get more than a few of us together, the names they gave us sound kind of ridiculous."

"Rescued us from the dirt and grew us into something useful," said Tamarind. The alumni of the PNLI had many puns around the names they were given as students at the Institute. Their first names were assigned when they arrived, and their surnames when they graduated.

"Meanwhile, I'm covered in regolith and surrounded by scientists a little too impressed with their usefulness." Kohlrabi rarely complained, so Tamarind pressed him for details.

"What's going on?"

"I love the science and the mathematics of experimental analysis, but there are days where the squabbles between the researchers make me wonder why I am here."

"You are there because you are a mathematical genius, can find research errors no one else can, and respected by every scientist and all the host nations. No need to wonder," Tamarind said.

"Thank you, my friend." Gathering himself, Kohlrabi turned the conversation. "Tell me, have you recovered from the wedding?"

"Not feeling so creative today, I haven't yet invented your drone transport." The technical problem was not the issue, and his friend saw through this.

"Flax and Almond are your best friends. You want to be happy for them, but it is hard when you are in love with Almond." Kohlrabi could always read Tamarind, evidently even from the moon.

In the long pause that followed, Tamarind shifted in his chair and considered denying this, but his friend's blunt directness had nailed it. "I'm so transparent. They are coming back today, and I'm not quite ready to see them. I realize that a lot of my motivation to excel was to impress Almond."

"Not transparent, but I've known of your love for her for years. You aren't the first or last man trying to impress a woman. There is no shame in the pursuit, at least up until their marriage. I'm sure it will bring awkwardness into your friendship for a while that none of you want, but they are your family and your closest friends. Don't run from your feelings or bury them. Turn your passion to acceptance and use it to nurture a crisp mindfulness." Kohlrabi subconsciously stacked his arms on top of each other when dispensing his Buddhist counsel.

"Passion to acceptance to mindfulness," Tamarind repeated, appreciating the friendship behind the advice without having any idea what it meant. "You were always the wise one among us," he said, grinning and bowing his head in mock respect.

"Wisdom? No, I've barely achieved Relevance," Kohlrabi said, grinning slightly.

Shifting uncomfortably in his chair, he changed the topic to the news he'd seen that morning. "Did you hear about the accident on the ISS?"

"No, what happened?"

"North Korea failed in its first docking procedure, killing both Korean pilots and three Japanese astronauts on the ISS. No room for errors in space. NASA shuttles our supplies through that station, and many of our staff here are from Japan or the joint Korea Federation. Could you see what you can find out about this for me?" Kohlrabi asked. Scientists on Moonbase Verity received news from biased national sources, limited by bandwidth and time delays. As governor, he often ended up as the peace-maker, needing more info than he could obtain efficiently.

"Will do. I'll know more on our call tomorrow. ERIWA, my friend."

"ERIWA, be well, my friend." They both ended with their Pan-National acronym of encouragement.

Tamarind usually enjoyed updates on the base's research progress, but today he was just ready to end the call. He picked up the cube of black ilmenite rock that Kohlrabi had sent him, twirling it on corners between his index finger and thumb. Someday it might become the source for much titanium and oxygen on the moon, but much must be done first.

After the call, he set up an AI newsagent to track, sift, translate, and sort news or responses related to the ISS incident from anywhere in the world to review during his breakfast the next day. Checking the time, he grew anxious, spinning the cube of rock faster between his fingers, realizing his management meeting with his returning DroneTech cofounders was near. He paused to compose himself before walking down the hall from his office into the meeting room.

* * *

Flax Venture ran with a steady pace, his tall, muscular frame glid-ing gracefully along the wooded path near their new Colorado home. He began as he usually did, considering the blessings in his life—his new mar-riage with Almond came first to mind. As he'd never known before, joy and peace filled him with a sense of hope for the days ahead. He considered his day's tasks, mentally sequencing and pacing each with the rhythm of his footfalls. Finally, he turned to the challenges before him, and his friend Tamarind was at the top. The three were close since growing up at PNLI, but now Flax had married Almond, despite the tension that his best friend loved her too. As he turned the final corner to his street, he saw Almond waiting for him on the porch.

Almond Brighten met him as he sprinted up the stairs. She placed a hand in the middle of his chest, "Need any help in the shower, husband?" She was satisfied with his blush at their new intimacy, smiling to herself as he sprinted up the stairs. She went into the kitchen of her house, full of plants, books, colors, and smells she had chosen. She knew she would need to change things to incorporate his interests as he settled in, but not today. His tastes were so bland; perhaps she could win him over to hers?

She clipped some microgreens from her garden wall and added them to the fruits and vegetables she'd collected for their morning juice drink. She hummed an ethereal tune as she moved gracefully around the kitchen, preparing for and excited for her day.

She could see Flax had business on his mind as he joined her for breakfast, but she didn't ask him about it. Now that they were married, they would have to find a separation between work and home life. They were business partners and long-time friends and would have to carve out time to learn to become marriage partners. He ate quietly, and she removed the dishes from the table as they finished getting ready to leave their house.

As they drove into the office together, Flax finally voiced his concern. "Do you think he will finally be settled?"

"When have we ever known Tamarind to be settled? His arc is always to infinity; he settles for nothing. I chose you, my husband, and now we must make that as painless as possible for our friend." She looked out at the crisp sky and snow-capped mountains, so different from their recent honeymoon.

They smiled through the greetings and cheers as they entered the DroneTech offices beneath the tall ceiling suspending the company's drones. Finally, Almond tugged his hand as they walked down the hallway, entered the conference room, and sat together on one side of the conference table.

* * *

As Tamarind entered the conference room a few minutes later, the newlyweds were seated on one side of the eight-person cherry conference table, turned toward each other with broad smiles, and still had a glow about them. Ugh. Flax's blond hair contrasted their newly tanned skin. Tamarind could smell Almond's perfume, a sweet smell of amaretto and cherry, as he stood in the entrance to the small room. They appeared to be holding hands under the table. Double ugh.

Mustering a smile, he walked confidently up to the table. With feigned seriousness, he said, "We have a company to run here, are you two engaged?"

"Not anymore," Almond said, holding up her ring finger with a smile. It sparkled against her skin under the bright LED lights illuminating the room. Flax stood and shook Tamarind's hand warmly, his eyes excited to see his friend.

"You enjoyed your honeymoon, then?" Tamarind asked. His eyes slowly moved from the ring up her bare arm before looking at Almond in the face. He blinked, flushing at the sudden intimacy of her eyes, and turned toward Flax for the answer, releasing his grip.

Almond also turned toward Flax, waiting for him to answer. The new groom grinned, "Oregon is beautiful in the summer. Beautiful beach, beautiful wife, gorgeous sunsets, what's not to like?" The couple gazed into each other's eyes for a long moment. Tamarind sat loudly in his chair and began picking at a string on his shirt sleeve.

Conscious of his friend's discomfort, the DroneTech CEO started the meeting on task. "How did everything go at the company while we were gone?"

"I checked in with each of the department heads during the week; they seem to be working enthusiastically on all the right things." Tamarind was vague but knew Flax was asking if there were any crises while he was gone.

What is the status of the opportunity for P291's at Verity?"

"Their need is real, valuable, and well-defined, but I haven't solved the propulsion problem. They certainly won't be standard P291 drones. Kohlrabi is anticipating a solution and is being patient." He realized he still had the black cube of ilmenite in his hand and was spinning it by the corners.

Flax proceeded. "You are the most creative person I've ever known. I'm sure you'll come up with something. Let me know if you need additional engineering resources. Almond, do you want to tell him about your new project?"

"Remember how I came up with our tranq dart formulation while studying the effects of curare on the central nervous system?" Tamarind nodded. "I'm now looking at how certain proteins can trigger hibernation in some animals and how animals and insects can be frozen and can completely recover. I hope we can develop a long shelf-life and safe medication to induce medical stasis during a hospital recovery or long-distant transport, perhaps even space flight. Not everyone can afford a chemically induced coma in a hospital."

"Sounds intriguing." Tamarind's bland response stilted the conversation. Glancing down the table, Almond shifted uncomfortably in her seat. Flax kept the meeting moving forward.

"Our communications drones are going through their final software test," Flax continued, "We should be able to deliver high-speed internet connections to the most remote and under-served parts of the planet very soon."

His cofounders beamed with energy about this, a long-held goal of the company, but Tamarind just smiled distantly while looking down at the cube. "That is good news. Do you mind if we cut the meeting short? I want to get back to this problem," Tamarind said.

"Is something else wrong, Tamarind?" Almond asked, her fingers scratching at the tabletop, hoping he didn't mention her in his answer.

He looked directly into her eyes and held her gaze silently for a long moment. "Kohlrabi is concerned about the accident on the ISS and how it might affect him at Verity. I've agreed to sift the international tensions related to this incident for him."

Seeing he wasn't his usual cheerful self, they waved him off with encouraging smiles. Their friend rose and moved off without further comment.

"Not very settled." Flax said.

"Give him time, my love."

CHAPTER 2

Escalation

"Conflicts only escalate with active participation by both sides." —Journal of Kohlrabi Trust

As he walked back to his office, Tamarind considered Kohlrabi's words—"passion to acceptance to mindfulness."

Does that mean I should think about my 'passion' until I accept the outcome? That will make me a more mindful person somehow? That didn't make any sense to him. Closing the door and sitting at his desk, he breathed in and out several times with his eyes closed, shifting his mind consciously away from his distraction back to the problem at hand.

Then he began brainstorming on Kohlrabi's drone request. One of the most dangerous and time-consuming activities on the moon was moving supplies from the landing site to the base, moving objects between the domes, and research excursions on the moon's surface. Last month's airlock failure, where a rover had bumped the loading door, had damaged their fresh food stores and given Kohlrabi the scar on his face. This accident had elevated the Moonbase governor's interest in the possibility of an automated drone taking over some of the base's routine transport tasks.

The central problem was how to provide lift on the moon. The default solutions of rockets and compressed gases have weight to payload issues, making them impractical. He couldn't think of any improvements or modifications to significantly change that. Dronetech's propellers wouldn't work without an atmosphere.

As he considered the goals and problem constraints, he began to resolve them with playful and fanciful solutions. He sketched the domes of the Moonbase and linked them with zip lines. He added drones with ion thrusters. Hyperloop underground monorails. Balloons. He spent some time considering creating an atmosphere on the moon or changing any of the other constraints. Didn't they use pneumatic tubes to deliver mail at some point a long time ago? Maybe a pneumatic or electromagnetic cannon and a net? He added each idea to the sketch, expanding across his holodesk. The net reminded him of a spiderweb, and he sketched a giant hairy spider crawling across the moon carrying a backpack. *Perhaps jumping spiders? If they got high enough, we could triangulate off surface features.* His drawing was covered with fanciful ideas. New connections appeared that he had not considered before. The project objectives and the problem constraints seemed to loom over his concepts, gliding in his mind toward the best fit. He stopped hearing the office sounds from the hallway, his cloud of emotions eased, and ideas converged toward an elegantly simple solution.

His AI agent had filled his feed the next morning with information about the ISS incident. He sat in his spartan apartment, filled with exercise equipment and dirty laundry, at his tiny kitchen table, watching the feed while eating his equally simple breakfast of twenty-grain bread and mixed fruit juice.

The Japanese honored their astronauts as national heroes and attributed their accidental deaths to the North Koreans' incompetence, incensing both countries' people.

Tensions were already high between the two nations in the weeks leading up to the space station's accident. North Korea had accused the Japanese of spying with their satellites, stealing intellectual property, and improperly leveraging their regional lock on satellite communications to keep them out. The previous week, an incident where the near-collision of Japanese and North Korean fishing vessels ended in threats.

The Japanese astronauts on the ISS were commanded to build a peaceful exchange by assisting the first North Korean docking at the station and symbolically welcoming them into the international space community. Now the astronauts from both countries were dead. The two countries' verbal exchanges had ratcheted up before the incident on the space station and hardened now to a fever pitch.

Tamarind read the subtitles as the Japanese Prime Minister, Kubo Takatomo, spoke, "Once again, North Korea demonstrates their incompetence, this time in space. Japan can no longer tolerate these supposed accidents, and we demand that they remain grounded until full reparations are made."

Profiles of the five dead astronauts cycled through the news feeds worldwide in various languages, all verbally translated to English by his AI agent, with added statistics and projections based upon the growing frequency of reports, the expansion into new regions, and the inflammatory words used. The rest of the feed was about the crash accident and the portion of the released video clip clearly showing the warning signals from the Japanese astronauts preceding the impact and the explosion. Analysts were all over this with drawings, frame by frame sequences, and talking heads debating what went wrong.

So many opinions, thought Tamarind. *from those who never are at risk.* He hated the talking head shows of experts that debated things and placed blame.

He scrolled through the AI agent's summary of statements by the pundits and analysts, each seeming to outdo the other by ever more fanciful projections. Could lead to war in the far east. Might disrupt the global telecommunications industry. Would the UN act, or would they wait until the conflict escalated as they usually do? One analyst predicted the destruction of all satellites just from the debris. Another predicted deaths on the ground from falling shrapnel. Another forecasted that this uncertainty would lead to an economic crisis. Tamarind finally stopped the feed, a look of disgust across his face as he packed his stuff for the office.

His red electric sports car was his one indulgence, and rather than driving the back roads into work, he set the autopilot and continued with his news feed, considering how he was going to communicate all this to his friend on the moon. The feed on his dashboard display stopped abruptly and transferred to a real-time picture of a series of rockets in the sky and an American news announcer's voice, "Japan has just launched ten or more rockets into space. These appear to be warheads. There was no announcement; this must be their response to the North Korean attack earlier today. More as it becomes available."

"What North Korean attack?" Tamarind asked. He'd programmed his AI newsagent to provide info on the ISS incident. Evidently, it decided the missile launch that destroyed a Japanese satellite a few hours earlier irrelevant.

By the time Tamarind commuted into his office, a global storm had erupted, and everyone was clustered around displays in the Dronetech offices and public spaces, murmuring about the crisis. Tamarind pushed through the crowded hallways and quickly activated his office holodesk with his door closed.

North Korea had launched a missile without any warning, destroying a Japanese satellite, and issued a seven-word press release. "A Japanese spy satellite was destroyed today."

The debris from the Japanese satellite had struck an orbiting Russian military command communication array, damaging it. The Russian military was on full alert but clarified that North Korea had the right to defend itself from Japanese aggression.

The image he'd seen while driving was the Japanese response—blasting all 36 of North Korea's military satellites out of the sky. A junior minister angrily said on the feed that the North Koreans should "stay on earth and squalor in the mud where they belong."

Within another hour, it became clear that the Japanese attack on the satellites was more than an international incident, and more even than a declaration of war between the two countries. It had generated a significant amount of space debris, destroying a second Russian military satellite and a Chinese communications array.

"This is insanity, slow down people," Tamarind said out loud to himself. Usually, international hostilities go through a progression of insults, accusations, defining boundaries, and threats expanding over weeks or months before they come to blows. Why would either country escalate this so quickly?

Since Kohlrabi Trust had members of each of these nations on Moonbase Verity, Tamarind contacted him immediately and brought him up to speed with what he'd learned.

"Kohlrabi," Tamarind began, speaking into his holodesk display, "I can't imagine Russia and China not responding in kind." He paused to allow for the communications delay to the moon.

The Moonbase governor ran his hand over his short afro and shook his head as he considered these actions' implications. "What are they thinking? This will elevate tensions here. What is the international community saying?" Small lines formed between his eyebrows as he spoke.

"Predictable accusations and counter-accusations and threats from the North Koreans and the Japanese. There have been calls for peace from several world leaders. The Russians criticized the Japanese for a disproportionate response and demanded sanctions."

"Do you think this will expand?

"It will expand. Normally, reasonable nations have diplomatic or verbal exchanges before something escalates to military conflict. I think the historical tensions building between these two shunted all those inter-mediate stages."

"Anything else I should know?" Tamarind spent several minutes summarizing and then forwarding what he'd learned from his AI agent. Kohlrabi took it all in, taking some notes, mentally preparing for the inevitable conflicts that might arise on the Moonbase. After the exchange, he pressed his spread fingertips together with his elbows on his desk, his face contorted with concern. "Do you have any good news?"

Tamarind smiled. "I also have an idea for your transport drones."

"Ah, your creativity has returned. Tell me," Kohlrabi seemed intrigued and welcomed the tenor change in the conversation.

"Think grasshoppers," Tamarind began. "Three legs mounted outside a cylindrical transport container, each leg activated by solenoid actuators and pneumatics. The low gravity will allow them to lift high off the ground. Compressed gas jets will allow side maneuvers while aloft just enough to avoid obstacles and optimize their landing site as necessary. The drones will partially recharge by storing the kinetic energy as the legs cushion their landing."

"Why three legs? Sending me mutant grasshoppers?" Kohlrabi smiled when he saw Tamarind grin.

"Three allows a stable planar base and can be used to induce a spin, using angular momentum to assist in keeping the container upright. Different forces applied to each leg for forward movement. Vision in-flight enables corrections in transit and location to physical features." Tamarind spoke succinctly with the confident knowledge that he'd considered many options, and this was the best one.

"I look forward to the specifications. Send along a sketch and some calculations, and we'll discuss it with our team. This will be a great help to us, Tamarind! Please come and visit us with the first completed unit!" He knew it would be almost impossible for his friend to get approval to bring something to the Moonbase.

"Will do. I need a vacation but might wait until this space fracas calms down. Too much testosterone floating around up there now." Tamarind mock-saluted to signal the meeting's end, and Kohlrabi smiled to see his friend had his humor back.

* * *

Kohlrabi settled into his other tasks for the day, reviewing his daily news dispatch informing him about the expanding space conflict's developments. Troubling as it was, it was also a cause for immediate action. He started searching through his files for a particular article.

Ah, yes, here it is, he thought, reviewing the *Space Physics* journal dated June 1978, by Donald J. Kessler, a NASA scientist. It was mandatory reading for anyone going to or through the ISS to Moonbase Verity. He plunged into the technical paper entitled *Collision frequency of artificial satellites: The creation of a debris belt.* Kessler analyzed the likelihood of satellites colliding and predicted a domino effect; a self-sustaining debris field would form, destroying all the human-made objects in a particular orbit. *He didn't, however, analyze the outcome of an intentional conflict,* Kohlrabi concluded to himself.

Kohlrabi then reviewed the paper's equations and worked to extend them to the current situation—intentional destruction, different orbits, explosions. Within a few hours, the revised model predicted a dire outcome with mathematical certainty that only he was aware of for now.

Next, Kohlrabi reviewed Verity's inventory logs, consumption rates, including those required for future research. Some of the scientific studies could continue for years with sufficient energy, water, and air supplies. However, critical shortages would disable most experiments within two months. Most critically, they would run out of food stores in 7 weeks. *Just seven weeks,* he thought. He created a second model, this time for the rationing of their food sources. He added in the food production in the

Nigerian dome and estimated a sustainable production rate for their crops. It would not be enough; they would need supplies.

CHAPTER 3

Fracas

"An insult morphs into an allegation, an allegation crystallizes into a fracas, and then reason dissolves and what emerges from the cocoon lacks all grace or beauty." —Journal of Kohlrabi Trust

Tamarind's 'space fracas' did not calm down. Other countries saw an opportunity amidst the conflict to disable threatening satellites, annihilating spy or commercial satellites that they perceived infringed on their business or national interests somehow. A whole arsenal of newly developed weapons for space warfare came out of the closet. Mysterious software attacks caused satellites to shut down, spin out of control, overheat, or simply explode. Attack satellites physically disabled others. Missiles from the ground or aircraft destroyed more. Tamarind's AI agent could not sequence the rapidly escalating events.

With 35 nations dependent on the commercial space industry's revenues, each having a significant number of satellites in orbit, each began taking actions both commercial and militaristic to protect their investments.

Before long, dozens of countries destroyed hundreds of satellites. Still, only a tiny fraction of the more than 100,000 in orbit had been affected. The United Nations Secretary-General called for an immediate cessation of hostilities and summoned all the space-capable nations to send representatives to Brussels to negotiate an end to this Space War. Tamarind's 'fracas' blossomed into a full-blown 'space war'!

Tamarind and Kohlrabi connected the next morning. His friend looked haggard and disheveled, unusual for him.

"News of the Space War reached our facility, unfortunately, filtered through the governments of fourteen different nations, all aggressors or victims in this conflict. Our thin veil of peaceful respect was nearly torn last night."

"How did you calm them down?" Tamarind asked.

"I reminded them of why we are here. Moonbase Verity is a model of a peaceful future where all nations can share equally in exploring and sharing space. I told them that we had to stand firm with this vision and call our politicians to a higher standard. Finally, I challenged them." Pretending to look severe, he said, "If athletes can compete in the Olympics during times of war and our politicians can meet in Brussels to negotiate peace, the genius scientists at this station should treat each other with civility. They became unified around their self-perception of superiority and universal disdain for athletes and politicians." The Moonbase governor chuckled at this observation.

Tamarind smiled at him encouragingly. "If there is anyone who can unify research scientists, it is you, Kohlrabi." Of all the PNLI graduates, Dr. Kohlrabi Trust was uniquely skilled for this situation. A prodigy in mathematics and experimental methods, he often was able to find bias or errors in scientific studies that no one else could see. After graduating, he'd used his PNLI grant to establish the KTrust Foundation, which analyzed published research, funded more statistically accurate repeat experiments, and helped scientists design better research avoiding their own biases. Getting a high KTrust score on a paper's conclusions had become necessary to get published in some journals. When it came to understanding people and their hidden motivations, his skills were equally legendary among those who had worked closely with him. The respect scientists had for him, and these unique abilities made him the obvious choice to manage Moonbase Verity.

"Thank you for your vote of confidence. It will take all my experience to navigate this. Please set aside the drone project; I need you to do two things for me," Kohlrabi again got severe. "I have calculated that the amount of debris generated by this war will trigger a Kessler syndrome event. I believe this will destroy the ISS and the communication satellites we depend on as well. I need you to find a ground-based antenna. Some of the older deep-space missions used direct signals without satellite relays: repurpose one for Moonbase Verity."

Kohlrabi knew Tamarind did not influence NASA but knew he could find ways to get things done. The request was unexpected, but after considering it, Tamarind nodded assent.

"Thank you. Secondly, I need you to figure out how to get critical supplies to us. We can grow some food here in our hydroponics lab, but our recent airlock failure damaged most of our fresh food supplies." He rubbed the scar on his cheek as if it were a reminder. "Most of our food, medicines, and lab materials still come from Earth. Sustaining ourselves after the Kessler Event will be difficult, and we need your help Earth-side to figure this out."

Although Tamarind loved space and thought about it daily since he was at PNLI, he wasn't a rocket ship designer. Kohlrabi must have been seriously worried if he was counting on him.

"Stabilize your situation there. I'm sure things won't get that bad, but I promise to dedicate myself exclusively to this if they do. OK?" Tamarind tried to deliver assurance but saw only concern on his friend's face.

* * *

Although the news filtering up to Moonbase Verity contained factual account summaries of events, Kohlrabi called together Verity's researchers to explain its meaning.

He thought of starting formally as he sometimes did as their governor, but this seemed inappropriate. "My friends, our situation here has become more perilous than our relative comfort would suggest. In trying to assert their rights in space, our nations inadvertently triggered a Kessler Event. You studied this; it was a requirement for you to do so to come here. What has occurred is far more severe than even Dr. Kessler envisioned. Reworking his mathematical models, I now believe that the ISS and all satellites in orbit around Earth will be destroyed in a matter of weeks." A shocked silence reverberated around the room. They all acknowledged Kohlrabi's math skills, and no one questioned his conclusion, muttering swear words in several languages.

"As you know, our supplies and our contact to Earth is through the ISS and satellite feeds. Their loss will temporarily cut us off until communications are reestablished. Following this meeting, please send me personal messages homeward, and I will try to find a channel before they are all destroyed," Kohlrabi remained dispassionate and factual.

"We are not without resources. We will ration food, medicines, lab consumables, and personal supplies, but we produce ample power, water, and air. The Nigerian team grows some of our food, and over the next few days, we will explore options to expand that work. If any of you store food in your labs or personal areas, please bring them to me for inventory."

"Beginning immediately, we will reduce our food to half rations. This will be a hardship, but it will stretch our resources as we plan for our future. I contacted partners on Earth to bring us supplies and restore communications. In the meantime, please focus on documenting and completing your research to a logical milestone." Looking around the room, most were accepting this reasonably, and he could only hope it would stay that way.

Kohlrabi was able to forward the personal communications to Earth as planned that evening but couldn't reach Tamarind the next day. He realized his chats with his friend was a piece of sanity and a source of hope in his day. He was confident that his friend was working on his two requests, as promised. Governor Trust began the most challenging cycle of leadership, waiting for hopeful news in a crisis.

CHAPTER 4

Hope

"As we envision the future, we enable hope. Hope is not a passive dream but the fuel for the action that seizes that future." —Journal of Kohlrabi Trust

Kohlrabi's words turned out to be prophetic. When Tamarind checked his AI news feeds the next morning, global headlines read '*Space War Triggers Kessler Event.*' *A Kessler Syndrome, or the Kessler effect, was first proposed by NASA scientist Donald J. Kessler in 1978. He predicted that once the space debris in a particular orbit exceeds a certain quantity, the likelihood of a collision with another satellite becomes statistically unavoidable. This would cause a self-sustaining cascading debris field that would progress throughout the affected orbit level until nothing could survive.*

A fragment of a satellite going 18,000 miles an hour is a powerful projectile. Each day, the debris from the initial missile attacks have damaged others of the nearly 100,000 satellites in space. Each impact generates even more fragments causing more collisions. The self-sustained debris field expands exponentially. Although Kessler's predictions were related to Low Earth Orbits (LEO), particulates will encompass the Medium Earth Orbits (MEO) and higher geosynchronous and geostationary orbits (GSO and GEO). Over the next days and weeks, a steady and relentless progression of satellites will be damaged.

Tamarind couldn't reach Kohlrabi, and as promised, began working on his two requests. Unfortunately, he couldn't get the attention of any person of influence at NASA. Debris struck the ISS multiple times with additional casualties, and their immediate focus was on getting astronauts off the station.

Tamarind contacted another Pan-National, Taro Search, Director of SETI.

* * *

Taro Search sat alone in his cluttered office at the SETI Institute, surrounded by models of other planets, spaceship concepts, 3D printed dolls of envisioned aliens, and maps of various star systems. When he answered the incoming call, his short hair stuck up at all angles where his hand had been resting.

"Taro, I need your help. The Space War knocked out Verity's connections to Earth. Some older space programs used direct Earth to mission antennas, which Kohlrabi wants us to re-task," Tamarind blurted out nonstop without his usual cheerful intro.

"Tamarind? Good to hear your voice! OK, OK, Kohlrabi is in trouble. Hmmm. How about if I walk you straight into the Director of NASA's office? Dr. John Lewis is a good man and very decisive."

"Great! Put me on your display and make the introductions," Tamarind said.

Taro's direct link to the space agency director allowed him to report on the SETI Institute's many projects under contract to NASA. Soon, Dr. Lewis's image appeared next to Taro's. "Taro, is this urgent? We're pretty busy here." His expression indicated he often tolerated Taro but had no time for him now.

Taro said quickly, "John, this is my friend Tamarind Chase. We are both friends with Dr. Trust at Moonbase Verity. Mr. Chase has a plan to restore their communications." Tamarind thought this was the fastest and most precise he had ever heard Taro speak. He had a reputation for meandering conversations and was easily flustered.

Before John could respond, Tamarind made his pitch. "Thank you, Taro. Director Lewis, Dr. Trust requested we direct a communication array at Verity."

John was brief and to the point. "Not our priority. We need to get those astronauts off the ISS, and then I'll get back to Verity. They are good for a few weeks anyway."

Tamarind persisted. "Dr. Lewis, I appreciate your situation; I'm sure you are understaffed in this crisis. Our talented communications technical crew at DroneTech will come and facilitate redirecting one of the available antennas from an old mission. We can be there tomorrow. Just give me the name of someone in your organization that can provide access and oversight."

Dr. John Lewis took a few seconds to consider this. "Reestablishing comms with Verity would be a win, and we need one. Your plan could work. Transport your crew to Kennedy Spaceport, ask for Miles Madison. Keep this out of the press. They're all over us. Do not disturb our team there."

Tamarind began to thank him, but he was already gone. "Friendly kind of guy, huh?"

"Efficient," Taro said with a smile. "Glad I could help. ERIWA."

Now Tamarind's difficult task would be informing Flax he needed to pull his entire checkout team during a product release to work on a mothballed antenna across the country. He walked into Flax's office as he was just finishing up a production meeting and waited in the corner until it ended. As soon as the last person filed out, Tamarind closed the door.

"Trouble at Verity. No comms and no idea when the next food shipment will come. Kohlrabi is trapped with two hundred twenty-four scientists from the fourteen countries participating in this Space War mess. Taro helped us get access to a NASA antenna that could connect them back up, and I'm going to need eight to ten of our communications technical team to head to NASA tomorrow and align the antenna."

Friends since childhood, they often joked around. Flax's expression suggested he thought this was a joke but changed as he searched Tamarind's face. The communications drones were the most significant project at DroneTech, and they were in the final drive for release. Considering the tasks left on the comm drone checkout and who from their team could go on short notice, he calculated the impact on the project.

"OK, I'll put together a list and have them ready to fly out first thing in the morning. Anything else we can do to help?" Flax asked.

"Maybe. Kohlrabi asked me to figure out how to get supplies to them. ISS appears unlikely, so we must come up with a rocket solution in a hurry that can make it to the moon through the debris field." Tamarind couldn't see any way this request was possible, and he didn't expect his friend to have any suggestions.

"We aren't rocket scientists here, no one on our team has that skill set, and no one has thought about space as much as you. There is one system engineer who could help. I'll have him on the flight with you. Take the jumpjet, should hold twelve of you, and get you there mid-morning." Flax assessed the need, decided, and was all-in.

Kohlrabi's daily rounds around the space station projected an image of normality, although nothing felt stable. Extra time in his morning Zen meditations helped him embody the peace and harmony he hoped to model.

The Nigerian dome was the most changed from his last visit, and the first thing he noticed was the smell.

"Ah, Dr. Trust, thank you for stopping by. We planted every seed for an edible plant from our stores and are converting inedible plants to compost. We are accelerating this with feces from sewage treatment. The smells will calm down in a few days, we hope!" Dr. Chibuagu Tinubu was buoyant as usual, and her team on 24/7 work crews were singing rhythmically as they worked. "C'mon people," she said, "we're losing daylight!" Of course, on the sunward side of the moon, the light poured in through the optical fibers and out of the UV LED lamps. The team surged to a steady beat, walking and working in sync as they labored away.

Kohlrabi smiled widely, despite the bite of the pungent stench of manure. "You certainly look happy and productive! Let me know growing times and estimated crop yields; this will be a big help if our supplies are delayed as we expect." He hadn't clarified how dire their situation was yet, still waiting for more news from Earth. He rubbed his nose as he left their dome, hoping to get the smell out.

As he visited the Russian dome, he felt unwelcome. "Governor Trust, excuse us, we are calibrating some equipment currently; perhaps we could postpone your visit until another day?" Their team leader seemed uncomfortable, as if there was something he wasn't saying.

Kohlrabi was offended by this apparent brush-off but worked hard not to show it. He stood there without moving for an uncomfortable amount of time. The Russians looked down at their shifting feet. Finally, he said, "I don't mind if you are calibrating equipment; why should that delay our daily visit? You expected results from your uranium surveys today?" Kohlrabi smiled, his manner indicating he wasn't going anywhere and expected an answer.

"Yes, that is... correct," The team leader responded in halting English. He was usually fluent and enthusiastic. "I'm sorry, the samples are encouraging but highly radioactive. We have put the dome on emergency protection status until properly stored and the equipment recalibrated. We should have more information for you tomorrow." He looked more confident with this answer.

"That is encouraging news. A major uranium find would increase our value as an outpost. Perhaps I will start my rounds here tomorrow." Not waiting for an answer, he continued, "Has your team responded well to the rations and supply delays?"

"Yes, for now, I do not see it as a problem. Our work does not require many consumables either, as you know, so we are well-positioned to finish our current work with our current resources."

As Kohlrabi left the Russian dome, he felt uneasy. *Have they received direct contact from Earth? Did their research uncover something important? Is there a critical resource they are hoarding? I'll begin with them tomorrow,* Kohlrabi thought to himself. This was the part of the work he disliked— quarrels, lies, secrets, elitism, nationalism.

He continued his rounds, finding nothing amiss. Some teams questioned him, but there were few he could answer at this time.

The next day, in fact, the entire rest of the week, continued the same way. He received no news from Earth, static on all channels. Each research team seemed to be working away happily. More questions he couldn't answer. The Russians showed him some encouraging results indicating a potentially rich uranium deposit, but nothing seemed amiss.

* * *

Telsun Filorini was first on the tarmac the next morning, along with ten members of the DroneTech comm team and a pilot, all ready to go. They boarded the company's jumpjet, and after a vertical takeoff and ascent to 10,000 meters, they stabilized the plane for the ninety-minute flight from Colorado to Florida.

Standing near the cockpit, Tamarind directed them, "Turn your chairs to face each other. Use your time on the flight to research old NASA missions that used direct communications from Florida to a deep space mission. Shortlist the most accessible antennas to redirect to Verity and make a checklist of the calibrations to make it operational. Have this list available before we land."

"On it!" said one of the more senior engineers on the team.

Tamarind sat down with the system engineer in the last two seats at the back of the plane. "What is your background, Telsun?" His lean, fluid movements and his gnarly forearm muscles were sure signs of a rock climber.

"Robotics, machine vision, system engineering. My work now is on improving autonomous drone flight using real-time information from machine vision, sensors, and uploaded data." The engineer was fit, smart, concise, and confident; Tamarind liked him already.

"Are you Italian?"

"I'm an American mutt, sir. Three generations of intermingled immigrants from Europe and Asia created this sculpted visage," he said, with a sly grin.

"We need to configure a spaceship that can fly through the debris field and deliver supplies to the moon within six weeks without stopping at the ISS. We need to design it on this flight."

Telsun opened his eyes wide and said, "Coolio."

They worked well together. Starting with an approximate weight of supplies they needed to move, they considered how they would harden the capsule to survive the debris field. Then they specified the rocket payload to get them off the ground. They tried to do some simple calcs to verify the basics—cargo, fuel, thrust, targeting, landing. By the time the jumpjet landed at Kennedy Spaceport in Florida, they had the requirements and the outlines of a basic design that might be possible if they could find the parts.

Miles Madison was waiting for them as they disembarked. He looked like one of those engineers in the control room for a 1960s Apollo Mission—white shirt, short haircut, thick black-rimmed glasses. "I work on special projects for NASA Director Lewis," he said, with a Texan drawl, directing them inside a decrepit-looking building.

Once inside, he brought them into a government gray conference room. "Restrooms are around the corner, some snacks and drinks on the credenza. Director Lewis brought me up to speed on what you want to do. There is an old S-Band antenna that could communicate with the moon.

It's a stop on the Space Center tour now and hasn't been active except for training since the Exploration Missions back in the twenties. The equipment is all there if your team can figure out how to turn it on." He didn't intend to question their competence, but the DroneTech comm team all took it that way.

Tamarind said, "Grab some snacks, and let's get started." Soon they boarded a shuttle out to the site. On the shuttle ride, he outlined the test plan the engineering team had put together. The DroneTech engineers clustered around them, clarifying points with animated arm movements and expressions. Miles moved with the shuttle's bouncing, nodded at each step, commenting only with corrections or alternatives on a few points.

Opening the doors into the antenna building felt like entering a museum; much of the equipment was from the turn of the century. The windows near the ceiling let in a filtered yellow light highlighting the dust they'd stirred up when they entered the room. Racks of equipment sat forlornly on the shelves like a quiet mausoleum of an earlier time. Fortunately, the DroneTech techno-geeks all loved a challenge. After some explanation and clarifications from Miles, they worked away on their plan. Within thirty minutes, they set up some staging tables and had equipment manuals spread out, and each person was working on an assigned task. One table focused on power supplies, oscilloscopes, and signal generators, another pouring over the manuals related to the racks of equipment that powered the antenna. There was a buzz and energy in the room with beeping equipment and the occasional pop and smoke of a failed component adding humor.

Taking Miles aside, Tamarind and Telsun asked, "Miles, assuming we can get this antenna connected, the first thing Verity's governor is going to give us is a shopping list of emergency supplies. We need to figure out how to get those there within six weeks."

"Unlikely." Then, with his head tilted to the side, he added, "In fact, there is no way." His head shaking sideways, he explained in his slow drawl,

"Our transport equipment is only suitable to get stuff into orbit or relay to the ISS, which is out of commission. We haven't built rockets for decades that can land on the moon after an Earth launch. Same with the other space agencies and companies. Even if we did, launch windows occur only once per lunar month. Verity's predicament weighs heavily on me. Those guys are in a heap more trouble than anyone knows."

"I can see we are talking to the right man for the job!" Tamarind turned up the charm and moved into his pitch. "Telsun and I have designed a ship that can deliver the supplies they need and be ready to launch within six weeks. We need your help finding some of the components." He laid out the drawing, the calculations, and the parts list of what they needed.

Miles looked over the sketches with casual disdain, scanned the calculations, and turned to Tamarind. "Mr. Chase, Director Lewis asked me to help y'all reconnect with Verity. Nothing was said about bringing HG Wells' moon cannon to life. No scratchpad designed rocket will lift off from NASA during a Kessler Event; it just won't."

"Miles, look, we're stuck here for a while until our team gets this dish working. Why don't we just look over the parts list and see what is in inventory? Leave it to me to get the approvals. The best and brightest minds from fourteen countries are on the Moonbase; I'm sure they will want to help. I think we can find a way to keep them from starving to death up there, don't you?"

Miles grabbed the notes from Telsun, pursed his lips in disgust, then looked down the list. "Fuel - yes. Rocket engines - no. Capsule - maybe. Nose cone - maybe. Heat shielding?" Pausing for a minute, he said, "Yes. Your real challenge is your time frame. New vehicles take years, sometimes decades, and even scheduled launches require large teams, huge budgets, and long planning cycles. Six weeks just doesn't work." Miles handed the sketches back to Telsun.

"Are there any missions already planned we could reroute?" Tamarind continued.

"China launched a ship for Titan, but it is too far away to get to the moon and, another in the works six months out. The US crewless Mars mission scheduled five months out meets the capacity requirements, but this Space War shut everything down, big-time. Russia, maybe, but unlikely. The other countries only possess orbital rockets ready to go within the next year or two, as far as I'm aware. The private companies are in a meltdown as their commercial contracts are dead, with their stocks plummeting amidst this Kessler Event. Rescuing the ISS astronauts is our only approved launch, and it is an emergency, with all our resources and a tight time frame. The Kessler debris field may consume the ISS even before the rescue." Miles was not annoyed anymore or dismissive, just addressing the facts. It was clear he'd thought long and hard about the scientists on the moon.

"Understood. What if we repurposed one of the old rockets, like Apollo, sitting in the museum? Clean it up, change the seals, add the capsule hardening so it can survive passing through the debris field, and load it up for a moon launch quickly? We could pull in the contractors from aeronautical companies on a humanitarian mission. There must be many engineers around who studied the old Apollo missions?" Tamarind knew he was reaching and sounding a little desperate.

As it turned out, Miles was one of those old engineers who grew up studying every aspect of the Apollo program. He loved the Saturn rockets and the landing vehicles. There were enough parts in space museums that maybe, just maybe, he could pull them all together and get one usable system. Smiling at Tamarind and Telsun, he said, "Maybe. Let's get this antenna working, and I'll talk to the director." The pair from DroneTech squeezed their fists up by their shoulders and went in for a high five when Miles said, "Now don't get yourselves all ready and raring to go. I just said maybe. Y'all need to calm down."

* * *

The S-Band antenna took most of the week to get out of mothballs and up and running. While not there all the time, Miles stopped in regularly with spare parts, delivered food, and checked on their progress. He was there the entire time of the alignment, calibration, and communication tests with Moonbase Verity. The equipment would allow video and audio compromised by signal delays, a snowy image, and lots of static. When they finally got a connection, the comm team cheered. Miles motioned for them to be quiet.

"Miles, is that you? Thank you, NASA!" The fuzzy image on the screen was recognizable. Long pause.

Miles said, "In this case, y'all can thank the team from DroneTech." Tamarind stepped closer to the camera, and Kohlrabi saw him for the first time in more than a week. A huge smile came across his face.

"My friend, I knew you would find a way. Thank you!" As predicted, the Moonbase governor immediately sent a supplies list via the data link and confirmed reception. "How is my space supply ship coming?"

After an awkward pause, "We've discussed some ideas with Miles. Lots of approvals and issues, but progress. How long can you last with what you have?" Tamarind asked.

"Everything that remains is being rationed. Maybe two months. The base was past due to receive a supply run before this conflict erupted. What is happening now? We haven't heard anything since we last spoke."

Two months. That seemed impossible. Deciding to be encouraging, Tamarind said, "The ISS is still operational; NASA is putting together a mission to rescue those astronauts. The governments involved in the Space War are meeting in Brussels to negotiate peace. We'll get started on filling your grocery list, OK? How are you doing at keeping peace on the base?" His smile was affirming despite what he was feeling.

"I have directed the scientists to continue their research, document their conclusions, and put their larger projects on ice. They are aware supplies may be delayed, but a rescue mission is in the works." Kohlrabi had done well to keep peace and to keep them working.

"Now that this antenna is operational, I'll return the DroneTech team, but as promised, I will work on this until you are all safe." Tamarind looked confident, and Kohlrabi seemed relieved. "Let's plan on talking every day at the same time. OK?"

"Miles, Tamarind, thank you so much. Please thank your whole team there. I can't quite see them in the image. You all have given us a most precious commodity—hope!"

CHAPTER 5

Opportunity

"There is a transcendent moment in every tragedy where an opportunity emerges to build a better world."—Journal of Kohlrabi Trust

By the time the jumpjet arrived back at DroneTech's facility in Colorado, the comm team felt invincible. Flax met them at the doors and said, "Success, I see! Come on in and let me fill you in on what happened while you were away." They headed into the largest conference room, where the management and the rest of the checkout team gathered.

Flax began with an animation of the objects in orbit. "As you can see, the Kessler debris field is expanding, and more satellites are damaged. At this point, the result appears inevitable—debris will destroy everything in orbit within a few weeks. I spoke this morning with the President of the United States and several members of his Cabinet. They would like a proposal for restoring the entire global telecommunications infrastructure using our new comm drones." Flax looked around the table to give them a chance to take in this announcement.

The team returning from Florida started pumping their hands over their heads—"Yeah!" The manufacturing manager slumped back in his chair but still looked excited. Tamarind held his hands over his face and was shaking his head. He didn't want to spoil the mood, but the gravity of this moment was overwhelming. The inevitable had progressed while he was gone.

Flax calmed the group and pointed to the other end of the table at his friend and partner. "Tamarind," he said, encouraging him to speak to the room.

Tamarind swallowed hard, and with a somber expression, said, "This is a tragedy of the highest order. It is a death sentence to those still alive on the International Space Station and most likely to the scientists on Moonbase Verity. Many countries are dependent on the revenues from their satellites and will plunge into an economic depression. Cars, planes, ships will be nearly inoperable, with navigation and weather systems destroyed. Business networks, agriculture, financial systems, the entire planet will be swept into a recession. The space industry might never recover. What a waste..." He tapered off toward the end, overwhelmed by emotion. He returned his head to his hands.

Flax stood, "He is right. DroneTech has been pushed to the forefront of the biggest humanitarian aid mission ever conducted. As we get our comm drones up, each of the inevitable effects Tamarind just described will be relieved by a small amount. This just became our company mission. Are we ready to rise to the need?" Flax was every bit the leader they could follow into battle. Heads nodded around the room. Tamarind excused himself and went back to his office, while Flax led the rest of the team through their government proposal details.

* * *

Kohlrabi would receive Tamarind's daily updates and relay the messages to the scientists. Each day, Kohlrabi became less hopeful, weaker, more resigned to the inevitability of the deaths of those on the base. He feared the tenuous cooperation on the station would break down, wrecking facilities, fighting over morsels, or worse. His peaceful resolve was breaking down.

Waking up one morning malnourished and exhausted, Kohlrabi realized over six weeks had passed since the start of this crisis. His meditations were distracted and did not quiet his mind. *I must buy time for Tamarind to get us help. I must keep Verity peaceful and productive. I must save as many lives as possible.*

He looked again, for the fiftieth time, at their dwindling resources and medicines. The Nigerian team was making heroic progress, but it was insufficient food generation to impact their outcome significantly. *Maybe a month. Maybe two months, if some people die.* He hated that he was thinking this way, but the math didn't lie.

He made the tough decision to be honest with the facts. Every manager and politician felt pressure to lie a little "for the good of the people," but he was first a scientist, and so was his team.

That night he got them all together. "Thank you all for working together peacefully, for staying engaged despite our challenges. I want to tell you what is ahead for us. Several of you know already that the medicines we depend on are running out. The Chinese team has been working on medicines, which we will test after our critical medicines run out. I suspect some of you with more serious medical conditions will be the first to die here, but unfortunately not the last." The room went silent; some put their heads down in despair.

"When you left Earth, you each shipped out with a body bag. You knew the risk and chose to come. We now ask that if it is your time, you choose to die with dignity and honor. Please place your body bags in a place visible from your bed and prepare yourself spiritually for this possibility." Kohlrabi paused to see if anyone asked questions.

"Is there no hope left for a supply or rescue ship from Earth?" One of the young engineers from the unified Korean delegation asked the question on everyone's mind.

"There is still reason to hope for the supply mission. A mission to evacuate us, I'm afraid, is a long time off. The supply mission is working through approvals and preparations, still more than a month away. I'm afraid that some of us will not make it until that happens." Kohlrabi spoke hopefully, but realistically as well. There was little discussion. The meeting ended with the scientists shuffling off toward their domes, this news adding to their malnourished exhaustion.

* * *

A few days later, while NASA was still organizing its rescue of the astronauts on the ISS, the ISS astronauts telecast a hopeful and thankful message live from the station. Tamarind and many others watching around the world saw a barrage of debris strike the astronaut's capsule. The ISS was spectacularly destroyed on the live telecast, killing the last nine remaining crew aboard. It was the final satellite broadcast he and many others received. Channels continued to blink out of operation as their relay satellites were destroyed.

The effects of the Space War and the resulting Kessler Event spread globally almost exactly as Tamarind feared. Governments banned auto-driving cars and trucks when they began crashing. Banks and stores could not verify credit transactions. Banking, business, mobile and military communications, weather tracking, navigation for airplanes and ships—all were suddenly, silently, and irrevocably destroyed. People who never thought about satellites or ever knew a world before they existed realized how much they depended on them. People who had grown up with self-driving cars and GPS had to learn to drive manually and read maps. Ship pilots navigated by lighthouses and compasses. Soldiers retrained to read charts and coordinate ops without satellite intel and remote-controlled weapons.

Everything.Was.Slowing.Down.

Tamarind could drive his car in manual mode, but many could not. As he went home, cars and trucks littered the highway, unable to move without satellite direction. He saw crowds pressing into banks and taking everything they could carry out of the few remaining grocery stores.

The automated warehouse stores were stagnant. With the inventory locations and orders kept on cloud computers, all unlinked by satellites, the automated forklifts, delivery vans, and drones could not complete even known orders.

His satellite radio had no working channels, and his car was too new to have old analog stations. At home, he had access to some local TV stations that had already set up some kind of station to station information shuttle system to provide something like national news.

The resulting financial, transportation, and communication uncertainty rippled through every market, disrupting food and goods' supply until all were affected by the crisis. The hotly contested, trillion-dollar communications industry was the largest industry for several nations, dependant on satellites. Now the industry was destroyed, and with it vanished the jobs, support industries, and all the many puzzle pieces that made that industry work.

Tamarind listened to how the global outcry about the war changed the political priorities of anyone who wanted to remain in office. The nations that participated in the conflict rushed to sign the Space Peace Treaty, ending the war and banning all further space launches indefinitely. Exceptions to the ban would require the UN Council on Space Affairs's approval representing the 35 space-faring nations.

Even after the ISS catastrophe, news outlets gave little attention to the situation on Moonbase Verity.

A few days after the ISS disaster, an article in the *International Times*, written by freelance reporter Jake Johnson, titled "Space War—what happened?" was picked up and translated worldwide, becoming the default description everyone quoted. An hour before his scheduled call to Verity, Tamarind sat in his office, reading the article a second time. He decided to contact the reporter first. Reporters are never too hard to find, and his AI agent reached him directly without difficulty.

"Jake? Tamarind Chase from DroneTech. Your article gets a lot right, thank you. I think you've underestimated the economic fallout and global impact which will occur, but that isn't why I'm calling."

Jake was pretty green as a journalist, and for him, the worldwide reach of his article in times like these was like winning a Pulitzer. However, he was still clear-thinking enough to ask questions when a business leader called him directly on the phone. "Mr. Chase, thank you for your comments. There will be follow-up articles, but how can I clarify the points you've raised?" He knew his caller would get back to his reason for calling. He might be able to squeeze in one or two questions before then.

Jake could not misdirect Tamarind. "It is your last two sentences I've called you about—*the fate of the scientists on Moonbase Verity is still uncertain. Resupply missions are currently forbidden under the terms of the Space Peace Treaty.*" He paused for emphasis and then spoke more strongly and deliberately, "I think you would perform a great service if you would draw the entire world's focus to saving the two hundred twenty-four scientists on Moonbase Verity."

Jake could tell he wouldn't get more out of his caller on this call. "I'll speak to my editor today. I'll try, Mr. Chase. Please send me any details you know to help me make my case." He was surprised when details about Verity arrived a few minutes later.

* * *

When Tamarind connected with Kohlrabi that day, all the hope he'd felt from their last exchange was gone, and Tamarind was fidgety, avoiding direct eye contact.

"Tamarind, what happened?" Kohlrabi asked.

"The good news is the signing of the Space Peace Treaty. Unfortunately, there is much bad news. The ISS was destroyed by debris; everyone aboard was killed. The treaty bans all space launches indefinitely, including any resupply mission to Verity. I want you to know that I am on this exclusively, but the hill we must climb just got higher."

Kohlrabi composed himself before replying, "Tamarind, please contact the fourteen host nations of our scientists. Tell them you have established a rudimentary connection and to relay messages through you for our people here. Please tell them the nature of our station's fragile peace and hope and ask them to ensure their messages are appropriate. I will tell our people you are continuing our resupply mission; we will expect the best. I believe in you, my friend!" Tamarind was impressed by Kohlrabi's composure with his own emotions barely in check.

"You know I am on it. I've asked a reporter, Jake Johnson, to write an article highlighting the resource situation on Moonbase Verity. I'll work with Miles Madison at NASA and coordinate with the other nations. I'll have more for you soon!"

* * *

Jake's article did raise awareness about Verity for a few news cycles, but the effects of the war were so profound and felt so personally that few could sustain concern for those so far away.

Miles did help Tamarind put together a proposal using museum-quality equipment repurposed for this mission. If it could get off the ground, the NASA engineers rated it a "very high risk" to make it to the moon. Approvals seemed improbable.

Every day, Tamarind relayed the messages to the scientists. And every day, he could see Kohlrabi look less hopeful, weaker, more resigned to the inevitability of the deaths of those on the base.

When Flax presented the DroneTech communications proposal to the President, Tamarind asked if he could insert 5 minutes at the end of the call to make a pitch for Verity. Flax was uncomfortable with this; their proposal was critical for DroneTech and the world. But Tamarind was his best friend and partner, and Kohlrabi was a friend, and he reluctantly agreed that they must try.

At the end of the meeting, the President looked around at his advisors. "Any more questions for the DroneTech team?" Then after a short pause, "Gentlemen, this proposal looks good. I'll initiate with Congress and request immediate funding appropriation for the US portion of this. I will recommend it to the other nations at next week's UN summit meeting. Thank you for your work." The meeting looked like it was about to end, but Flax intervened.

"We have one more matter to bring before you, Mr. President," Flax said.

Tamarind bent forward. "I've been working with NASA on an emergency supply mission to Moonbase Verity. I have been in daily communications with Governor Trust there, and the situation is growing desperate. We would like your support to bring this before the UN Council on Space Affairs during your meetings there next week." Tamarind pitched it with hope and confidence, expecting approval.

"Dr. Lewis mentioned your work with the antenna and your idea to get supplies to Verity. It's creative, and I appreciate your initiative. However, even if we could get unanimous support from all 35 nations, John tells me there are even odds that the mission would fail." The President spoke knowledgeably about the possibility and the risk. "OK, work with John to prepare the proposal, and I'll see if we can get a vote on it at the UN Council on Space Affairs. Good day, gentlemen." He cut the link quickly as if to prevent further requests.

Tamarind was encouraged, thanked Flax, and sailed out of the room. As a partner at DroneTech and the VP of Business Development, he should have been elated by the massive government contract they had just snagged. However, his joy was almost entirely about the potential launch.

* * *

Tamarind was excited to provide some positive news on his call the next day with Kohlrabi. When his fuzzy image came up, his friend looked even frailer.

"Good to see your face, Tamarind. Three people died here, not from starvation or suicide yet, but just weakened immune systems and lack of medications. The scientists still strong enough are documenting their research for those who come after us. Gallows humor is spreading around the place. Any good news for us?" Kohlrabi was still expectant despite the challenges they faced. Pause.

"NASA approved the viability of the plan, and the President agreed to present the proposal to the UN Committee on Space Affairs next week. Miles Madison is pulling together a launch bay to assemble the parts, and I have begun procuring your grocery list. There is still hope, Kohlrabi!" Tamarind was as buoyant as he'd been on any call since this started, and Kohlrabi couldn't help but be encouraged.

"What is your best guess for a launch date?" Kohlrabi asked. They were already close to his two-month time frame and were still a long way from a completed vehicle and approvals. Long pause.

"I'll know more in a week, but no sooner than three weeks, if all goes perfectly."

"I know you well enough to appreciate your answer, and also well enough to know neither of us believes it. I'm not sure there will be anyone left here when you get here, but I will get you a summary of our health status for your proposal." Looking sincerely into the display, he said, "ERIWA, my friend." Tears filled his eyes, and he broke the comm signal before Tamarind could reply.

ERIWA was a Pan-National phrase encouraging each other to their best, but Tamarind couldn't help hearing it as Kohlrabi saying goodbye.

* * *

Once the President agreed to present the proposal, Dr. John Lewis went into high gear at NASA. He applied all his resources to get parts into the launch bay and pull together the plan for the President. Miles collected almost 90% of the Apollo materials and had the rest fabricated on accelerated schedules. Tamarind sourced all the supplies for timed deliveries scheduled over the next two weeks by the time of the UN meeting.

The proposal from NASA was impeccable. The presentation from the President was moving, compelling, and called for decisive action. The council agreed to vote. All 14 of the nations with scientists on the moon voted affirmative. The other 21 countries represented in the UN committee without researchers on Verity were harder to convince. Discussions continued for much of the day and spilled into the next. Finally, they received the votes to proceed.

* * *

When the Moonbase governor received the call from his friend a week later, he could see the excitement in his eyes. "Kohlrabi, we got approval! NASA is on track to launch in two weeks. All the materials on your grocery list are at the site, and the work is proceeding as rapidly as is humanly possible." Pause.

Tamarind had become so personally invested in this process. Kohlrabi realized for the first time that if this failed, his friend would be alone to live with the result.

"Tamarind, I knew we could count on you! Please thank Miles and the crew at NASA." Tamarind could feel his friend's love as he wiped a tear out of his own eyes. He wasn't sure if it was because of the new hope or because his friend was so proud.

Tamarind's next question grounded him. "How are things there? Can you make it for another two or three weeks?" He feared the answer to his question.

"Several more have died, these from malnutrition. To be honest, I don't think we can, but we will try. Thank you for giving us hope, a most precious commodity in this time of scarcity," Kohlrabi said.

After the call, Kohlrabi began his daily rounds. His weakness slowed the progress but being able to bring encouraging news was helpful. Most of the domes had at least one death at this point, and all were severely malnourished, but they courageously worked away at their research despite their hunger and fatigue.

The Chinese reported on their medical research. Their medicines had slightly extended the lives of the team members who had run out of critical supplies, and they provided comfort and reduced despair. They had learned a lot from human trials. The UK team had samples of their regolith hex bricks, but they were all too weak to lift them now. Working with the Japanese scientists, they'd developed a process to 3D print a building from the regolith material. The Nigerians were ashamed that their crops had not been more productive at alleviating their hunger but believed they would provide a more sustainable yield after the first harvest, probably by the time the supply ship arrived. While there, they offered Kohlrabi one of the first radishes.

Kohlrabi brought the scarlet radish up to his nose and inhaled the rich earthy scent, commenting on the tangy, spicy overtones. Then he bit into it; the crisp snap of the chunk was almost as pleasing to his ears as the spicy warmth to his tongue.

"It has been a long time since I have had a radish. This is undoubtedly the best one I have ever had. I feel guilty for eating it," Kohlrabi was a little embarrassed by his emotions about the humble vegetable.

The Nigerians laughed heartily. Kohlrabi hadn't heard a good belly laugh for weeks, and he realized that it had healing powers too. He chuckled with them.

He continued his rounds to the other domes, a little lighter on his feet. Most were wrapping up their current research, noting the urgency to finalize their results. More than one commented they felt like they were writing their will, and they should put them together in a book of the dead.

CHAPTER 6
Collateral Damage

"Leaders use the euphemism, 'collateral damage' to mask the killing of innocent civilians, the destruction of the environment, and the waste of useful resources. Ultimately, it obscures their failure as leaders, but by illumination, we prevent future folly." —Journal of Kohlrabi Trust

Kohlrabi encouraged the scientists strong enough to come to the commons dome and watch the launch. The hollow looking researchers shuffled in, some with cobbled together canes and crutches to help them walk the short distance.

Ironically, the first DroneTech communications drones came online to enable television coverage of the NASA launch in the 14 countries with scientists at Verity. Since the ISS destruction, the world had only seen local cable news, so Earth was looking to space once again. Those watching silently counted down with the announcers and cheered when the Apollo Verity mission took off, celebrating the event. Each stage separation and each flight milestone brought enthusiastic support on the ground, and after a delay, at Moonbase Verity. The fuzzy picture was unclear at the moonbase, so Tamarind acted as a commentator and described what he perceived to those at the Moonbase.

"Liftoff is beautiful, fire and smoke against the blue sky," Tamarind said. "The first stage separation looks good. Apollo Verity is leaving the lower atmosphere, approaching 50 km. The second stage separation looks perfect. The camera image on the module is beginning to show stars, and wait, I see the moon! It is on its way!"

The split-screen sowed the cheers at Verity. On the live image of the rocket, he saw a burst of light that filled the picture. The announcers were saying some type of unexpected explosion had occurred. Tamarind remained silent.

The split-screen showed him that they were still cheering at Verity for nearly a minute after the explosion had already occurred when someone pointed to the blurry image on the screen. Their joy turned to despair and moans as they clustered around the small screen to understand what had happened.

Somewhere near the exit of Earth's orbit, debris impacted the final capsule's fuel tank, causing a massive cascading detonation that suddenly converted the rocket and the Moonbase's supplies into more space debris.

The Apollo Verity mission was a spectacular failure with the whole world and the Moonbase watching.

Tamarind's botched rescue meant the scientists at Moonbase Verity would most certainly die.

The transmission continued, but Tamarind was overwhelmed with grief and a sense of failure. The scientists on Verity had gone quiet, except for moans of overwhelming anguish.

The announcers played a recorded message from the UN Council on Space Affairs directed at the viewing audience.

"NASA's bold plan was always unlikely to succeed, and even if successful, would have only extended the misery of those on Moonbase Verity. Those heroic scientists should not die with misguided hope. They should know they will be remembered for their bravery and acknowledged by all nations as unfortunate collateral damage of the Space War."

It was over. Tamarind slumped in his chair, all options gone. NASA ceased transmission, and with nothing more to say, he too terminated the connection to Verity.

* * *

Kohlrabi, however, had prepared for this. He kept the team on Verity talking late into the night, their worst fears now confirmed. Then, sometime in the night, the mood shifted. In all the years of the Moonbase, there had been fourteen separate cultures, ethnic and language distinctions, national priorities, uniquely personal and professional pressures that kept them separated. Kohlrabi had always remained aloof, maintaining independence to allow him to unify them all. Now he opened up about his fear and desire to die with honor and forge their deaths into something meaningful and be surrounded not by colleagues but by friends. As the night wore on, their bonds with one another deepened, and cultural and national walls came down.

They spoke of their reasons for coming to Verity, their sadness, those they'd leave behind, and their sense of fulfillment in completing their work. Sharing their most secret research, they found significance and unusual connections among their results. The camaraderie deepened; they were pioneers, they were ambassadors, they had finished well.

* * *

Their scheduled call the next day was not initiated by Tamarind but by Kohlrabi.

"I'm so sorry, Kohlrabi, I don't know what more I can do." Kohlrabi could see the fuzzy tears running down Tamarind's face. Pause.

"Tamarind, you have done more than anyone else. You were our champion, our hope, our ambassador to the world. Please feel no guilt, and know you have the genuine appreciation of every scientist here." Pause.

"My friend, is there anything more I can do for you?" Tamarind's face was contorted, trying unsuccessfully to hold back tears. Kohlrabi was not crying and rallied a bit for his next words.

"We ran out of food here but have heat, air, and water. We've lost many colleagues. After the explosion yesterday, a beautiful unity happened here. Those strong enough to participate shared their research findings honestly and openly. We've formed a greater allegiance to each other than our nations or our rights to our science ownership. We voted not to send any of our findings to Earth." He spoke with joy and pride in his voice.

"Tamarind, we've discovered something here—something game-changing—and we voted to ask you to come and receive it. When you come, bring those grasshopper drones," he smiled a bit at this but then got serious. "Bury us with respect and use our findings to rebuild Moonbase Verity." Clearly, Kohlrabi prepared for this call, never expected a successful supply mission, and rallied his team impressively to a unified end. Pause.

"Kohlrabi, I don't know how long it will take or how we'll even clear the debris field. I promise you, I will personally come to Moonbase Verity. ERIWA, my friend. Finish well." Tamarind raised his arm in a way that would have ended in a clasp of hands if his friend was close, his face covered with tears. He had just said goodbye to a friend and committed his future down an uncertain path.

"ERIWA, my friend!" Kohlrabi raised his arm to complete the gesture, and with those final words, Kohlrabi ended the call. He did not call again. He felt the harmony flowing from unity, purpose, completeness, and the release of remaining burdens. He left his office for the last time and spent his final hours with the disparate group of scientists who had finally become his friends.

* * *

Tamarind tried every day for a month but did not speak to another person at Moonbase Verity ever again.

Kohlrabi sent one more communication to Earth, picked up by most major news outlets in dozens of languages.

To: UN Council on Space Affairs and the worldwide space industry

From: Dr. Kohlrabi Trust and the "collateral damage" of MoonBase Verity

> *We are not the collateral damage of the Space War. Our deaths are the inevitable result of the space industry and 35 space-faring nations that have continued to place spacecraft into orbit while ignoring their contribution to the unavoidable Kessler Event. Humanity has never been good at sustainably managing the use of resources. Like oil, water, the oceans, rainforests, the air, we continued to consume and pollute until wars and catastrophes sealed our fate. Space could not sustain the continued launching of satellites without commensurate responsibility for cleaning up the junk left there.*

> *We are not collateral damage; we are victims of gross negligence from our leadership. True leaders sustainably achieve progress without destroying resources shared by all. It is good that the space-faring nations signed the Space Peace Treaty to establish clear accountability for future failures in leadership. We call on the people of the world to hold this council accountable for any plan that enters space without a clear plan to clean up the resulting debris such a launch will cause. We ask, no, we demand, that no ship leave Earth until the debris field is cleared and the regulations and technology are in place to prevent any future waste, destruction, or collateral damage from ever occurring again. As you on Earth suffer through the prolonged effects of this mismanagement of space, we ask you to demand better. This is our final request; this is our last will and testament.*

The document ended with the signatures of the final eight members of MoonBase Verity "representing the 224 scientists of this base".

CHAPTER 7

Grief

"Grief consumes as embers, crests in waves, and exhausts as a relentless summer heat. It will not be satiated, bargained with, or ignored. It must run its course completely or die with its victim."
— *Journal of Kohlrabi Trust*

Tamarind wanted to take some time off to grieve and think. The PNLI requested he come to a special celebration honoring Kohlrabi.

The jumpjet to Hope Island was only six hours but seemed to take forever. Circling the east side of the island, he could see the huts in the thick jungle where he was raised—his earliest memories. As the jet descended toward the volcanic island, he could see the twin lakes in the caldera where Kohlrabi had once saved his life. He directed the jumpjet to land near the buildings on the more barren west side of the island that was his home and school during the final part of his training where Kohlrabi, Taro, Almond, Flax, and he had found their missions, their faiths, and prepared to fulfill their potential.

He walked across the low cliff face where the Institute had recently added a jumpjet landing site. The short walk allowed him to drink in the ocean smells and sounds below him and look up at the sparsely covered hillside of the volcano above him. The small campus was a cluster of white buildings clinging to the low cliffs above the beach and surf below. As he entered the three-story white stone building that housed the student-filled halls of his alma mater, scents and memories flooded back, reminding him of his time there. They had learned much and were given a great privilege as unwanted orphans from many countries and cultures.

Professor Lambardi met him in the hallway and silently moved him toward the cafeteria, set up for Kohlrabi's memorial. Other teachers and alumni were present, and Tamarind felt encouraged to see old friends and overcome grief. The professor motioned for people to find seats and moved to a podium adjacent to photos and displays of Kohlrabi's life and life work.

"My friends, ERIWA!" He spoke in a loud voice as if giving a command and demanding a response.

"ERIWA," the audience responded in one voice.

"We gather to remember the life of Dr. Kohlrabi Trust, to honor his mission and life work, and to mourn for our friend. I remember the day when his mathematical genius began to show as he parsed complex statistics and saw almost musical patterns in numbers. He digested technical papers like a child's storybook and seemed to inhale the charts and graphs and equations. It did not take much to direct him toward life missions that might use those gifts."

"His work at the KTrust Foundation became both relevant and respected among the research community, and he had the unusual gift not of just finding errors and biases but also selflessly and humbly guiding researchers to see them without feeling attacked. This is a gift I wish I shared; I've been hard on some of you over the years."

Quiet laughter rippled through the room.

"Kohlrabi did not want to go to the moon and sought my counsel when offered the job. I do not regret encouraging him to go—he was the perfect choice to bring unity and clarity of purpose to a disparate group of researchers. His last days were no doubt unbearably difficult, and yet he led those scientists under his care to their best possible end, unified, at peace, and bound by brotherly love. In his most difficult moment, he was heroic. It was his best moment. Kohlrabi was the best of us, compassionate and wise, competent, and kind. ERIWA!"

Others shared stories, both humorous and profound, of their memories of Kohlrabi. As the memorial wound down, Professor Lambardi came alongside Tamarind.

"Tamarind, could you come to my next class? I want you to meet some of my students in their Life Mission Class." He didn't give him any time to object.

In their early teenage years, the two dozen students were eager and happy, standing next to displays addressing world problems and debating potential solutions. After a brief introduction, they were full of questions about Tamarind and his choices, faith, and life mission. This class of students was named after useful rocks and minerals, and he smiled as he listened to Salt, Granite, Shale, Silica, and Mica present their life mission presentations. As he interacted with them, his own sense of purpose and mission seemed lacking.

After the memorial and class, he walked back to Professor Lambardi's office. "Professor, thank you for your kind words at the memorial. It was good to remember Kohlrabi as both a hero and a man wise beyond his years."

"Call me Luca, Tamarind," he said, crossing the room for a handshake. "ERIWA."

"ERIWA. Your students have reminded me of my purpose."

"They do that to me each day," he said with a warm smile. "Tamarind, you were heroic in your efforts to rescue Kohlrabi. You honored him with your valiance."

"But it wasn't enough, was it?"

"None of that was your fault. Kohlrabi correctly blamed the leadership of the space-faring nations, and his message is being heard."

"Posthumous impact—how very like him."

His final stop was at his house parents' hut on the west side of the island. It took him most of the day to ascend the volcano and hike down through the jungle on the other side. Martin and Clarissa were in their hut eating dinner, surrounded by six new students who looked seven or eight years old.

With tears in their eyes, Martin and Clarissa rose from the table and crossed the small room when he arrived. They group-hugged each other and reminisced about their deceased friend for a few moments before the din of the household broke them up. Martin offered to put the children to bed, and Clarissa motioned for Tamarind to walk with her.

The intoxicating smell of the jungle and the cloudless sky at sunset heightened the intensity of his emotions.

"The hut seemed a lot bigger when I was last here."

"How are you doing, Tamarind?" Her voice filled with compassion and her face with concern, her hand resting on his shoulder.

"What am I doing, more like. Nothing seems important. I failed to save my friend when he needed me most. Where can I go from here?"

"Kohlrabi never wanted you to feel guilty or to do anything but be all you could be. Grief is like a dark cloud, but you will see the stars again."

They walked in silence for a while, and he drank in the sounds and smells. He felt the touch of Clarissa's arm on his shoulder and tasted the warm, salty tears as they ran down his cheeks.

* * *

The long flight home the next day gave him time to think. When Tamarind returned to DroneTech, he struggled to reengage; his heart was not in it. One evening, he asked Flax and Almond to meet with him after work.

"My friends, when we left PNLI, we started this venture to begin the pursuit of each of our missions. Flax, you succeeded in using drones to make police stops safer for all involved. Almond, you pioneered non-toxic pesticides for agricultural drones that revolutionized the growth of food. This new communications contract has put DroneTech on the frontlines addressing the fallout from the Space War and destined it to become one of the most important companies globally. Our work together became relevant. But, as you know, my mission has always been in space. Please allow me to sell you my stake in DroneTech and pursue my mission." Tamarind's voice held resolve and a tinge of excitement.

"Oh, Tamarind," Almond said and then stopped, her hand covering the quivering in her lips and chin, her eyes welling up with tears. "Kohlrabi doesn't want you to leave your life and friends behind. You've done more than anyone could have—you owe him nothing."

"I owe him my life, Almond, and I made him a promise."

Flax went rigid next to her at his words, looked at him stone-faced, but said nothing.

"ERIWA, you know we love you," she said, giving him a long hug, her shoulders shaking with her sobs.

Flax could see no way to dissuade him and had seen this coming since the Space War began. He went through the mental calculation of the practicalities—fair market value of shares, the work Tamarind was in the middle of, how they could afford to buy him out. "Of course, we will purchase your shares and help you in any way we can in your pursuit. I'll have the details drawn up with legal and get you an initial transfer based on cash on hand. Might take us a while to buy you out completely, but we'll make it happen." They slapped their arms together in a raised arm lock and pulled each other closer. "ERIWA, my friend!"

Tamarind left the building feeling relieved and yet anxious. Grief, the daunting task he'd committed to, and the derailment of his plans had his stomach tied in knots. The memory of Almond's tender frame sobbing in his arms haunted him.

He packed some equipment and clothes and headed for the nearest airport. He booked the first flight to Islamabad, Pakistan. Distance—he needed to get far away from here, from his failure to save Kohlrabi, from Almond.

Tamarind had an athlete's fitness level and often worked out his stress with the most strenuous exercise. He had hiked or climbed the peaks near his home on weekends and had sparring partners to hone his martial arts. He wanted something more, much, much more.

He decided climbing K2, the world's most dangerous mountain, was just what he needed right now.

Twenty-four hours later, he had checked into a room at the Islamabad Serena Hotel—he found its aging elegance acceptable. Since the Kessler Event, the hotel had no internet connection, and none of his usual communication devices worked. He hand wrote a fax to Dronetech and headed up to his room for bed, the day of travel and grief catching up with him. He ordered Rosemary Kebab and Maghaz Masala off the Sindhi cuisine menu and some Tandoori Naan bread. He added hot chai tea, realizing that there was no alcohol listed like in many Muslim regions.

He had vivid dreams that night. A gaunt and withered Kohlrabi appeared at the door of his room. "Save me, Tamarind. You owe me. I saved you." He repeated this in a ghostly voice over and over while Tamarind lay in his bed, unable to move, speak, or respond.

He struggled to get up when Almond's arms grabbed him from beside him in bed, sobbing and holding him and whispering, "Don't go. I love you."

When he awoke sweating, both from the heat and humidity and the specters that had robbed him of restful sleep. He felt dehydrated and jet-lagged, his head hurt, his stomach felt unsettled.

There was a tentative knock at the door. A diminutive local boy dressed in a hotel uniform looked up at him with big brown eyes. "Mr. Chase? We have a letter for you." It was placed on a silver tray, held high by his white-gloved hands.

Tamarind took the letter and closed the door with a nod and a tip. Wrapping the now stale naan bread around some of the leftovers from his evening meal, he downed them with some of the lukewarm tea. It did not make his stomach feel better.

The letter was a fax reply from Flax on Dronetech letterhead. Despite working there for years, Tamarind had never seen a fax from the company, a sign of their post-satellite world.

Hello, my friend. Islamabad? Attached is the shares sales agreement, as discussed. We got a quick valuation on the shares by legal, based on an update of our 409a with the government contract inclusion. Almond and I added an extra 15% since you are allowing us to pay you over time. I found an old-fashioned way to make an international wire transfer—$50k will be transferred by courier to your hotel, which should cover your immediate plans, and the rest will be deposited in your bank account here until paid in full. Let us know you are all right, and please keep in touch, so we know you are ok. Love you, brother!

- Flax

Tamarind read it twice and noted the switch to "us" when it came to personal concerns. Almond cared; Flax cared but was glad to have him gone, at least for a while. He read through the contract, signed it, and headed down to reception to send the return fax.

The front desk treated him entirely differently today. The $50,000 transfer through the ancient Western Union cable lines and delivered by courier was noteworthy, and he was suddenly a VIP at the hotel.

After sending the fax ending his ownership in DroneTech and partner-ship with his two best friends for life, he felt a burden off his shoulders. He was extremely wealthy, was in excellent physical condition, and had no responsibilities.

That giddy lightness lasted a full three minutes before the grief of his failure, loss of his friend, and his final promise to come to bury him on the moon caught up with him and weighed him down once more. He checked out of the hotel, rented a jeep, and began the long, uncomfortable ride to Askole.

The roads in Pakistan were not like Colorado. Even with the vibra-tion dampening system on, it was a bumpy and grueling drive. He tried the autodrive once but was quickly reminded the vehicle had no satellite GPS, and the sensors could not correct for the lack of visible road, which often resembled the gravel and desolate landscape on either side. The New Silk Road initiatives of the previous decades had improved the area somewhat but not much. Tamarind drove manually for hour after hour, his mind consumed by the monotony of gray pavement and the barrenness of the rocky landscape around him, with dust hypnotically blowing on the path before him.

It was dark when he reached the Naran Kaghan Valley, and he was unable to see the beautiful river and mountains covered with greenery on each side except in the headlights of the jeep. He found an old hotel with a Chinese-style roof—stacked ceramic tiles that swooped up at the corners. The room was modest but adequate, and after dropping his bags, he wan-dered out on the streets looking for a meal. He felt tired in his soul and fatigued in his bones.

The 2400 meter elevation, the icy crispness of the high mountain air, the roar of the river running through the valley, and the smells of the community reminded him of how far he was from any place he'd been to before. No one spoke English or the other languages Tamarind knew, so he depended on hand gestures and pointing to order his food. Many establishments were closed for the evening, but he found a restaurant with a local din and too bright lighting. He wasn't sure what he ordered but received an entire chicken baked and stuffed with rice and vegetables, satisfying his weariness.

As he sat there, listening to the sounds of the locals, he considered his future. The love of his life had married his best friend. Another friend who had once saved his life, he had been unable to rescue. Before his friend's death on the moon, he requested Tamarind bury him and restart the Moonbase. The debris field from the Space War blocked access to space. He had left his employment, and his life plan to mine asteroids seemed farther away than ever. Ugh.

Kohlrabi's final request had three parts to it. First, he had to clear the debris field in space. Then he had to get to the moon with a team that could stay there for a while. In addition to burying the 224 scientists, he also needed to take possession of what they had discovered and somehow use it to rebuild MoonBase Verity. It was too daunting to think about all of that in his current mental state. Double ugh.

Focusing instead on his immediate challenge of climbing K2 helped him clear his head. He'd need gear, supplies, and a plan. As he walked back to his hotel through the thin, crisp air, he got excited about the adventure ahead.

* * *

By the end of the next day, he had his jeep full of high mountain clothing, gear, and supplies. The total weight of everything was pushing 100 Kg, more than he could carry. He decided to purchase a SherpATV—a narrow track automatically guided vehicle that would follow him up the trail, lug at least half his supplies, and had a self-charging power source and inflatable tent. The ATV should be useful until the K2 base camp, still many days away.

The next morning, the air was clear, and the wind was light. The final drive to Askole took him the daylight hours. The road was well-paved, being the primary destination for the region's highest peaks. The Eight-Thousanders, so named, were more than 8000 meters, with K2 the highest in the Karakoram range at 8611m. Askole was the end of the road, where all expeditions began.

As he drove, the surrounding scenery was stunning—trees, green hillsides, roaring rivers, rocky cliffs, icicle-clad waterfalls, and snow-capped mountains. Being raised on a tropical island at the PNLI, Tamarind always appreciated mountains, snow, and cold, crisp air. By the time he arrived in Askole near dusk, he felt refreshed and eager for the adventure ahead. He'd booked a small stone hut with a garage to secure the jeep while he was on the mountain. It was far more rustic than he'd been told, with an old wood plank bed frame and table being the only furniture, hand-pumped water, and a basic toilet. It did have a solar panel on the roof, providing electricity for lighting, heating, and cooking during the daylight hours.

He registered his solo climb with the authorities and declined to hire a local Sherpa, which was almost a crime in the impoverished village dependent on wealthy foreigners like him.

"Sir, you must hire a Sherpa for your safety," the official from the Ministry of Tourism pleaded.

"No, thank you."

"You come here to die? Hundreds die on K2, one of four, and you climb over bodies on way to summit. One of four!" The official punctuated his staccato, heavily accented English with arm gestures aiming the back of his hand toward the mountains.

"Yes, I've heard that. No, I do not plan to die," Tamarind spoke confidently but thought to himself his life problems might be resolved if he died up here.

"No good. Stupid man to go alone." With that, he angrily stamped his permit and sealed a tracking bracelet with his details onto his wrist. "No remove until back here."

Finally, Tamarind packed his gear for the trip, stowed the rest in the stone hut for the way back, and headed out. He followed one of the traditional routes on a moderately-trafficked access trail to established campsites along the way.

The SherpATV carried 60kg of gear and followed a tag on his backpack loaded with 40 Kg of supplies. The nearly silent electric motors followed him tirelessly, its hyper-efficient solar cells recharging as they progressed. He saw no one on the trail and no animals throughout the day after he left the village. After a few hours, he found his body getting into the steady rhythm of the hike. The traditional trek into K2 base camp is 7-15 days, and he was hoping to do it in 5, but perhaps that was too ambitious.

The long, steady daily hike allowed him to reflect on the many challenges ahead of him. He broke the long list into sections in his mind and spent each day working through one part in as much detail as he could. His engineering mind naturally broke problems into 'Given, Required, Solution' format. Each day began with a hearty breakfast, loaded up for 5-8 hrs of hiking, and started with what he knew about the problem. He delved deeply into how he would mine asteroids, his long-held dream, and then each day; he considered one of the other issues—getting to the moon, Kohlrabi's puzzle, restarting Verity, clearing the debris field. He contemplated the technologies for asteroid mining, the Moonbase, and for going into space at all. He imagined a future past Almond and a basis for a new friendship with Flax and Almond. He decided to leave that one until the last day, which allowed him to systematically put it out of his mind.

Each day's journey relieved his burden a little. Korofong, Bardumal, long day to Khoburtse, Urdukas, long day to Concordia, and his final push to the 5400m base camp on K2. The physical details of the trek, the mental challenges working through each problem in his future, the spiritual challenges of his multi-layered grief, failure, and loss eased as he plodded on—therapy at 5000m.

CHAPTER 8

Repurposed

"Are not all problems and failures just opportunities waiting to be repurposed?" —Journal of Kohlrabi Trust

Telsun Filorini was sitting at his desk at Dronetech with both the satisfying feeling of completing a significant project and the unsettling discomfort of having nothing essential to do. Cleanup tasks remained after every engineering product development, but his communication drone development and checkout role was substantially complete. The discomfort made him subconsciously itch, and when Flax came to his desk, he had just inserted a ruler down the back of his shirt to scratch the center of his back.

"Solving an important problem, I see," Flax said, putting a hand on Telsun's shoulder.

"It seemed like the highest priority I have to work on," he replied with a shrug.

"We have a new project for you that we hope you will find… elevating. Can you join us in my office?" They walked together down the hall to Flax's office, and Almond was sitting in one of the two brown leather wing chairs in front of Flax's slab maple desk. It appeared made out of a single slab—the sides and top were continuous grain mitered at the corners.

Telsun hadn't been to the CEO's office before and ran his hand appreciatively across the desktop. "Coolio."

Almond held out her hand to him as she motioned for him to sit in the other chair. "Telsun, good to meet you. My name is Almond. Flax tells me you are the best person for this job." She had a welcoming smile.

"Hi, Almond, I know who you are, of course. Good to know I'm the best. What's the job?"

Flax sat down behind his desk and said, "We'd like to sponsor you for a climb of K2."

"Fractal!" Telsun exclaimed, his nodding head affirming that he was intrigued by the idea. "Er, why me?"

It was Almond who answered. "We're worried about Tamarind Chase. We have reason to believe he is attempting a solo climb of K2, and well, he wasn't in the best mental shape when he left. He was pretty upset about his friend's death on the moon, and he resigned and sold his shares in DroneTech. We know you worked with him for a while on the Moonbase rescue plan, and we were hoping you might, I don't know, help him to be safe and make new plans?" Almond folded her hands in her lap, her forehead lined with concern.

In a more encouraging voice, Flax added, "I've heard stories that say you are quite the climber?"

Telsun said, "I love climbing. I run marathons to stay fit, do rock climbing, ice climbing, or summiting almost every chance I get. Colorado has over fifty peaks above four thousand meters, and I've summited about half of them. K2 is every serious climber's dream."

"I thought Everest was the tallest—why K2?" Flax asked.

"You are right, but Everest is a well-trafficked mountain and not as wild. Nearly ten thousand have summited Everest, but less than a tenth have climbed K2. I don't know if I can help or encourage Tamarind, but I'd love to attempt K2!"

"The planet is reeling from the Kessler Event, so communications and travel will not be easy. DroneTech sold search and rescue drones to the Pakistanis last year, and I met one of the commanders of that unit. I'm trying to reach him via short wave radio to see if we can track Tam's whereabouts and get you faster to base camp. I'm afraid you won't have the usual time to acclimate. If you want to make a list of the gear you'll need, we can have it on a plane with you by day's end. That is if you accept?"

"You had me at K2!" Telsun grabbed Flax's hand firmly.

Almond promised him she would have two letters for him before leaving, one for Tamarind and one giving him background details. "Thank you, thank you for doing this; it means so much to us."

Telsun owned most of the equipment needed, and the rest was procured for him and delivered by courier. Flax had found from his business contact that Tamarind had left Askole for K2 base camp about a week ago. The plan was to fly to Islamabad and hitch a ride on a K2 rescue helicopter to base camp.

* * *

After more than a week on the trail carrying a heavy load, Tamarind was physically relieved to reach base camp, but it was bitterly cold, the wind ripping through the edges of his gear to find his flesh. His SherpATV had performed admirably, and his four-person tent was inflated and anchored for whatever weather might come. The SherpATV had a built-in cookstove, electrical charger, LED lights, and if he only used those capabilities, it would recharge using the solar panels. It also could provide heat, purify water, and generate pressurized oxygen, but these would drain the batteries more than he could recharge in a day. He had four weeks of supplies, which, weather permitting, should allow him to summit and return to the stone hut in Askole. Huddling around the cookstove for heat and devouring a hearty beef stew, he wrapped up in his sleeping bag and fell asleep.

The sound of the helicopter delivered a thumping pulse to his chest. It was just past dawn on his tenth day out of Askole when he heard it, and like the dozens of others at base camp, he came out of his tent to see what was going on. A climber had fallen on an acclimation climb and was unable to hike out without assistance. Four members of the Pakistani rescue team descended from the helicopter and headed off across the base carrying a stretcher. One additional man carrying a climber's backpack and two duffel bags of gear climbed out on the other side. Tamarind watched as the pilot pointed toward him while looking at a handheld device.

When the man had reached him, he pulled back his hood, shivered, reached out his hand, and said, "Tamarind?"

"Telsun? What are you doing here?" He was puzzled; he hadn't seen him since their trip together to Kennedy Spaceport.

"I was wondering if I could join you on your K2 summit?" His white teeth showed from his smile, and his hand was still out for a handshake.

"Come inside, you look cold." Tamarind grabbed his hand and directed him toward his tent, curious but not surprised. "Almond sent you?"

"Flax and Almond asked me to look you up, yes. They were worried about you."

Tamarind studied him for a minute after they sat cross-legged on the tent floor. "Flax was worried, or Almond was worried?"

"They both expressed concern and agreed to pay for my trip to join you on the mountain. I've brought my gear and supplies, and I am an experienced climber with twenty-plus climbs above four thousand meters."

"Right now, we are at fifty-four hundred meters, higher than any point in the contiguous United States. You up for this?"

Telsun exuded confidence and said, "I've dreamed and prepared for this for years. Whether anyone is up for K2—we'll see on the mountain, I guess."

"Humility is a good answer. Ok, you're in."

As before, they worked well together. Telsun knew much more about climbing and had years of research into the K2 trail. Tamarind knew the people at the camp who had K2 experience. There were no satellite phones or internet connections anymore, so they depended on radioed weather forecasts, Sherpa-knowledge, and climbers who had been here for a while. Communication between the camps on the mountains ensured they could make decisions each day.

There were three teams at base camp planning for a K2 summit—the Russians, the Norwegians, and the Dutch. Adding in the Sherpas and participants from other countries on these teams, about 40 people were at the camp. Of those, no one was supportive of the Tamarind-Telsun summit plan. Elite climbing teams all knew each other, had sponsors, and philosophies about the best way to climb. Tamarind and Telsun were nobodies in the climbing world. The Sherpas didn't like them because they hadn't hired any locals.

"I expected a spirit of comradery of fellow adventurers in this camp, but we appear to be outcasts," Telsun said, after leaving one of the mountain conditions briefings given to the climbers daily in the radio tent. It was the one place in the camp where all the climbing teams or at least the team leaders gathered each day.

"We'll just have to win them over with our grit, wit, and cheerful optimism," Tamarind said.

"Apparently, each of the teams is doing siege style summits, with equipment caches along the way. Are you still thinking of Alpine style climbing?

"We certainly don't have the support crew or equipment to do caches. The gear and food we have we intended to carry, so I say we go for it."

"Oxygen?" Telsun asked, without sounding concerned either way. They both knew that at about 8000m, usually called the "death zone," there isn't enough air to support life. Some have made the ascent without oxygen. Many have died trying, often on the way down.

"I can generate it here with the SherpATV. We'll need it if we are carrying our gear. You've heard them talk about the different routes and what they have planned; what do you think is the best for us?"

"The most common is the Abruzzi Spur route, which has four camps between the Advance Base Camp and the summit. The route is long and has many perils, and the Dutch team is doing it, leaving tomorrow, weather permitting. The Cesen Spur is considered safer and joins the Abruzzi, skipping a few of the perils. The Norwegian team is set-up for this route later in the week. The Russian team is attempting the Magic Line up the Southwest pillar, which many consider borderline suicidal."

"Despite rumors to the contrary, I'm not suicidal, so what do you think of tagging behind the Dutch or the Norwegians?"

Telsun agreed, and they went to each group separately. Neither team was willing to allow them to join their teams, so they decided they would do the Cesen route a day or two ahead of the Norwegian team. They packed ten days of food, Telsun's much smaller two-person tent, and all the ropes, axes, O2 tanks, and equipment they thought would be useful. They checked in with the Dutch team by radio the night before they left and got the latest on the weather and conditions on the mountain.

Dirk Van Dijk, the Dutch team leader, answered in his broken English, "Conditions gut. We thinkst ya go home best, no?"

"No, we'll see you on the mountain," Tamarind said. Looking at Telsun, "We're a go for tomorrow."

With the gear packed and loaded before sunrise, they secured their base camp supplies for their return. The first day's climb took them about four hours up to the Advanced Base Camp, shared with the Abruzzi Route. Some of the Dutch team's debris was there, and their path up the mountain was visible. There had been only light winds and no snow that day—if anything, they got sweaty and hot and had to remove layers.

On their second day, the relative warmth of the previous day was gone. Their eyebrows, eyelashes, and lips froze instantly, and they wore every layer of clothing. Splitting off the Abruzzi path, they followed a ridge at the edge of glacial flow. While the route avoided some of the Abruzzi Spur route's technical and perilous challenges, it did not have established camps until it reconnected above the shoulder. They set ropes into the exposed rocks on the ridge because of the steepness and stayed roped together. The minimal oxygen, the technical difficulty, and heavy packs ensured that they kept conversation to a minimum. They had helmet comms and would check in verbally every half hour or so, but the biting cold hurt the lungs and made conversation beyond short phrases painful.

By the middle of the afternoon, Tamarind suggested they search for a campsite. Today had been slower, with them taking diagonal steps and then zigging for three more. This technique allowed them to evenly use their muscles and rest on one side a little. Their hiking slowed to 8-10 steps per minute. Each time they zagged to the right, Telsun would scan the rocky mountainside looking for a place to tie in for the night. He finally identified a jutting rock about 20 meters above the path that had a tiny ledge behind it, a challenging vertical climb at the end of a tiring day. The pillar gave them a break from the wind and had absorbed heat from the Sun during the day, providing warmth and a place to anchor the tent. Once set up for the night, they melted some snow for their dehydrated meals, ravenous after the day's climb. The night sky was spectacular, and they were able to sit back against the pillar of rock and look up at the stars and the tiny sliver of a moon.

Telsun pulled out a flask, "Imported."

"Bootlegged, you mean." Alcohol was only readily available in Pakistan in 5-star hotels and then only by the glass in the hotel bar. Tamarind took a small sip. Aged bourbon. "Do you have a girlfriend?"

"Am I limited to only one?"

"Integrity and character limit us to things that align with our life purpose and values. Do you have a purpose?"

Telsun thought about this for a moment and then said, "Not really. I love my work, adventure, and dating. I suppose *carpe diem* is my purpose. You?"

He pointed up at the moon. "My next summit."

"Almond told me that Dr. Trust had asked you to come to bury him. How do you plan to do that?"

"I've been thinking about that since I left the company. All I must do is clear the debris field, restart the space industry, build a rocket, fly to the moon, and flip on the switch at Verity first. Easy." Telsun could detect the sarcasm.

"I've heard you like a challenge," Telsun said, after a long sip. "Which part are you having a problem with?"

"Clearing the debris." As if on cue, a series of shooting stars began sailing across the sky. "There goes one of those dead satellites now."

Telsun pulled out a tiny green pointing laser and pointed it up into the sky. "I wonder if you could estimate the mass of a shooting star based upon how long it takes to burn up, given its velocity and angle."

"If so, you could also calculate how much energy is needed to destroy the debris. Can you do that math for me?"

Telsun took the line and ran with it. "You can't easily destroy metal debris, but could break it into smaller fragments, or vaporize it into a gas or form a plasma. Most metals would vaporize below three thousand degrees Celsius. Less or more in a vacuum?"

Tamarind put his gloved hands behind his helmet and leaned back fully on the rock. "Much less, perhaps a fourth of the temperature required, so much less energy. How powerful is your laser?"

"It is a ten-watt military signal laser. It can start a fire but can't vaporize metal."

While they were talking, a much larger piece of debris entered the atmosphere. It was fast, low in the sky, and looked like it was coming right toward them, growing larger as it approached. Telsun grabbed his phone to video the speeding fragment that struck below the peak above them, triggering an avalanche high on the mountain.

"Quantum! Fractal! Coolio!" He had jumped to his feet and continued recording the event. The moonlight made the avalanche look like a magical ocean wave of blue as it tumbled down the mountain.

"Avalanche above us, Telsun!" Tamarind was less interested in the recording and more in their survival. As they watched, the thunderous sound of the avalanche beat in their chests. Huge sky-blue boulders cascaded down the mountainside, following the path of the glacier flow they had hiked up that day.

Telsun dove into the tent and activated the base camp radio. "Satellite debris impact about two thousand meters above ABC, avalanche heading your way!" He got a double click indicating receipt but no other answer from base camp. He looked up at the avalanche, gauging its depth, speed, and trajectory. "I think we are good at this height?"

Tamarind had come to the same conclusion. "However, we may get dusted pretty heavily. Let's get in the tent and buckle in." The tent was anchored firmly to the rock on both ends. They clipped their climbing belts onto the central line, grabbed their oxygen canisters and masks, tightened their helmets and facemasks, and huddled against the pillar rock.

The roar got louder, and the Earth rumbled. A shockwave of air, dust, and powder hit their position with full intensity, nearly collapsing the tent with them inside. For the next several minutes, all they could do was hold on. The sound was deafening; they could not hear each other even with their helmet mics.

As suddenly as it began, everything went silent and dark, with not even the light of the moon getting through the tent walls.

"You ok?" Telsun whispered.

"No injuries. You?"

"I'm not hurt, but we're buried under the snow." The avalanche compressed the tent's crisscrossed arched ribs into a teardrop shape about as tall as where they were sitting huddled on one side. Telsun's headlamp illuminated the far end of the tent, lighting the collapsed entrance. Pushing up against the top of the tent, all they could feel was snow.

"Ok. Don't panic. Equipment check. Oxygen tanks for 5-6 hours each, check. No injuries. Air cavity for perhaps 2 hours without CO2 buildup? Light – check. Water – check. Food?" He reached the top of one of the backpacks buried under the end of the tent and patted it. "Check. Safety?" He pulled on the anchor rope that had kept them on the cliff, "Check. Radio?" He had pulled it out when he signaled base camp. Where was it now? "Ok, no radio. No GPS satellites. No rescue teams coming to look for us; we are on our own here."

Tamarind watched Telsun work through his checklist, realizing how much more prepared for this his new friend was. The wisdom of this trip now struck him—foolhardy, more fool than hardy. They couldn't have predicted this avalanche, but they were willingly submitting themselves to innumerable deadly obstacles on this ascent. For what? They were talented with had much to live for; what were they doing buried under the snow on this mountain? The exhausting efforts of the day and their current situation's futility left him with little but fatigue.

"What do you say we get some sleep and address our predicament in the morning? We are warm, safe, and exhausted."

"No sleeping until we get access to outside air."

Tamarind groaned and steeled himself. "Can we tunnel out? Or at least dig until we find the radio?"

"Maybe. Usually, avalanche snow compresses into a cement-like mixture. But we have some room to work, tools, and we know which way is up."

They began by lying on their backs and pushing up on the ceiling. They were able to depress the snow above their feet slightly. They slowly moved along the tent, gaining tiny amounts. As they got toward the entrance, they wiggled out the backpack between them and the door. A small cavity remained, but they couldn't get the other pack uncovered, nor find either radio. As they unzipped the front door, the packed snow was almost as hard as ice. Taking turns and using the crampons in their hands, they chipped away small amounts with short, piston-like arm movements.

After a few minutes, they realized their efforts were useless. They leaned back against the rock and discussed a Plan B.

Removing his glove to touch one of the metal supports in the tent, Tamarind asked, "What are these made of?"

"Titanium tubes rated for two hundred kilometers per hour winds, which was the highest rating I could find the day I left. The fabric is virtually indestructible unless you are wailing on it with an ice ax. Evidently, with our climbing rope for support, the tubes and tent formed a sort of protective igloo."

"Your tent saved us; thank you for that. How reflective is titanium to a green laser beam?"

Telsun caught his idea immediately. They slid one of the three-segment titanium support tubes out of the loops in the fabric. Telsun directed the laser into one end, and the light beam came out almost unaffected on the other end. They positioned it against the ceiling and began drilling upward using the twisting motion and the laser's heat to cut through the snow above them, catching the dripping water in their water bottles. After the second segment was attached, the beam punched through, and no further water came down the tube.

"Fractal! We're through!" They took turns inhaling the fresh mountain air through the tube. "Well, at least we won't suffocate." They could see that it was dark outside and hear that the wind was blowing lightly, giving a whistling noise down the shaft. They proceeded to remove the other titanium supports carefully, and the igloo seemed to be self-supporting above them. They continued to drill holes and insert them until the air was noticeably better.

"Is there any chance we might get rescued?" Tamarind asked.

"They probably think we are dead by now. They haven't contacted us since my avalanche warning. Even if they sent a search party, they wouldn't know where to look. We are twenty meters above the trail buried under the avalanche." Telsun summed up their challenge.

"What about our wrist bands?"

"Detectable within about five to ten meters. Useful for finding our bodies, but not for finding us. The other groups are one to two days away. The Dutch probably decided to descend after the avalanche and might arrive at advanced base camp today if they aren't injured. The Norwegian team was geared for heading up our route but won't start unless they know we are alive. My radio may be outside the tent; yours is pinned under that corner of the tent somewhere."

"I've got an idea." Taking off his thermal jacket, Tamarind detached the electronic tag attached to the bottom seam. Turning it over in his hand, he saw four arrow buttons and a button marked 'Test mode.' "This is the controller for the Sherpa ATV. It has redundant comm systems and can be operated at a distance with a VHF radio link. I think the feature allowed you to send the SherpATV back down the trail to another user and pick up more supplies. I think we could use it now."

"It is a powerful tool, but I don't think it is going to come to us up here on the mountain?"

"No, but we might get it to move a little, as a signal." They discussed how they might move it and decided an SOS pattern of movements might signal that they were alive. Using the controller to send a message, they moved the SherpATV forward in three short steps, backward in three long steps, and forward again. Morse code for SOS ... --- ...

"Hopefully, they will figure out we are still alive. Now to signal where we are." Telsun took the laser and pointed it up through one of the tubes, flashing out the same SOS pattern with the bright green beam into the night sky. "If they look up, they should see it."

After ten minutes, the SherpATV remote battery was dead, not designed for continuous long-distance use. They decided to save the remaining life of the laser in case they needed it again.

"What if we used our ice axes to dig straight up through the tallest part of the tent?" Tamarind asked.

"Quantum. Gives us more leverage, shorter distance. Good idea." After a quick snack, they began chipping away at the ceiling, taking turns every 5 minutes. The person resting would move the snow out of the way, drink water, and breathe some oxygen to recover for their turn. Progress was faster but still chipping away millimeters with each stroke.

As they worked, they began talking about their next steps. The CO_2 buildup in their snow cave gave them a headache, and the tubes could not refresh the air very quickly. If they did get out, they would be exhausted and have only gear for one person, no ropes, no radios, and no tent—just one pack, an ice ax, and with one sleeping bag, they would not survive a night on the mountain without more protection.

The realities of their situation changed their attack, switching to 20-minute bursts with their oxygen masks on, with the person resting trying to sleep. Despite the adrenalin coursing through their veins, they fell asleep fast during their rest cycles. The thin, cold air, exhaustion, full stomachs, and total blackness overwhelmed them.

Kohlrabi appeared in Tamarind's dreams.

"Tamarind, we've found something here, something game-changing, and we want you to come and use it to rebuild Moonbase Verity." He was in the room with Kohlrabi under the station's white domes instead of the tent buried in snow.

"I don't know how to get there," Tamarind muttered in his sleep.

"You have resources, intelligence, and creativity; use them. Exhaust yourself getting here. It will be worth it."

"It will take everything. What have you found?"

"Come, Tamarind. Make it your dream."

Tamarind awoke to Telsun's shaking. Their snow tent was still almost as dark, though it must have been close to daylight outside—the snow depth was blocking all light. Considering the dream and their predicament, he aggressively tore into the ceiling. Gazing down the hole at his sleeping comrade, he realized they might be dead without this man's skills and preparations and worked through the next shift as well. Confirming it was just past sunrise, he gently shook him awake.

"Good morning, sunshine. Ready to go home?"

"The name is Telsun. I used to have a cat named Sunshine." He sat up, ran his hand through his thick hair, and drank some water. "Ok, let's do this. Let's first eat a hearty breakfast. Any brilliant ideas in the night?"

Working through the night, they had chipped a hole one meter above the top of the tent but still were not through. Their hands and arms knotted from the constant effort, their feet and legs cramped by the space further constricted with the snow from the hole, CO_2 poisoning only held off by their rapidly draining oxygen canisters and the small air tubes they had drilled to the surface.

"I could use lasers to destroy the debris field in space," Tamarind said, knowing he wasn't answering the question.

"Coolio, that could work. Any ideas on how to get out of here?"

"So, two pole segments suggest we have about 1 meter more to the surface. The CO_2 situation is getting worse here. I don't think we can last another day?" Tamarind had already calculated the answer but waited for confirmation.

"Agreed, we must go faster today, somehow, or we will suffocate. The air holes are blocked; it must have snowed in the night." Inserting his laser, he quickly cleared the tubes and could see the blue sky above. If they didn't exit today, they'd be there until next spring.

The ice ax's handle was also a sharp point, and they inverted it to drive it into the ceiling of the shaft above them. Highly motivated, working through exhaustion, they used their legs and arms in rhythm to jackhammer through the snow. The snow density lessened as they neared the surface. Soon they could scoop it with their hands. They had summit fever, and getting out became their summit.

When they burst out mid-afternoon, Telsun emitted a cry of joy halfway between a Tarzan yell and an alpine yodel. "They should hear that in base camp," he said, as he hoisted himself out of the tunnel of their igloo. The avalanche's scale was now visible; this part of the canyon had filled 20 meters since they climbed. The freshly fallen snow had smoothed the surface and covered any chasms beneath. "Weather is clear, and we have some hours of daylight. I think we should get as far as we can."

Tamarind passed up all the remaining gear and cut out the last bits of tent and structure. The hole was over 2 meters deep; he had to use the footholes to climb out.

Telsun revisited their equipment check. "One sleeping bag, signal laser, no tent, no radio, no oxygen, a few meters of rope, one pack of food and gear, and one ice pick. We must climb down before we freeze or starve to death."

"Unfortunately, I'm feeling the effects of CO_2 poisoning. Weakness, breathing twice as fast, head hurts, dizzy, nauseous, and my arms and legs feel like jelly. I don't think I can safely climb down." Tamarind felt as bad as Telsun looked.

"Copy that. This new snow gives us another option. Ever glissaded?"

Telsun laid out the titanium tent poles aimed downhill and threaded them through the fabric tubes in the tent. He tied the three tent poles together at each end and then secured the remaining rope to the front triad. Then placing the backpack with their gear below him on the tent and holding the ice ax behind him like a rudder, he said, "All aboard!"

Sitting in the front, Tamarind kept the bow of their glissading raft from digging into the snow. The tent poles acted like a keel, keeping them going straight.

Telsun hung off the back, using the ice ax as a rudder and a brake. "What can go wrong?"

The mountain in this section was nearly 45 degrees, too steep for safe glissading. Locking his legs around Tamarind's waist, Telsun pushed them off their perch and then leaned back, digging the ax into the snow as a rudder. Tamarind lifted the front of their canoe to his nose and tried to steer around obstacles by tilting the front section and his body.

Soon they were going so fast that they were screaming like kids getting airtime off bumps and crashing down, knocking the air out of them on impact. Still, they gained speed.

"Put your heels in, but don't let them catch!" Telsun yelled over the roar of the descent. They each put their feet up high and then slowly brought them down until they were just skipping across the top of the snow. Still, they were gaining speed. He leaned all his weight into the ax, now burrowing a deep rut in the snow while somehow also keeping his feet digging in.

Tamarind could see a colored tent far down the hill. "ABC!" he yelled, steering the front slightly. He used one hand to dig into the snow, but they gained speed. Surveying the terrain ahead, he could see they were passing the end of the ridgeline they had followed and that a hard left would direct them up the trail. He pointed, and they tilted left as he steered slightly in that direction, cutting a large curving arc up the incline. Finally, they started to slow and then stop. They laid back, the adrenalin and vibrations taking what energy they had left after the cold.

"That was glissading, huh? Beats walking."

Telsun laughed in relief.

It was a short walk downhill to the orange domed tent at the Advanced Base Camp. Dirk Van Dijk came out and looked at them as if he'd seen a ghost. "We coming to rescue ya!

"We need it. Can we come into your tent?" Tamarind gave him a bear hug and said, "I told you we'd see you on the mountain."

"Ha, ya."

* * *

It took them two weeks to recover entirely and trek back to Islamabad. Each party along the way wanted to watch Telsun's video of the satellite impact and hear his increasingly dramatized story of their narrow escape.

When they finally reached the airport, Telsun asked, "Are you sure you won't come back to the USA with me?"

"No, I have some companies I need to acquire. The space industry is in freefall right now, and I'm going to need a ship to get to the moon."

"You are doing all this because your friend saved your life?"

"Not just for that reason. Which reminds me, thank you for saving mine. I owe you one."

"I thought you saved mine, but I'll take it. Give me a call when you are ready for your moon trip. Sounds fractal."

Tamarind waved and walked down the concourse toward his gate. He heard his name paged to the information desk. The man behind the counter handed him a phone.

"Tamarind Chase? This is Jake Johnson. I have some questions for you."

"Jake, I'm boarding a flight. What is it?"

"Do you feel responsible for the destruction of Apollo Verity?" the reporter asked.

"No," Tamarind said, not believing it himself.

"Were you trying to kill yourself on K2?"

"No, of course not."

"Why did you sell your shares in DroneTech?"

"I have new plans for my future." Tamarind felt vague in his answers and wanted to end the call.

"What plans? Were these plans given to you by the leadership of the PNLI?" Jake did not cease.

"What? No. You'll have to wait and see. I need to go now, Jake." Before the reporter could ask more questions, Tamarind handed the phone back to the clerk. He could still hear Jake talking when he hung up the phone.

He boarded his flight. He had a lounge seat in first class, and after a nice meal, fell quickly asleep thinking about his journey ahead. He had a mission and a plan, and now he needed to build the tools to make it happen.

He dreamed of Kohlrabi talking to him in his office at Verity. "What is your plan, Tamarind?"

Tamarind explained the plan in detail.

"How will you accomplish it?"

Tamarind talked about his ideas, the steps he'd thought through, the ones he had not.

"Why are you doing this?"

"I promised you."

"No, that isn't it. Why are you doing this? Is it to win Almond's respect? Is it guilt? Why?" Kohlrabi's specter menacingly stared at him, demanding an answer.

"This is my mission..." His voice fell off, his words not even convincing himself.

"Your mission. No. You know what and how, that will have to do for now. You will need to know why Tamarind. Why will define your purpose."

PART 2:

LIGHTSTAR

CHAPTER 9

Launch day

"Mankind's greatest accomplishments began as one person's wild idea" —
Journal of Kohlrabi Trust

Launch minus 30 seconds.

Under the terms of the Space Peace Treaty, it was another six years before an approved launch of any vessel or satellite into space.

"This is the moment, this moment, that the entire world has been waiting for," Tamarind Chase spoke confidently, his arms out wide. The audience became quiet as he took the stage in the center of the room.

A silky, transparent cylindrical screen descended from the ceiling, stopping just above his head. The real-time images of the rocket were displayed all around and underneath it, giving the impression of the launch vehicle itself dropping into the room. The Dark Matter Ventures CEO seemed to relish the moment, the fulfillment of a long-held dream.

"The Space War affected us all, and with the launch of Project LightStar, mankind can resume our exploration of space." He placed his hands on the ceremoniously oversized red button in front of him. The cylindrical screen and visuals made it look like Tamarind was standing right under the rocket on the launchpad and said, "Wherever you are on planet Earth, count with me—five, four, three, two, one!" And as he pressed the button, throughout the room and all over the world, people yelled, "Blast OFF!"

Dark Matter Ventures designed the facility for this day. It was multiple stories high with live images displayed on the cylindrical chamber walls, on the floor, and the central rocket display. The rocket display screen in the center rose as the rocket lifted off, and warm air blasted down on the crowd. The engines' roar, flames billowing, above, under, and around the room, was loud as thunder and jarring as a lightning storm. The sensation of standing on the launchpad was unsettling for the people onsite or viewing through the VR headset app available globally. As the rocket rose, the ceiling filled with a cloud-like fog. Green lasers projected out from the nose cone amidst the smoke, highlighting the vital work of Project LightStar as it lifted off the ground. The launch, the cheers around the room and the planet, and the celebrations which followed made this a moment no one could ever forget. Tamarind's ambition to clean up the accumulated space debris that had shut down space exploration and satellite communications had finally begun.

Though visibly the celebrity of the moment, the Dark Matter Ventures CEO made his rounds through the crowd of guests, humbly thanking each of them for their service. Most were high impact leaders of organizations addressing world health needs, social or economic inequality, environmental problems, or other world issues.

"Dr. Cole, your work to end homelessness is an inspiration to me. Thank you."

"Mr. and Mrs. Abercrombie, your legal efforts to end the slave sex trade are working. Thank you for making a difference in the lives of those most in need of your protection."

"Lucille, your idea to restore the ozone layer using sunlight-activated photocatalytic coated fabrics held aloft by weather balloons... love it, I wish I'd thought of it!"

Tamarind moved through the gathering, purposefully shaking hands. He encouraged those present to make a difference. He thanked them for their organizations' work and reminded them anything was possible through creativity and perseverance.

When he stopped at reporter Jake Johnson, he gave him a warm handshake surrounding Jake's hand with both of his.

"Glad you could come today, Jake!" Tamarind said. "Keep asking those tough questions—a free and penetrating press is essential for a free world."

Everything about him screamed authenticity. Even Jake was having a hard time being skeptical, but as his mother always told him, "If something seems too good to be true, it probably is!"

Jake replied, "I will, I will. Can I set up a meeting to ask you some of those tough questions?"

Tamarind smiled, nodded, winked, and introduced him to his assistant. Tim Garner was following him, ready to record any assignment Tamarind gave him as they meandered through the crowd gathered for the event.

Impressive, Jake thought. Jake felt appreciated, respected, and genuinely believed he would get the interview, despite his ever-present skepticism and cynicism at all displays of power and significance.

Jake Johnson recognized only VIPs around the room and realized he was fortunate to get an invitation today, unusual for a freelance reporter. He primarily submitted articles to the *International Times*, but sometimes to other outlets. Jake was about the same age as Tamarind, early to mid-30s, but they looked very different. Tamarind looked healthy, polished, with South Asian features—dark skin, black hair, and medium build in a perfectly tailored, charcoal black suit with a white shirt and a colorful tie with rocket flames around a Dark Matter Ventures logo. The image of an accomplished, self-confident CEO.

If he was honest with himself, Jake was trying too hard to look like the historical, classic, iconic reporter. He had scraggly brown hair, a well-used tweed jacket with folded up articles, pens, and notepads stuffed in his pockets, and penetrating brown eyes behind durable-looking glasses. Holding his pad and pen was a leather messenger bag draped across his chest. In an age when articles were recorded and imaged immediately, he had gone out of his way to symbolize the more in-depth research required to get the story behind the story. Journalism today was not about images and opinions. These were commonplace. It was about the background and more profound connections that told the underlying story.

Jake had done a series of penetrating articles on the Pan-Nationals, especially on Tamarind Chase, even before Project LightStar. This rocket ship transported the world's most powerful laser aimed through a spinning crystal at the nose cone. It was the culmination of the work of about a thousand of the smartest people on the planet. If everything went as planned, it would simultaneously identify and vaporize debris in space and continue to do this while orbiting indefinitely, being recharged by the Sun. The cargo and technology were shrouded in mystery, and Jake hoped to shed some light on that too.

Jake watched Tamarind closely as events progressed during the launch. *Man, he is smooth in a crowd. Is that arrogance? Smugness?* Jake thought to himself. No, just that competent, purposeful, joyfulness so characteristic of all the Pan-Nationals he had researched.

There was something else—it took Jake longer to put his finger on. The satisfaction that comes to those who complete an essential step in a long-held dream. That was it. But why? Sure, LightStar will benefit humanity, but how does it profit the mysterious Tamarind Chase? That thought nagged at him as he continued to watch at a respectful distance.

After completing his walk through the standing-room-only crowd, Tamarind returned to the small center stage raised a few steps above the people buzzing around the room. The hour preceding the launch had included a video highlighting historic missions in space, a summary of the causes of the Space War, the resulting debris field and deaths on the ISS, and at Moonbase Verity. Background on Dark Matter Ventures and the objectives of Project LightStar were overlaid with the countdown clock. Once launched and the vehicle tracked into orbit, Tamarind loosened his tie for the post-launch celebration.

Jake saw that Tamarind's friends, Flax Venture and Almond Brighten, had joined him on the raised dais. Flax and Almond were also Pan-Nationals and had cofounded DroneTech with Tamarind years earlier. Flax was taller than Tamarind with an infectious smile. Almond exuded enthusiasm. Jake moved closer to see if he could hear what they said to each other.

Flax leaned into Tamarind and gave him that special forearm lock handshake resembling an arm-wrestling match in the air. They each said a cryptic phrase while looking into each other's eyes, "ERIWA, my friend!" Jake was close enough to hear them despite the noise in the room. Almond hugged Tamarind with a beaming smile and tears of pride in her eyes, and then she repeated the handshake and the same phrase. All the Pan-Nationals used this cryptic, symbolic phrase with each other, and no one seemed to know what it meant. Various meanings were proposed, some noble, some crude, and some suspicious. Maybe Jake could unravel this as well. He had formed his own conspiracy theories about the Pan-Nationals.

His research had concluded that Tamarind was in the first class of the orphans who graduated from the PNLI. While most had taken influential roles in society, his path was unique. After starting DroneTech with his best friends Flax and Almond, and after growing it to billions in revenue, the cofounder resigned. He suddenly and mysteriously sold his share and spent years purchasing up what remained of the stagnant space industry crippled by the Space War.

Jake's early career blossomed during the brief but destructive Space War, which ended six years ago—about the time his first major journalistic article went global. Jake's initial contact with Tamarind was a call where the latter had told Jake he had understated the war's impact. In retrospect, Tamarind was right.

The global satellite industry's value before the conflict exceeded $1 trillion, and for several countries, it represented the most substantial part of their economy. The telecommunications industry, including phones, television, GPS for road and rail, maritime, and aviation, space communications, were all made possible by satellites. Agriculture, environmental monitoring, disaster detection and response, Earth and space science were also linked to essential satellite data.

In the decades leading up to the war, almost all internet traffic, business, military, and phone communications migrated to satellite networks. These were more secure, faster, and lower cost than optical cable, wire, and radio-based telecommunications. Low Earth Orbit (LEO) satellites significantly shortened the time delays associated with satellite communication, making them competitive with line-of-site and cable systems on the ground. Developing world countries skipped wired connections and went directly to these networks. Militaries, governments, banks, and large businesses moved to the highly secure direct laser with quantum entanglement validation connections on proprietary satellites impossible to hack.

The Space War's impact was profound, blowing the world back to an earlier age, where international data transfer depended on undersea cables, wired optical cable hubs, and line-of-sight towers. DroneTech reconnected the globe with its communication drones, but a sustained recession followed as the communications and space industry's value plummeted.

The ESA, NASA, Russians, and Chinese developed ground lasers that were slowly destroying large fragments in orbit. Project LightStar was the first approved vehicle to begin to clean up the debris field from space. This was quite a bit faster than the 'decades' Jake had initially predicted in his article because of the incredible genius of Tamarind Chase and his team at Dark Matter Ventures.

* * *

That night after the launch parties had wound down, Tamarind invited Flax and Almond back to his home for a quiet drink. The house was modest or extreme, depending on your perspective. He lived in a cement box, more than half-buried in the ground near the top of a small hill. The roof had a central skylight that allowed a clear view of the sky from within. Bioswale grass covered the rest forming a part of the house's water collection and treatment system. The mostly-buried building needed no heating or air conditioning, maintaining a constant temperature of 20C with no direct connection to the sewer, water, or power grids. He loved to explain the complex thermionic energy conversion system, which exchanged heat, purified water, and generated electricity, but few beyond Flax and Almond fully appreciated it. A "shoebox system with net-zero environmental impact," he called it.

The remainder of Tamarind's property facing the roadway was landscaped with Golden and Alphonse Karr bamboo, fed by a drip irrigation system. A solar-powered LED-lit path meandered through the bamboo to his front door. The backside looked out over the desert. The windows were 1.5 meters above the floor and continued up to the ceiling, allowing a view outside slightly above ground level. Half the windows viewed bamboo tops, and the rest displayed the blue Nevada sky or distant mountaintops. Inside, his home had every modern convenience, but it was sleek and understated. They sat on a black leather sectional around a transparent aluminum coffee table, directly under the skylight view of stars.

"Why do you love bamboo so much, Tamarind?" Almond asked.

"It is the only thing I could get to grow here that reminded me of our home growing up. Not that the barrenness of eastern Nevada is anything like the dense jungles of Hope Island," said Tamarind, looking much more relaxed than the polished image of confidence he exuded at the launch. "I lack your touch with plants."

"Most of the world lacks her touch with plants," Flax said, with a grin. Almond's expertise in botany was legendary.

"Have you made progress on your medical stasis drug you were working on when I left DroneTech?"

"Medical developments are slow going, but we are ready for human trials. I just returned from Africa, where we successfully induced hibernation in primates that don't normally hibernate. It isn't as deep as a medically induced coma or as systemically overwhelming as a tranquilizer, more like a chilled sleep for weeks at a time. We demonstrated its benefits for animal transport, a good start while we are completing the human trials."

"Almond's shown some real genius with this work. Leading scientists are following her work with sustained interest," Flax added.

"Have you heard from Martin and Carlissa?" Almond deftly moved the topic off herself. The three of them and three other orphans had lived with this loving couple as their house parents during their first years at the PNLI. They represented the closest any of them ever had to parents.

"I chatted with them yesterday. Our house parents were "excited about the launch, proud, and send their love to each of you." Tamarind quickly summarized the ten-minute exchange, imitating their lilting Irish accents. He tilted his head and winked the way Martin always did when he approved of something they did. They all laughed.

"The launch went well today, didn't it?" Flax asked. He settled on the couch with his arm draped casually around Almond's hips. Even after all this time, Tamarind felt a little jealous of their relationship.

"Thanks to impressive displays from DroneTech cameras!" Tamarind said, raising his drink as a salute to their role in the day.

"A few of them got a bit crispy in the rocket exhaust, but we were glad to be a part of the effort. I know this was an important step in a life-long dream of yours, Tamarind," he said, raising his glass to toast his old friend.

"Hear, hear," Almond added.

"ERIWA, my friends," Tamarind replied, drinking deeply from his glass. "Still much to do to re-open space, but today was an important first step. Hopefully, my life-long dream won't take the rest of my life."

Tamarind reached into his pocket and took out the black Ilmenite moon rock he had carried with him all day and placed it carefully in the center of the table. "Kohlrabi would have loved to see this day."

"Any more insights into his cryptic last words?" Almond asked.

"We've found something game-changing here... yes, I've considered it, as perhaps he knew I would. I've tried to understand what each of the countries was researching. I'm sure their work will be vital in colonizing the moon and furthering our exploration of space, but game-changing? I guess I'll find out if and when I get there. Perhaps he just enticed me with a secret treasure because he knew I would love the chase."

"To Kohlrabi, the wisest of us all!" Almond made the toast, and both Flax and Tamarind nodded with respect and drank deeply. "Are you still having the dreams?"

"Yes, he seems to be guiding me forward in my mission."

"What does your doctor say?" Flax asked.

"My psychiatrist, you mean? She wants to medicate me. Seeing a dead person is not unusual for a few months after a close friend's death, but six years has me skirting the lunatic fringe." Tamarind looked resigned to his condition.

"Why not take the meds, Tamarind? Perhaps they will give you some peace?" Almond leaned forward, her hands clasped together as if pleading.

"Perhaps I need his wisdom?" He looked up through the skylight, making a mock toast toward the stars. The moon was nearly full tonight, illuminating the few clouds from behind. Hidden there were the mysteries of Moonbase Verity.

CHAPTER 10

Interviews

"Where is the one who turns over the rock, who scrapes the gloss off the deception, who pursues the difficult question until answered, and coura- geously stares down the faces of power? There is the hero of our times."
—*Journal of Kohlrabi Trust*

Launch plus 18 hours

To his surprise, Jake was given time the next day on Tamarind's sched- ule, for a full hour, no less. He reviewed his background research on Tamarind Chase, Dark Matters Ventures, and the Pan-Nationals in preparation.

Most people now had nothing but praise for the Pan-Nationals, but it didn't start that way. The Pan-National Leadership Institute (PNLI) was founded after a pandemic in 2030 had drastically increased the number of orphans worldwide. Every nation was affected, and while there were some new orphanages built and aid packages put together, it became evi- dent that humanitarian concern for these orphans was inadequate to the problem. With all the conflicts going on in the world, those growing up without parents got lost in the mix. There was a growing perception that children bereft of parents were the inevitable products of their impover- ished countries, genetically damaged in some way, inherently useless, and untrainable. Most nations considered the orphan issue a sad reflection on their struggling governments.

The Pan-National movement began when a group of prestigious adults orphaned as children, many of them billionaires, came together to address the problem. They decided world borders, perceptions, and theories about the value of orphans prevented the kind of concerted action required. The founders decided a systemic solution outside of the existing government and non-government organizations was necessary. Additionally, they found the nature vs. nurture debate about orphans somehow being genetically inferior particularly disgusting.

Initially, they began with a media campaign highlighting the value of influential leaders in history who lost their parents as children or were raised without them. These included Confucius, Aristotle, Dante, Eleanor Roosevelt, Nelson Mandela, Tolstoy, Malcolm X, JRR Tolkien, and Henry Ford. Their media campaign summarized these famous orphans' contributions, encouraging people to imagine a world where these voices went unheard. They then called for a worldwide response to the orphan crisis. They followed this with celebrities raised as orphans, including Marilyn Monroe, Ray Charles, Babe Ruth, Ingrid Bergman, Ella Fitzgerald. The campaign created sympathy for orphans initially, but it also created a backlash. Critics pointed out the infamous children raised without parents like Adolph Hitler, Genghis Khan, Saddam Hussein, John Wilkes Booth, and Ivan the Terrible. The Pan National leadership attempted to make light of the infamous examples by highlighting fictional orphan heroes— Superman, Batman, Spiderman, Harry Potter, Anne of Green Gables, Cinderella, Tarzan, Frodo. In the end, the group abandoned the media campaign and turned their efforts toward establishing the PNLI.

The founders located PNLI on an isolated island off the coast of New Zealand and asked each country to transfer the responsibility for raising the orphans they couldn't or wouldn't care for themselves. PNLI would provide a loving and nurturing environment, excellent health care, education,

and training to allow them to become world leaders. Almost every country participated, though there was some skepticism about the outcome. The final agreements included that each of the graduates of the PNLI would be citizens of all the countries participating in the contract—Pan-Nationals.

The PNLI initially took orphans seven years old or younger and offered them the absolute best education, training, and medical care possible. The overall aim was that these "worthless" orphans would become world leaders, taking on humanity's most challenging problems, and prove the worth of every person.

As Jake reviewed his notes on the Pan-Nationals, he couldn't deny that the results were impressive. The Pan-National graduates had founded companies that addressed world problems and emerged as thought leaders addressing intractable issues. Others grew into world leaders who had negotiated peace and environmental agreements and implemented solutions reducing poverty, disease, climate change, and other previously deemed unsolvable problems.

DroneTech, for example, was founded by Tamarind, Flax, and Almond to address police brutality by providing drone camera tracking at every police stop. Their drones' capabilities expanded to improve farming, enhance communications in remote areas of the world, and facilitate responses to disasters. DroneTech pioneered drones to dispense medicines, monitor the environment, reduce violence using drone-based non-lethal crowd control, minimize school shootings, and other ground-breaking initiatives.

Without a doubt, the Pan-National movement had demonstrated that every orphan had value, and given the right opportunities, could excel in character, leadership, and almost any field of endeavor. That hopeful message alone had raised experts' expectations in several areas, leading to improvements in pediatrics, childcare, and education globally.

But Jake couldn't shake the feeling that a network of super-trained, mission-driven leaders, funded by billionaires, networked together, with access to any country, was a part of something altogether more sinister. In his widely published series of articles, he put forward this idea. Perhaps his rare invitation to the launch and now this immediate follow-up interview was intended to change his opinion.

I need my wits about me today, Jake thought. *Few get this kind of access to Tamarind Chase.* After reviewing his earlier notes and background work, he wrote out questions as they came to mind:

PanNats all have names formed from a useful plant and an action word. Why? How were they chosen?

PanNats never seem to remember where they came from. Why? Three to seven-year-olds should have memories, some scarring, perhaps.

PanNats all seem to be healthy despite coming from diseased, discarded, injured, abused backgrounds. How is that possible? Did some die? Were the disabled healed?

What was so different about their education? Why do they all share the same values? Brainwashing techniques?

What does the acronym 'ERIWA' mean?

What is the laser technology on Project LightStar? How is it deployed and recharged in use? What happens if it gets hit by debris?

How will it clear the debris field? How long will it take?

How will Dark Matter Ventures benefit from Project LightStar?

Many other questions came to mind, but he grouped them into background questions, technical questions about the project, and impact questions. He researched previous articles on the company, so he was careful not to tread old ground. He crossed out some and scribbled notes by others. Jake insisted on doing prep work in a paper notebook. He found that the physical process of writing things down added some structure to his interviews and visually showed the interviewees the progress as he turned pages, which in his experience put people at ease. He also inconspicuously

imaged and recorded everything using state-of-the-art technology, with permission, of course.

* * *

Dark Matter Ventures' offices were near the launch site, so he had a short commute from his hotel. They were expecting him in the lobby and directed him to the CEO's office. "Thank you, Mr. Chase, for agreeing to meet with me," Jake began.

"Please, call me Tamarind," shaking his hand with both of his and gesturing toward leather chairs by the window.

Jake wasn't seated opposite Tamarind's sustainably harvested bamboo desk, but casually next to him. The office was efficient and elegantly simple, almost no personal mementos, except a younger picture of Flax, Almond, and himself cutting a ribbon at the opening of the expanded offices of DroneTech. One wall was a window overlooking the Dark Matter Ventures facility, the Nevada hub of Tamarind's dispersed space and terrestrial mining business. Another whole wall had a moving image of the wind blowing through a jungle scene, the buildings of the PNLI visible in the distance.

Jake looked at the moving jungle image and asked the celebrity CEO, "Did you like living on a tropical island at PNLI?" It was an awkward question that didn't lead to anything useful. Tamarind just looked at him, indicating he should continue.

Jake quieted his mind, took out his notebook, and proceeded with the interview. "Our readers will want to know a little more about you. Do you mind if I ask some background questions?" Tamarind nodded for him to proceed. "How did you get the surname Chase?" Jake asked.

"Probably because I was always chasing after Flax, who was much faster than me," Tamarind said, smiling. Jake was glad this question had put the Dark Matter CEO at ease. He'd often found getting his subject in good humor essential to getting an honest interview.

"What is your earliest memory of PNLI?"

"It is running after Flax in the jungle."

Jake continued with a string of other questions about Tamarind's early years, but after several stilted answers, the persistent reporter received little information that was useful or insightful. He wrote down *evasive about personal details but careful not to lie.* Tamarind either didn't know the answers, was sensitive about them, or was not interested in revealing the details. His black hair and South Asian or Indian features *only narrows things down to about 1/4th of the world's population*, Jake thought. Jake gave up on the tack and moved on.

"We spoke years ago about Moonbase Verity. Did you know Dr. Kohlrabi Trust personally?" Jake could see from Tamarind's expression that he did.

"Kohlrabi was a close friend; we grew up together at PNLI," Tamarind said, with emotion in his voice.

"Did you conceive of Project LightStar because of his death on Moonbase Verity?" Jake asked.

Tamarind smiled and said, "The Space War certainly changed my priorities. The resulting collapse of the commercial space industry motivated me to use my resources to acquire and sustain a portion of those companies. Most analysts questioned my choice to abandon DroneTech as it entered the Earth-based communications market to purchase the remains of a space industry banned from space by international agreement."

"Most people questioned your entry to the space industry during the launch ban," Jake restated his words, hoping Tamarind would continue with the train of thought.

"I questioned my decision many times over the years. To reopen space, we must clean up the mess in orbit around the Earth. Several national space agencies were attempting to reduce space debris but were making slow progress. However, as the Space War's effects persisted, eyes turned toward the solutions proposed by Dark Matter Ventures. Now, six years later, we've launched Project LightStar to place the first communications satellite back into orbit, restore critical communications, and most importantly, to clean up the debris field."

"Your team has the right to feel very proud of that."

"Our team discussed various paths through the Kessler Field," Tamarind continued.

"The space debris field caused by the Kessler Syndrome Event..." Jake often found restating the obvious helped the conversation continue.

"Exactly. We ticked off dozens of ideas which wouldn't work," The Dark Matter Ventures CEO held up another finger as he explained each of the ideas he considered. "Waiting for all the debris to enter the atmosphere and burn up—far too long—decades, even centuries." He raised his left index finger. "Send up toughened satellites to get above it all and ignore it—this would violate the terms of the Space Peace Treaty, and it might be impossible to create a stable asynchronous orbit this way. For geosynchronous orbits, the debris field would still be in the way. Delay times for communications to these higher orbits would be inadequate." His left middle finger went up. "Use an electromagnetic field to collect debris—most of the debris is not sufficiently polarized or magnetic to attract and is spread over too large of an area." Third finger. "Use space nets made of super fibers as a collection filter—many of the particles are too small, the surface area required far too large, and the required fiber strength too high." Fourth finger. "We also considered an explosive event to vaporize material in a region large enough to create a hole—we'd never get that one approved, and it wouldn't be a clean enough or a big enough hole to do anything but get through it." With the fifth finger raised, he motioned with his arm as if he had just thrown those ideas out the window.

"Finally, we settled on the fact that we'd have to destroy all the particles in the debris field or make them so small that they couldn't cause much damage. Pulsed lasers of sufficient intensity could do that. We considered locating them strategically on the ground as NASA, ESA, and the Russian Space Agency have been doing, but going through the atmosphere and tracking from the ground loses a lot of functionality. However, if we used a very high-energy, ultra-short pulsed laser and located and recharged it in space, we could keep doing that indefinitely until space is cleared. Thus, began Project LightStar."

"How long will it take to clean up the debris field?" pressed Jake.

"If there were 100 billion particles in the debris field, and Project LightStar could vaporize one every pulse at 100,000 pulses a second, it would only take a few weeks. However, there are a lot more particles than that. Some will take more than a single pulse, and the laser needs some charge time, so it cannot operate at maximum pulse rate all the time. More realistically, several years. But we may be able to get some hardened satellites up there once we've destroyed the largest pieces." Tamarind spoke clearly and confidently on scientific and mathematical details and project outcomes. He had done his homework.

"Tell me about the laser technology," Jake asked.

Tamarind smiled at him and raised one eyebrow. "The specifics are a trade secret of Dark Matter Ventures. There may be military applications of the technology which we want to avoid," Tamarind replied. The Pan-Nationals were all pacifists, though each of them knew at least one martial art. Jake had found reports of examples where Pan-Nationals had been attacked and had rendered the attackers harmless.

"I can say it is the most powerful laser ever created in the ultraviolet portion of the electromagnetic spectrum, which is essential to its functionality. We based the laser on proprietary crystal technologies that can generate terajoules of energy in nanosecond pulses to ablate or to vaporize matter." Tamarind was adept at explaining complex concepts succinctly and at a level appropriate to his audience. He acknowledged Jake's technical background with his answers and phrased things to address Jake's eventual readers. "The computing system uploads location and trajectory information from Earth-tracking stations and uses this information plus onboard machine vision recognition. The system tracks objects in their proximity and signals the pulses and intensities sufficient to destroy each fragment. The spinning faceted crystal in the nose cone directs pulses at targets within the full field of view."

"Ultraviolet lasers? I saw green lasers during the launch?" Jake was quick to notice the discrepancy.

Tamarind paused and smiled mischievously before continuing. "We generated a little extra smoke and added a green laser light show just to make the take-off more spectacular!" He shrugged guiltily and smiled. "Did you like the launch?"

"It was the most spectacular show this reporter has ever seen," Jake enthused, smiling widely, hopefully enough to disarm Tamarind for his next question. "The rocket seems excessive for a single satellite. Is something else in there?" Jake suspected the CEO would evade but thought he might slip it in there at a lighter moment. There had been some speculation on the net that there must be more inside the rocket than just the Project LightStar satellite.

"It's a very powerful laser. Did I mention that?" Tamarind chuckled, and then narrowing his eyebrows sarcastically, added, "or do you see a dark conspiracy hiding in there?"

Jake did wonder but decided his interviewee might evade another question. Nothing false, just no information. He decided to give the topic one more poke.

"There have been discussions on the net that Dark Matter Ventures also has a large military contract," Jake injected provocatively.

"No. Nothing about Project LightStar is funded by or achieves any military objective."

"What happens if a large object hits Project LightStar?" Jake asked.

"It will never get that close," Tamarind said confidently. "We did extensive wind tunnel testing before we received approval. In those tests, we put the equivalent of an automobile of debris into the wind tunnel at Mach 2 and then measured the particles' size coming out in sequential filters. Everything ended in the HEPA filters—micron and sub-micron-sized. Nothing will get close enough to hit LightStar.

Smugness? Competence? Jake wrote in his notes. "But what if it did?"

"Objects in space move very quickly but at a tiny fraction of the speed of light. To the LightStar, which is also moving, they are almost standing still. They won't get close." Tamarind spoke with infectious confidence about this.

"So how does Project LightStar benefit Dark Matter Ventures?" Jake asked.

"We are restoring critical communications to the planet, cleaning up the mess of the Space War, and giving all humanity a chance to reach outward again. Those are benefits for us all," Tamarind answered sincerely and sounded genuinely philanthropic in his goals. Still, Jake knew this project had to cost an astronomical amount of money and assumed the financial rewards must be equally immense. There must be an unstated way to make a sizeable return on the investment.

"Is your intent in cleaning up space to capture a significant share of the communications industry?" Dark Matter Ventures would have a temporary monopoly on space communications and would also be well-situated to launch additional satellites to form communication arrays. "DroneTech has become a significant global player since the Space War. You are well-positioned to displace their dynasty."

"We are not a communications company. We may assist others in placing satellites in orbit, but that is not our primary objective either." Tamarind nixed two obvious opportunities but also hinted there was a primary objective.

Jake decided to take a different tack. "What is ahead for Dark Matter Ventures after the success of Project LightStar?" Jake hoped if he opened the door, perhaps Tamarind would walk through it.

"Clearing space isn't a done deal yet. We have several years of work ahead of us. But once space is open, we hope to get back to Moonbase Verity."

"You are hoping to expand your terrestrial mining operations to the moon?" Jake conjectured.

"Perhaps," Tamarind answered, "but we must also restore communications to the many deep space missions idle since before the Space War."

While many deep space missions by various international agencies and commercial enterprises were still operating outside of the Earth's orbit throughout the solar system, information from them was limited. They depended on using the orbiting satellites to relay communications. These agencies had wanted this first mission to restore their links to these space programs outside the Earth's atmosphere, which were undamaged in the Space War.

"Why did you decide not to reconnect them to Earth with Project LightStar?

"We gave priority to critical communications on Earth." Tamarind's definition of "critical communications" differed from some nations and many space programs.

"Why was restoring communications to deep space programs not considered critical?" Jake asked. Without those connections, Dark Matter Ventures owned solo access to any of the information from these long-distance space programs, further fueling Jake's conspiracy theories. It all seemed too convenient. There were no checks and balances on Tamarind's space communications monopoly over the next few years.

Tamarind nodded his head, expecting this question. He leaned back in his chair and said reassuringly, "I understand the concerns expressed by many about this. It would be easier for me if I did choose to prioritize these developed nations' science projects. However, the loss of satellite communications most impacted the developing nations, and the people living there deserve to have their communications restored ahead of first-world scientific concerns. You know I am a space scientist at heart and will rejoice when we restore communications to these deep space missions. Most have data protocols that allow efficient storage of data for up to ten years without having a download link, so hopefully, we can restore communications before any data they have collected is lost."

"I suspect it will be amazingly profitable to control space, communications, and the world's future," Jake said, with a twinge of cynicism in his voice.

"Great endeavors require great risks, and hopefully, result in commensurate rewards," Tamarind spoke calmly, assuming everyone agreed with such a statement. "However, profits will be directed toward other endeavors to help humanity."

"It seems that Project LightStar means more to you than just a significant accomplishment. What does it mean to you?" Jake prodded at the question that had been nagging at him. Jake noticed a subtle flex in the muscles of his face as Tamarind paused before answering.

"As you mentioned, Dark Matter Ventures has terrestrial mining interests. I didn't buy up the space industry to dig in the dirt on Earth. Ultimately, opening space opens the opportunity to expand operations to the moon and beyond. Space mining has been a personal dream of mine since a very young age."

Jake continued to ask questions, and Tamarind either answered or evaded them until they both noticed that the hour was up and stood up from their chairs. Jake asked one more question on the way to the door.

"What does 'ERIWA' mean? I noticed all the Pan-Nationals say it to each other."

Tamarind put his hand on Jake's shoulder and said, "It is an encouragement to be our best. Thanks for coming by today, Jake," and with that, the interview was over.

Tamarind's assistant, Tim Garner, met him at the door. "Nice to see you again, Mr. Johnson," Tim said respectfully and briskly escorted him to the VIP elevator and rode it down with him.

Jake looked back and saw Tamarind head off in the other direction, already walking with purpose surrounded by a group of suits. Several delivery robots moved to the side of the hallway as Tamarind walked by, and Jake thought, *Even the robots show deference to Tamarind Chase.*

Jake turned to Tim, who was in his mid-20s, way-too-eager, and asked him, "What is it like to work for Chase?"

"It is the most amazing experience of my life. He's a true genius," Tim answered with bubbly enthusiasm.

Jake smiled. *Not much here*, he thought.

Jake concluded he wouldn't get a Pulitzer for the article he would write, but he had thoroughly enjoyed the research, launch, and meeting. He still had a few support interviews with professors and an industry expert, which might shed light on some of his unanswered technical questions; maybe he'd turn something up there. He hurried back to his office for the scheduled call.

* * *

The professor and the two industry technologists all joined the conference call at the scheduled time. The conference call room in his office was his one real luxury. He had virtual conference tables on his wall displays, so each participant appeared to be sitting in the room with him. His imaging computer picked up additional details: book titles, notes on their desk, twitches in their eyes or hands, dilation of their pupils. The microphones picked up every sound in each of their offices while Jake was interviewing them. His analytical tools could interpret the truthfulness of their statements and tell him what the background noises were.

"Lasers don't necessarily get bigger to create higher pulse energies, and their size doesn't scale linearly," said the professor from Cal Tech. "No way that capsule contains just a laser." Professor Alexander Thompson was gray-haired and looked academic with a worn, brown jacket, and practical, plastic-rimmed glasses. As he stood to pace around his dark-paneled office, which he said helped him think, Jake heard his chair squeak. Jake wondered, *why do scientists and engineers not just lubricate their chairs occasionally?*

"I concur. I did some calculations on the thrust used in the lift-off, and the weight of the cargo is far larger than is reasonable for a satellite." From Lawrence Livermore Labs, Dr. Ken Watson was one of the leading US authorities on astrophysics who was not working at NASA or directly on Project LightStar. He spoke as a person who was always the room's expert and with a slight English accent. "Even if the satellite was hardened, there is more than enough payload in there for a second satellite." He shifted in his seat, and Jake could see and hear he had bumped one of the voluminous stacks of journal articles piled around his desk.

Amazing that anyone would have that much paper in his office, Jake thought. "Are you saying it possessed twice the thrust needed for the launch of Project LightStar?" Jake asked.

"Oh, more than that. From what I can infer from the scant design information Dark Matter Ventures supplied, the satellite would account for one-third of the payload of that rocket," Dr. Watson stated provocatively. Jake glanced at Professor Thompson, who nodded in agreement.

"What else might be in there, or what would the purpose be of that second satellite, in your opinion?" Jake asked.

Like most scientists and academics, Dr. Watson quickly back-tracked when things got speculative, "I was merely conjecturing that the available payload was sufficient to allow the second satellite, not stating a conclusion of its existence. The difference could be for redundancy, or perhaps I've underestimated the mass of LightStar," he said.

Jake looked to Professor Thompson to expand. He did not speculate on what else was in the capsule or offer any conjectures on what the extra payload might be. Jake always found it challenging to get newsworthy quotes out of academics and scientists without many caveats.

Dr. Michael Martin, the Chief Technical Officer for Maxwell Energy's solar energy and storage division, did have something to add. Dr. Martin was well-tailored in a dark grey suit and a white shirt with no tie, his black hair perfectly manicured. He looked the part of the technical spokesperson, exuding confidence, and used to giving interviews discussing technical topics in any level of detail. "When you do an energy balance for Project LightStar, the numbers don't quite add up. We don't know much about the proprietary laser. Still, if you estimate a conversion efficiency, a pulse rate, and an energy per pulse to achieve ablative energies, the rocket doesn't need to be as large as it is. If we also consider the solar insolation in space and estimate a maximum possible solar collection area and factor in energy conversion efficiencies, the numbers don't stack up."

Jake looked at him expectantly, encouraging a conclusion.

"There is no way he could generate enough power using solar collection to fuel that laser. Essentially, LightStar needs another power source. I'm thinking a Thorium nuclear fission power plant is filling the remainder of the payload."

"There could even be two Thorium reactors, a second satellite, and a second laser," continued Dr. Martin. "Perhaps it is redundancy designed into the project in case of failure."

Jake knew that multiple redundant systems were vital to space reliability and wished he had pressed Mr. Chase about that earlier.

"It would also make the ensuing restart of the space race surprisingly one-sided, should it be a military-guided laser," Dr. Martin conjectured.

Bingo: a conspiracy theory with a direct quote from a leading scientist. Jake followed up. "Why a thorium reactor?"

"Thorium reactors have the potential to provide a significant amount of energy over a long period without outside assistance or additional materials. If I were powering a high output laser in space, I would use a Thorium-based nuclear reactor." Dr. Martin spoke confidently, implying that it was probably the best idea if he thought so and looked to the other scientists for confirmation. Each nodded in turn.

You have to love engineers, Jake thought, *no fear of making conclusions.* The other two scientists continued to nod their heads in apparent agreement and added nothing further to the conversation. Jake thanked them and ended the connection.

After the conference, Jake's real work began. He remembered the relative simplicity of that first major article on the Space War years ago, how it was about interviews, research, facts, and conjectures. Now, he created visual simulations of everything, linking together the video footage he recorded, overlaying audio interview comments, and finally, adding a simulation of the rocket and the possible dual satellite deployments. For modern journalism to compete with video feeds and reporting bots, he needed unique content.

Broadcasts of the live event had appeared on every media outlet by the time Jake finished his article and simulations. One simulation showed the rocket engines ceasing and deploying the solar cells, the spinning crystal, and the lasers destroying debris. A second simulation showed the second satellite and then zoomed in to see the thorium reactor supplementing the solar cells. His article included video quotes from Tamarind Chase and leading scientists linking together his simulations. It was provocative, and he suspected it would command some airtime.

CHAPTER 11

Deployment

"There seems no end to unwinnable causes, arguments that never sway, perspectives that never shift, and creative deceptions that distract. Their ubiquitous persistence suggests that we believe they are essential to accomplish anything of significance. Are not transparency, reason, and truth tools powerful enough to achieve any just cause?"
— *Journal of Kohlrabi Trust*

The initiation of Project LightStar's mission had been one of the most highly anticipated events in media history. The DroneTech cameras monitored the lift-off from every angle, capturing the thunderous and fiery display, creating unprecedented images watched repeatedly, topping 100 million media views within 24 hours, swelling to over 1 billion within the week. Additional cameras mounted on the LightStar satellite showed its deployment with equal clarity, continuous audio, and a text feed clarifying details.

Once deployed, live space images seamlessly integrated with real-time simulations highlighted the destruction of particles too small to be seen. Invisible ultraviolet nanosecond laser pulses rendered as purple beams blasted thousands of particles per second, sometimes with slow-motion playback. It was mesmerizing to watch. The coverage showed that Project LightStar's launch was a success, and debris destruction was in progress.

Over the first few weeks, critical satellite communications started blinking on, showing, of course, the spectacular images of the preceding days.

* * *

Tamarind reviewed Jake's article—"Project LightStar Launches New Space Era, Questions Remain." Jake speculated in the editorial that Project LightStar had a secondary agenda and that it might contain a second satellite with a thorium reactor powering another unrelated mission. Perhaps that mission pursued another Dark Matter Ventures project or a US military communications or weapon system, despite Tamarind's denials.

Tamarind watched Jake's simulation of the rocket separation and launch of not one but two satellites. "Not bad, Jake. Not correct, but close." He again wondered if he should have chosen transparency in this quest, and yet confirmed in his mind that the second stage couldn't have happened if he had.

What was not seen from the launch videos, what no camera or simulation showed, was the ongoing trajectory of a secondary capsule, taking the rest of the rocket's payload out of the atmosphere, out of orbit, deep into space. Phase 2 of Project LightStar had also deployed, and only a handful of the most loyal at Dark Matter Ventures and a few key investors knew anything about it. It was not a second satellite, as Jake's article suggested, but a deep-space mission. Tamarind's magic used the launch as the distraction to hide his sleight-of-hand, even from his executive team.

A second laser powered by a thorium nuclear reactor was mounted on the back end of the cylindrically shaped capsule. Side thrusters extended out of the rocket, and when fired, it accelerated deeper into space. The laser beam, emitting pulses straight out of the open maw of the capsule's front, kept searching, detecting, firing, and approaching its eventual target. The world's first fully-automated asteroid survey and mining system was launched in secret, without any fanfare or approvals.

* * *

Alone in his secured control center, Tamarind looked forward to watching a daily summary after completing his regular workday. "It will be years before anyone will even know about Phase 2 if the secret holds, and hopefully by then, they will see the genius of my idea. It's always easier to get forgiveness than permission," Tamarind spoke out loud to himself. History has shown the future is not imagined by rule-followers but by those who find a way to break free from the thinking which created the existing order. Tamarind delighted in being that man.

He had much to complete before his phase two objectives could be revealed. In addition to the survey laser, which searched for the perfect asteroid, the capsule contained mining and processing equipment. These were based upon Dark Matter Ventures' terrestrial mining capabilities adapted for space. Not all the problems associated with mining, processing, and retrieving materials had been solved at the time of launch, so some intelligence and adaptability were also integrated to implement solutions when developed in the intervening years.

It had taken considerable skill to make the entire world, and especially his management team, believe that there was only the Project LightStar satellite in the capsule. He'd tasked the LightStar team with the construction of two matching satellites and then had the extra one routed to Arizona for analysis by the terrestrial mining team. He'd assigned one member of his LightStar team to modify the laser and one member of his terrestrial mining team to oversee the parts' assembly and insertion into the mining capsule. In the end, only the three of them had clarity on what they were doing. Even they did not know precisely what he had done.

CHAPTER 12

LightStar

*"Lasers were the greatest invention of the 20th century, but it took until
the 21st century for us to realize it." —Tamarind Chase*

Launch plus 18 months

While Project LightStar was Tamarind's vision, there was no doubt who the optical genius was that made it work, at least within the team at Dark Matter's Launch facility in Nevada.

Paul "Scarecrow" Moncrief was tall, unbelievably thin, and undoubtedly smart. With dual master's degrees in electronic control systems and mathematics and an intuitive grasp of laser optics, he was an early hire at Dark Matter Ventures. He relished the kind of technical problems that would scare most away, digging into them like a dog searching for a bone. His team was responsible for implementing the targeting and control system for Project LightStar.

His nickname came about two years before launch while explaining to the engineering team that there was no possible way to reorient the satellite, fire the laser and direct the beam using galvo optics as the laser optic team proposed. Galvanometers with optical mirrors mounted on each rotating axis, or galvo optics, were the standard way of directing lasers at very high speeds.

"Look, guys," he said in the Dark Matter Ventures engineering meeting, "there is a lot of stuff up there, flying at tremendous speeds, and that stuff already demonstrated its assassin capabilities by destroying all the satellites in the history of the world. The laser optics solution proposed does not pulse fast enough, and your optics can't respond fast enough to give our satellite a hope of surviving in debris-filled space." The team looked at him expectantly but unconvinced. "Imagine my body is the laser, my left hand one galvo mirror, and my right arm a second galvo mirror." At this point, he raised his arms above his head, pointed his face at his left hand, flickering his left hand spastically, and then swung the laser pointer over his head with his right. He moved his body in short arcs to imitate repositioning the satellite. Everyone cracked up laughing.

"That should scare the crows away," one of the team said, adding to the giggles around the room. Paul blushed and scowled. The name just stuck. "Scarecrow" Moncrief was born. After a good laugh, Tamarind calmed the team down and asked Paul to explain his proposal.

"We must deliver the energy to vaporize an object in a nanosecond pulse," he began, still flushing a little from embarrassment and the exertion of his demonstration. "At any given moment, thousands of chunks of debris could be flying toward our satellite, which itself is oscillating and traveling at high velocity, so traditional mechanical methods will not be fast enough to respond. However, a combination of a pair of piezo mirrors and a very high-speed, spinning, hemispherical, or parabolic fly's eye lens will allow the beam to target any position in a one hundred-twenty-degree spherical arc. The satellite will move with the debris field but at a slower velocity and positioned so its backside is never vulnerable to debris impact."

"Can you demonstrate that, Scarecrow?" Tamarind quipped, and the room again erupted in laughter.

It was this idea, however, that made Project LightStar possible. Scarecrow, the nickname the team gave Paul, was able to do the spinning axis coordinate transformations and translations and the control system algorithms to position a pulse anywhere in its 120-degree access cone. The satellite itself oscillated in a narrower cone, allowing the full field to approach 150 degrees in the final implementation.

The laser optics team was led by Dr. Xiang-Ling Xu, who'd been in charge of the development team at Yongzhu Crystal Laboratories before joining the Dark Matter Ventures team. The tall Chinese optical physicist who'd pioneered several UV laser crystal developments had been a great hire. He had previously led the development of the high-energy mining lasers used in Dark Matter's terrestrial mining operations. The requirements of Project LightStar were both challenging and exciting to him. He carefully led his team through significant breakthroughs in laser system design to deliver enough energy into a single nanosecond pulse. Additionally, once Scarecrow's vision was fully understood, the team developed the impressive multi-faceted spinning crystal at the tip of the launch vehicle.

Tamarind suggested adding the green laser to aid in visualization and target illumination and, of course, to enhance the show used in the launch. Dr. Xu scowled at the perversion of his pristine optic with a green laser primarily for marketing purposes.

"Mr. Chase, your green laser is possible but not desirable. I would prefer not to add unnecessary components into an already complex laser optic system." Xiang-Ling spoke with a heavy Mandarin accent, but his intent was clearly understood.

It took some effort for Tamarind to convince him. "Xiang-Ling, those of us here at Dark Matter Ventures, know of your amazing accomplishments, but no one else will be able to see your UV laser or optics before or during operation. Adding a little green color will allow the world to see your genius, and everyone will know the name of Dr. Xiang-Ling Xu." Tamarind could see this appealed to Xiang-Ling's ego, but his pride would not allow him to yield even then. Finally, with feigned reluctance, he agreed to add a small green laser into his optics train.

Xiang-Ling's acceptance came with a technical poke at Tamarind's optical competence. "Of course, I will have to correct for the prismatic deflection—the UV light and green light will not hit the same point after passing through the prism due to the variation of the index of refraction at the different wavelengths. However, I have an idea for how to solve this problem, which you did not appreciate when proposing your solution."

Tamarind smiled. He often worked with experts and geniuses in their field, and many of them were also divas. He appealed to Xiang-Ling's "greater understanding" and thanked him for his "inventive solution to this problem." Tamarind suggested one more idea to help secure the decision across the line. "We'll use the green laser for video tracking, but we will use image processing to render the laser light in dark purple to represent the UV laser." Xiang-Ling agreed to this, and Scarecrow affirmed this was possible.

* * *

Every day after launch, the team tracked the progress of the Project LightStar, making sure the targeting information was uploaded to the satellite, updating performance metrics on the key components, and measuring progress metrics on the clearing of the debris field.

To keep the public interested in Project LightStar, Tamarind included specialty cameras capable of monitoring a few hundred more substantial debris destructions per day. Converting these to spectacular images with slow-motion replays and sound effects continued to generate interest worldwide. Most people knew sound doesn't travel in space, but the movie industry had prepared them to accept and even expect the added sound effects. While not as technical as the Project LightStar team, his video production crew created a 24/7 live feed of the command center, the debris field, and the debris destruction simulations.

He hired the appropriately named Galactic Marketing to assist his video team in presenting the Project LightStar story to the world. They would add subtitles about the debris field, like "Approaching debris field from Russian Satellite Mionosk-6," and overlay an original satellite image. Tamarind's idea to add meaningful numbers, "billions destroyed," "% cleared," etc., became buzz-statistics that most people knew. Some even celebrated as each milestone was achieved.

Every week, Tamarind's split his time between overseeing the terrestrial mining business of Dark Matter Ventures located at their Arizona facility, monitoring his secondary project from his hidden control room, and managing the progress and communications about Project LightStar. When in the LightStar office in Nevada, Tamarind would wander through the command center, reviewing mission stats, chatting with key team members about their personal lives, and checking in with each team leader. After returning from Washington, DC, where he was painfully working toward his asteroid mining legislation, he decided to spend a little extra time on the floor.

"How is she flying today, Scarecrow?" Tamarind asked.

"Everything is operating within normal parameters," Paul answered. "As we thin out the debris field, we have been able to increase the pulse frequency four percent and expand the field of view by three degrees." Paul was always searching for slight improvements and was relentlessly on task. Sometimes, at the end of his shift, Tamarind had to remind him to go home. Scarecrow was the one person from the LightStar team involved in designing the asteroid mining portion of the project.

"Every great accomplishment in history required someone like you who is committed to its outcome. Thank you, Paul," Tamarind said, acknowledging his contributions to both key projects. Paul nodded and then turned back to his work. Scarecrow was not doing this for praise.

Tamarind had been monitoring the video feeds and decided it was time to turn things up a bit. Walking into video production, the visible difference between the marketing and engineering teams was noticeable. The engineers on the floor dressed a little nerdy-chic, but in video production, people dressed like they enjoyed social lives outside of this place, at least as much as you could in a remote location in eastern Nevada.

Calisandra Spencer, the CEO of Galactic Marketing, arrived at Dark Matter Ventures for their scheduled meeting with a fashionable leather shoulder bag carrying her work materials. She preferred to be called Cali and walked with the confidence of a woman whose time was valuable to her, and the team in video production performed at the top of their game when she was around.

"How's the buzz out there, Cali?" Tamarind asked as they moved toward the conference room she used for her office on the days she was at his office.

"We get regional interest spikes when we are destroying debris from that country's satellites," she answered.

"I guess people like to see their government's stuff blown up," Tamarind said with a chuckle.

Tamarind noticed her eyes dilate whenever he spoke to her and suspected his did as well. Their mutual respect and attraction remained unspoken; their interactions were always professional and friendly.

Cali had worked for NASA before the Space War and had overseen public relations and marketing associated with NASA's many global missions. After she left to start Galactic Marketing, many of the industry's companies hired her to communicate about their latest developments, satellite launches, space voyages, etc. Galactic Marketing expanded rapidly until the Space War messed up the industry.

Tamarind met her when DroneTech hired Galactic Marketing to get out information about the communication drones. After starting Dark Matter Ventures, he stayed in touch and hired her to assist them with the complicated media events around the launch of Project LightStar.

Cali smiled warmly and continued, "Unique views are up twenty-five percent over last quarter, and our core users remain steady at two hundred thousand, ninety-seven percent of which keep the feed on round the clock. "Whenever a celebrity visits the command room, or larger debris is destroyed, we get media comments and retweets. We have daily video links to classrooms worldwide, and we have a series of information videos used in schools. We get pictures incoming from groups celebrating when we hit a new performance milestone." Photos from these "percent parties," when the mission ticked over a percent, Cali would integrate into the daily feed. The world was still interested, and Cali made sure there was always something fresh to bring the story back into the foreground. Every few months, she'd strategically introduced competitions that gave prizes predicting the sequence of satellites destroyed or timing of a milestone achieved. She'd timed press releases on the heroes of Project LightStar, and her coloring book, *Satellites and Lasers,* was well-received in children's classrooms. Once Cali finished her update, Tamarind made a new proposal.

"Cali, I think it is time to start a countdown timer aligned with a press release. In a hundred days, the debris field will be sixty-eight percent cleared, and we will be ready to start launching hardened satellites. Let's tell the world we are ready for them."

Tamarind had been working internationally to restart the communications satellite industry, which was still much needed. Several governments and commercial teams globally unrelated to Dark Matter Ventures were developing hardened satellites and preparing them for the go-ahead approvals to launch. Dark Matter Ventures was not the one approving the launches, which required the sign-off by a consortium of international space agencies, nor would their rockets be the only ones putting them into orbit, but all waited for the safety reports from Tamarind's team to proceed. NASA scientists calculated 68% of the debris field cleared before launching a hardened satellite with minimum risk, and >87% removed to open space to non-hardened satellites safely.

"I'll get started on that tomorrow, OK?" Cali replied, packing up her leather satchel. "I have a board meeting at Galactic Marketing, and I need to get back to Denver and to prepare."

"I'll walk you out," Tamarind said with a smile. She nodded.

Out of the corner of her eye, Cali noticed one of the ladies on the marketing staff move her arm rapidly. As she looked over, she saw her fending off one of the engineers' unwanted attention, a rather large, red-bearded engineer, a part of the manufacturing engineering team.

Is that Kern? Tamarind thought as he followed her view. Tamarind remembered his name because he had asked Kern to take down inappropriate photos prominently displayed on his desk a few months back.

Kern was bending over her and had one hand on her shoulder. She did not like it and was trying to discourage his advances with her arms. Tamarind decided he needed to step in, but before he had, Cali moved quickly down the aisle toward the cubicle to position herself in an aggressive position between Kern and the young lady.

Tamarind saw the engineer put his fingertips on the lady's face and say something crude to her. She rolled her chair back, stood, and raised both hands defensively.

Tamarind stepped into the cubicle and spoke with authority to the engineer, "Step back."

"This is none of your concern, Chase," Kern said, casually. "We were having a personal discussion."

"It looked to me like you were harassing her." Tamarind looked at the young marketing professional, who was bright red and uncomfortable by this attention. He looked at Cali, and she nodded in agreement.

"No, just being friendly," Kern said, defiantly. No embarrassment, no concern, no change registered on his face.

"You're fired, Kern. There is no room in our company for anyone who disrespects another person as you just have." Tamarind said. Cali put her arm around the young woman, who started to cry.

"Fired? For what?" Kern turned away from Tamarind and stepped closer to Cali, clinched both hands, his face flushing with the heat of anger.

Tamarind did not look the least bit fearful. "Please leave quietly now. Personal items will be returned with your final check." Tamarind pointed toward the exit with an open hand, standing beside him, next to Cali and the crying woman.

Kern was quite a bit larger than Tamarind or Cali and moved angrily toward the young lady, saying, "Now look what you've done."

Cali was between them, and he moved his arm sideways to shove Cali out of the way. "What are you going to do?" Kern asked.

Cali deftly stepped back in time to avert much energy from the push and then stepped between Kern and the distressed woman.

"Kern, don't make this worse than it is." Again, Tamarind opened his hand and directed him toward the exit, positioning himself to step in to protect the ladies.

Kern thrust an open hand at Cali's shoulder. She stepped sideways, grabbed his hand at the wrist, pulled his momentum forward, and with one hand behind his elbow and one on his wrist, swept his feet out from under him with her leg. He fell loud and hard to the ground emitting a painful grunt.

Tamarind deftly caught Kern's head before it hit the carpet, and folding Kern's arm firmly across his chest, pinned both arms, and said, "That was Aikido. Are you done?"

Kern was not hurt, but Cali and Tamarind's moves were so fast, he reconsidered the wisdom of another attack. He didn't answer, but once Tamarind felt his muscles relax and saw the fire had gone out of his eyes, he let him up. By this point, there was a small crowd, and Kern moved passively toward the exit, his face nearly as red as his hair, shoulders slumped, rubbing his wrist. Tamarind watched as he left the building.

Tamarind turned first to the young lady from marketing. "I'm so sorry."

She nodded, sobbing, and walked back to Cali's office with her. Cali calmed her down while Tamarind dispersed the crowd.

Remembering that the Galactic Marketing CEO had an urgent appointment and he had offered to walk her to her car, he stood by her office until the young lady had calmed. She again collected her things and walked with him out of the office. During this exchange, he noticed she had never acted in anger, never appeared fearful, and unruffled from the exertion. *Impressive*, he thought.

"Thank you for your help, Cali," Tamarind said, with a genuine look of appreciation in his eyes. "What was that—Jujitsu or Krav Maga?"

"The latter. So, you know Aikido?" Cali thought he was probably more comfortable handling the angry engineer than comforting the crying woman.

"We should spar sometime, might be fun," Tamarind said.

They walked without speaking down toward her car, and she looked around the parking lot to make sure Kern had left. He had.

Tamarind wanted to end on a positive note. "It has been eighteen months since Launch Day, and by every measurement, Project LightStar has been a success. Soon, the world's communications will be restored. Project LightStar will continue, but interest will subside as other communication satellites are launched. However, you've done a great job keeping the world's attention on space, Cali. It is important work as the world once again looks to the stars."

She smiled as she thought how positively he switched back to the business after that scuffle and that he was thinking about her needs.

"Tamarind, I share your passion for space. There is no project I would rather be on," she said sincerely.

As she drove away, she watched Tamarind confirm that Kern had left the area before heading back into the office.

That afternoon and evening, Tamarind continued to walk around the office until he'd said 'goodnight' to each member of his team.

Everyone at the Nevada facility of Dark Matter Ventures knew that Tamarind had an elevator in his office. They knew that he sometimes disappeared and assumed his disappearance was to work on one of his other vital priorities. He might be off to a Congressional meeting to give an update on Project LightStar, or to establish the criteria to end the ban on future space launches, or to negotiate the future of the space mining industry. He might be headed to his terrestrial mining business operations, or to meet with investors, analysts, or the press offsite. After a few years at Dark Matter Ventures, the team had grown used to this.

But tonight, after being in DC for much of the week, he had another priority in mind.

CHAPTER 13

Phosaster

"It is our secrets that worm deep inside of us, feed our fears, and isolate us from our friends." —Journal of Kohlrabi Trust

Tamarind's elevator also descended to his secret underground control center. When Tamarind leaned into the retinal scanner on the elevator's control panel, it dropped to an underground floor. It opened into a circular room about 15 meters in diameter with a ceiling 3 meters above the plush carpeted floor. The front half walls were covered with displays facing a leather couch in front of a single desk in the center. On the back half of the room was a bathroom with a shower, a closet with a few changes of clothes, an exercise station, a bed, and a kitchen with prepared meals he could reheat. The cafeteria staff delivered the meals to his office, and he would carry them down to the room each day and bring up the waste. Although underground, the displays and the sheer size of the place made him feel comfortable and unrestricted in his thoughts and movements, and he could move freely around the room while looking at the displays.

Removing his shoes and socks upon entering the room, he turned on jazz music. It always helped him relax, and the improvisations stimulated his creative thinking. With colorful wall displays and music surrounding him, he felt like the conductor of an epic space opera.

Tamarind examined the five-day backlog of data from the latest asteroids, the favorite part of his work. As was often the case, he might end up sleeping here tonight.

* * *

Although he loved his work, it led to a spartan lifestyle—daily exercise, void of entertainment or hobbies unrelated to exercise, or deeper relationships. Occasionally, he'd watch a sci-fi movie about space here in his bunker. While they'd taught the Pan-Nationals a lot and had given them valuable skills at PNLI, relationships and love were mostly talked around. Sure, they'd learned conflict resolution skills, active listening, recognizing others' strengths, and reading about love stories and human physiology. Still, Tamarind had felt overwhelmed and unprepared when he'd fallen in love with Almond Brighten. Her silky black hair, engaging brown eyes, and alluring curves initially attracted him, and her wit and shrewd intellect drew him in. But it was her playful spirit that had captivated him; she was always game for an adventure and could draw Flax and him out of a sullen mood with a mischievous smile.

Flax, Almond, and he did everything together at PNLI and raised as siblings in the home they shared on the island. Typically, Tamarind had crazy ideas, Flax led the bold endeavors, and Almond was the joyful, playful, funny one who made it so enjoyable to be together. Both Flax and Tamarind adored her, but they had an unspoken agreement that their great friendship came first, and they should not risk that with anything like romance.

When the three of them founded DroneTech together, Tamarind's idea of dual counter-rotating blades on a programmable flexing shaft gave their drones a significant edge on payloads maneuverability. Like most startups, DroneTech had struggled at first as they tried to implement their company vision. Flax used to say, "Product development is like peeling an onion: there are many layers, and each makes you cry." They'd had some limited success with their first drones, which monitored every police engagement to document and minimize police brutality.

The real breakthrough came when Almond, a brilliant biochemist, had synthesized the potent but safe drug used in their security darts. The idea was to render the offender, or an out-of-control officer, harmless as quickly as possible, giving them just enough control to catch themselves as they fell to the ground. The drone went up during any police engagement and could be remotely monitored by more senior officers, who could control the situation if things escalated. Adding the tranquilizer darts to their security drones had been the breakthrough that had secured the first significant security orders for DroneTech.

The three of them continued to work together well, but slowly, their "unspoken agreement" to avoid romance began to break down.

Among the PNLI graduates, Flax Venture stood out—he was taller and a natural athlete. His wavy blond hair and bronzed physique might have been Northern European. He was always eager for an adventure, was the first to take a risk, and was typically the best at every sport. But it was his faith and character that had won Almond over.

A thread throughout their PNLI training was the ongoing challenge to choose a belief system. While contrary to the prevailing trend of secular education, the Institute promoted faith, noting that history's great leaders were driven by high ideals practiced wholeheartedly. Tamarind's self-confidence, understanding of science, and his ability to make informed decisions led him to Deism, like Benjamin Franklin and Thomas Jefferson. A vague acknowledgment of a providential hand but a stronger belief in science and human intelligence. Kohlrabi had chosen Buddhism. Christianity had gripped almond and Flax, and for each of them, it had become a defining and sincere faith that affected every decision they made. For Flax and Almond, their Christian faith shaped their character, morality, business ethics, and compassion for others.

It became apparent that Flax and Almond shared something Tamarind did not. They married before he left DroneTech but had remained good friends ever since. Tamarind was happy for them, but he just couldn't shake his love for Almond, or maybe the idea of Almond, even after more than six years.

Keeping the second phase of Project LightStar secret also contributed to his loneliness. It made him feel duplicitous. It required him to hold back. He had considered a relationship with Cali, and they had enjoyed some meals together and flirted a bit. He couldn't get past the fact that she wasn't Almond and that he wasn't willing to be fully transparent. So, relationships were just on hold for now.

He decided to call the second phase of Project LightStar, Phosaster. In Greek, the word 'phos' meant 'light,' and 'aster' meant 'star.' The investors had liked the name, and in his mind, the fact that it rhymed with 'disaster' reflected the inherent risks and personal impact the project had on him. Tamarind glanced longingly at the photo of the three of them at Flax and Almond's wedding sitting on the corner of his desk. After a little too long in this indulgence, he said out loud to himself, "Get back to work, Tamarind," using a firm voice reminiscent of one of his teachers at PNLI.

With a flick of his hand across his holodesk, the asteroid data projected on the wall displays. Tamarind liked to get 4 or 5 of them up on the wall and then walk around the room and look at the data. Asteroids rotated in the images just as they did in space. Dimensional overlays provided size, speed, distance from Earth, mass, orbit trajectories, and composition summary information. Color simulations within the semi-transparent images showed mineral deposits' locations, mine-ability analysis, and ease of recovery. The potential value of the asteroid was displayed and based on up-to-the-minute valuations of each mineral.

Each of them had tremendous value, billions, or trillions of dollars, in fact. The challenges included mining the asteroids and either transporting the material back to Earth or processing them and using the materials in space. If their orbit period was too long or their rotational frequency too fast, they were impractical to mine using current mining technology. Tamarind would review each one, analyzing the data, and assigning it a single number on his own Chase Scale of Viability. The five currently displayed included three S-Class asteroids he'd rated 2.0, 1.8, and 2.4; one C-class measured 3.7, and an X-class he'd scored 6.1. He searched for an X-class asteroid that was 9.0 or better on his Chase Scale, indicating a high recovery value, a reasonable orbit period, a practical rotational frequency, and a viable near-Earth orbit to facilitate recovery.

"Each of you lovely ladies will be attractive to someone," Tamarind said to the displays, "but none of you has my heart." *At least I can still joke about it*, he thought, as he took another look at the picture of Almond.

* * *

Tamarind thought back to the meeting a few years previously that entrapped him in his current duplicitous and solitary condition.

The investors in the Phosaster portion of Project LightStar were the five PNLI founders who had co-invested in several PNLI graduates' projects before, but never at this level. Phosaster was one of the more expensive projects in history, making it challenging to keep it a secret. They'd met to discuss the project at one of the PNLI's annual on-site board meetings. After a tour of new parts of the facility, students' presentations, and a review of the Institute's progress to their stated goals, Tamarind hosted a special event to discuss the Phosaster project. The five founders of PNLI and he were all billionaires, and all had demonstrated unwavering support for PNLI over many years.

No one came to the remote island where the PNLI was founded unless invited. The board members and other distinguished guests had completed the tour, and only the board members remained for Tamarind's special meeting. They sat in the conference room at PNLI. It was a comfortable but modest room considering the combined wealth of those around the table. The PNLI was never about comfort and worldly criteria of success but about improving the perception of the world's orphans and training leaders for the world's challenges.

"Ladies and Gentlemen," Tamarind began, clinking his glass. He had arranged for after-dinner drinks to lubricate the discussion, including the Irish whiskey, Italian liqueur, and other beverages he knew each person favored.

"As you know, space has been closed for many years, and my company, Dark Matter Ventures, will be launching Project LightStar to re-open space for communications and development."

"Hear, hear," one of them toasted, raising his glass. Tamarind smiled and continued.

"I would like to invite you to participate in the confidential second phase of this project, which promises to both secure the long-term future of the Institute and also to help our planet solve one of the most pressing problems of the next decade." At this point, none of them had heard of the Phosaster project, though they were aware of Dark Matter Ventures' Earth-based mining interest, Project LightStar, and Tamarind's ultimate hope to mine asteroids, a dream he had had since his days as a student.

"The Phosaster capsule phase of Project LightStar is about surveying, selecting, and drilling into a valuable asteroid with a reasonable orbit period, and preparing the materials for use on Earth. Many elements that are critical for renewable energy development, electronic products, and advanced lasers, for instance, are becoming harder to find in the mineable regions of the Earth's surface. Their availability on the planet is not uniform, leaving some nations like China controlling a significant amount of these precious and rare Earth metals. Phosaster will identify and survey enough asteroids to generate interest in space mining. Phosaster's ultimate goal is to mine one asteroid and return enough of these precious metals to Earth to positively affect global supply. This should end extreme mining on Earth, and potentially, the conflicts over excessive pricing or limited availability of these precious metals.

The final phase will be an extremely profitable business-peace initiative, which will provide critical metals for sustainable energy solutions of the future, while also providing an investment trust for future PNLI projects."

He then detailed the impending world shortages of certain precious metals and the inevitable resulting conflicts between nations. "In conclusion, I plan to both prevent these shortages and proactively avert these conflicts by mining a single asteroid," Tamarind said.

Knowing they were industry leaders with significant experience handling substantial investments, he had planned to finish by summarizing his investment request and the expected returns. He would include the medium-term profits for the asteroid data, which would fund a new generation of space exploration, and the longer-term, higher-risk prospect of mining an asteroid remotely. However, his wrap-up was interrupted by a technical question.

"How much of this technology exists, Tamarind?" asked Karl Oakley, a pioneer in household robotics.

"We've succeeded in developing the lasers, sensors, and the mining robots as a part of our terrestrial mining work at Dark Matter Ventures and our development work on Project LightStar. Yet to be developed is the power source and post-processing capabilities for the robotic mining on an asteroid. It is that part of the project that we are seeking funding for," Tamarind concluded. He decided now was the time for his funding pitch.

"We will need sixty billion dollars to complete Phosaster development in time to include in the launch of Project LightStar. We anticipate a trillion-dollar return on mining an asteroid, if successful and between forty and one hundred billion-dollar return on the asteroid survey data sold to other companies entering the space mining industry."

There was an audible inhaling sound as the room collectively responded to the investment scale and the upside. Most of them had done multi-billion-dollar deals before and had invested hundreds of millions in various projects of PNLI graduates, but a $60 billion stake in such a high-risk venture was new to them.

"In summary, the proposal is that your investment will cover the actual program costs of the Phosaster Capsule unique developments. Thirty percent of the profits and the technology will remain with Dark Matter Ventures, thirty percent to this investment consortium for your risk, and forty percent to form a fund to support PNLI and graduate investments for the foreseeable future." Tamarind did his best to smile confidently and look at each person individually as he completed his pitch.

The investors asked additional questions confirming the metals' potential market value, clarifying and debating the split of profits, and how PNLI would use such a significant investment. Finally, the proposal came to a show of hands vote. Amazingly, they all agreed to participate and split the investment evenly. They gave him two caveats, as stated by Mr. Oakley.

"Tamarind, first, we want you to achieve the objectives for forty-five billion dollars instead of the sixty billion you proposed. Secondly, we want this mission to be kept completely secret. You know how much scrutiny and how many dissenting voices you had to work through globally to get Project LightStar off the ground. Phosaster can only succeed if you don't repeat that approval process. If it fails, only us in this room will know of our folly. If it succeeds, everyone will praise our foresight."

* * *

Since that day, he'd discovered creative ways to work within their proposed budget. He had reluctantly agreed to the second stipulation, and that decision had haunted him over the years since.

Now Tamarind hoped he could deliver on the promise of return-ing the projected revenues the investors had irrevocably committed to investing in the future of PNLI and other high-value PNLI graduate projects. He hoped that the end would justify the means, and if the high-risk enterprise failed, all involved would keep it hidden.

For the last 18 months since the launch and separation from the Project LightStar satellite, Phosaster had surveyed asteroids within about a 30-degree spatial arc of the capsule trajectory. The Phosaster's path took it in a broad elliptical route skirting the edge of the asteroid belt, near known Trojan asteroids, and near-Earth objects. It was targeting X-Class asteroids but was surveying any asteroids of a mineable scale within its spatial arc.

As the laser beam hit an asteroid, it would drill deep into it, sending up a plasma plume from the drilling debris, emitting spectrally and sequentially in the characteristic wavelengths of the asteroid's materials. It was like taking a core sample at a great distance. Phosaster fired a sequence of laser pulses until it generated a picture of the asteroid's composition. As high-value precious metals, like palladium, platinum, gold, etc., were detected, additional laser pulses fully characterized the asteroid. In this way, the Phosaster capsule achieved a mining survey of hundreds of asteroids of the right size and potentially the right materials suitable for mining.

Realistically, all asteroids contain commercially valuable materials. C-Class asteroids include the most precious substance in space: water and its constituents, hydrogen and oxygen—two useful fuels. Other marketable elements, like phosphorus, are often present. S-class asteroids are predominantly silicon-based and may have value for manufacturing integrated circuits, glass, or solar cells in space. Neither of these asteroid classes was the objective of this project.

The Phosaster investment team had decided that a survey of 300 C, X, and S-Class asteroids would be sufficient data to make the project's research objectives profitable. This data, relayed through the Project LightStar satellite, would provide the next generation of asteroid mining information. The investment team would decide when to go public with the data.

For Tamarind, that day could not come soon enough.

No man is an island, Tamarind thought. Once the public knew about the Phosaster capsule and its objectives, he could fully and transparently resume his life. Until then, he would learn to live with his choices.

CHAPTER 14

Contact

"Exploration is one of the most foundational drives of humanity and the key to unlocking our fastest and most meaningful times of learning. Great education must channel our innate desire to explore."
— *PNLI Education Manual*

Launch plus one year 11 months

Astronomers classified hundreds of thousands of asteroids based upon their dimensions and optical properties in the decades leading up to the Space War. They correlated their spectral properties to their composition, but it was at best a crude estimate. The very few probes which successfully landed on an asteroid had proven these approximations could be significantly different from reality, enough that an individual asteroid mining activity might flip from being hugely profitable to a financial disaster.

The Phosaster asteroid survey gleaned a massive amount of physical data from the surface and probing relatively deep into the asteroids. Tamarind was excited to share what they had learned, and the new technologies developed to characterize and value asteroids.

It took less than two years for Phosaster to survey 300 asteroids, the targeted "cash-flow-break even" number for the project's survey phase and completed just in time. NASA and several other countries had hardened communications satellites beginning to go online and might have detected the encrypted communications between LightStar and the Phosaster capsule.

It would be a hardship to reveal Phosaster before we are ready, Tamarind thought. He knew an honest and full disclosure announced by him when they had achieved some success was essential to complete the project's outcomes and secure his future.

The asteroid mining capsule used encoded data communications that were "dark"—encrypted, with signals transmitted once per week at random and coordinated intervals and frequencies. The idea was to prevent detection until the success of Phosaster, giving Tamarind time to secure the suspension of the Space Peace Treaty ban on future launches and acceptance of a new space mining treaty.

Now it was time to choose an asteroid and begin mining, but in the first nearly two years since launch, no asteroid had met his requirements. Finally, after surveying 321 asteroids, an asteroid matching most of his criteria received an 8.9 rating on his Chase scale. *Close enough,* Tamarind thought, *time to begin drilling!* He had made hundreds of go/no-go decisions over the last few years, and the Phosaster capsule was traveling on a trajectory just inside the asteroid belt that did not allow it to go back to earlier finds. It was always difficult to let another opportunity go by hoping a better one was still out there. He was relieved that he had finally found what he was looking for and could proceed to the next phase.

Contact with the asteroid worked perfectly, the capsule landing vertically aligned with the center of mass of the asteroid on its open front end. Hydraulic clamps anchored it to the surface. Phosaster deployed solar and communication arrays in concentric rings around the capsule. These would supplement the optimized thorium nuclear reactor, which had successfully fueled the system thus far and was designed to sustain it for years to come. Once the arrays were secured and the comms deployed, Tamarind sent the engage code to begin grinding into the asteroid's surface.

The capsule slowly ground through the asteroid using conventional bore drilling tools lightened for deployment in space. Diamond-tipped titanium teeth could gnaw through virtually anything. Sensors examined the mine tailings and updated the trajectory toward promising mineral deposits, and the smelting of raw metals began.

The Phosaster cylinder's core had various analysis, separation, and processing technologies mounted peripherally around the wall. While in space, the grinding and processing tools remained retracted, allowing Phosaster's laser to be positioned on the back end a clear line of sight through the open mouth of the capsule's front. Now that mining had started, the cylinder was filled with the processing tools, progressively processing the material into usefully separated compounds.

* * *

Tamarind's seemingly random purchasing of companies in the space industry eight years earlier had, of course, not been accidental. He acquired businesses with 3D printing technologies that could print rocket engine components, companies with launch facilities, and start-ups in the early stages of asteroid mining and remote surveying. Investors poured hundreds of billions into these companies before the Space War, and the technology existed to select an asteroid from the Earth using probes in space. Initial landings and samplings on asteroids had been completed. However, after the Kessler Event, these companies stood idle, and the probe communications severed. Now, eight years later, Tamarind feared the probes were lost along with the information collected. However, Project LightStar had reinitiated contact with several probes and integrated their data into the Phosaster survey database. Unfortunately, none of these pre-Space War sampling robots were still in operation, and some data lost: a small but expected setback.

Refocusing the mining teams had been more problematic. Engineering teams had scattered, and it took a while to regroup enough of the teams to identify what remained. Tamarind tasked them with a terrestrial mining project, drilling with integrated sensors that could self-direct toward deposits and then complete an in situ smelting operation before returning to the surface. The teams could see the obvious connection to future asteroid mining and worked enthusiastically toward this objective.

The commercial success of terrestrial mining had been minimal but close to breakeven. But the project had been an excellent testing ground for asteroid mining. At this point, to most financial analysts, Dark Matter Ventures was a poor investment: the folly of an overly ambitious Tamarind Chase. To Tamarind, however, Project LightStar, and the Phosaster mining capsule development, were precisely on track.

Mining on Earth has not changed much for thousands of years. Dig holes in geologically promising locations. Follow veins to precious deposits. Blow up or dig out the ore and remove it from the site. Concentrate the ore by cleaning or by various chemical and mechanical methods. Heat the final product to smelting temperatures, and separate and purify the resulting elements into ingots used in processing steps. The equipment had become more substantial, and the processes slightly more efficient, but were not optimized for outer space.

The design of the Phosaster capsule had to address the practical differences between asteroid mining and terrestrial mining. First, asteroids pre-selected on his Chase scale had metal densities far higher than the most productive mines on Earth. Second, processing would be in situ—no rough collection of ore for remote processing. Third, mining and processing would be in a vacuum, so no oxides are formed, and heat transfer excludes natural convection. Fourth, gravity is significantly less than on Earth, so the rotating asteroid's centripetal forces would dominate. Fifth, getting equipment to the site and getting ore back would be the most challenging part of the project.

The eventual goal of all Dark Matter Ventures activities was asteroid mining. The terrestrial mining activities on Earth, the legislative work on asteroid mining, and Project LightStar were incremental steps toward Phosaster and that objective.

In the six years between the Space War and the launch of Project Light Star, Dark Matter Ventures' technical team began concept development on Phosaster. Pulling the engineers from his terrestrial mining division in Arizona into a conference room one day, he wrote the above five environmental differences on a wall display. He started a brainstorming discussion on modifying their terrestrial mining equipment for use on an asteroid.

Stacy Norton was the lead engineer and had worked on asteroid surveying before the Space War and had a graduate degree from the Colorado School of Mines. She offered her thoughts first. "We'll have to lighten the structure significantly. On Earth, we use a lot of iron and carbide and oil-based lubricants. In space, we would change the cutting tools to titanium with diamond tips and solid or impregnated lubricants."

Other team members commented on how the drilling power source had to be self-contained, likely nuclear, and recycling heat in processing steps. All were logical but somewhat predictable proposals.

"How can we utilize the unique properties of space to our advantage?" Tamarind asked.

"I think we would want to pursue shaft mining and drill perpendicular to the rotational axis of the asteroid. The rotation would give us a small centripetal force, which we could use for the separation of materials," Stacy suggested.

"How so?" Tamarind asked.

"Are you familiar with fluidized beds?" Stacy asked. Tamarind nodded that he was.

"We could crush all the ore to a small, relatively uniform size, say, 500 microns. Then we would bubble a heated gas through this bed of particles and into a tube parallel to the axis of the shaft," Stacy said.

"I see where you are going with this. The particles would slowly separate according to their material density in the fluidized bed. Since we are talking about relatively heavy metals and lighter silicates, we should be able to achieve high purity separation by elements or compounds," Tamarind caught on to what she was proposing quickly, "Why a heated gas?"

"The heated gas would allow us to transfer heat from the motors and drill directly into the fluidized bed, preheating the particles for later post-processing. We probably will be able to find neon, argon, krypton, or xenon gases and release them through the mining process." Stacy said.

"Excellent, so we could cool the equipment with the gas and transfer the heat usefully to preheat the mined materials. Can we test this on Earth?" Tamarind asked.

"Yes and no. On Earth, the pull of gravity dominates, and the centripetal force due to the Earth's rotation is minor. On the asteroid, depending on its rotational velocity, the centripetal force might dominate. It will depend on the properties of the asteroid somewhat. We can test separation by a fluidized bed in situ in terrestrial mining, but we'll have to modify the equations to make it work on an asteroid." There were some discussions and calculations among the other engineers, but Stacy dove toward conclusions.

Tamarind continued, "Intriguing. So, we will have a fluid-like flow of pre-heated particles of each material. Could we tap these off individually and use them directly in the post-processing equipment?"

A heated discussion ensued. Some of the team thought that just placing the particles directly into cylinders for transporting. "Imagine a cable linked train of cylinders filled with these particles. They could float out in space like this until we are ready for transport. Then we could power this entire train back to Earth and into orbit," one young engineer enthusiastically proclaimed. Several liked this "cable-train" idea.

A creative systems engineer on the team had a different proposal. "We could just flow the particles directly into mesh bags and have the individual element bags within a larger mesh which could be pulled by a rocket back to Earth. We could just tether these mesh bags to the surface until ready for transport." There wasn't as much support for this idea, which one of the male engineers derogatorily called the "bag-lady concept."

Tamarind ignored his comment and embraced her idea. "Good idea. Let's keep going. My question was about processing the materials on site. Let's discuss this further," Tamarind kept the meeting moving, the ideas flowing, stopping anyone from shooting down any ideas prematurely.

"I think extrusion is the most obvious post-process. We could make pipes, channels, I-beams, tubes, wire, cylindrical ingots, etc., by just changing the extrusion die shape," Stacy said. "We could tap off one stream of fluidized metal particles, for instance, flow them into a heating chamber to a molten state, and then rotate in an appropriate extrusion die to form spools of wire or whatever."

"Could we use 3D printing of metals or ceramics, or produce polymers to make useful components in space?" Tamarind asked. Some team members had been a part of a company which 3D printed critical metal components for rockets before the Space War. Dark Matter Ventures routinely used these capabilities in the mining business unit, and all were familiar with them.

After some discussion, Stacy concluded, "Generating polymers on site is probably impractical. 3D printing on Earth of metals and ceramics requires pure material sources, intricate control of heating and cooling processes, and depends on surface tension, gravity, and air pressure considerations. It will take some development to adapt these to space environments, but it is not unrealistic. I'd love to work on that project."

"I'd like you to lead it, Stacy," Tamarind said. "Specifically, I'd like you to start with five hundred-micron preheated particles of mined materials separated by the proposed fluidized bed, and develop the system for printing components from these materials, first on Earth and then for space.

Next time I'm here, I'd like a specific proposal of what resources you'll need and a project plan, OK?"

Stacy couldn't restrain her enthusiasm. "Wow! Yes, OK!" Several of the other engineers looked at her, sneering with jealousy. Tamarind quickly took the team back to the next question at hand.

"Now, how might we use a powerful laser in post-processing?" While the team did not know the specifics of what capabilities Tamarind intended to put into the Phosaster module, it was reasonable for them to consider laser processing in space.

"Lasers could cut materials to almost any shape," suggested Doug Anderson. Each engineer in the room had become more engaged after seeing Stacy given her own assignment.

"Lasers can also make a plasma of the particles, sort of like a charged gas phase of the element. We could use this plasma to make coatings," Benji added. "Hmmm. A plasma of a compound could further refine it, or simply deposit it along the walls of a tube to form a pure ingot of the material."

"Laser refinement and deposition, good idea, Benji," Tamarind said supportively.

The meeting went on for a few hours, and the team regrouped over several days for similar sessions. Brainstorming with Tamarind was exhilarating and productive. Before leaving the Arizona office and heading back to Nevada, Tamarind thanked everyone and praised their specific contributions. He asked Stacy Norton to hang back in the conference room for a private meeting.

"Stacy, I have a top-secret project for your eyes only. I want you to make two prototypes of a space version of our terrestrial mining module, and I'd like to include one in our launch of Project LightStar as a separate capsule. Assume a nuclear power source and a high-power laser will be available and add in the fluidized bed separation module, extrusion, laser processing, and 3D printing capabilities. Make the capsule flexible enough to use any of the transport ideas we have discussed. Our system engineer on Project LightStar, Paul Moncrief, will assist you on the laser and optics integration."

"Can I clarify which part is secret? Everyone will see and know what I'm working on." She was right to clarify this point; the team was too close for complete secrecy.

"Thanks for asking. The fact that we are working toward asteroid mining and you are leading that effort is understood within the company. The fact that we are planning to integrate it into Project LightStar is the secret."

She accepted the appointment. At that moment, Stacy became the Future Asteroid-Mining Project Leader and the only member of the terrestrial mining team that knew she was working on what would become the Phosaster capsule. Her work assignment began immediately, and Tamarind gave her the authority to hire external contractors to develop some of the needed modules confidentially.

She began by building super-lightened versions of their terrestrial mining robots. Dark Matter Ventures terrestrial mining already used vertical hole drilling and grinding equipment, so she adapted those for space. She chose 3D printed titanium throughout, which lightened the materials and minimized corrosion and thermal damage. The cutting tools used synthetic chemical vapor deposited diamond cutting tips, the most durable material for long-term use. Diamond cutting tools have two weaknesses—machining iron and titanium, two elements they were likely to encounter in asteroid mining, so she added a second set of blades coated with cubic boron nitride (CBN) for cutting these materials. She designed the cutting tips to be replaceable by vapor depositing new diamond or CBN tips with the post-processing equipment. She decided that synthetic diamond and cubic boride nitride could not be mined on-site, so she included those in the list of materials shipped into space.

The most technically challenging part of the project had been to develop the processing capabilities of the module. The fluidized bed concept

Stacy had proposed simplified the separation and concentration processes. Smelting and refining of molten materials allowed separation by density and boiling point. Processing the resulting metals was more challenging. Stacy decided to extrude cables, tubes, beams, and ingots of raw materials, and to move them up the shaft was the most practical solution. She included robotic assembly, 3D printing, and laser processing in the capsule's equipment. Phosaster could build simple structures, fabricate metal shapes, and manufacture simple components using the materials mined.

Benji's idea of using the Phosaster laser to generate any element's plasma state was also quite useful. It allowed thin coatings to be deposited on any surface uniformly in the vacuum of space. His idea enabled a wide range of dielectric and conductive coatings to be vacuum-deposited in layers and imaged by the laser to form simple circuits and simple controls. Working with Paul Moncrief to fully understand the laser and its capabilities, they also developed a laser-generated plasma process that enabled electro-magnetic refining.

Tamarind kept one of the asteroid mining prototypes at the mining facility in Tucson, Arizona. It was a visible reminder to the team that eventually, they would be mining in space. The other was transported to the Project LightStar facility in Nevada for the integration of the laser, computer controls, power source, and other capabilities needed for the Phosaster project.

Tamarind outsourced the Thorium salt fusion nuclear reactor to a Nigerian company run by another Pan-National, Mace Power. This project was a significant step for Mace's company tasked with building three units and supplying them to Dark Matter Ventures mining facility under a strict non-disclosure agreement. One reactor was kept in Tuscon with the asteroid mining prototype. The other two were sent to the Nevada facility for integration into both Project LightStar and the Phosaster capsule.

Tamarind had integrated the drilling/sensing technology, the laser from Project LightStar, and the processing capabilities with artificial intelligence computing technology he had adapted from one of the asteroid surveying companies he had acquired.

The AI company had developed an extensive suite of AI tools to sift information and adjust probe research objectives when supplied with new data from Earth. Phosaster could change its mining, smelting, and processing algorithms based upon updated information received en route on processing optimizations. Phosaster could adapt its mining and processing objectives to what would be of greatest value to Earth. This might be as simple as changing mineral processing priorities based on Earth pricing, but it might also mean adding new processing technologies or solving the as-yet-unsolved challenge of getting the mined materials back to Earth.

Tamarind hoped that this AI algorithm would maximize the value of the asteroid's yield and enable the capsule to create some useful equipment that might help with the conversion of the asteroid and make it easier to retrieve. However, the algorithm was open-ended, and he uploaded a massive amount of data about Earth into its computers. "Greatest value to Earth" could become almost anything, and he hoped it would surprise him with ideas he hadn't thought of yet.

These Phosaster innovations had been successfully integrated into Project LightStar by the day of the launch.

* * *

Once deployed on the asteroid, Tamarind, working alone in his control room, monitored the mining, smelting, and processing results. Phosaster was fully automated. The distance and infrequent communications allowed him to make only occasional and slight corrective commands. He updated Paul and Stacy monthly, and they informed him of new ideas, processing optimizations, and helped him keep the company focused on their short-term objectives supporting their long-term needs.

Phosaster had progressed exceptionally well through the surveying phase and started well once it landed on the asteroid. The robotic mining, smelting, and forming portions of the capsule continued to perform admirably. The 2km diameter X-class asteroid chosen had a mineral value of over one quintillion dollars—more than enough to exceed the project objectives. More importantly, it had the rarer compounds in sufficient quantities to affect the supply of materials that were becoming critical on Earth.

The orbit of the asteroid chosen had a round trip cycle time of 7.93 years. For the first two years after contact, each weekly update was the favorite part of Tamarind's week. He'd pore over the data, noting the high levels of iron and nickel and useful levels of aluminum and copper. He'd also review the intriguing levels of platinum-class metals – platinum, iridium, ruthenium, rhodium, and palladium, which estimates suggested exceeded the entire amount ever mined on Earth. There were also gold and other precious metals with high commercial value. In addition to these, Phosaster had started producing small machinery from the iron, including a rail system to move smelted deposits to the surface. Phosaster extruded conductors into long coils and formed cylindrical containers to transport material to the surface. Simple components were printed to replace those worn by abrasion. The solar array was expanded using simplified solar cells processed on-site. Everything was proceeding better than he had hoped and much better than he had promised.

Then one day, inexplicably, the Phosaster capsule did not check-in. It missed the next scheduled communication as well. Tamarind investigated whether the commlink was broken from the LightStar satellite, or if from the capsule, or if perhaps it was a sync error. Troubleshooting an encoded 'dark' randomly synced comm was nearly impossible. Phosaster had gone dark, and Tamarind had to quietly explain to his investors that it still may be doing something useful but that they wouldn't know for up to 4 more years. He would then launch a probe to intercept the asteroid and reconnect with it well before that date. He scaled back some of the company's other projects to retrieve the metals from space, switching them all over to the comm probe.

He hoped that once the survey objectives were complete and the mining started, he could announce what they had accomplished to the world. The loss of communications had complicated that. The investors asked him to hold off on the announcement of Phosaster until he had reestablished a link. In the meantime, all he could do was prepare and wait frustratingly alone. Weeks stretched to months, months to years, and there was still no contact with Phosaster.

Tamarind stuck to his routine. He visited the terrestrial mining offices and continued speaking engagements that fueled the interest and technology for "future" asteroid mining. He regularly traveled to Washington DC to push on the asteroid mining legislation. At his home base in Nevada, he worked patiently with the Project LightStar team. He enthusiastically kept others' spirits high. Inwardly, he grew more frustrated, more isolated, and more uncomfortable with the lack of transparency with his friends and his team.

CHAPTER 15

Nightmare

"Some days, I feel in control of my fears, my choices, and successful with my responsibilities. But when sleep comes, my nightmares tell me otherwise." —Journal of Kohlrabi Trust

Launch plus six years

Tamarind's business colleagues would describe him as a self-confident, worry-free, outgoing person. But tonight, alone in his bedroom, he was restless. He was feeling vaguely guilty about Phosaster, the money he had raised to pursue it, about his public duplicity, and hiding it from even his closest friends. The dreams of Kohlrabi often returned, reminding him of his promise and all he had not done.

There didn't seem any way to make it right. He reviewed all the reasons which led him to project secrecy and reminded himself it was a requirement from his investors. He considered all the good he had planned with the revenue. But now, the uncertain outcome fed his unease.

When he finally fell asleep, he drifted into a dream, replaying one of the defining moments of his time at PNLI. Professor Lambardi had tasked the students with writing a research paper on a historical figure who had made a positive change to the world, focusing on their motivations and strategies. Class members chose politicians, entrepreneurs, thought leaders, writers, heroes, religious leaders, and philanthropists. When it was Tamarind's turn to present to the class, the Professor asked, "And how about you, Tamarind?"

"Ghengis Khan," he said, provocatively.

"Most historians would consider him a genocidal warlord," the Professor asked calmly, "why did you choose to write about him?"

"He created a Mongol ethnic unity and formed an empire that ruled over much of Asia. He opened the Silk Road, promoting trade and exchanging ideas between the East and West. Khan practiced religious tolerance and established a meritocracy promoting the competent rather than family members. These were great and lasting accomplishments." Many in the class squirmed in their seats, awaiting the Professor's response.

Professor Lambardi responded quietly. "He also condoned the butchering, rape, and enslavement of millions of people to achieve those objectives, did he not? What do you have to say about how he accomplished these things?"

Young Tamarind was feeling rebellious when he chose Khan and decided not to retreat now. "The results of what he accomplished are a greater good than the bad things he did along the way."

Professor Lambardi knit his massive eyebrows together, leaned forward on his podium, and looked around the class, disregarding Tamarind. Tamarind began to shrink in his dream, smaller and smaller, until he was half as big as everyone else in the room.

"How you each choose to address the question of good and evil is the most important part of your training here at PNLI. Do the ends justify the means? Can you achieve good results with a bad character? How can you overcome the evil tendencies inside of each of you and replace them with good desires? The faith you choose to follow will inform your understanding of this, and how you respond to good and evil will determine the kind of leader you will become."

Then, turning to Tamarind, Professor Lambardi said, "Tamarind, your boldness will serve you well if your pride and rebelliousness are replaced by humility and clarity of purpose. Choose wisely when you repeat the assignment tonight." Tamarind's face grew red, and the class uttered a hushed moan sharing his pain. For years after that, whenever he was overly ambitious, rebellious, or argumentative, his classmates would quip, "You going Ghengis, again?"

In his dream, the class and Professor Lambardi all circled around him, pointing at him. "What were you thinking with Phosaster? You had so much promise, but to waste yourself and all these resources—why? Ghengis—Ghengis—Ghengis," they chanted and pointed.

Tamarind awoke, covered with sweat, his skin hot to the touch, but with a shiver of fear running down his spine. "No, that is not who I am," he repeated out loud to himself. He would find a way to make this right.

Rather than dwelling in the spiral of his darkest imaginings, Tamarind decided to get up and think through his options.

His first option was to come clean about Phosaster by public announcement. He had proposed this to his investors when he had told them about losing communications, and had repeated it recently.

"Despite the achievement of the survey phase of the Phosaster project, we'd like you to continue to keep it confidential for now," Karl Oakley spoke forcefully for the group.

"That is not what we agreed upon," Tamarind objected.

"Losing contact with Phosaster changed the parameters. We'd like you to keep Phosaster confidential until you've reestablished contact with Phosaster or you have negotiated the signing of the asteroid mining agreement and the Space Peace Treaty constraints are lifted." Karl again confirmed the two conditions they had given him previously.

Tamarind looked around the room, connecting with each investor eye to eye. He considered each of their commitment to the project and that their reputations were also on the line.

"I'll continue to keep it quiet until one of those has occurred," he said. When he had initially agreed to this, he hoped to reestablish comms quickly.

After revisiting the discussion in his mind, he decided again that he would have to remain silent.

His second option was to tell some close friends and get their input as he thought this through. He was afraid his dishonesty in concealing this would injure his relationship with Flax and Almond, but he could think of no one else he could trust with this information. However, it felt selfish to bring them into a secret weighing so heavily on him. They knew all his investors personally, and he would be burdening them with keeping both his secret and that he had told them. He set option two aside for now.

His third option was to redouble his efforts to make Phosaster a success, which required re-establishing communications with the capsule. Tamarind reviewed the possible reasons why the data stream was broken and assigned a likelihood to each possibility. Most of the reasons listed for the failure of the capsule implied the mining had ceased as well. Even if significant minerals were ready for collection, he had not yet worked out the plan to recover them. The asteroid would pass its closest approach to Earth without any fruitful result.

No tangible result anyway, Tamarind thought, *but we would have demonstrated the potential of asteroid mining, and we'd have another eight years before Phosaster's next Earth approach to consider how to unload the materials.*

Realistically, Dark Matter Ventures would still have the data on more than 300 mineable asteroids and have developed and demonstrated the technology to mine an asteroid remotely. Tamarind hoped this would be enough to prove the value of asteroid mining and restart space exploration. Even if it took eight more years to capitalize on Phosaster's mining results, if he could regain comms and download a summary of results to-date, he could make his announcement, and others would choose to invest in the future of asteroid mining.

He set his mind and an increased portion of his Nevada staff on developing the communication probe, which could land on the asteroid and reestablish the comms link. Most of Dark Matter Ventures's team had seen the prototype Stacy Norton had designed for the asteroid mining module. They knew Tamarind was negotiating asteroid mining legislation, so ramping up a project aimed at landing a probe on an asteroid was a logical next step, which didn't raise any questions. The team didn't quite understand the urgency after years of delay, but Tamarind was firm in his meetings with them, driving them to get this ready for immediate deployment.

He also pushed vigorously for the asteroid mining legislation, which had been slowly moving through government channels. The space industry worked feverishly to rebuild the satellite communications industry and launch the pent-up queue of NASA and other global research projects. The treaty's launch bans relaxed as Project LightStar cleared enough debris for relaunching satellites. Asteroid mining, however, appeared years away to legislators since they didn't know about Phosaster.

Separately, he tried from his command center each day to reconnect directly with Phosaster. He used a newly launched satellite to verify Project LightStar's communication array and attempt a separate link to Phosaster. Nothing he tried worked.

Despite this clear plan of action, the nightmare returned a week later. Tamarind again awoke in a sweat. This time, he rolled out of bed, put on a Transdermal Electromagnetic (TEM) suit, set it to maximum, and considered what athletic endeavor to select on the Virtual Stimulated Reality (VSR) headband. He often practiced Aikido, but that was too restrained for how he felt. He set it for rock climbing and chose the summit, Half Dome, in Yosemite. The TEM suit pulsed his muscles in sync with the VSR images.

At this setting, this climb would be painful and exhausting; it was just what Tamarind needed.

* * *

However, for the next 3.5 years, there was no contact with Phosaster, and the asteroid mining legislation floundered in a sub-committee. Fortunately, the intercept probe was moving forward and would be ready for launch well before Phosaster's upcoming Earth approach.

Tamarind's nightmare recurred in different forms in those intervening years. Each time they drove him forward, not giving in to his fears but fueling his pursuit to make things right. Sometimes, however, he felt trapped between the specters that haunted him at night, his isolation, and the unsolvable problems facing him by day.

PART 3:

APOLLYON

CHAPTER 16

DroneTech

"Of all the things I miss of Earth,
The birds, the fish, the trees,
It is the mystery of the swarm,
And the music of the bees."
—*The Journal of Kohlrabi Trust*

Launch plus nine years, seven months, four days

Telsun, Jimmy, Cecilia, and Ardwana were all engineers at DroneTech. They also spent most of their weekends together. They weren't double dating, exactly, but they liked to hang out together. Telsun was the project leader of the Swarm Team. Drone swarm communications were a new field DroneTech had sponsored when the numbers of drones grew to millions.

Jimmy—Dr. James Calhoun—had done his Ph.D. thesis on simultaneous swarm communications. He was tall, thin, and walked tilted forward like he was always in a hurry to get somewhere.

Cecilia and Ardwana, both accomplished computer scientists and mathematicians, worked on the coding, which formed the swarm software base. They were also housemates and best of friends but very different in many ways. Cecilia's flaming red hair highlighted her pale skin and blue eyes, complimenting her cheerful and musical voice and outgoing personality. Ardwana was more reserved with darker features and subtler expressions, which belied her competence and outspoken confidence. They were both engaging and adventurous, rare qualities for programmers and mathematicians.

Telsun's vision for the group went beyond drone collision avoidance to swarm collaboration, and it was this vision that drew the group together. At the basic level, with two objects hurling towards each other, collision avoidance was complicated but straightforward using simple physics. At the swarm level, it was significantly more complicated. Telsun's machine vision/robotics system engineering background enabled him to envision the architecture allowing a drone swarm to work together to accomplish an objective. Telsun had worked for Flax since the "early days" of DroneTech, initially implementing the mob track and control feature in their police drones. He was the oldest member of the Swarm Team in his late thirties. It had been nearly 15 years since Tamarind had left, and the company had grown massively since then. He loved working with Flax and the Swarm Team but missed that smaller, aggressive start-up team and the focused vision of those earlier days.

Jimmy asked over lunch if anyone had a plan for their weekend.

Telsun said, "What about borrowing some transport drones and taking ourselves down into the Grand Canyon?" Smiles all around, but also some nervous facial expressions. He tried again. "What about ice-climbing the constructed columns at the Tetons?" Telsun liked to push the safety envelope; the rest liked more controlled thrills.

Cecilia had a counter-proposal. "Did you hear the Rock Drones are in town? They are doing a classic rock concert at the waterfront."

"I love them," Ardwana agreed.

"You wrote most of the code that lets them fly, so I bet you love them," Jimmy added.

Telsun eventually caved and agreed that exploring the Grand Canyon or the Tetons could happen any weekend, but a Rock Drones concert was a rare event.

The concert was in an outdoor amphitheater at the eastern base of the Rockies outside Loveland, Colorado. The smoothly contoured lawn sloped down to the stage, which backed to the mountain stream flowing from the mountains above. The crowd of ten thousand spread out over the large area but increased in density near the stage.

"It appears to be a Gaussian distribution; perhaps we should sit a few sigmas out?" Cecilia said it with an impish smirk, and they all nodded and moved up the hill.

They ordered a picnic dinner for the concert, spreading out a blanket on the grass. Cecilia arranged for drone delivery of the group's food and drinks about ten minutes before the show, knowing it would be a no-fly zone once the music got underway. The picnic delivery was generously stocked with summer fruits, sliced artisanal cheeses and meats, charcuterie, nuts, crackers, chocolates, and lots of wine sticks. Wine sticks allowed a person to drink wine while lying on their back—essential for aerial Rock Drone concerts.

Telsun noted that the only lighting was along the path to the parking lot.

"The Rock Drones will generate their own light. You better stay close, so you don't get lost." Ardwana replied, motioning him closer to her on the blanket.

While the Swarm Team always affirmed that they were colleagues who were friends and not dating, their arrangement on the blanket and their interactions suggested otherwise. That tension seemed to elevate their enjoyment of being together.

As the dusk deepened, the concert began with a 10-meter-tall Elvis rising out of the river to take the stage to roaring applause. "Thank you, thank you very much," he said and started the first set. He was formed from a swarm of microdrones so dense that he looked solid, and despite his magnified scale, his movements were convincing. Each drone had multicolor LEDs that gave his skin subtle shading, lasers that came out of his sequins, and micro speakers that put out plenty of intense, perfectly tuned music optimized for this outdoor venue. Elvis never looked or sounded better!

The concert continued with a steady procession of performers from rock and roll history, with ever-increasing special effects. Pink Floyd had a rotating prism with lasers projecting up to the sky throughout a *Dark Side of the Moon* montage. When *Money* was performed, cash appeared to drift down all over the venue, only to vaporize as the microdrones flew away when they neared the ground. Jimi Hendrix riffed with an oversized guitar; his fingers literally flew across the strings. Later, he joined the Beatles to play *While My Guitar Gently Weeps* in a duet with George Harrison. As they slowly descended into the river in a *Yellow Submarine*, the Rolling Stones materialized on stage singing *I Can't Get No Satisfaction*. The cheers of the crowd amped up with the volume of the music.

Prince took the stage singing *Purple Rain*, and as he sang, thousands of microdrones with purple lights fell like rain across the crowd.

About halfway into the concert, out of the corner of his eye, Telsun noticed a couple of drunk fans climbing onto the stage, trying to snag some of the microdrones forming Cher's legs.

"Uh-oh," Telsun pointed. "This won't end well," He was kind of sad to disturb everyone as both women were snuggled up to him, one on each arm.

"Moron," Ardwana said. "Don't they know DroneTech was first a security company?"

As the giant-sized Cher danced across the stage, a part of her leg peeled off, the microdrones reconfiguring as a human-sized security officer. The other drones readjusted, with Cher not missing a beat as she sang *Gypsies, Tramps, and Thieves*. She looked over at the drunk fans, flung her hair over her shoulder characteristically, and continued with the song.

Directing the fans back to their seats, the drone security officer gave them a second warning, while the fans charged him, grabbing at the microdrones for souvenirs. The security officer evaded their grasp and then dropped them both with well-placed drone tranq darts. Both fans, both adult males, fell instantly, harmlessly to the ground. The crowd cheered.

"Coolio. Those darts are effective," Telsun noted, "and entertaining."

He was about to turn his attention back to the concert when all four of their silenced phones vibrated simultaneously.

"Fractal, an emergency back at DroneTech, and they want us all in there immediately."

"An emergency? Could we just pretend that the concert was so loud we couldn't hear the phones?" Cecilia asked.

"Probably just a glitch in the code," Telsun said, rising slowly.

"Not my code," said Ardwana, elbowing Telsun in the ribs as she quickly rose to her feet.

"Code Red," said Jimmy. At that, they moved toward the exit as quickly as the wine sticks, the darkness, and the press of the crowd would allow.

CHAPTER 17

Sighting

"Don't fear the alarm or the disaster, fear the leader with a slow response."
—*Journal of Kohlrabi Trust*

The DroneTech Swarm Team had been called in because the sensor-tracking net they'd set up for NASA/SETI a few months previously had issued a CODE RED alarm.

Now that satellites relaunched worldwide, ground-based operations were reconnecting with near-Earth object tracking satellites and SETI communication arrays. NASA contracted DroneTech to link them together in a swarm to monitor space more cooperatively, maximizing deployed equipment. While each had a limited image of space from a single point of view, they formed a combined mosaic with resolution, depth, and trajectory. Flax had promised SWARMNET would be an early warning system protecting America from "debris falling from space." This reference was both to the failed Space War and to a recent report, which predicted a substantial asteroid impact was possible within the next few decades.

When the Swarm Team arrived at the automated tracking station within DroneTech, they found racks of equipment and monitors flashing CODE RED - IMMINENT THREAT! The SWARMNET satellites had discovered something. Big and moving toward Earth. DroneTech was completing a trial run, preparing for the training phase to transfer full control to NASA. The team quickly alerted the DroneTech CEO before they had even confirmed the sighting or begun analysis to determine what had been detected. Flax Venture, DroneTech's CEO, was among the first to know about the space anomaly.

"Proceed with the confirmation protocol and send me your analysis as soon as you have it," Flax said calmly into the conference phone to the Swarm Team. "And keep this under wraps until our government decides what information to release."

Flax was a confident leader and undaunted in the face of significant challenges. After Tamarind had left DroneTech, Flax's role as CEO expanded to become the company's business visionary and managed the rapidly growing business's operational details. With the eyes of the world on him in the weeks after the Space War, Flax had led DroneTech to set up drone comm hubs, which quickly replaced much of the critical satellite communications. Starting with government and military, and expanding to essential commercial enterprises, the manufacturing ramp-up and field deployment had gone exceptionally well. Although no one ever said it to his face, his nickname at DroneTech was 'Flax the Unflappable.'

This SWARMNET contract with NASA/SETI was a logical extension of the Swarm Team's coordinated drone communications. They weren't controlling satellite motion but coordinated the data collection, allowing a stitched view of the planet and space. Flax Venture had negotiated it with NASA/SETI himself and met President Jaspar during the final stages. Once the Swarm Team confirmed the sighting, Flax immediately alerted her.

* * *

President Laura Jaspar quickly assembled the commanders who had authority over space capable weapons. After the Space War, the US had begun to develop both ground-based and space arsenals and defensive capabilities to prevent future catastrophes. The terms of the Space Peace

Treaty had increasingly relaxed the launch restrictions as the debris field cleared. Although space-based weapons were still banned under the treaty, the US would not be caught unawares again. Hopefully, this alarm was not the first volley in another Space War, but if it was, the US was better prepared.

It was nearly midnight before everyone was in the room and waiting for her. President Laura Jaspar rose from her chair in the Oval Office and performed her pre-meeting ritual. She smoothed her gray wool skirt, adjusted her white blouse and Navy jacket, checked her auburn hair and makeup in the small mirror she had requested hung on the wall near her desk. She took another long drink of her coffee, straightened her shoulders, put on a practiced smile, and walked swiftly to the Security Briefings Room, where everyone stood and greeted her with deference.

She had never liked the title Madam President— it made it sound like she was running a brothel—and instead preferred Ms. President. Those that got it wrong did so at their peril. It was not only her position and title but also her six feet enhanced by two-inch heels and confident bearing, which commanded respect in any room she entered.

The Presidential Security Briefings Room was located almost directly under the Oval Office and was more heavily protected. The room was added during a previous administration's call for increased security amidst terrorist threats. It had been repurposed after the Space War with both state-of-the-art security and display capabilities. The room was dominated by the massive mahogany conference table that could seat 20 people.

President Jaspar called the meeting to order and asked everyone to be seated. "John, your briefing."

Dr. John Lewis had been the Director of NASA for two decades. After the Space War, Space Command made him their Space Security Advisor. Despite his commanding presence and deep voice, he was more of a scientific leader reflecting the civilian departments he coordinated. After the Space War ended, NASA's purview had expanded to include the "development of space assets," and they had co-sponsored the development of SWARMNET with SETI. NASA wanted to track their projects and the natural objects in space, SETI searched for intelligence. Space Command monitored threats to space assets, including any of the above plus missiles launched from Earth. Although SETI began as a private organization, it was now incorporated into NASA, which had historically provided most of its funding.

"I've included the CEO of DroneTech and the four members of the SWARMNET Team in this briefing as they made us aware of this threat and have supplied much of the technical details we will discuss," the NASA Director began.

President Laura looked at Flax on the commlink display and said, "Thank you for joining us Flax, good to see you again."

"Thank you, Ms. President," Flax said correctly.

Dr. Lewis continued, "Six hours ago, SWARMNET picked up a large, almost perfectly spherical object on an Earth collision trajectory. The size of the object—nearly 2 km in diameter—the estimated density, and the speed, make it a double threat." He sequenced through images first to show the object, then to indicate the trajectory, appearing from behind the Sun and passing near the Sun on a direct path toward Earth.

"Why double threat?" President Jaspar asked.

"The object's path takes it within the corona of the Sun. Its speed, mass, and density could trigger a solar flare of a magnitude which could cause significant Earth effects." Dr. Lewis continued, "Secondly, the current trajectory results in a perpendicular impact on Earth, which would have global consequences."

"How significant? What kind of global consequences?" President Jaspar pressed. She liked succinct answers with clear-cut conclusions.

"A solar flare of significant magnitude with accompanying Coronal Mass Ejection (CME) would release an Electromagnetic Pulse (EMP) that would disrupt radio communications within ten minutes and continue for weeks, potentially damaging electronics in satellites in higher orbits. Anyone in space could receive critical radiation doses. If the CME is ejected toward Earth, we'll have half a day or so to make additional preparations. It could also cause electrical grid effects, causing fires, explosions, and regional power outages."

Dr. Lewis continued solemnly, "An impact of this comet is still a few months out, but only five days after the projected CME. A straight-on impact of this magnitude could become a mass extinction event over much of the Earth."

Silence spread across the room, and everyone turned to look at President Jaspar.

"Not on my watch," President Jaspar said, with the enthusiastic confidence that had got her elected and helped her to win support for many initiatives. "This object is a clear and present danger to national security and our citizens at home and abroad. This information is classified Top Secret—this room only and those on your team with appropriate security clearances. Flax, that includes your team as well. Since our SWARMNET detected this, let's assume that no one outside this meeting knows anything about it at this point, and let's keep it that way. We are at the idea and information collection and analysis stage of this threat. Before our next meeting, I want each of you to work independently using the skills, information, and tools at your disposal. I want your impact analysis, simulations, and response recommendations by oh-seven hundred tomorrow. We've got this, people. Earn the trust that our Nation and this planet have put in us. Dismissed." It was just after midnight in DC; it would be a difficult night.

Flax was in the visual conference room with the Swarm Team when they participated in the call. When the display went blank, Jimmy, Cecilia, Ardwana, and Telsun looked at each other wide-eyed. Flax spoke to the group without any appearance of stress or concern.

"Team, your developments have given us the first alert and time to respond to this threat. The President has also invited us to participate on the front lines of the response. I'm sorry to ask you to work through the night on this. Keep the information contained to the people in this room and work on the tasks she described—impact analysis, simulations, and possible responses. We'll regroup an hour before the call to discuss and format the information you've gathered." With that, he gave tasks for each member of the Swarm Team.

"OK, Jimmy, download the data we have on speed, trajectory, size, composition, etc., and forward what we know to each of us. Cecilia, you focus on the likely impact location on the current trajectory and then correct it for the possible bending due to the Sun's gravitation impact. Ardwana, work up a simulation image of this, including the size of the impact zone. Telsun, work on options to eliminate the threats. I'm sure every other government department represented in that room will be doing similar things, but let's get ahead of this. Keep a lid on your emotions, people, and let's work quietly, focus on facts and options. It is going to be a long night; I'll put on the kettle and coffee pot." His positive, decisive direction put everyone at ease.

* * *

Telsun carried his large, black mug of coffee emblazoned with 'SPACE NERD' and constellations to his small office, the walls covered with images of space and pictures of him summiting mountains. He initially focused on the Coronal Mass Ejection (CME) and resulting Electromagnetic Pulse (EMP). He estimated the potential EMP scale, went through the SWARMNET satellites list, and considered which could handle such a pulse. It might be possible to adjust the orbits of those that couldn't, or perhaps orient them for minimal damage or shade them behind the Earth or the moon partially during the initial burst. However, he couldn't think of any way to eliminate that threat, which was the first part of his task. After listing his ideas and listing the affected satellites, he shifted his focus to the second, more severe threat—avoiding the impact.

Sungrazing comets were usually significantly affected by their proximity to the Sun. This one would pass through the photosphere, the nearest region to the Sun's surface at perihelion, its closest approach. Historically, the effects of such a near approach included destruction, reduction of mass, change of trajectory, or fragmentation.

Any of these could reduce the threat, Telsun thought, *but if it doesn't, what could we do?*

He wondered if there was any way to preheat the object before it approached the Sun so it would maximize the damaging effects of passing through the photosphere. Perhaps he could modify the object's surface to absorb the Sun's heat more effectively? After considering this awhile, he couldn't think of any way to affect the Sun's influence on the object before perihelion.

Perhaps after it had passed perihelion? Telsun's first thought was about Dark Matter Ventures' Project LightStar—it was still in orbit, vaporizing garbage in the upper atmosphere. Telsun was one of those real-time video addicts who always had LightStar images going in the background. *Could it be redirected to aim its powerful laser at this comet?* Telsun wondered. He calculated the energy emitted by the laser and estimated that it could reduce over five days between the Sun and the Earth but not deflect or destroy a comet of this size. He'd have liked to bring Tamarind in on this but knew he couldn't until authorized.

His thoughts then moved to weapons launched from Earth. A rocket with a nuclear payload could intercept a comet and detonate, potentially diverting it. He didn't know if any government had nukes in space, so he assumed the ground arsenal was what he had. Most nukes had been destroyed under previous peace agreements, but surely some were still in play, so he started calculating what might be available, how far out it could reliably intercept, and if it could destroy or divert the incoming comet. The answer was mathematically challenging, so he decided to set it aside and ask Cecilia or Ardwana to assist with the calculation.

Thirdly, he explored kinetic impacts that might fracture or alter the course of the asteroid. The billiard ball problem, with a very fast-approaching ball. He roughly calculated the distance out, mass, and velocity of the impact required to divert the comet. Unfortunately, there was nothing in deep space that he knew of that could accelerate that large of an object at that high of velocity with that kind of accuracy. *Where is an orbiting rail gun or photon torpedo when you need one?* Telsun thought, *or a Death Star might be handy.* His love for classic science fiction often showed in his speech.

Finally, he considered a gravity tractor, the idea of pulling a space vessel alongside the object, allowing the relatively small gravity attraction of the adjacent space vessel to shift the trajectory over time. The concept was feasible, but making and deploying such a device would take much longer than the remaining time until impact. He set that one aside.

Time was up. Telsun regrouped with his team, synced up their presentations and conclusions, briefed Flax on their findings, and got ready for the call scheduled for 5 am in Colorado. As the emotionally and physically exhausted team members stood and stretched, they looked out at the lightening Colorado skyline. They thought not of the coming day but the impending impact.

CHAPTER 18

The Plan

"They say that great chess masters can see 10 or 15 moves ahead. Life is not as well-defined as a chess game, and we all play it by different rules. The best plan is decisive and yet allows us to adapt to new information and developments." —Flax Venture

LightStar Launch plus nine years, seven months, five days

Object Impact minus 53 days

At 0700 sharp in DC, President Jaspar called the meeting to order, calling for reports from each department head. "Since we are discussing strategies to eliminate a threat in space, I'd like General Sharon Ward, Director of Space Command, to discuss our analysis of strategies to understand and eliminate this threat."

Gen Sharon Ward, the youngest female officer to be promoted to a full General in the country's history, had been appointed as Director of Space Command, a new position created during the Space War. Although the shortest person in the room, her bearing and presence were formidable.

"Thank you, Ms. President. I want to begin with a refined statement from our consultant from NASA." She motioned for Dr. Lewis to speak.

Dr. John Lewis, Director of NASA, began. Dr. Lewis stood over 2 meters tall, was black with graying in the temples. A respected astrophysicist, he had led the organization well for more than 20 years, carefully balancing NASA's military, commercial, and research objectives.

"Ms. President," he began, carefully using Laura Jaspar's preferred designation. "Due to the proximity and urgency of this object, we decided to suspend traditional numerical designations and give it a name—'Apollyon'—for reference."

"What does Apollyon mean?" the President asked.

"From the Bible, Apollyon is the Angel of Death in the book of Revelations."

"Appropriate. John, what do we know about Apollyon?" President Jaspar asked with a staccato rhythm, conveying urgency and precision.

Dr. Lewis continued, "Apollyon is one point nine six kilometers in diameter, and unusually spherical, implying that its origin is not from a fragment of a planet or comet. It has not been detected before despite fifty years of monitoring space objects with equipment that should have detected it, so if it is in orbit, it has a very long period, perhaps hundreds of years. My team is working on some possible orbit trajectories, but that isn't our immediate concern today."

General Ward looked at him, acknowledging with a nod her approval at leaving out unnecessary details and encouraging him to continue.

"Unlike most comets which have a visible tail—a stream of loose ice, gas, and debris—this one has no visible tail. This suggests Apollyon is mostly metallic and tightly bound. Many of the measurement techniques we use to determine composition look at the tail and dust cloud, so we can't use them on Apollyon. The information we have so far is based on optical measurements. Its surface brightness is on the high end of the measurement scale, almost mirror-like. Astronomers, perhaps even amateurs, will be able to detect it within a few weeks. Apollyon exhibits the highest albedo, that is, optical intensity, ever recorded, the second puzzle as to its origin. This might imply a pure form of a single metal or alloy, as we might see from an Earth satellite or space vessel."

John looked uncomfortable but shifted on his feet and continued. "The velocity is five hundred forty-six point three kilometers per second, which is significant, as it suggests it may achieve escape velocity as it passes the Sun. Depending on its mass and composition, it should deflect slightly from its current trajectory, but if we assume a heavier metal, like gold or iridium, the gravity of the Sun will only bend the trajectory inconsequentially."

Dr. Lewis continued, "Apollyon will graze the photosphere of the Sun and will be superheated, perhaps causing destruction or fragmentation. However, our analysis suggests it will remain intact, retain most of its mass, and cause a significant Coronal Mass Ejection, or CME. It will continue close to its current trajectory toward Earth. We have forty-seven days until it achieves perihelion, the closest approach to the Sun. The resulting CME will arrive 4.8 days before Earth Impact. I'm sorry, Ms. President, that we don't have better news," he said, and then sat down abruptly.

The simulation of Apollyon's trajectory he referenced during his discourse was still displayed. Apollyon passed through the Sun's outer edges, triggering a massive solar flare approximately perpendicular to the Sun's surface before impacting the Earth.

"Thank you, Director Lewis," General Ward said, standing to speak. While the NASA Director had addressed everyone in the room, General Ward spoke directly to the President. "We are currently working between agencies to orient and focus NASA, SETI, and other satellites within SWARMNET to gather additional information to help us monitor Apollyon's progress and to learn more about its composition, which could suggest different strategies.

"Space Command has significant threat simulation resources, and at this moment, my team is evaluating several options for eliminating this threat and minimizing damage. We have two nuclear warheads in space today, which we can deploy at your command. Because of the Sun's gravity and potential changes at perihelion, we recommend waiting until after it grazes the Sun, and we have a fuller analysis of its composition and trajectory." She changed the display to show Apollyon coming out of the Sun and the sequential impacts of two nuclear explosions. "Depending on the composition and construction of Apollyon, several post-detonation scenarios are possible. If it does not fragment, the explosions will shift the trajectory so that Apollyon would miss Earth. Fragmentation or destruction is more likely, with the result that only debris would enter the Earth's atmosphere. Larger fragments would cause local damage, and we would only have a few days to evacuate those areas. Smaller fragments would burn-up on entry to our atmosphere or result in minimal damage on Earth."

Her simulation showed the most likely scenario her team had calculated, which had a large fragment striking the Earth, and smaller pieces impacting a wide area. The rest of Apollyon had deflected away from the Earth from the impact of the missiles.

"Hitting this target at this distance is completely within the capabilities of Space Command, even if we do lack practical experience in space detonation. It is not, however, our only option for eliminating this threat."

"What else have you got, Sharon?" President Jaspar asked.

"We suspect but cannot confirm that other countries have nuclear warheads in space. We recommend alerting the Heads of State of space-capable nations, informing them of our discovery and analysis, and ask what they can do to assist."

President Jaspar and the Secretary of State looked at each other and exchanged a meaningful glance. Telling other nations of an impending impact and the US' nuclear missiles in orbit would be a series of challenging calls.

"Additionally, Project LightStar, owned and operated by Dark Matter Ventures, could reorient its laser to destroy comet fragments further," General Ward said. "I recommend we commandeer their space assets for this mission."

President Jaspar smiled. "I've met Tamarind Chase; I have no doubt he will offer his assistance as soon as he finds out about this threat. I doubt "commandeering" will be required. Flax, could you contact him and bring him up to speed before our next meeting? Does your team have anything to add?"

Flax was not used to political-military briefings and was honored to have a voice at the table. "Certainly, Ms. President. I agree that Tamarind Chase will want to assist. Our team has similar conclusions to the ones presented and additional suggestions for protecting space assets from the CME, which we agree is likely and unavoidable. I'm sure General Ward has considered the effect of the initial pulse on the ground to space communications, implying that the missiles would be in flight during the CME and would have no contact with Earth during the resulting solar storm."

General Ward nodded but did not reply.

"We also considered the option of kinetic impactors on the comet, Apollyon, that might divert it or slow it enough to miss the Earth. We don't know the assets in space, of course, but if those that can maneuver are aimed at the object, it would collectively contribute to shifting it off course. We agree, reaching out to other space-capable countries would be worth adding to that analysis."

"Kind of like throwing pebbles at a charging bull," General Ward said dismissively.

"We also believe DroneTech could re-establish Earth-based communications with a Drone Swarm after the CME as we did after the Space War, which will minimize communications problems. It will take weeks to reroute banking, GPS, cell phone, and other critical systems unless completely set up before the CME."

"Thank you, Flax; those are useful contributions. Please have your team detail out the specifics of the Drone Swarm communications and summarize your other suggestions for Space Command."

"Certainly, Ms. President," Flax replied.

President Jaspar divided the problem into sections and assigned responsibilities. They discussed possible impact sites, evacuation and readiness plans, damage minimization, threat elimination options, and timing of expanding the number of people told. The President decided to keep it Top Secret, except for adding Tamarind at the next meeting. The Secretary of State, Space Command, and the President would meet offline to discuss contacting other worldwide space powers. She set a new date and dismissed the current session. If the mark of a good leader in a crisis was the ability to break a problem into definable chunks, put them in sequence, and bring all the best thinking and resources to bear without wasting energy on emotions, then President Jaspar had demonstrated excellent leadership.

* * *

Only Flax from DroneTech was in the conference with the President, but when the call was complete, he gathered the Swarm Team, briefed them on the meeting, and assigned them all new tasks.

A few hours later, at the DroneTech office, Cecilia turned up the volume when she saw President Jaspar speaking at a press conference. The President spoke widely and animatedly about economic and peace initiatives, an industry stimulus plan, and addressed a broad range of questions with a lively, often joking banter with the press.

Cecilia commented, "She is a cool one: business as usual. Personally, I'm having a hard time not breaking down in tears."

Jimmy gave her a firm, sustained, side hug, and encouraged them all to stay focused on their tasks. Admittedly, their duties weren't the most critical, so he thought about recommending they rest and come back fresh tomorrow.

Telsun was thinking the same thing. "Why don't you all come over tonight? I'll cook something. A few pints and a movie might be just the thing," he said. They'd been working almost thirty-six hours straight and knew they needed some rest.

"Sounds good; maybe we can get our mind off our work with an apocalyptic sci-fi movie about a comet heading toward Earth," Cecilia said sarcastically. They all smiled and started throwing out various B-movies on this or other disaster themes.

Telsun thought, *it's good to see them smile a bit,* and said out loud, "How about an old-school horror movie *It Came from Outer Space.* We could turn out all the lights and have just one candle."

"Wooooooooo," Ardwana said, "It's a date. I better pick the food; I don't want eyeball soup on the menu."

CHAPTER 19

Starlight

"When the rainbow breaks through the storm or the vast starlight illumines the darkest night, when I explore the creative variations in all of nature, I see the God of mystery and love, and am renewed in faith and hope." —Almond Brighten

Impact minus 53 days

The Swarm Team all rendezvoused at Telsun's house that evening.

DroneTech was just outside Loveland, Colorado. After the Space War, it had grown so fast that there weren't enough homes in the area to support it. The company decided to partner with one of the PNLI's other graduates who had developed Bucky-Pods to address the worldwide need for affordable, energy-efficient, and environmentally responsible housing. Bucky-Pods now scattered across Loveland's high plains, and most DroneTech employees lived in them, including each of the Swarm Team members.

Bucky-Pods were built on the geodesic dome concepts of 20th century architect Buckminster Fuller. There had been a fan following among futurists and hippies since the 1960s, but they weren't that easy or efficient to build. Most sheet materials were fabricated in 4 by 8-foot sheets and challenging to use in dome construction. However, in the third decade of the 21st century, the whole world transitioned to metric. For efficiency, panels of almost all materials—plywood, glass, metals, solar cells, etc., had switched to a 2m x 3m sheet and produced in continuous rolls 2m wide. This made triangle constructions based on 1m and 2m edges much more material-efficient. Extra pieces were used for external shades and reflectors and internal hanging joists. The structural design problem was solved by an innovative anchor system and slide-together joining method that allowed anyone of reasonable skill to build their home in a week or so, choosing from a wide range of readily available triangles constructed for different purposes. Doors, fixed or opening windows, opaque and semi-transparent walls in various colors and materials, solar panels, vents, and panels with integrated facilities (water, electrical, HVAC) were all available. Interiors were more traditional, often with a central rectangular area with rooms radiating out for different purposes. To expand or modify a module's size, a person could exchange 1m triangle panels, which were always in high demand, with larger 2m triangles.

Telsun had been at DroneTech the longest and had helped each of them build their Bucky-Pods when they had joined the team. He had a single pod expanded to 2m triangles constructed upon a cylindrical tube, so all the facilities were under the floor in the foundation. It was much larger than the other team members' homes, so they often met at his place.

Telsun was also an excellent cook with a stocked wet bar, which made it more inviting. The large living/eating area had a centrally mounted wall display so his guests could eat, drink, play games, watch movies, or lounge around, and often did. They were all giddily tired when they got over that night after the last few days of craziness.

"Knock, knock," Cecilia said, as she entered without waiting for a response, holding two bottles of wine. Jimmy followed her in with a tub of Neapolitan ice cream and a few movie cubes.

"Ardwana is just pulling up," Telsun had set out some pita bread, hummus, tabouli, a variety of drinks, and Ardwana came in with a heaping platter of shawarma.

"Ardwana's Shawarma, that rhymes," Telsun said flirtatiously, licking his lips.

"The movie isn't about space cannibals, I hope?" she said playfully, eyes widening, pulling away in mock fear, and turning to Jimmy, "what did you pick for us tonight?"

"No peeking," said Jimmy.

Cecilia was bouncing on her toes, looking at the food, and trying to get a glimpse of the movies.

They all sat on the stools or leaned against the kitchen bar. As the food disappeared, Telsun refilled the glasses, and they moved to the leather sectional wrapped around the central display. The random, cheesy gore in the space horror movie made them all laugh, and sometimes the frights made them snuggle into the nearest person. But soon, the wine, their missed night's sleep, and the craziness of their last few days took their toll, and Telsun looked around to see they all had nodded off. Jimmy and Cecilia were sitting slumped on the floor with arms around each other, their heads against pillows leaning against the couch. Ardwana had her head on the other end of the sofa, and her feet resting on Telsun. Gently lifting her feet, he covered each of them up with blankets and went up to his loft.

The transparent ceiling panels in his loft allowed an excellent view of the night sky. He had developed an imaging system that made the stars a little brighter and more colorful, like the way you might see them through a telescope or if you were out in space. With DroneTech's leadership support, he tried to commercialize his idea, selling them as skylights or Bucky-pod windows. He didn't sell as many products as he hoped, so his enhanced star-viewing system became a hobby, sold to other stargazers like himself. He did like to fall asleep just looking at the stars through his StarViewer Skylight, and tonight, it didn't take very long.

Telsun awoke to the sensation of someone standing close by. Ardwana stood next to him, looking up at the stars. Telsun silently appreciated her shapely legs, enhanced by her black leggings. His gaze traveled up to her loose-fitting blouse outlined against the stars.

"Pretty heavenly view," Telsun said, eyebrows raised.

"This is amazing. Is this what you fall asleep thinking about every night?" Only after she had spoken did Ardwana look down at Telsun and realize the view from his perspective and the implication of what she'd just said.

"Tonight is much better than other nights," Telsun said, with a big grin on his face. She kicked at him playfully, and he grabbed her foot and held her leg by her calf. They looked at each other until they could feel the heat on their faces. Telsun stayed frozen, still grasping the calf of one leg. It was Ardwana that decided to act.

"Would you like me to improve your view?" Ardwana asked seductively, her hands unbuttoning her top button and stepping across him with her other leg. He grabbed this leg as well. She looked over the edge of the loft at Jimmy and Cecilia, who were dead asleep, and put her finger to her mouth, motioning for him to be quiet. Without waiting for a reply, she kneeled and kissed him passionately.

He looked up at her, the stars coming through her long, brown hair, and thought to himself, *Heavenly, indeed.*

Jimmy woke later in the night and saw that Cecilia had snuggled into him and had her arm laid across his waist. He glanced over at the couch where Ardwana had been and saw the covers pulled back. He glanced up to the loft and thought, *About time!*

They all slept soundly and rose refreshed to address the challenges awaiting them.

CHAPTER 20

Reunion

"Through our friends, our character is honed, our flaws are rubbed smooth, our ideas catch flame, and our best selves shine through."
— *Professor Luca Lambardi, cofounder of the PNLI.*

Impact minus 52 days

Most people thought that Tamarind's company, Dark Matter Ventures, was based upon the universe theory that postulated that dark matter, though undetected, made up nearly 85% of the mass of the universe and that somehow the company would discover or harness this resource. Flax Venture, Tamarind Chase, and Almond Brighten knew better.

When the three of them co-founded DroneTech, they needed a place to unwind and discuss their ideas. Over time, they started hanging out in brewpubs, cafes, and coffee shops, but none of these places were ever quite right. Thus began the early days of Dark Matter Café, a coffee shop, and a cafe that got everything right in their minds. Who started the idea was lost in time, but they all actively contributed to the concept whenever they tasted a perfect chocolate dessert, coffee drink, or dark stout beer. "Mmmm, this is good enough that we could serve it at Dark Matter Café." Over time, these jokes and images grew to a shared vision of their imaginary café and their mutual attraction to chocolate, coffee, and beer—all as dark as could be found. They decided that these were the fundamental elements that held the world together, and they had discovered the real dark matter of the universe. This little game continued for years until they decided to go for it and start Dark Matter Café in Loveland, near the offices of DroneTech. It remained a favorite meeting place between the three of them. When Tamarind sold his shares in DroneTech and moved to Nevada, he had named his solo venture, Dark Matter Ventures, as a homage to his friends.

This morning Flax and Almond settled in over a Black Hole Dark Coffee and a zucchini chocolate chip muffin for a coffee break at the café.

"I sure hope most of the universe is made of this," Almond said as she chewed on her muffin and gazed into her coffee, and then suddenly lifted her eyes and asked excitedly, "have you heard from Tamarind this week?"

Flax shook his head, "I need to make a trip up to visit Tamarind today for a government project DroneTech is working on." The President had not included her in the top-secret loop, which was awkward.

"Would you like me to come? she asked, adding, "It would be great to catch up with Tamarind."

Flax shook his head. "I need to talk to him about a technical project for the government related to SWARMNET. I think we won't have much time to chat. I'll invite him to come over and stay for the holiday weekend, OK?"

"That would be great! Tell him if he doesn't say 'yes,' then I will program a drone with one of my magic darts with his name on it." She seemed satisfied with his answer, though aware that something was unsaid, she kissed him, turned, and walked out of the café toward the office. "Have some fun with your friend, Flax!"

Flax headed off in his Nostradamus and set it on auto. He was so glad that enough satellites had been launched to allow auto-drive again using GPS. *Not much between Loveland and Tamarind's place in Nevada; I might as well let the car do the driving,* Flax thought. Loading the data from the briefing into the car's heads-up display, he reviewed the Swarm Team's info. Then he called Tamarind to set up the meeting.

"Flax," Tamarind said, "good to see your gnarly face. How's that beautiful wife I set you up with?"

"Fortunately, she chose this gnarly face over your polished mug," Flax answered, smiling. "Hey, I'm going to be there shortly, and I have something important I must discuss with you."

Tamarind could see by the concerned look on Flax's face that it was something important. When he considered he was driving from Colorado to talk to him about it with no advanced warning, he knew it must be urgent, critical, and confidential. He glanced at his scheduler and quickly slid his one appointment into the re-schedule column.

"Sure, my time is yours. When will you get here?" Tamarind asked. He could see that Flax was traveling at 400km/hr on the I70 superhighway from his display, with an estimated arrival of 67 minutes.

"About an hour, and you know how hungry I can get. I need a completely private location; your house good?"

"Come to my office; there is something I want to show you when you are here," Tamarind said. *Time to come clean on Phosaster*, he thought.

* * *

Flax arrived, appearing more rested and relaxed than he did on the call.

After a man hug and a brief mutual update, Flax got straight to business.

"Tamarind, what I am about to tell you is top secret—a matter of global security. President Jaspar asked me to include you in the loop."

Tamarind immediately wondered what DroneTech's top secret project was and why his friend, the President, didn't call him directly. But he just looked at Flax and nodded.

"A previously unidentified object, code-named Apollyon, is on a collision course with Earth. It's big, nearly two kilometers in diameter, and appears to be solid metal, traveling fast enough to cause an extinction event. It hits perihelion in less than two months, and Earth about five days after that. Sensors detected it thirty-six hours ago with our recently uploaded SWARMNET software, just in time, I guess," Flax said, ominously.

"Just in time for what?" Tamarind asked, eyebrows raised at the corners. "That was quite a bombshell you just dropped; I see how you got the nickname 'Flax the Unflappable.'"

If Flax was aware of this nickname, he didn't comment on it but instead continued his explanation.

"As the terms of the Space Peace Treaty relaxed, the US, and perhaps other countries, began deploying some nuclear missile-capable satellites in orbit. Space Command intends to use the only two missiles currently deployed to intercept Apollyon after it passes the Sun, hoping to destroy or deflect it before it strikes Earth. We're alerting other space-capable governments to see what assets can be brought to bear. President Jaspar would like Project LightStar positioned to destroy fragments that make it past the initial attack." Flax looked at him somberly.

"That is a lot to take in. Has your team done the calcs to say this plan can work?" Tamarind asked.

Flax toggled his hand and said, "Fifty-fifty chance. Its tangential proximity to the Sun will likely create a CME. LightStar would have no ground communications for a while."

"Then it's a blindfolded quick-draw with a mean dude that is sure to kill us if I miss," Tamarind said. "You never bring me any easy stuff, do you?" Flax completed downloading the information and analysis, finished up the meal Tamarind brought in and stood up to leave.

"Tell the President that we will get right on this and will have information on the anti-fragment capabilities of Project LightStar in two days.

Before you go, Flax, I have something to tell you that you aren't going to like."

"Wonderful," Flax was already carrying a heavy load, and Tamarind thought about leaving it but decided he had to do it today for his own peace of mind. He walked over to his private elevator and motioned Flax to join him. They made the quick descent to his Phosaster command center. When the elevator doors opened, Flax became the only other person to be in the bunker for nearly ten years since the Phosaster project began. Flax looked around dumbfounded and then back to Tamarind.

"What is this?" Flax asked.

Tamarind explained his work the last several years on the Phosaster project, the PNLI founders' support, and why he'd kept it quiet all these years, even from Flax and Almond. Flax shook his head slowly from side to side and said predictably, "You going Ghengis on us again, Tamarind?"

Ouch.

Tamarind explained the vital data collected, the plans to restart the deep space industry, and increased funding to PNLI. Of course, none of that mattered if Apollyon hit Earth.

"I've launched a communications probe to intercept Phosaster, and to reconnect communications with Earth, hopefully in a few days. Perhaps Phosaster's laser is still operational and could also be aligned toward Apollyon?" Tamarind offered.

"Perhaps," Flax said. "Review the materials I've given you and send me your analysis on what you think LightStar and Phosaster can do against Apollyon. I'll send you the details about the next meeting."

"Done. We good?" Tamarind asked expectantly.

"You are my best friend, and as a Christian, I believe in love, forgiveness, and redemption," Flax said, with a smile. "But do work on being redeemable. I know you Deists are flexible on morals, but..."

"Practical and rational, not flexible," Tamarind countered. He thought he might add "and not mystical like you Christians are," but instead said, "Thank you for your understanding, your friendship, and your forgiveness. I see why she chose you. ERIWA, my friend."

"ERIWA, my friend." Flax grabbed his forearm and hand and then instead pulled him in close for a full-body bear hug.

Remembering Almond's request, he added, "Oh yeah, Almond requires your presence next weekend at our home and threatened drone darts if you said anything other than yes."

"Yes," Tamarind made like he was turning a key with his fingers over his lips and then feigned to throw away the key.

Flax and Tamarind had been two of the business community leaders who had written to the government in support of building a superhighway for the vehicles that could manage it. Flax considered how tired he felt and decided he would be safer if he let the car drive. He set the autopilot to home and max sensor mode and figured he could rest until he neared Denver. Soon he was fast asleep.

Flax woke with a start as the vehicle maneuvered through a mountain pass before descending toward Denver. An alarm was going off on the dashboard. Not loud but persistent. Putting him back in control, the car quickly brought his chair up to drive position and slowed to 100 km/hr. He looked down at the display and saw it was one of Almond's nature apps. A herd of mountain goats was detected on the mountainside. None were dangerously near the road, or the alarm would have been louder and more urgent.

Flax slowed the vehicle further and looked at the mountain goats grazing on the precarious hillside. A doe gracefully leaped up from rock to rock on the cliff face as her fawn followed less nimbly behind her. He wondered at their remarkable agility, which must take a lifetime to gain. He took a picture to share with Almond when he got home. She'd appreciate that her app had awakened him from sleep to enjoy the beauties of nature.

The DroneTech CEO was too much of a pragmatist to dwell on dark thoughts, but he did wonder if they would be able to save these noble animals or the people who appreciate them. He wondered as he watched the doe and fawn if Almond and he would ever have children. He reminded himself that God is sovereign over the universe and has their best interests at heart. He prayed for wisdom, perseverance, unity among the world's leaders, and that God would save them from Apollyon.

Switching to manual mode on the back roads to Loveland, he took the time to fully appreciate the scenery: sharp mountain crags silhouetted against the skyline. Deep blue, pink, and gold colors illuminating the evening sky. The snow on the hillsides gradually engulfed in shadows in the fading light, and the grasses of the high plains moving rhythmically with the breeze.

CHAPTER 21

Suspicion

"My end is near and inescapable. I choose to face it with peace, purpose, and clarity."--Journal of Kohlrabi Trust

51 days until Impact

Poring over the data Flax had given him, Tamarind recalculated each conclusion and simulated each predicted outcome again. He saw no holes in their analysis, but a 50/50 chance of success was generous. He needed to find some answers and options that would help them improve the odds. Dark Matter Ventures had significant simulation capabilities for space events, likely more advanced than those of the government.

While he often worked without AI support to keep his brain sharp, now there was too much data, too little time, and too many questions in his mind.

"Athena, show me a holograph of the solar system and overlay info we have on Apollyon," Tamarind said to his holodesk AI assistant.

"Yes, Tamarind," Athena said, as a small holograph image of Athena, goddess of wisdom, appeared on the corner of his desk. Above her, she displayed the solar system with every known object moving precisely as it was in space.

"Fast-forward to the potential impact on Earth," Tamarind said. The image animated forward until Earth impact. Athena anticipated his interest in the trajectory of Apollyon and overlaid both the measured and projected path.

"Project Apollyon's trajectory in the past," Tamarind said. Athena used the known data points and extrapolated a path backward before the measured data collected by SWARMNET. "Considering the estimated mass of Apollyon, what would be the gravitational effect from the planets it passed along the way?"

Interestingly, the extrapolated path took it near other planets, which had curved its trajectory. A comet of this size would have to have an orbit of hundreds or thousands of years to have been undetected. "Athena, show me Apollyon's possible orbits based on this trajectory." The results showed orbits that either seemed impossible for a newly discovered object of this size or unlikely for an asteroid.

Tamarind had an extremely unpleasant thought.

"Athena, overlay the orbit of the Phosaster asteroid." Suddenly, he could hear his pulse as he said, "Project possible scenarios from the time we lost contact with Phosaster, exploring the possibility that Apollyon launched from the Phosaster asteroid." The display started projecting conceivable launch points, trying to get a trajectory that aligned with Apollyon. The simulation continued, marking each iteration as failed. Each successive iteration came closer to a possible origin point for Apollyon.

"Oh, Divine Providence, please don't let me be the cause of this!" It was the closest Tamarind had come to an actual prayer. How could the programmed directive to a mining capsule to provide "the greatest value to Earth" result in launching a killer object right at the Earth's core? "Surely not," Tamarind said, weakly.

He continued to watch as Athena projected all launch points and projected trajectories, and each one failed to intersect with Apollyon. Having exhausted the options, Athena concluded, "Tamarind, it appears impossible within the required input parameters to resolve a trajectory between Apollyon and Phosaster," she stated with her calm, unemotional voice. Tamarind breathed out heavily, his shoulders slumping, with his eyes closed. He was a little unsettled by the caveat "within the required input parameters." He considered the unlikely possibility that Phosaster developed Apollyon with an engine that redirected it under power toward Earth. He decided not to waste additional time exploring his fears and moved on.

"Athena, assume Apollyon came from outside our solar system, project its path out to 100 light-years from our Sun." The scale changed, and new solar systems emerged in the display. The route Athena drew didn't seem to pass near any stars or star clusters.

Tamarind continued. "Increase the mass +/- 20% of the NASA estimate for Apollyon, and project this range of paths as a band." The change in mass altered how the trajectory was affected by planets along the way. This band overlapped three distant solar systems, some with known planets.

"Interesting," said Tamarind out loud to himself. "Apollyon, are you an interstellar object that escaped the gravity well of another solar system? Or were you sent here?"

"Athena, calculate the time from each star at Apollyon's current velocity." Interstellar distances are vast, and as Tamarind thought, Apollyon was not traveling fast enough to achieve these distances, even in millennia. Sure enough, as Athena overlaid the paths, the times were unrealistic to consider that Apollyon had been "sent" to Earth.

However, there were several things about Apollyon that seemed inconsistent with a natural object. First, Apollyon's albedo, or its optical reflectivity in the visible spectrum, was unusually high, suggesting an almost polished surface, or a metal that ideally reflected visible wavelength bands. Secondly, it was unrealistically spherical. Tamarind considered that if it began as molten metal, surface tension could theoretically achieve those conditions. Still, there wasn't anything about the trajectory that suggested it had been superheated en route.

Thirdly, the likelihood of a random interstellar object being on such an accurate course toward Earth while avoiding every other entity in the solar system was astronomically unlikely. He couldn't figure out a way to estimate the odds of that. *Maybe I could, but let's not get distracted*, Tamarind thought. Finally, the mass and speed were just enough to escape falling into the Sun and just enough to cause an extinction event on Earth.

When he considered these factors together, he decided that being under attack from another star system was more realistic than a naturally occurring event. He looked again at the star with the shortest distance to Earth. Over 2300 years to reach us at Apollyon's velocity. *Who would want to kill us in 200 BCE?*

Tamarind went back to the idea he had rejected earlier related to a Phosaster trajectory. "Athena, consider Apollyon as having a means of propulsion, allowing it to travel much faster on the trajectory from the closest star." Tamarind looked at the name of the closest star, Proxima Centauri, and considered that if it traveled 100 times faster than its current velocity, it could get to Earth in a few decades. While more advanced than current Earth spaceship technology, that was still far less than light speed.

"Radio and television signals could have been detected a few decades ago, which might explain how aliens knew we existed and why they'd want to kill us." Tamarind shook his head, recalling that the first international TV broadcast capable of penetrating the ionosphere was a speech by Adolf Hitler.

He used the mass that Athena had calculated that correlated closest to the trajectory from Proxima Centauri. "Athena, given that mass and Apollyon's current velocity, show how the Sun's gravity will affect it." These calculations showed Apollyon escaping the Sun's gravity. If it had once been a molten ball of metal, it was unlikely that it would break up at that point. The trajectory shift from the Sun's gravity deflected Apollyon only slightly, bringing it to a straight-on impact on the planet.

"Athena, project the location of impact and simulate the extent of the damage." The simulated projection showed the object hitting the Earth between China and India and the impact wave enveloping the world. There was a small point in South America where human survival might be possible, but the resulting earthquakes, mudslides, and atmospheric debris would further diminish survival odds. As if that wasn't enough, a global ice age would follow, lasting for millennia.

"A frighteningly effective weapon," Tamarind found himself leaning toward the alien assault theory and couldn't help but admire the sheer genius of the weapon.

"Athena, using the mass and dimensions you estimated, predict the composition." Ten seconds later, Athena displayed the results. Assuming it was a single element, the average density would be nearly 140 molecular weight. That meant it would be denser than iron, nickel, or silicon—common asteroid materials. Athena proposed possible compositions constructed by higher molecular weight metals like lead, gold, platinum, and iridium. As an asteroid miner, Tamarind couldn't help but be impressed by the immense wealth generated if these metals could be safely steered into orbit around Earth.

"Athena, using the albedo and sensor information, predict the most likely composition of the surface materials." Gradually, he refined Athena's estimates and compositions until he had an iron core ball with the heavier metals on the shell.

"Athena, predict the first point when Project LightStar could fire at Apollyon. Could we get enough of a pulse to predict the composition accurately?" While Tamarind's team designed Project LightStar to destroy objects near it, the laser was similar to the one on Phosaster and could be redirected for near-Earth object analysis. Athena's model suggested Tamarind could position the LightStar satellite to get a material analysis of Apollyon shortly after it passed perihelion and came closest to the Sun.

"Athena, if LightStar fired continuous pulses at Apollyon, could it shift or slow its trajectory?" Athena began analyzing the amount of material that would be ejected by each pulse. Newton's laws required an equal and opposite reaction, so the tiny plumes caused by the laser pulses hitting Apollyon's surface would result in a little explosive push in the opposite direction. He first looked at whether head-on blasts could slow Apollyon enough for it to miss the Earth. Then he looked at whether side blasts would offset the course. Neither was sufficient to affect the object's path.

Tamarind launched Athena on enough other simulations and graphical representations to keep her working through the night.

Tamarind moved toward his sleeping quarters. He had spent many nights sleeping in his bunker over the years, and he often left the displays on in night mode. Tonight, he didn't need this; his dreams were full of the images of Apollyon hurtling toward Earth.

* * *

He awoke around dawn to his commlink, indicating a call from Jake Johnson.

"Jake, it's early. What can I do for you?" He flattened his hair with his hand and directed his display to show the least sensitive part of the room.

"Mr. Chase. Flax Venture has been seen entering the White House and then coming to your office. Would you care to comment?

"Good morning, Jake. I don't think a comment is required." Tamarind tried to look casual and slightly disinterested.

Jake was looking around at the room behind him.

"Where are you?" Jake asked. The walls appeared to be cement and had a curvature, and there were no shadows from sunlight.

Silence. "Are DroneTech and Dark Matter Ventures cooperating on a government project?"

"Flax and I are friends; we usually have much to talk about."

"I doubt he left his office and drove there during a workday just for a chat."

Jake was beginning to annoy him. "We also had a meal when he was here. Would you like to know what we ate? I thought you gave up on your conspiracy theories after your conjecture of the second satellite in Project LightStar."

"I was wrong about that. I now think Project LightStar was a cover to launch something outside of a planetary orbit for asteroid mining or military uses."

"Ah, that is a new one. You are trying to tie Flax's visit to a military contract?"

"Would you care to make a comment on that or make a definitive statement refuting that assessment?"

Tamarind considered that he was working with Flax on a military project—shooting down Apollyon. He also was mining asteroids. He couldn't refute either charge definitively. He thought about just saying "No" but decided instead to answer with cynical wit.

"I admire your dogged reporter instincts, Jake. I've told you before that I have never engaged in a military contract, and you've watched for years as Project LightStar has diligently cleaned up the debris from Earth's orbit. You have also followed DroneTech as Flax led them to restore Earth's communications through a government contract. You have no new facts that could infer anything untoward. Do you think perhaps your instincts might be misguided?"

"That is not a definitive refusal," Jake said, with a steely gaze.

"Have a nice day, Jake. We're done here." Tamarind ended the connection. Having a nosy reporter watching their movements would make things more difficult. He decided to try to get another hour of fitful sleep before his day began.

Jake reviewed the call recording. His equipment did not detect intentional falsehood in Tamarind's statements, but his instincts told him there was something he was not saying. He analyzed the background—edge of a bed, cement wall, only artificial light, ceiling outside of the field of view. The curved wall was the most puzzling, and his analysis suggested more than ten meters in diameter. *Where was Tamarind Chase on this call?*

CHAPTER 22

Camaraderie

Leaders build teams to accomplish objectives. The best leaders create camaraderie along the way.—Flax Venture

51 days until Impact

Flax asked Telsun to come to his office early before everyone else had arrived for the day. The President's classified assignments required much of DroneTech's resources. However, they had to find a way to divert the resources without revealing any Apollyon details to the rest of the company.

They decided to present the company with the prospect that they would submit a proposal for a government project. It would use their latest drone technology to instantly re-establish the world's communications grid, should there be another Space War-type scenario. The plan would be to use DroneTech communications drones to reestablish the global network quickly. An emergency backup grid was a plausible story, conveying the urgency to get the info rapidly together. It didn't involve saying anything untrue—one of Flax Venture's requirements when communicating with his team.

As the team started arriving, Flax called an urgent meeting of department heads and announced the plan. They met in DroneTech's sprawling

Leonardo Da Vinci conference room, which was more like a gallery with pictures of DroneTech projects and one of Leonardo's first sketches of a helicopter. DroneTech had thousands of employees and frequent visitors to this room, designed to inspire the team and market to customers. Staff meetings were usually in the smaller conference room near his office, but he thought this room would help sell the terrestrial communication grid proposal to his team.

"Thank you all for coming on such short notice. We have been invited to put together a proposal for the government to build an emergency backup communication grid in case there is ever another Space War that affects the world satellite communications network. We have twenty-four hours to come up with the proposal. While we are clearly in the best position to fulfill this contract and have years of experience in government contracts, we may not be the only bid, so we want to do our best. I've asked the Swarm Team to lead this effort. Please give Telsun's team any resources he requests today."

Mike Stapleton, who led their Drone comms division, asked several clarifying questions. "Should we restrain drone launch locations to US military sites globally, or could we expand to include DroneTech and other secondarily secure sites?"

"Don't constrain the locations, but define an optimum grid," Flax added.

Mike continued, "Should we assume existing designs to fulfill this contract, or can we develop new drones to supply the contract?"

Flax clarified, "Since this would be a global emergency, assume that we would appropriate any relevant DroneTech assets. Assume only six weeks to fulfill the contract using existing inventory and designs, giving priority over other manufacturing and deployment requirements."

At this, the Comms Division Manager spoke up, "That is quite a constraint. Six weeks is insufficient to manufacture and deploy enough drones to reestablish a secure global comms network." Then, turning to the Swarm Team said, "Telsun, our team will get right on this with the obvious analysis and questions. Stop by when you are ready to discuss specific requirements."

Law Enforcement, Underwater Drones, BioTech, Agriculture, Environmental Monitoring, and Transport departments did not have the right kind of equipment or resources to assist with this project. Flax asked each of them to consider how they might contribute and how their departments might address the fallout resulting from such a situation.

Telsun made a specific request of the IT division's leader, Aislinn O'Malley. "Aislinn, a critical part of this, establishing secure communications with the global resources that currently use satellite communications. Can you help us figure out which organizations and with whom we'd need to interface? We want to demonstrate our understanding of the problem in our proposal, so please be as specific as possible."

Aislinn, who'd been a part of the team that had set up and managed the Drone Communications Network after the Space War, had been intricately involved in the transfer back to satellite communications in recent years.

She spoke confidently. "No problem. I think I'm on a first-name basis with most of the parties." She inherited her relationship skills from her Irish father and her calm efficiency from her German mother. Her slight lilting accent must have been something she picked up from her father or her many trips to Ireland to visit her extended family.

"I can believe that, thanks, Aislinn," Flax responded. Wrapping up the meeting, Flax glanced at his watch and said, "We have twenty-three hours and thirty minutes left; let's get started." Everyone bolted out of their seats and rushed out of the door.

Almond, head of the biotech division, hung back and smiled at Flax at the meeting's end. "This is what has been distracting you in the last few days? Why not just tell me?"

Flax smiled back at her and tenderly put his hands on her shoulders. "This isn't the whole story; it is only the part I can tell you about now. You know how governments can be with their security." Flax shrugged and tilted his head to one side like it was out of his control.

"I'm not sure I like you keeping secrets from me, but I'll trust you for now," Almond said seductively. "Just don't push it, mister, I'm watching you." With that, she turned and walked away, dragging her index finger across his chest as she left. Almond was more openly affectionate at work. Flax was always concerned that his HR manager would get complaints. Most employees thought it endearing and strangely assuring to know their founders were in love.

Almond went back to her lab and began mixing up a concoction in test tubes and beakers. Soon she had a vial filled with a blue liquid and one filled with a faintly yellow liquid. She smiled as she held them up to the light.

"That ought to do it," she said.

* * *

Telsun pulled together the Swarm Team, the only DroneTech employees who knew almost everything that was going on. They all looked rested, and there was a bit of awkwardness as they looked at each other and contemplated their new relationship changes from the previous night. Telsun thought about acknowledging this somehow but instead decided to get straight to business, breaking everything into defined task assignments.

"Cecilia, will you work with Aislinn and the IT team on comm uplinks?" Cecilia nodded affirmatively.

"Ardwana, I'd like you to design the swarm network using our new software and communications algorithms." These SW tools weren't available at the time of the first Space War and made things much more manageable.

"Sure, boss man," she said playfully.

"Jimmy, will you work with Mike Stapleton and the Comms Division to figure out the hardware requirements?" His enthusiastic nod confirmed his agreement.

"I will coordinate the various tasks with the department heads and work with them on the manufacturing challenge. I'll also write-up our proposal and integrate anything that comes up along the way. Remember, everything we know is still highly classified, so be careful to work within the framework of this being a contract bid." Telsun restated their agreed actions and the constraints as he did at the end of every meeting.

Ardwana said with mock seriousness, "Agreed. Some things should remain secret on a need-to-know basis." She and Cecilia grinned knowingly while Telsun blushed.

"Thanks for having us over last night, Telsun," Cecilia said, and then looking at Jimmy, "but next time, I'm going to pick the movie."

"Get to work," Jimmy said.

The next 24 hours were a blur, but they pulled it all back together and presented a credible proposal for a global Drone Swarm Comm Network, which they could implement within six weeks. The Department Heads shared high fives and cheers and celebrated their completion of the task, heading off home exhausted but relieved. Little did they know their relief would be short-lived.

CHAPTER 23

Connection

"Happiness is the intersection of mystery, mastery, and purpose." —
Journal of Kohlrabi Trust

50 days to Impact

Tamarind woke again, now eager to see the results of the simulations and analysis he'd tasked Athena with the night before. Overlaid on top of these answers, he had an image from Phosaster—his communication probe had re-established the link with the asteroid.

"Yes!" he shouted to himself, pumping both fists. This moment he had worked toward for so many years. Setting aside the impending destruction of the Earth by Apollyon, his curiosity consumed him.

Years of data reports from Phosaster were streaming in, monthly updates on asteroid mining results, which had continued all these years. There were new constructions and mechanisms on the asteroid. It turned out a sophisticated communications control relay had failed, as had the redundant module, but it was too advanced for Phosaster to manufacture the damaged part. They'd put many advanced manufacturing capabilities in the processing modules, but computer-controlled electronics were beyond its ability. Tamarind shook his head at this oversight and his presumption that only one redundant module would be enough. The angst his oversight had cost him all these years!

Tamarind's communications intercept ship had rendezvoused, re-established the comms link using the lower data rate internal comms link. It now was broadcasting the data to him via the Project LightStar satellite.

The amount of data was impressive and overwhelming, and from a project point of view, all the news appeared good. Tamarind started considering the implications. Now that they had a connection with Phosaster again, he could finally come clean on the whole program, per his agreement with his investors. The Phosaster project was now a success, and his investors would be pleased.

Even more than that, he considered the implications for himself. He could aggressively and openly pursue his dreams of space mining, fulfill his promises to Phosaster's investors and Dark Matter Ventures employees and Kohlrabi, and he could have a life outside of this bunker. He spun around in the center of the room, feasting his eyes on the displays around him.

"Won't matter if we don't survive this asteroid," Tamarind's mood shifted quickly from joy to sober consideration of the implications of Apollyon's impact. But Tamarind was determined not to get lost in his dark thoughts but to use this challenge to energize him toward solving the problem. "Perhaps Phosaster can help us with Apollyon?" he said aloud to himself.

"Athena, show me the trajectories of both Apollyon and Phosaster," Phosaster was nearing its approach to Earth, and Apollyon was directly on an impact course. They would be closest to each other when Apollyon passed perihelion in about six weeks but would still be hundreds of thousands of kilometers apart.

"Athena, can we reposition Phosaster, so it's mining laser can target Apollyon?" Athena overlaid the angle of the mining laser on the spinning asteroid and considered where there might be a clean shot at Apollyon. There were six points where Phosaster could blast Apollyon. Unfortunately, that wasn't enough to have any significant effect. The speed differences, the diverging trajectories, the rotational spin of Phosaster, and the narrow targeting angle made a more extended sequence of clean shots impossible. He considered how he might adjust the targeting angle of the Phosaster laser or slow the rotation of Phosaster. Athena's computations found none of those ideas had any significant positive effect. He narrowed his focus in on the timeframe right before and after Apollyon approached perihelion, where the two objects would be almost in parallel. He concluded he might be able to do a single blast to determine the composition and perhaps three to five more at debris after perihelion, which might deflect or damage larger fragments. He wouldn't know until the fragment trajectories were assessed after the perihelion exit zone.

Finally, he reluctantly turned back to the simulations Athena ran in the night.

Athena began reporting, "Tamarind, your first question was 'what is the largest size object that Project LightStar could successfully deflect with its laser along the Apollyon trajectory and current velocity.' My conclusion is that an object fifty meters in diameter could be successfully deflected or destroyed by this method."

Good, thought Tamarind, *at least we can deflect some of the larger debris if it breaks into fragments.* Then he said, "Proceed."

"Your second question was about the effect of known space assets if launched at Apollyon debris." Athena then displayed the space assets which could be directed into the debris path. Athena had considered each satellite's maneuverability, the mass, and the velocity each could accelerate to, and then estimated the most significant piece of debris it could fragment or deflect. The results were encouraging. More than 1,000 chunks of Apollyon between 30 and 300 meters in diameter could be diverted or damaged, albeit at the cost of much of the world's newly launched communications satellites.

"Maybe we could get more hardware in space in the time remaining," Tamarind said out loud to himself. That idea triggered another question. "Athena, how many Earth-bound rockets could be launched in the next forty-five days?"

"I have insufficient information to calculate accurately. Many countries and private corporations have such capabilities but have not gone public with their data." Athena extrapolated from known ground-based assets and suggested 50% on top of what is in space could be initiated from the ground by that time. Some of those could be launched with explosive payloads, expanding their repulsion capability.

"Perhaps the President can get us a more accurate list. Time to get ready for our meeting," Tamarind pulled together the most useful data and prepared an executive summary. He knew the President liked to get straight to the point.

Reconnecting with Phosaster and reviewing the results of the night's simulations had left Tamarind as hopeful as he had been in many years, despite everything that was going on.

* * *

Before he left for the meeting with the President, he decided to have one more meeting with Cali. He finished getting showered and dressed, had a quick breakfast, and then took his elevator into his office. Once there, he called her in.

"Hi Cali," Tamarind said tenderly, "could you stop by my office?"

Appearing in his doorway wearing a sleeveless, belted, red linen dress complimented with a Celtic design silk scarf, she took the seat next to him by his jungle image wall.

"Cali, have you noticed the level of encrypted communications passing through LightStar?"

She nodded. "I figured you would tell me if you wanted me to know more details."

"I think it is the time that the whole world knows what is in those encrypted communications. I'd like you to hunt down Jake Johnson and set up a meeting later this week for an onsite interview."

Cali opened her eyes wide in surprise by Tamarind's suggestion.

"Jake Johnson? Wasn't he the guy that wrote those conspiracy theory articles about you several years ago? Surely there are better reporters to make a press release through, or perhaps we should do a press meeting and invite top reporters from all the agencies?" Cali was correct from a strict marketing perspective, but Tamarind had other reasons for asking for Jake.

"We'll do that too, but first, I have an idea of how we can get the President's endorsement when we go public with this information. However, Jake Johnson was right enough in those reports he wrote that he deserves to have the first crack at the story."

Cali's eyes opened wide. "He was right? There was a second ship with a secret military mission? Is this going to be a PR disaster for us?"

"He wasn't right on everything, but I appreciate the work he did to explore and challenge me on this. Leaders need people that support them and people that challenge them to be better. Jake is one of those who keeps me honest." Cali slumped a little in her chair. She still didn't know anything, and so far, he'd only asked her to set up a single interview.

"Cali, I've always considered you as a peer and respect you as a CEO of your own company. I appreciate that you took the contract with Dark Matter Ventures; your work has made us matter in the world." He paused and took a deep breath, "and taking off my Dark Matter Ventures CEO hat for a minute; I'd also like to tell you that you look stunning today. That is a beautiful outfit you are wearing."

Cali blushed, taken aback by this change of direction. Tamarind never commented directly on anything she wore or how she looked.

"Thank you," she said, with one raised eyebrow suspiciously.

"I'd like to ask you to consider doing one more thing," Tamarind said, pausing as he reconsidered the line he was crossing. Cali sensed the tension and shifted in her chair expectantly. "Would you have dinner with me this Friday night?"

Cali was already a little confused by this conversation and decided to ask for clarification. "So, we can go over the press release?"

"For a date," Tamarind replied with a smile, "if you'd like. I understand if you feel us working together makes anything personal too complicated..."

He could see her pupils dilate and her face flush as she leaned forward in her chair. "I'd like that." She held his gaze for a long moment. Then she stood and walked toward the door turning back to smile as she left the room.

Tamarind smiled back, sincerely. Despite everything going on, the planet in danger, Phosaster's newfound success, he was most energized by the thought that she had accepted his date proposal. He was anxious as well. He hadn't been on many dates in his life. He realized he was more nervous about that than his upcoming meeting with the President.

"Priorities, Tamarind. Stay on target," he said to himself, slapping his cheek with a grin on his face.

Before he left for the meeting, he sent a quick communication to the Phosaster investor team. "Phosaster comms reestablished, project data amazing, more soon."

CHAPTER 24

Command

"Leaders cannot wait, there is never enough information or resources, and the timing is never exactly right. Instead, we begin where we are, work with the tools available, and hope better information and tools will be found as we move forward." —Journal of Kohlrabi Trust

49 days until Impact

Everyone stood as President Laura Jaspar entered the Security Briefings Room and called the meeting to order. She motioned to them to sit but remained standing herself. Around the table were the General of Space Command, Director of NASA, the Joint Chiefs of Staff, the Secretary of State, Tamarind Chase, and Flax Venture.

She began the meeting with the end results in mind.

"At the end of today's meeting, we will take action to save our world and our way of life. Now is not a time for more analysis, more discussion, or more committees—it is a time for fast, decisive, and coordinated action. Make your comments appropriate to this outcome. Sharon, please begin," she motioned for her to take the floor, and then she sat down.

General Sharon Ward of Space Command stood to address the group. "The President, Secretary of State, and I have informed each of the world's nuclear powers about Apollyon and the threat of impact, and we have secured an agreement to cooperate on a coordinated response. The Japanese, French, and Russians each have confirmed one nuclear missile on a satellite in orbit. With our two, this gives us five nuclear weapons already in Earth orbit, which will be sufficient to deflect Apollyon or to fragment it into smaller pieces, whichever we decide." She made a motion with her hands, and displayed above the table were holographic images of five missiles deflecting or fragmenting the asteroid. There were murmurs of approval around the table and some muffled comments and "yes," but she raised her hand to silence them.

"Fortunately, each nation hardened their armed satellites against an EMP, but communications to the satellites will be affected. We have only a few days to reconnect, calculate trajectory modifications, or respond to any other changes, such as multiple fragments. For this reason, we recommend pre-programming each missile for an inline direct impact trajectory rather than diverting Apollyon with a side impact." General Ward sat down and transferred her simulation of the direct impact trajectory from the center hologram to one of the wall displays.

"What is the likelihood that Apollyon could fragment on its own as it passes the Sun?" President Jaspar asked.

General Ward stood again to answer the question. "Ms. President," she began, "our analysis suggests an eighty-two percent probability that Apollyon will remain intact through the perihelion zone and will not lose significant mass and an eighteen percent probability that it will fragment into two or more pieces. If it fragments, the explosion of that event will deflect the remaining mass, so that they are less likely to hit the Earth." Her simulation took center stage, with two fragments splitting and each chunk deflecting away from the Earth.

"Can we plan our assault near or at Perihelion to maximize the likelihood of such fragmentation?" President Jaspar was quick to grasp the technical aspects and see the strategic advantage of forcing this outcome.

"Unfortunately not, Ms. President," General Ward continued. "The nuclear missiles are neither fast enough, nor do they have enough fuel to impact at that point, and they would not survive the heat on approach. If we wait until we know what happens to Apollyon after exiting the Perihelion zone, the missiles launched will impact Apollyon only seventeen hours from Earth. It would be desirable to launch earlier, but we may not reestablish communications in time for any trajectory corrections. Therefore, Space Command recommends launching our missiles as Apollyon passes perihelion, where we have exact coordinates of our target. If the target has fragmented, we can split our missiles in-flight, among the remaining fragments, once we have comms reestablished after the CME." Her simulation moved from the central hologram to a second location on the wall displays. The room nodded general approval for this plan, not that it was up to a vote.

"Flax, talk to us about comms," the President said.

Some in the room shifted uncomfortably because two business leaders were at the table for such a critical decision. Still, no one could doubt their competency or relevant resources and experience.

"President Jaspar, Directors, Commanders," Flax stood and said formally, "we have proposed the optimum positioning of our SWARMNET satellites to minimize damage during the Coronal Mass Ejection (CME) and resulting Electromagnetic Pulse (EMP)." Flax presented the satellite SWARMNET grid's movements so satellites not hardened would be hidden behind the Earth during the EMP, improving their likelihood of remaining active. "From this, we believe we can reposition the satellites and reactivate the SWARMNET grid within forty-eight hours of the event. We cannot predict or guarantee how ground communications or other comms to the satellites will be affected or restored."

"Separately, our team has proposed a DroneNet to reestablish terrestrial communications immediately following the EMP." A second image appeared within the hologram of the Earth and SWARMNET of Satellites, this time showing the DroneNet grid's locations, all connected with red lines forming triangles that cover the significant landmasses almost uniformly and the seas more sparsely. "We have only enough DroneNet class assets to do approximately twenty percent of this today, but with an immediate production launch, we could get near one hundred percent and distribute the drones globally by the time of the pulse. As you know, DroneTech has done this successfully after the Space War, and some of our team members worked on that implementation. Dronetech's previous experience reestablishing Earth communications, technological expertise, and manufacturing capabilities ensure we can accomplish this. We recommend allocating three hundred million dollars to DroneTech for the immediate launch of this network." Flax sat down, and as with previous presenters, he transferred his hologram simulations to wall displays.

General Ward responded while sitting, "President Jaspar, this would result in DroneTech having control of the entire planet's communications network, as well as their current SW control linking our satellites. This is an unacceptable security risk. I suspect every other nation's security advisors will see it the same way."

"I appreciate your concern. Certainly, these times are unprecedented. Do we have another proposal?" She looked directly at her and paused until she confirmed she had no other proposal. "Dr. Lewis, SWARMNET was under your department. I'd like you to work with Flax to get him this money for a DroneNet." Then turning back to General Ward, "Incorporate the locations of the satellites with nuclear missiles into Flax's SWARMNET simulation, and coordinate with the Secretary of State to present this proposal to every other Head of State." Then turning to Flax, she said, "Please start production immediately."

Flax nodded in affirmation.

General Ward knitted her eyebrows and looked at Dr. Lewis, who seemed to share her disapproval.

Ignoring them, the President turned to the other side of the table. "Dark Matter Ventures have significant assets in space. Tamarind, what do you have for us?" It was an open-ended question, but Laura Jaspar and Tamarind Chase had known each other for many years, and she respected his ability to creatively solve problems and bring resources to bear in unexpected ways. President Jaspar had once offered Tamarind a place in her administration, but he had decided to focus on "the important work of Dark Matter Ventures," as they agreed to say in the press release. Despite the backlash from some that the Pan-Nationals were not "true Americans," she had successfully appointed other Pan-Nationals to positions in her administration.

Tamarind smiled and stood to address the meeting, speaking confidently. "First, let me show how Project LightStar can help," and immediately motioned for a hologram of Earth with only the LightStar satellite orbiting it. Laser pulses were destroying fragments of Apollyon. "LightStar can pivot over a wide arc and target any remaining debris still Earth-bound after the nuclear attacks. It can significantly reduce debris between twenty-five and fifty meters in diameter. Debris less than twenty-five meters should burn up in the atmosphere, or at most, cause minimum damage upon impact. Unfortunately, LightStar's laser will be relatively ineffective on larger debris." Tamarind paused and then put up a second hologram.

"However, we have analyzed the number of satellites that have enough maneuverability to be positioned into the path of debris and then estimated the size of fragment each could destroy. We have concluded that about a thousand satellites are available and could address targets between fifty and three hundred meters in diameter," The display showed SWARMNET satellites and other commercial satellites leaving orbit and blowing up against fragments of various sizes. A scrolling list confirmed each satellite's name and the mass of the objects it could destroy or deflect.

"There went SWARMNET," President Jaspar said, and seeing the opportunity for a little levity, turned to Flax and said, "I thought the two of you were friends?" The room chuckled nervously. "Continue," she said, looking back at Tamarind.

"Yesterday, I reconnected with an asteroid surveying and mining asset called Phosaster that was launched concurrently with Project LightStar," Tamarind said with no introduction.

"What? You've been mining asteroids for the last decade without approval? This is a violation of many international agreements, including the Space Peace Treaty," General Ward glared menacingly at Tamarind and slapped the table as she spoke. She sat red-faced next to Dr. Lewis of NASA, whose clenched jaws pulsed in anger.

The President turned to Flax with a question mark in her expression. "I just found out about this yesterday when I read him in on Apollyon," Flax said.

Tamarind spoke in his defense, "Technically, I had received legal approval to launch Project LightStar, and nothing in the treaties specifically limited the deployment of a surveying tool outside of Earth's orbit..."

The room got louder with the murmur of side comments at his words. President Jaspar raised her hand for them all to stop this side squabble. She was legendary for her ability to shut-down secondary issues that distracted from the agenda.

"Tamarind, presumably, you've brought this up now because Phosaster can help us?" She glared at him tight-lipped.

"Possibly," said Tamarind. "Phosaster has a similar laser to LightStar but is configured for longer duration pulses suitable for surveying and mining. It doesn't have any mobility while attached to the asteroid, but its natural rotation will result in the ability to shoot pulses at the larger debris occasionally. It is traveling on an almost parallel trajectory to Apollyon at perihelion. It may be able to deflect or damage several large fragments in the ten to one hundred-meter diameter range," Tamarind smiled hopefully. "It will also have the capability to get an up-close image and survey

Apollyon as it exits the Perihelion zone, so we should know what we are up against at that time."

"That will be helpful. Anything else?" President Jaspar asked.

"Yes. We believe that there are a significant number of rockets, probes, and space assets in both corporate and government inventories we could deploy to block incoming debris. I'd like to propose a global contest with the prize being ownership of one of the asteroids we've surveyed to any group that can launch an asteroid-capable rocket within the next six weeks. That should bring out every available asset currently hidden in development somewhere and get them motivated for launch without revealing anything about Apollyon until necessary. Then, once we have functional teams working on this, we can assign them a chunk of debris to target. We estimate another fifty percent of the smaller debris could be targeted this way."

"You want us to participate in your bait and switch global contest, and then for those who sacrifice their development hardware, you can withdraw your promised asteroid? Ms. President, I must protest," General Ward stood and slapped her hand on the table again, and then, realizing she had overstated her position, sat down.

"I like this idea," President Jaspar announced. Tamarind looked relieved. "This will get the whole world focusing on space, engaging in something positive, hopeful for the potential, and prepare them for the tempest ahead. Crowdsourcing a global army of spaceships," and then looking more positively at the Dark Matter CEO, she said, pointing at him, "Brilliant."

Then turning to her chief of staff, she said, "Set up a meeting announcing that the US will be signing the asteroid mining agreement and reopening space for commercial development. Tamarind and I will have a press conference together about this global contest, and he can come clean on the world stage about Phosaster and the asteroid survey data he has collected. I expect widespread support, except the Chinese and Russian governments, who won't like that we might have new sources for the precious metals they currently hold over us."

Most of the people at the table were surprised by this enthusiastic turn of events. Flax smiled at Tamarind while shaking his head from side to side.

President Jaspar ended the meeting with authority, clarifying each decision made, with tasks for each person. "We can do this, people," she concluded. Amazingly, what had seemed like a resigned resolution to ultimate destruction only a few days ago had turned to a glimmer of hope.

As they walked out of the room, Flax put his arm on Tamarind's shoulder. "Well, you certainly pulled that poker out of the fire at the right time. Congratulations on Phosaster; I know you have been working on that one for a few years. Let's hope it has a chance to make the difference you had in mind."

"Thanks, Flax. Congratulations on your new DroneTech contract. We were both skirting the ire of some of our military leaders in that meeting." They were both upbeat as they wound their way back through the security systems and long hallways connected to their meeting room.

Once they were outside, Tamarind handed Flax a memory cube and said, "Walk with me? There is one other thing I wanted to run by you for confirmation before I present to this group. Do you have a few minutes?"

"Don't tell me you have more confessions?" Flax asked.

They walked through the mall from the White House toward the Washington Monument. Once they were well clear of anyone, Tamarind said, "There are aspects of Apollyon that just don't make sense. It is so unnatural, the trajectory so direct, the characteristics of Apollyon a little too perfect."

"What are you trying to say?" Flax turned to look at him directly.

"I believe Apollyon is an alien attack, initiating from Proxima Centauri," Tamarind began.

Flax stiffened, and then realizing Tamarind was serious, said, "I can see why you didn't lead with that in the Situation Room. Do you know how crazy that sounds?"

Tamarind said, "The trajectory extrapolates backward to align with Proxima Centauri. The path was designed optimally using gravity-assist from planets to pass close to the Sun and then directly to Earth. Apollyon has so many properties that just don't seem natural. With the triggering of the CME taking out comms and the precisely aligned killer trajectory, it is a perfect weapon."

Flax nodded in affirmation, going along with this line of thinking, "It is pretty amazing, designed to kill us but not destroy the planet. But wouldn't that mean it would have been launched hundreds of years ago?"

"Thousands, in fact, at current velocity. Apollyon would have to have accelerated and then decelerated for this crazy theory to make any sense, which is why I didn't speak up about it. We don't have any evidence it has changed velocity. It also raises another concern. If our existence is known and someone went to this much trouble, perhaps they could have anticipated that we might come up with a response. I wonder if Apollyon might be equipped with countermeasures?" Tamarind looked at Flax with concern on his face.

"Tamarind, let's not get ahead of ourselves. I'll look at the data you have and see if it holds together, then we can decide what to bring to the President. Remember, God has a plan for our welfare, not for our destruction so that we can have a future and a hope." He smiled reassuringly at Tamarind.

"Christians," Tamarind said, shaking his head and smiling. He gave Flax their traditional handshake, and said "ERIWA, my friend," and then departed. As he walked away, he turned back to say, "Give Almond my love, and tell her I'm looking forward to catching up."

Tamarind made his way to his jumpjet that had brought him to this meeting across the country. He would be back in Nevada later this evening and found himself getting excited for the day ahead.

CHAPTER 25

Revelation

"Of all the spiritual disciplines, meditation has been of the most benefit to me. Next to that is the discipline of confession. Acknowledging to another our mistruths, our injuries, our wrongs allows us to achieve freedom."
— *Journal of Kohlrabi Trust*

47 days to Impact

Tamarind passed through the office more quickly than usual, touching base with each team. Everyone knew he had been in Washington for an important meeting and was hopeful his work on the mining treaty had finally paid off. In response to their question, he didn't say anything but gave them a thumbs-up and then put his finger to his lips to tell them to keep it a secret for now.

When he walked into the media department, Cali casually acknowledged his presence.

"Good morning, isn't this a lovely *Friday* morning? What have you got for me today?"

Cali raised one eyebrow, wondering if he had intended a subtle double entendre, and decided he probably hadn't. "Jake Johnson from the *International Times* will be coming in at nine-thirty this morning. I'd like to discuss our plans for the press release if you'd step into my office?" Tamarind nodded, heading into the conference room she used as an office, and waited until she had closed the door.

Before she had a chance to speak, he said, "The President has agreed to sign the asteroid mining treaty early next week. I will be with her at the press conference and reveal Phosaster, the second stage of Project LightStar. Phosaster is an asteroid survey and mining project which has been successfully operating for the last ten years." He paused to give her a chance to respond.

"W-W-What?" she stammered, and then recovering her professionalism, said, "OK, this is big. Presumably, you are going to start by telling Jake Johnson about Phosaster?"

"Yes, and I'd like you to sit in on that meeting. I want to be sure that I tell you both the same details. After the meeting, prepare a press release with the key points. Jake will get his scoop, and we'll ensure everyone knows about it." Cali nodded that she understood his request and agreed to his plan of action.

"The investors in the Phosaster part of the project are primarily interested in jump-starting the asteroid mining industry and shunting the major conflicts in the world brewing around access to precious metals. Phosaster has surveyed over three-hundred asteroids, all with market values of billions or trillions of dollars. The President and I agreed to announce a worldwide contest concurrently with the signing of the treaty. The organizations that demonstrate they are ready to pursue asteroid mining by launching a relevant space vehicle within the next five weeks, Dark Matter Ventures will grant mining rights on an asteroid." Tamarind was efficient with his words but paused again to make sure she was taking it all in.

"Sounds like the next five weeks will be busy for Galactic Marketing and the Media Department. How many teams do you think might enter?"

Cali kept up and was also anticipating developments and enthusiastic about being on point in this unprecedented media opportunity.

"Hard to say, I'm hoping there are several hundred teams that can get something in space in the next five weeks," Tamarind said.

"Wow," was all Cali said, smiling. "I knew our terrestrial mining work and Project LightStar were preparing us for asteroid mining, but I had no idea your vision was so far along. You've been collecting precious metals from an asteroid ever since Project LightStar took off?" Tamarind was concerned she might respond negatively to his long-held secret, but she seemed to be even more impressed with him if that was possible.

"The investors considered Phosaster a dangerous endeavor, both as a financial investment and politically. They insisted on total silence until the project's survey phase was complete, which took about two years, and until we had selected and started mining on an asteroid. That was nearly eight years ago, but we lost contact with the asteroid until just this week. You won't believe what Phosaster accomplished during those years of silence." Tamarind looked excited, which was both infectious and attractive. Cali held his gaze with excitement and a broad smile before transitioning to the practicalities of their evening.

"Have you been able to make any dinner plans for tonight with all this going on?" Cali asked.

"Yes. I thought we'd start with a ride in my private elevator," Tamarind said secretively, with a mischievous grin.

"Just what every girl wants to hear on her first date," Cali said playfully.

Tamarind winked at her, and said, "Let's get ready for Jake." As he walked out of Cali's office and headed to his own, Tamarind read the personal message he'd been expecting.

The Phosaster investors are pleased with the successful reconnection to the asteroid. We agreed to allow the complete release of information about the Phosaster project, including the specific mention of each of us in the announcement. Good job, Tamarind; it is a tribute to your perseverance, creativity, and integrity that you have succeeded in this venture despite the personal cost. We hope that Phosaster has the Impact that you envisioned so long ago.

"Yes," Tamarind exclaimed. A few in the office heard his unexplained outburst and smiled. Tamarind was particularly pleased with two words—'integrity' and 'Impact,' and noticed that they had capitalized the second word with a smile.

* * *

Jake Johnson arrived looking a little older than the last time they'd met, with a bit of graying at the temples, but still clad as the retro journalist: notepad in hand, tweed jacket with leather patches on the elbows, a thin, black, loosely-knotted tie, his leather satchel slung across his chest and glasses sitting on top of his head, messing his hair a bit. No one needed to wear glasses anymore as laser surgeries and implants could correct any anomaly, so Tamarind assumed Jake still used them for effect or for recording conversations. In fact, both were true.

Tim Garner, Tamarind's long-time executive assistant, had escorted Jake to the room. Tim asked them if he could bring them anything to drink, then quickly responded to each of their orders before they had finished their greetings. Experienced at anticipating and responding to Tamarind's requests, he prided himself on his speed.

"Jake, my friend, good to see you again," Tamarind grabbed his hand firmly and then encased it in both of his hands and shook vigorously. "Please, have a seat. Let me introduce you to Calisandra Spencer, CEO of Galactic Marketing, who is consulting with our media department and will be joining us today."

Tamarind placed a seat beside his desk for Cali, behind her the wall display of the jungle danced in the wind. He noticed how beautiful she looked against this backdrop, the waves in her hair and her curves set amidst the jungle's colors.

"Thanks for inviting me, or summoning me perhaps?" Jake opened.

Tamarind shook his head and said, "No, no, not a summons. You were invited here because of your excellent journalism."

Jake's lips tightened; he knew when he was being played. Realizing this, Tamarind held up his hand as if to acknowledge Jake's skepticism and began again.

"Jake, you were right. There was a second part of Project LightStar all those years ago. I feel I owe you the opportunity to report to the world what you have long-suspected."

Jake sat back in his chair dramatically and let the notebook and satchel in his hands flop over the arms of the chair. This revelation was like a punch in the face. Although he'd previously worked as a freelance reporter, after that LightStar launch, he'd joined *The International Times* full-time to continue his investigative series. He thought back to the flack he'd taken in the office for those articles he'd written about what was in the second satellite. Finally, his editor had pulled his resources and told him to drop his conspiracy theories or lose his job. He hadn't expected this interview, but in some ways, he'd been preparing for it for the last decade. He sat up straight and nodded his head, indicating he was ready to proceed with the interview.

Jake slid his glasses down, leaned forward in his chair, and asked, "What was in the second satellite?"

Tamarind responded directly, "Actually, it wasn't a second satellite, but a second rocket which continued beyond the Earth's orbit toward the asteroid belt. As you reported, it included a second laser and a thorium reactor to power it. The project is called Phosaster."

"'Light' and 'Star' in Greek—nice. What was Phosaster's purpose?" Jake asked bluntly, his head still spinning. He had been right all these years, even on many specifics, and had taken so much criticism for it. He flexed his hands and clenched them into fists and breathed in sharply through his nose, a little discipline he used to increase his focus.

"Phosaster used the laser initially to survey asteroids encountered in its flight path. The laser remotely drilled a hole in the asteroid's surface, and from the rocket, we visually examined the asteroid and the plasma plume ejected from the hole. From this, we generated a very accurate spectro-photometric analysis of the material makeup of the asteroid and measured its surface, orbit, velocity, and rotation. Finally, it summarized this information in a rating scale Dark Matter Ventures developed and sent all this information via the LightStar satellite back to Earth, back to this facility."

Both Jake and Cali looked surprised at this revelation. Cali immediately wondered where in the building this information could be going, then glanced over at Tamarind's private elevator, suspiciously. Jake jotted notes and continued with his questions.

"So, it has been up there, what, like ten years since launch day? What has Phosaster discovered?" Jake asked.

"For the first few years, Phosaster surveyed hundreds of asteroids, and it finally identified one close enough to our target, based on our rating scale. At that point, the project changed to a robotic asteroid mining operation. As you know, Dark Matter Ventures has deployed mining lasers and robotic processing in many terrestrial projects over the last fifteen years. We incorporated these capabilities and more into the Phosaster capsule. Phosaster has been mining an asteroid for nearly eight years. The asteroid's orbit is finally bringing it near Earth." Tamarind said this enthusiastically, but he sensed the conspiracy theories forming in Jake's mind, along with many other questions.

"Doesn't Phosaster violate international space agreements? Is that why you kept it quiet all these years?" Jake asked. He stared straight at Tamarind, making sure his face was centered in his imaging system, looking for any twitches, perspiration, or skin color changes that might hint at deception. None was detected.

Tamarind said, "Technically, I had the approval to launch Project LightStar under the terms of the Space Peace Treaty, with the whole world's support. The Space Peace Treaty was initially about launches of objects into near-Earth orbit, and Phosaster went on into outer space and landed on an asteroid orbiting the Sun. The numerous treaties going back to the *Outer Space Peace Treaty of 1967* granted rights to explore for all human-kind's benefit. We've adhered to the *1986 Principles On Remote Sensing* and the *1996 Principles On The Use Of Nuclear Power In Space*. As you know, we've been working toward a consensus for a comprehensive asteroid min-ing agreement over the last several years. At the time of launch, the 2016 Luxembourg agreement acknowledging the ownership and exploitation rights to celestial bodies, was the prevailing legal guideline approved by most countries."

Once again, Jake was impressed by Tamarind's immediate access to information and his ability to sift, sort, and present it succinctly to max-imum effect. All three of them were familiar with the space agreements referenced, and Jake could see no apparent holes in Tamarind's logic.

"We have a major announcement that I will make jointly with President Jaspar early next week. Jake, we are on the verge of a new age of space exploration." Tamarind's enthusiasm was infectious, and Jake was aware that both he and Ms. Spencer had leaned forward with grins on their faces.

"I can't tell you the specifics of the President's announcement, but I wanted to give you a heads-up so you can move on this quickly before that date."

"What has Phosaster mined over these eight years?"

"We had communication's array failure on Phosaster, which was repaired in the last week. Mining has been progressing according to Phosaster's priorities during this time. The asteroid selected is an X-class with a significant amount of precious metals in its core. For some elements, Phosaster will yield more than has ever been mined on Earth. I'll provide you both with a complete list of mined commodities later today."

The reporter was surprised by the transparency; he saw no signs of the evasion he'd sensed in earlier discussions. *Better dig deeper,* he thought.

"You mentioned that Phosaster's mining was directed to specific priorities—what were those priorities and who set them?"

"Because of its autonomy and distance from Earth, we created the mining system with artificial intelligence. We, er… I programmed it to seek the "greatest value to Earth." Phosaster set its own priorities and has been mining based upon market values and global technology projections, and potential international conflicts. The communications array failure may have prevented it from optimizing according to Earth's most current needs, but we've reconnected it now."

"How do you intend to get the mined materials back to Earth?"

"Unfortunately, that part of the project is underdeveloped. We had to shift our funding and focus on regaining communications, so we haven't developed a complete plan for recovering the mined assets." The Dark Matter Ventures CEO shrugged his shoulders. "Perhaps other companies out there will be able to help us."

"You mentioned funding—who funded Phosaster, and who has the most to benefit from its success?"

"Yes. Good question. Our employees and I hold Dark Matter Ventures's shares. Phosaster had special funding from the founders of the PNLI, who rightly perceived that space mining could prevent future global conflicts over precious metals. Any profits from the venture are split between the investors, Dark Matter Ventures employees, and a future fund established for financing PNLI and its students' enterprises. I'll provide you a complete investor and stakeholder listing with the other information later today."

"Do you have any graphics or images to provide more details of Phosaster?"

"Yes, I do have images we can get to you. First, I want them reviewed by Cali, who, like the rest of the company, has been in the dark on Phosaster. I'll work with Cali and get you something shortly." Leaning back in his chair, he subtly indicated he was done with the prepared part of his disclosure.

Turning to Cali, he asked, "Will you work directly with Jake on this and let him know your timeline?"

"It would be my pleasure," she said, grinning widely.

As the meeting ended, Jake left with more questions than answers. That minor frustration was offset by his recognition that this was both a career-changing article and a validation of so much of the research he'd done. He decided to ask one more question as he stood to leave.

"Why now? Why stay quiet on Phosaster for so long and tell the world about it now?" Jake pressed.

"The investors required confidentiality until we reconnected with the asteroid. I think the President's announcement will answer your other questions."

Jake understood that he was getting first access to this announcement but might only be "included" in future press releases. Tamarind grabbed his hand and patted him on the shoulder. "Thanks for asking the tough questions all these years. You have earned my respect, and you deserve to have the first crack at this story."

Jake worked in an industry where praise came rarely and was taken aback by Tamarind's kind words. "Thanks for the opportunity," was all he could muster as he left the office. His instincts told him there was more to this story, and perhaps it would develop as he fleshed it out.

* * *

"How do you think that went?" Tamarind asked Cali as the reporter left the room.

"The information is astounding; this will be the highlight of his career. Mine too," she said, enthusiastically.

They spent the next hour crafting the Dark Matter Ventures press release, the Phosaster details they would release, and the competition plans and next week's press conference with the President. Cali had been working on a press announcement that they'd hit another significant milestone on Project LightStar, making it once again safe to launch objects that were not hardened into orbit or beyond. That goal that they had worked so long to reach seemed so insignificant now, but they decided to incorporate it into the formal announcement. It was nearly lunchtime by the time they had finished.

"I need to call our Phosaster investment team, give them an update, and bring the team up to speed with these developments. I will skip lunch. Could you pull together the exec team, including the LightStar and terrestrial mining departments, and maybe have a cake and champagne delivered? Short notice, I know, but this is a day to celebrate," Tamarind exclaimed.

"Agreed. Boardroom at three-thirty?" Cali proposed, and he affirmed. "Can I suggest we also plan an all-employee meeting as soon as possible?"

"Great idea. How about next week after the President's announcement?" As he walked over to stand near his private elevator. "Have a nice lunch, save some room for cake and dinner. I'll see you back here at six, OK?" She looked at him with some questions in her eyes, and he added thoughtfully, "You don't need to change or anything. You look perfect just as you are."

She smiled, brushed her hair back with her hand, and said, "Well, alright then." She had already planned to go back to her office and change before the evening.

CHAPTER 26

Friendship

"Friends remind you that the best is yet to come."
—*Journal of Kohlrabi Trust*

For Cali, the afternoon had many details, with phone calls, meetings, food deliveries, questions, answers, and celebrations, but she returned to Tamarind's office just a few minutes after six. She was wearing a new, light green dress and the Celtic scarf she'd worn earlier in the week, the day he asked her out. She was also holding a blue denim jacket. Not sure what type of shoes she should wear, she wore comfortable, low-heeled shoes. She was pleased to see that Tamarind had changed the white shirt that he had rolled up at the sleeves and worn around the office all day and was now wearing a crisp, white shirt with a stylish sports coat.

"Good evening, Cali," Tamarind greeted her, "ready for a ride in my elevator?" He opened the door and ushered her in. It was a small elevator, only meant for 1-2 people; he could smell her perfume as they stood close together facing each other. "I have two rides planned, and you can choose the order. Would you rather go up or down?"

Cali thinking that this wasn't like any date she had ever been on before, was quick to respond, "I think we should go down into your secret Phosaster command center," she ventured with a grin.

Tamarind raised his eyebrows, impressed at her guess, and then leaned forward to the retinal scanner on the button panel. The elevator immediately started moving downward. "A fine choice, miss," he said, sounding like a waiter in a classy restaurant.

Cali's eyes widened when the elevator opened to Tamarind's Phosaster command center. As she stepped into the circular room, she saw half the room's walls covered from floor to ceiling with colorful visual displays. She quickly scanned them to take in the information about Phosaster and other asteroids. Tamarind's desk in the center and the couch in front of it seemed to function as a divider with the living area: a small dining table, a chair, bed, bathroom, kitchen, and gym in the back half of the room. She stepped forward to his desk. On it was a chilled bottle of this year's French Beaujolais Nouveau and an assortment of appetizers. The room smelled like he had been cooking.

He pulled out his desk chair, and she sat. He remained standing, poured her a glass of wine, motioned for her to choose from the tray, and then poured himself a drink as well. "Cheers," he said, clinking her glass with his. She'd half expected some romantic toast, but the casualness of his toast seemed appropriate for their first date.

For the next hour, he walked from image to image, moving his hands to zoom, change pictures, or point out something in accenting color. He talked through the whole Phosaster project with unfiltered excitement.

Cali found it exhilarating to hear his discourse about the fulfillment of his hopes at Dark Matter Ventures. "All your Christmases have come together," she said, quoting her father's oft-used Irish phrase for unexpected positive developments.

He smiled, walked back to the desk where she was sitting, and standing at the side of the table with his arms crossed and looking pleased with himself, said, "Are you ready for what comes next?"

Cali glanced back toward the bed against the back wall, and looked up at him with one eyebrow raised, and said, "You promised me dinner, I believe?"

Tamarind blushed, realizing that she had misunderstood his intent. He hadn't been on many dates and felt awkward; his confidence swept away. He recovered quickly and said, "Exactly, now we will take the elevator up." Walking around the desk, he pulled out her chair, grabbed a briefcase, and proceeded to the elevator. He pressed the button for the roof.

As they stood close together in the elevator, Cali said, "Thank you for taking me to your secret lair." Tamarind smiled at her and reached out to take her hand. Other than a professional handshake, it was the first time they had ever touched, and it felt electric.

The door opened on the roof, and standing there amidst the vents and solar panels was a DroneTech personal transport. Cali had heard of these but had never ridden in one. She'd heard they were a little dangerous and required some skill.

"I have mastered these; you can trust me," Tamarind affirmed. Still holding her hand, he assisted her into the transport, then climbed in himself and placed the briefcase between his feet. It was much smaller than the elevator; they were face to face and nearly touching. "Hold on," he said. She considered grabbing him around the waist but decided he meant the two vertical bars like the one he grasped. He spoke a command, the motors started, and soon they lifted off the ground. "Just don't make any sudden shift in your position, and let me steer us," he said, reassuringly.

They rose vertically, and as he leaned toward her, they began moving backward, right off the building and out over the Nevada desert. She gasped a little, but then she surveyed the Bucky-Pod homes, buildings, and commercial centers that had grown up around Dark Matter over the last decade. As they continued to rise, Cali looked toward the surrounding hills that began to dominate their view. She could see they were going to land on a nearby mountaintop.

Tamarind set the transport down smoothly, helped her out, then opened his briefcase. He pulled out a picnic blanket, plates with lids on them, silverware, cloth napkins, a small bottle of wine, and glasses. It was a warm fall evening, and Tamarind invited her to sit down facing west where the sunset had just started shooting flashes of orange across the sky.

Tamarind uncovered the dinner plates and presented her with an artfully arranged meal with chicken Veronique, rice pilaf, and sautéed summer vegetables.

"When did you have time to do this?" Cali asked.

Tamarind moved his hands as if to say he conjured it by magic. "I've been thinking about tonight for a long time, Cali. I wasn't ready to ask you until Phosaster made contact again. I didn't want to start a relationship feeling like I was hiding something from you."

"Then let's toast to Phosaster, your integrity, and your courage," She said the last word playfully with extra emphasis.

Tamarind dipped his shoulders, embarrassed but then toasted with her.

They both savored their conversation and their meals. Cali told him of growing up as the only daughter of military parents who had moved from base to base during her childhood. They were both officers in the Air Force, but her mom had transferred to Space Command after it was formed. Her father retired from the military and founded and ran a military hardware supply company.

"It was my mom who gave me a love for space, and that is why I first chose to work for NASA. It was my father who gave me the desire to take what I'd learned and start my own company." He listened attentively as she spoke.

Tamarind told her about growing up at PNLI and about Kohlrabi and Moonbase Verity. Looking up at the moon, he said, "I must get back there and complete what Kohlrabi started." She was surprised that this successful CEO at the cusp of his long-planned success had even higher ambitions. Then, as she considered Tamarind, she realized she should not be surprised.

They leaned against each other and quietly watched the sunset. The temperature dropped rapidly in the fading light, and they put on their jackets and packed up the picnic. Wrapping the blanket around her for the return trip in the drone transport, he leaned in for a tender first kiss. They were silent on the ride home. They exchanged meaningful glances and allowed their bodies to bounce together as they shifted directions.

"I'm spending the weekend with Flax and Almond, but I look forward to seeing you on Monday, OK?" Tamarind said, after walking her home to her apartment near the office.

"OK," she said, "thanks for a lovely evening." She kissed him, longer this time, and then went inside, looking back with a smile as she entered the door.

* * *

Tamarind didn't have any unpleasant dreams that night. In fact, he couldn't remember ever feeling quite this good.

Waking up feeling rested, he grabbed a few things in a sports bag and headed off to Flax and Almond's place. He got there mid-morning, and as planned, met them for coffee at Dark Matter Café.

Almond ran across the Café, threw her arms around his neck, and with her toes stepping on his, gave him a long, heartfelt hug and a kiss on the cheek. "Tam, I'm so glad you're here," Flax and Almond were the only people that called him Tam, a nickname she'd given him in school.

"Careful, Almond, Flax will figure out that you love me," he said playfully.

"Oh, he knows you were my first love," she said, taking his arm with both of hers and leading him back to the table where Flax was sitting.

Flax did not look the least bit concerned by this public display of affection but stood, smiled, and said, "Tamarind, thanks for coming."

"I couldn't miss my favorite holiday with my favorite friends now, could I?"

Since the kids at the PNLI were all orphans and all from many countries and had chosen different religious traditions, there weren't any holidays they had in common that made sense to celebrate. The founders invented 'Friends' Day,' where PNLI friends got together, exchanged gifts, renewed their ERIWA pledge, and talked about the challenges and successes in their lives.

Almond enjoyed organizing these celebrations and always led them into her unique set of foods and events she planned for the weekend. The three of them celebrated Friends' Day together every year since they were seven years old.

While Flax was the boldly-lead-anywhere executive manager, Tamarind, the high-risk creative entrepreneur, it was Almond's brilliant bioscience that put DroneTech on the map. She was also the connector that unified them together—her love for life was infectious.

From the earliest days at the Institute, Almond loved nature. She was fascinated by the properties of plants, how they attracted pollinators, their medicinal value, the symbiotic relationships between them. Her brain was an encyclopedia of the natural world. At PNLI, she spent every moment she could outside, exploring, smelling, tasting, studying, and learning about every plant and animal on the island. She combined both lab and field studies for her formal research and became an innovative leader in her field. Her research labs at DroneTech allowed her to explore in ways never possible before. She possessed an insatiable curiosity, an infectious love of all things living, and an intuitive ability to synthesize biochemical combinations. This latter skill led her to the stun darts used in their police and riot control drones.

As Tamarind looked at her sitting with Flax at Dark Matter Café, it reminded him of that day years ago when she told them of her breakthrough at that very table. They were sitting there having a coffee break, and he and Flax were discussing floating down the Colorado river or going for a hike over the weekend. They seldom talked about anything related to DroneTech during a coffee break. She tilted her head abstractly and appeared to be listening.

Suddenly she blurted out, "I think I can modify a curare derivative to be a non-polarizing neuromuscular blocker which could be tuned to quickly achieve skeletal muscle paralysis without inhibiting spontaneous ventilation or unconsciousness!"

They both turned to her with confused expressions on their faces.

She said, more slowly this time, "I think I can make a tranq dart that can disable someone while leaving them conscious and breathing, and I can make it programmable for speed, duration, and body mass."

Tamarind remembered how they all had laughed as he responded, "That is why both of us are afraid to date you, Almond."

Almond's discovery was a breakthrough in policing. If a suspect, crowd, or even a police officer got out of control, they could be swiftly, safely, and temporarily immobilized. Their drone cameras had already reduced the use of excessive force in police altercations. By adding the tranq darts, an officer could remotely take control of the entire situation. The darts were harmless, hundreds were mounted on the drone, and the effects were temporary, giving the onsite officer a tool for containment. Their use had expanded to include VIP protection, shooter, and hostage situations. Even now, DroneTech made more profit on the tranq darts than they did on police drone sales.

The BioTech department, under Almond's direction, had also made breakthroughs in safer pesticides for crops, aerial treatment during mosquito-borne disease outbreaks, in situ water quality analysis in rivers, and other advances enabling DroneTech to enter many new markets.

Almond noticed Tamarind's distant stare and probed, "Usually, my kisses don't paralyze my victims. By the way, how long has it been since you kissed a girl?"

Tamarind focused on her face, smiled, and said, "Would you believe about twelve hours?" Flax and Almond were surprised; it had been so long since Tamarind had dated anyone. "It was just a first date, but it ended well, and I don't think it will be our last." Almond clapped her hands together rapidly, and they both rejoiced at his news.

"Tell me everything, Tamarind," She grabbed both of his hands and pulled them across the table toward her with a big smile on her face. He haltingly told them about Cali and insisted it was too soon to say much.

Satisfied, she outlined her plans for their weekend. They left the café and headed over to her house. Flax and Almond were married and lived there together, but they always referred to it as her house. As you drove into the driveway, the yard was a jungle of plants, and there was a large greenhouse in the backyard. Inside, the house had such a variety of plants that you felt like you might be in the greenhouse. It all spoke of her love of nature, and despite their years of marriage, it didn't reflect Flax in any way. They had the resources to live anywhere, but they chose to live modestly in keeping with their PNLI and Christian values.

After steering Tamarind and Flax to sit together on a loveseat in the center of their living room, Almond brought them what looked like a pale-yellow iced tea.

"A new concoction I've been working on, please drink deeply," she said.

"Wait, aren't you working on that coma-inducing medication?" Tamarind asked.

Flax said, "This isn't like that numbing pepper you gave me once that had me slobbering with my tongue hanging out, is it?" They both peered doubtfully at the tea in their hands.

"My puppy dog peppers. No, nothing like that. Drink up," she implored. They both dutifully tipped their glasses. She waited until they had each consumed at least half of the glass before she took her seat in the chair across from them.

"What have you done to us this time, Almond?" Tamarind asked.

"Both of you have been acting secretive lately, and I know you both were just in DC. I've just given you my truth serum tea. I don't care what the national secret is or what will happen to you if you tell me. Neither of you is leaving this room until you reveal everything." She held up a small blue vial. "This is an antidote, but I'll warn you, if you don't start talking, you will soon have a rash and a nasty case of diarrhea." Both Flax and Tamarind were feeling the heat in their skin and noticing some tingling in their fingertips. Their eyes widened, and their pupils dilated.

"Speak," she commanded.

Flax and Tamarind looked at each other, and Flax said, "But the President..."

"—isn't here, and I am, and trust me, boys, you have more to fear from me than from Laura Jaspar. Speak!" Almond looked at them fiercely.

They felt their faces flush and began to feel itchy on their arms and legs due to what felt like insects crawling on their skin.

They told her about Apollyon and Phosaster and all the secret plans on which they'd been briefed.

"Finish your drinks," she said, and they reluctantly downed the rest of their glasses, which tasted sweetly familiar.

"Is there anything else either of you is keeping from me?" she said. They both shook their heads.

"Drink the antidote, and let's have dinner." Almond was visibly shaken by all the information but reaffirmed that they all needed a relaxed and enjoyable weekend, especially considering what she'd just heard.

After downing the contents of the blue vial, Flax asked the question both he and Tamarind had been wondering. "What did you put in our drinks?"

"Just chamomile tea and a harmless but significant dose of niacin," she said. "Nothing that should have induced you to release top secret information to a civilian. The antidote was just a placebo—blue agave water. You boys really wanted to confess to me." She had an ornery grin but quickly turned away into the kitchen.

Almond had prepared a ceviche of fresh fish, roasted squash and salad greens from her garden, a dressing from her herbs, and forbidden rice. They had a chilled Pinot Gris from Oregon. Except for the wine, she had tried to present food like they might have eaten during their school years on the tropical island. As they ate, the effects of the niacin wore off, and they all settled into their weekend together.

Over dinner, Tamarind asked how the Dronetech staff had received the new contract.

Flax said, "The team is enthusiastic. It is a significant project for DroneTech and a real ramp in drone production. It utilizes the recently optimized swarm software and implements improvements we've worked on in the years since we last installed a comm net. It will be hard work, but the team is energized, and hopefully, it will stay that way until fully deployed. Of course, they don't know about Apollyon yet. How did your team take the news about Phosaster?

"It was a bit of a bombshell that they have been working toward asteroid mining for a decade only to find that we'd already achieved several major milestones. However, once we got past that hurdle, the office turned into quite a party yesterday afternoon, at least among the executive team and some of the key players who had quietly participated in Phosaster. Next week is the all-employee meeting, and I'm sure there will be lots of questions and more celebrations."

"I can imagine," Flax said. "Congratulations again, Tamarind, that is a huge accomplishment."

Almond waited patiently until they were done with this brief business update and then redirected their conversation to their schedule for the weekend. She had a few hike options planned and had purchased a strategy game about survival on a tropical island. She followed dinner with one of Dark Matter Café's ridiculously dark chocolate desserts.

The rest of the weekend, they did not mention DroneTech, Dark Matter Ventures, Phosaster, or Apollyon, even once. They hiked, told stories about PNLI friends, ate great food, exchanged gifts, and played a few board games. For Tamarind, this was the first time in a long time that he'd been able to put his burdens down temporarily. He felt fully rested the morning he planned to go home at the end of their weekend. Almond had made coffee and had laid out three of Dark Matter Café's Flax, Almond, and Tamarind muffins.

"You know, I just told you my darkest secret, but I don't remember you two ever admitting to doing anything wrong. I think it is time to 'fess up." Tamarind had nothing in mind with this line of conversation but thought it might be entertaining to see them squirm.

"Oh, we all have dark secrets, Tamarind, even from each other," Almond spoke calmly while pouring herself a cup of coffee.

"Like what?" Flax and Tamarind asked simultaneously.

She sat her cup down and looked at them somberly. "I can remember fragments of my life before PNLI. I think I killed my parents."

"What? No, none of us can remember anything about whatever traumas we experienced before we awoke at the school." Flax said.

"I can. I'm Japanese, I think. My father scolded me severely. I got one of his chemicals with the skull and crossbones on it and poured it into their teapot. That is all I remember." Her eyes filled with tears. "I don't know why I've never told you."

Flax moved over to hold her, and she buried her head in his shoulder and sobbed. He kept whispering, "It's ok; you were only a small child and didn't know better."

Tamarind was aghast at this disclosure and didn't say anything. After a long silence, he turned to Flax and said, "I bet you can't top that."

Flax faced him and said, "Actually, I can." Almond lifted her head, and they both looked at him with surprised expressions.

"Do you remember that day on top of the volcano?" he began.

"The day when Kohlrabi saved my life?" Tamarind asked. Flax nodded.

"We were throwing the football around between the two lakes. One lake was cold, and the other boiling hot. You were making athletic catches over the other kids, and I got jealous seeing that Almond was eyeing you and cheering for you. I purposely threw the football, knowing you would do anything to catch it." Flax looked uncharacteristically sheepish, waiting for them to make the conclusion.

"You intentionally threw the ball into the boiling water, hoping I would try to catch it and fall in?" Tamarind became angry at the realization.

"Kohlrabi saw the ball's trajectory and selflessly jumped into the water and shoved you to the shore before you fell in. His legs were horribly burned that day." Almond put her hand over her mouth in disgust.

"You tried to kill me? I thought you were my best friend! Was your jealousy why you proposed we all remain friends and not date Almond?" Tamarind's voice rose accusingly. Flax just nodded.

"Forgive me, Tamarind, please?" Flax spoke humbly and with remorse in his voice. "It was a long time ago."

Tamarind bolted up from the kitchen table with his hands in the air, pacing around the room. "I've lived for years with the burden of the promise I made to Kohlrabi—a promise I owed him because he saved my life. You tell me this now?"

"Please forgive me, Tamarind!"

"Forgive you? Redemption and forgiveness are your faith, not mine. I believe in rational cause and effect. You were deceptive about Almond, tried to kill me, and the course of my life has been committed to the promise I made to the man who saved me." Tamarind started to grab his belongings and stuff them into his backpack, preparing to leave.

Almond came over and put her hand on his shoulder. He shrugged it off. "It would appear you two deserve each other. I have a promise to keep to a friend." He stormed out the door and to his car and drove away with them standing and pleading from the porch.

CHAPTER 27

Distraction

"I've observed political leaders in many situations. War depends on deception, politics on distraction, but positive change requires coordinated action." —Journal of Kohlrabi Trust

Impact minus 42 days

President Jaspar hoped for a few weeks of relative peace while they pulled together their plans to address Apollyon. The generals and others on the team were implementing their strategies. The public remained unaware of the threat to planet Earth. She knew it wouldn't last, but she had learned the importance of capturing celebratory moments in the time between crises in her presidency.

One such opportunity was the press conference with Tamarind to announce the International Space Mining Treaty's signing and the rocket competition kickoff. Even Tamarind exuded nervous awe standing next to her at the podium emblazoned with the Presidential Seal. About 80 news agencies worldwide were in the room with others connected in for the announcement, asking questions remotely using the universal translators.

With the hum of motorized zooms, shutters, and camera drones around her, President Jaspar began, "Today I'd like to announce that we have just signed the International Space Mining Treaty, which establishes the rights, responsibilities, and laws regulating the mining of asteroids. It was approved by all the countries that are members of the United Nations. The treaty establishes that the first organization to make physical contact with an asteroid has ownership of the mineral rights. We believe the world's future depends on our ability to successfully mine asteroids for the precious metals and compounds necessary for Earth's population to thrive and support our future expansion into space."

Then, turning to Tamarind, she said, "No one has done more to get us to this day than Tamarind Chase. Project LightStar launched nearly ten years ago and succeeded in clearing the accumulated space debris field. Tamarind has worked tirelessly toward the signing of this treaty for nearly that long. Launching Project LightStar was also significant in another way, and I'd like him to tell you about it." She stepped out of the way and motioned for him to take the podium.

The crowd clapped, and the room buzzed with the sound of drones as he took the stage, unusual for press conferences. Although drone cameras were commonplace, they were not allowed inside the White House press conference room, so this event was in a public event room nearby.

"Thank you, Ms. President. Your visionary leadership in enabling space initiatives has brought us to this day. When I founded Dark Matter Ventures after the Space War, I hoped to hasten the day we could again explore space, specifically mine asteroids. When Project LightStar launched a decade ago, it also deployed a second capsule that continued into deep space. Over the past decade, this capsule, which I named Phosaster, has surveyed and made physical contact with over three hundred asteroids." He waited for the significance of this revelation to sink in. "Most of these asteroids have mineral content worth hundreds of billions of dollars if they can be utilized in space or transported to Earth. Dark Matter Ventures initiated exploratory asteroid mining activity on one of these asteroids, and the results are impressive."

As he spoke, a display behind him showed highlights of the Phosaster mission from the separation with Project LightStar, the laser survey of asteroids, the rocket landing, and the mining operation. "If we can overcome the significant challenges of getting those mined materials, mostly precious metals, back to Earth, they will dramatically improve our access to the materials critical to so many of our advanced technologies. However, in discussion with President Jaspar, we believe that for us to benefit from asteroid mining as a planet, we need to jump-start the mining initiative with a contest," Tamarind said, clearly enjoying this.

"Each organization, whether government, university, or private company that successfully launches a rocket outside the Earth's orbit containing equipment capable of surveying or making physical contact with an asteroid can enter. Those that succeed will receive exclusive mineral rights to one of the three hundred asteroids Dark Matter Ventures has surveyed. The more capability each entry demonstrates, the larger the value of the asteroid awarded, with a minimum estimated value of fifty billion dollars." At this, there were collective oohs and aahs across the room. "There is one caveat. The launch of your entry into the competition must leave the Earth's surface and achieve an altitude outside the atmosphere within five weeks from today. Five weeks to acquire the greatest treasure chest any explorer has ever found." Text appeared on viewing displays listing the full details for entry, and a countdown clock appeared showing the days/hours/minutes to the launch date.

President Jaspar again took the podium. "Thank you, Tamarind, for your generous contest, which we hope will bring new space entrepreneurs out of the proverbial woodwork. With the signing of this treaty and the announcement of this contest, I now declare space open for business." With that, President Jaspar cut the ribbon on an out-of-scale Solar System. The room erupted with the sound of claps, and the associated website got a massive surge of activity. Hands shot up across the room to ask questions. President Jaspar confidently answered each one, even those aimed at Tamarind, but paused for effect when one question was asked.

"Jake Johnson, *International Times*. Many precious metals critical to our electronics and sustainable infrastructure are in short supply and controlled by countries that have not always traded fairly. Do you see this new supply of resources from space as destabilizing these regimes and causing global conflict?"

"Thank you, Jake, for raising that question. The distribution of resources on Earth has never been fair and has led to many conflicts throughout the centuries. With the signing of this international mining treaty and the launching of this contest, we offer any organization or government access to the rights to an asteroid they never surveyed. We are giving the whole world equal access to space, equal access to the wealth it holds, and a level playing field for commercialization. Our past was determined by the land we could control. The future is for those bold adventurers who, through merit, are able to grasp it." She completed that comment by holding up her right hand and grasping at the air by making a fist.

With that, she held up both hands to stop questions and moved quickly to the exit. Tamarind followed her security detail, and once out of public view, she slowed and signaled him to catch up. As they were walking down the hall, she said, "Mr. Chase, let's hope there are some space-ready organizations out there. Hopefully, your little distraction will allow us the time to avoid destruction."

By the end of the day, every news agency worldwide had headlines about the Race for Space contest, which even eclipsed the International Space Mining Treaty signing. Each nation included any possible entries from their country or region. By the end of the day, more than one hundred organizations stated their intent to have one or more rockets in space within the next five-week period.

* * *

When he arrived back at the office, cheers went up around Dark Matter Ventures. They knew of his work for years on the Space Mining

Treaty and his visionary positioning of Dark Matter Ventures to participate in that segment. They did not know about Phosaster or the contest until the announcement. No work would get done until they had heard every detail.

Cali ushered those waiting for Tamarind in the lobby into the manufacturing area where she'd staged the all-company meeting. She began by announcing the Race for Space contest entries, showed a map of where all the entrants were from, showing images of some of the asteroids available to win in the contest. No one had thought about asteroid mining more than the people in this room, and each asteroid dataset was met with oohs and ahhs from the crowd. Someone asked, "Can we enter?" and there was laughter around the room.

Tamarind followed Cali's introduction and said to them, "Thank you, team. My original commitment to our investors required I keep you all in the dark about Phosaster until now. But believe me, the success of Phosaster depended upon all your work since the founding of the company. Phosaster is a triumph for us all."

"Many of you worked on key elements of the mining capsule without knowing the details. We had a special group of investors for this project who insisted on complete confidentiality until success was clear. I want to acknowledge the amazing work of two team members who did know and have coordinated and integrated all our work. Stacy Norton and Paul Moncrief." Stacy, who had flown up from the Arizona facility for the meeting, smiled broadly and waved her hand. Paul, slightly hunched forward and looking uncomfortable, raised one arm slightly to acknowledge the crowd.

Tamarind then displayed a summary of the mined resources so far on Phosaster. The results were almost unbelievable to the Dark Matter Ventures employees. "Don't worry, even if we give away some of the asteroids, there is plenty for us to do. The value of the minerals mined on Phosaster so far is over one trillion dollars. Our next task is to figure out how to get them off that asteroid and back to Earth. I'll need your help to do that!" The crowd laughed, whistled, and cheered, and the rest of the day was all about food and celebration. None of them ever envisioned working for a trillion-dollar enterprise.

Eventually, the festivities died down, and the technical discussions about the work ahead moved down the hallways and into the office spaces. Leaving the manufacturing floor, Tamarind pulled Scarecrow aside. "Hey Paul, now that LightStar is nearly finished cleaning up debris, do you think we could reorient it to target incoming debris from outer space? No rush, just think about it when you get a chance..."

Tamarind knew Paul "Scarecrow" Moncrief well. He had just tapped the most creative mind on his team to address Apollyon fallout and had no doubt Paul would come up with a solution better than any he could imagine, and sooner rather than later.

* * *

He didn't go to his control bunker that evening. However, he went for a walk with Cali, and after a wind-down of their exciting week, their conversation moved to personal matters.

"You were raised as a military brat?" he asked. "Is that why you know Krav Maga?"

"My parents were both military, and we moved around a lot. One of the hobbies that I could pursue at every base was self-defense. How about you? Why did you learn Aikido?"

"I'm a pacifist. Aikido's goal is to render an attacker safe to themselves, you, or others. It seemed like it fit my world view."

She told him about growing up in eastern Washington, her mom's frequent flights to DC for meetings at Space Command, her dad's company that sold aircraft parts to Boeing and other aircraft manufacturers. She talked about running down the rows of grapes in wine country, rafting in white water rivers, hiking in the Cascade mountains, and swimming in cold mountain lakes.

Tamarind listened raptly and asked questions about her parents and childhood since he had never had a family like that. It was just two people getting to know each other. She didn't know about Apollyon or his argument with his friends. For now, he was content to be with her and enjoy her company.

CHAPTER 28

SETI

"Mathematically, it is a near certainty that there is intelligent life in the universe. Practically, it is inevitable that another intelligent race of explorers like us will reach out. Surprisingly, we haven't had any contact yet."
—*Journal of Kohlrabi Trust*

Impact minus 41 days

Flax Venture was upset at how things had ended with Tamarind, but he didn't have any way to change that right now. He reviewed the information that Tamarind had given him and checked some of the calculations. He didn't have his friend's space experience, analytical tools, or knowledge of asteroids and comets. Still, he had found after years of working together, he could sometimes see holes in Tamarind's logic. This was one of the things that had made them such a good team. This time, however, Flax's review led him to the same conclusions Tamarind made.

Flax decided to run his conclusions by their old friend Taro Search.

Director Taro Search managed SETI, the Search for Extra-Terrestrial Intelligence. Another of the Pan-Nationals from PNLI, he was smaller than most students, had very fair skin, dark hair that usually stuck out at all angles, and little brown eyes. He was one of six children in their house at PNLI, so Flax and Tamarind knew him well. While not as adventurous or athletic as Flax or Tamarind, or Almond, for that matter, Taro was always looking up at the stars seeing the potential for life. If anyone could analyze this information, it was Taro.

While at the PNLI, students were tasked with solving one of the enormous problems facing humanity. Rather than choosing from the list provided, Taro decided "to make first contact with an alien race." The teacher challenged him on his choice, but Flax remembered when Taro stood in class and said, "What could further the development of humankind more than connecting them with an alien race? No matter what the outcome of that interaction, humanity would pull together, forget their terrestrial disputes, and would no doubt engage and learn new science and technology."

The strategy he proposed in his report to the class was straightforward. "SETI has focused on radio band and other signals for detecting and communicating with extraterrestrial life. These bands dissipate rapidly with their distance from Earth and would be so weak that the time they reached a planet with life would be almost impossible to detect. I would use a laser to direct a high intensity, visible light beam to each star cluster and each known planet in our galaxy, encoding information in the beam. Starting with those closest to Earth, there might be a chance of getting a reply in my lifetime. After I graduate, I will work at SETI and develop a detector for a laser-based reply." Years later, at PNLI, he constructed his laser signaling system, and every night he went up on the roof and aimed his laser at another star, planet, or galaxy. At graduation, he was appropriately given the surname Search.

Taro had joined SETI and stayed on when they merged with NASA under Space Command. His responsibilities had grown; eventually, he became the Director while overseeing the work to detect laser signals from planets and stars. While no response had been received during the decades-long SETI program, Taro always held out the hope that an alien message was imminent.

Flax decided a face-to-face meeting was essential, so he traveled to the SETI facility in California, a short hop after checking in with one of the nearby DroneTech manufacturing facilities that were ramping up for their government project. He caught Taro at his holodesk and asked him to close the door to his office before proceeding.

"Hi Taro, how's work at SETI? Found anyone yet?"

Although they were old friends and his visit was unexpected, Taro stayed sitting and got straight to the point. Flax smiled knowingly.

"Actually, Flax, ever since I was read-in on Apollyon, I have been thinking obsessively about where it came from."

"Of course, you have," Flax said, with a smile.

"...and I believe it might be an alien artifact," Taro said. "I wanted to talk it through with you before discussing with Director Lewis."

"Funny you should say that," Flax said, "Tamarind sent me a packet of information with the same conclusion, and after reviewing his analysis, I agree. I wanted to run it by you for your opinion. If we are going to mention this to the President, I think it should come from you." Handing him the information, Taro placed it on his holodesk and immediately started his review.

"No time to chat, I guess?" Flax said.

"This is clear data and analysis, Flax. The trajectory, timing, materials, construction, velocity, essentially everything supports the conclusion that Apollyon is of alien construction. Tamarind's data confirms and even extends my analysis. I must inform my chain of command."

Hearing a pacifist scientist like Taro Search speak of his "chain of command" reminded Flax again why he disagreed with having space research under a military command structure.

"Taro, before you present this to Dr. Lewis, you should think through the questions he will ask. When would aliens have launched this at us, and why would they do it this way? Is their purpose to destroy us?" Taro nodded approvingly and breathed dramatically like he was steeling himself for some rough internal discussions, where he would, no doubt, be mocked or challenged.

"OK, good point. I'll think that through before my meeting." Taro was a shy, nervous kind of person. Despite being Director of a large research organization, he was more comfortable with his head deep in the data and issuing directives via email. After an hour or so of role-playing as NASA's director and throwing tough questions at Taro, Flax was convinced he was on the right track and said his goodbyes.

CHAPTER 29

Perihelion

"The sun in all its glory shown,
Imparting life upon its own,
Wander close to its rays,
Consuming fire will end your days."
—*Journal of Kohlrabi Trust*

Impact minus ten days

Tamarind and Cali worked together to manage the contest as entries came in from all over the world. Large and small businesses, universities, governments of all sizes, and even some wealthy individuals worked on getting something up in space, demonstrating some capability, and claiming a piece of the asteroid-mining prize. Media coverage talked extensively about the potential value of a space-mining endeavor. Coupled with this, the data about Phosaster fueled stock market speculation as investors analyzed the companies which might benefit from this new industry.

The contest application required each team to identify themselves, declare their interest, and clarify what they would demonstrate with their launch. Explaining the contestant's technology, launch vehicles, surveying tools, or other proprietary details was not mandated. No intellectual property was disclosed in their applications. Tamarind added that Dark

Matter Ventures would not steal their technology or prevent any team from entering.

As the entries came in, he did a background check on each team's members. He consulted public records, disclosures, and professional journals and associations to assess their skills, accomplishments, and contributions. He then developed an algorithm to evaluate a team's success potential to complete a launch and target a chunk of Apollyon. The analysis appeared promising on paper, but it was all wild extrapolation at this point.

Separately, he worked with Paul Moncrief on the LightStar problem.

"After some analysis on the question you asked, yes, we can reorient LightStar to fire out into space. If the direction of an object's approach is known, we might want to position the satellite into a different orbit. Objects in near space are primarily in solar orbits, whereas our laser will be in Earth orbit, so there will be times when incoming debris will not be accessible by the laser. However, given enough notice, we might be able to overcome that." Paul methodically detailed the conclusions of his analysis.

"What about the LightStar prototype," Tamarind queried. "Could it be launched on the opposite side of the Earth, so we get better coverage?"

Paul looked at him uncomfortably. "Do you have a specific target in mind, Tamarind? That prototype is ten years old, and we've tested a few engineering mods on it through the years."

"I can't discuss a specific target at this time," Tamarind said but added, "considering the number of craft this contest is putting in space in the next few weeks, it might be good to be able to vaporize any that get out of control."

"You want to launch a second LightStar satellite in less than two weeks?" Paul asked.

"I should have thought of it sooner. Let me know if it is possible in eight days," Tamarind answered.

Paul raised his eyebrows, at the same time acknowledging to himself that this was more important than Tamarind was letting on. "I'll have a complete answer within twenty-four hours."

Analyzing the LightStar prototype, Paul could see the modifications engineering had made over the last decade. Parts were disassembled on a workbench, fingerprints on the optics, some mods half completed. Assembly and testing this system, assuming they had all the missing pieces, would be difficult in the time available.

Next, he went to the rocket area. Rockets typically took about six weeks to go through their assembly and test procedures. There were several missing parts, and he wrote down their part numbers for his analysis. He checked on the 3D metal printer, which could print most of the components of a rocket assembly. He went through the startup sequence on the printer and checked the materials inventory. It appeared to be working correctly, but he started its recalibration cycle and self-diagnostics, just to be sure.

Next, he checked the thorium reactor power cell visually. The energy source appeared in good condition but would need a full power-up and check-out sequence, and likely some parts would need to be replaced.

Finally, Paul looked for capsule components. Stacy Norton had moved the prototype to Arizona for sizing for future asteroid mining operations.

"Hi Paul, how are you doing?" Stacy asked when Paul contacted her.

"Stacy, can you tell me the status of the capsule prototype we sent you? Tamarind wants me to investigate if we could launch it quickly." Paul was always straight to the point.

"We've put some holes in it and mounted mining and processing gear on the side walls. I didn't know you would want it back," Stacy said.

"Neither did I, until today. So, it's not available. Thank you," Paul summarized and ended the call.

Paul took his list of missing parts, the required calibration sequences, and check-out tests and headed back to his office. After several hours of poring over the requirements and sequencing them to be completed in 8 days, he was confident of the optimal time frame. Sitting back in his chair, Paul thoroughly considered again what Tamarind wanted and double-checked his conclusions. Then, he went off in search of his boss and found him in his office.

"There is no possible way to get the prototype reassembled and launched into space in eight days." Paul looked severe; he didn't like to say things were impossible.

Tamarind said, "Even if your life depended on it?" As he spoke, he had a little smile on his face.

Paul shook his head from side to side. "Eight days is impossible, and six weeks would be pushing it." Then Paul tilted his head to one side and added, "However, we might be able to disengage the laser on the Phosaster asteroid; we do know it works and has similar capabilities. It is in a solar orbit and might fit your objectives better?"

Tamarind's face brightened noticeably, and he said, "You could do that, Paul? That would be awesome! Can you start on that immediately?" Paul nodded without speaking and walked off, satisfied he had addressed Tamarind's needs, and began analyzing the tasks ahead.

PART 4:

IMPACT

CHAPTER 30

Discovery

"We refer to the process of identifying something that already existed as a discovery. It existed, and our eyes didn't change it in any way. However, discoveries require that we see differently and open ourselves to new perceptions and connections. Ultimately, aren't all discoveries our internal process of accepting that what we perceive is true?"
— *Journal of Kohlrabi Trust*

Impact minus nine days

A week before Perihelion, a professional star photographer renting the telescope at Mt Lemmon Observatory in Arizona identified and took photos of Apollyon. To secure his right to name the discovery, he immediately released the information, without considering its trajectory. By the next day's science news cycle, the announcement of a giant comet turned eyes excitedly toward the skies.

Over the next week, astronomers repeated the discovery, adding an analysis of the flight path. Once the public realized that the asteroid was heading toward Earth, excitement turned to panic. The impending disaster began headlining every newsfeed, repeated in every language, and confirmed by scientists in other countries.

The discovery triggered the transition of the Apollyon response plan from top secret to public release. The President issued a communique to each head of state of the world's nations as a coordinated message. In the US, President Laura Jaspar held a press conference in the White House press briefings room and presented the details as agreed.

"Ladies and Gentlemen, US Space Command's SWARMNET had detected this comet before the recent civilian sighting. We informed other countries, and scientists and world leaders are working together on a strategy for protecting our planet from this threat. In six days, this comet, which we named Apollyon, will pass close to the Sun. At that time, we anticipate this approach will trigger a CME from the Sun, which will emit an EMP that will affect global communications. We are repositioning satellites for their protection and installing a backup communication grid to minimize impact from this pulse."

"Apollyon will also be affected by this close pass to the Sun. It will be destroyed, break into fragments, or its size or trajectory affected. Once we know Apollyon's condition, we will launch nuclear missiles to destroy or divert Apollyon or its fragments away from the Earth. Should any Apollyon pieces survive this attack and still be headed toward Earth, we have initiated plans to use the space laser systems LightStar and Phosaster and ground and space-based rockets to destroy the remaining pieces. The world's governments pulled together to face this threat, and we are asking the world's citizens to work with us by following the guidelines provided after this broadcast. This exact message will be repeated in every language and nation. We will not be taking questions today. Additional information will be provided following this announcement as to how individuals can help at this time." President Jaspar ended, saying, "May God bless and protect the United States of America."

As she was leaving the room, reporters were shouting questions in her direction.

"How long have you known about this, and why was this information kept from the public?"

"Is a nuclear response likely to succeed?"

"What is the expected impact of the CME?"

The questions continued until she left the room and repeated by news reporters echoing the unanswered questions.

After the broadcast, a government press release restated the official announcement with additional clarifications confirming that the EMP would not harm people, plants, or animals. It also recommended that people unplug electronic equipment and prepare their households with food, water, and supplies typical in any natural disaster. Specific guidelines were provided for hospitals and people with electronic implants or dependent on medical devices. It ended by asking people to remain calm and help others who needed assistance in their neighborhood.

"Get the Apollyon response team to the ready room," the President told her Chief of Staff as she walked from the news conference.

When they had all appeared in the Security Briefings Room, she said, "Report."

The US military joint chief General Corey Breckinpaw was to her immediate left and was the first to respond. "Ms. President, we've deployed National Guard troops to protect critical assets and are coordinating with local law enforcement to maintain peace, protect electrical infrastructure, advise on the protection of business and household electronics, and to facilitate the flow of supplies. Commercial air travel will be suspended for twenty-four hours, beginning six hours before the EMP. We will have at least a few hours warning of the arrival of the geomagnetic storm and temporarily shut down the power grid. Automobiles manufactured after the 2026 EMP protocol should be protected, but we expect five to ten percent of all vehicles will be disabled if the event is severe."

"All active military personnel will be activated immediately and deployed across the nation before and two days after the EMP. We will keep order, Ms. President, upon your command." General Breckinpaw was a classic, aging military commander, assuming the worst and preparing for it. He looked the part - sixty-seven years old and still built for action with a grey crew cut and square jaw. His keen strategic mind was what elevated him to joint chief. President Jaspar was not expecting riots or destruction of military facilities, but there was no harm in being prepared.

"General, are civilians at personal risk from this event?"

"Some are, Ms. President. The electromagnetic storm may cause fires or accidents but should not directly affect people, except those with pacemakers or dependent on electrical devices. We will recommend they be off the road, unplug their electronics, place them in Faraday bags or wrapped in aluminum foil, and stay away from metal objects. We will have the army medical corps and the corps of engineers deployed and first responders activated. We will bring the grid back up as soon as we can."

"Proceed," said the President, and then turning to General Sharon Ward of Space Command, "Report."

General Ward stood and spoke directly to the President. "We've positioned our satellites around the planet to maintain critical communications and protect all space assets not hardened for an EMP. Several deep space missions within the EMP radius may be damaged, but more than ninety percent can be hidden behind a planet or the Earth for the pulse duration. Since a geomagnetic storm interacts with the Earth's magnetic field, repositioning them behind the Earth may not be adequate. Some will be damaged even on the dark side of the Earth. The damage will depend on the magnitude and duration of the storm."

"After the EMP, we will need to assess the condition of Apollyon and plan our response accordingly. The nuclear missiles in space are in hardened satellites and are programmed to fire directly into Apollyon's oncoming trajectory unless new commands are issued. Our simulations show that we have the firepower to destroy Apollyon and that less than ten percent of the fragments will proceed on an Earth-bound trajectory. Satellites will be repositioned following the pulse to be available for kinetic impact weapons on larger fragments if required. We will deploy on your command, Ms. President."

"Proceed as planned," said the President, turning back to the joint military chief of staff and adding, "General Breckinpaw, after the EMP, I want all military personnel reassigned to ground response should any debris hit the planet."

"Yes, Ms. President," he replied. Her request would extend all military personnel's activation for another few weeks, not a trivial operational task. However, he would oversee their readiness.

When the President got to the civilian business leaders, she changed her tone. "Mr. Venture, what is the condition of the Drone Comm Network?" she asked.

"DroneTech has been able to accelerate the manufacture of our M38 Comm Drones. At this point, ninety percent of the grid, as agreed, has been deployed around the world. We're ready to complete the transfer of the communication, banking, and GPS grid globally upon your command. The system won't be complete by the time of the EMP but will be before Apollyon landfall." At this point, no one in the room had ever said the word *landfall*, and there was a moment of silence and shifting in seats.

Rather than addressing everyone's fears, the President said, "Thank you, Flax, I'm sure General Ward and your friend's laser system will prevent landfall. Proceed with your plan, and coordinate through my Chief of Staff on the transfer of comm codes." Flax nodded in affirmation, embarrassed by his choice of words.

The President noticed that Tamarind and Flax were not sitting next to each other as they usually did and had hardly looked at each other since they had come into the room. "Mr. Chase, what do you have for us?"

Tamarind spoke as succinctly as those before him. "Both Project LightStar and Phosaster have shielding and will not be affected by the EMP. We will reposition LightStar to start destroying debris once coordinates are available. Before that, it can place a targeting pulse on Apollyon that could improve missile targeting. Secondly, I've just had confirmation this morning that we may be able to disengage the Phosaster laser system from the asteroid. If successful, we would effectively have a second laser not bound by Earth orbit available for firing continuously at incoming objects."

General Ward nodded her head at the revelation of more weapons in the fight.

"Thirdly, before it separates from the asteroid, Phosaster will be aligned to provide an assessment of the makeup of Apollyon just before perihelion, and will be the first asset to have a good look at Apollyon after Perihelion. It can relay targeting information via LightStar as communications return after the EMP. Finally, we have a significant number of rockets in the asteroid competition, which we will now redirect toward fragments. We don't know how many of them can successfully make a space launch or what their capabilities are, but we have over two hundred entries of all shapes and sizes." Tamarind looked at Taro, decided to say no more, and finished with, "We'll proceed if you so command, Ms. President."

"Please proceed," and then looking around the room, the President asked, "Does anyone else have recommended actions or actionable information not presented?"

General Ward motioned to Dr. John Lewis of NASA and SETI Director Taro Search to proceed.

Dr. Lewis spoke, "Ms. President, this is Director Taro Search of SETI, who has additional information on the origin of Apollyon, which might affect our course of action."

Taro stood uncomfortably and took a deep breath. "Ms. President, our analysis suggests that Apollyon is not a naturally occurring comet, but rather an alien construct directed here from Proxima Centauri." His holographic display tracked a red path for Apollyon back to a planet in that star system.

"What, now we are being attacked by aliens?" President Jaspar spoke sarcastically, and everyone in the room chuckled uncomfortably.

Taro had anticipated that and answered confidently, "Essentially, yes, the data overwhelmingly supports this conclusion. However, it may not be meant as an attack to destroy the Earth. We believe it was sent in response to a signal sent from Earth and that it accelerated and then decelerated to its current velocity. It could be a test to evaluate our defenses, communicate or warn us, a gift to initiate a trade, or meant to terraform the planet for their colonization. Whatever their objective, it suggests that they are an advanced civilization and that we should not conclude that Apollyon is merely a rock flying toward us. There could be structure or purpose beyond simply a kinetic weapon."

President Jaspar glared at Dr. Lewis and Gen. Ward and said, "Do you agree with this analysis? They both nodded their head.

Tamarind also spoke up, "Ms. President, I separately came to this conclusion and thoroughly reviewed the analysis."

At this point, President Jaspar's forehead creased in anger, and she scowled at Taro. "You mentioned they responded to a signal from Earth— what signal?"

"I sent laser pulses directed at this planet a few decades ago while in school and have been monitoring for a response ever since. I expected an optical rather than a physical response." Taro said apologetically.

President Jaspar shook her head. "This information is filled with conjecture and is not actionable. Extraordinary claims require extraordinary proof. We are not going to discuss or act on this "alien theory" unless you come back with actionable information and undeniable evidence. Understood?"

IMPACT

Taro Search slumped in his seat and resolved to himself to find the proof that the President needed.

CHAPTER 31

Storm

"A storm strikes one with fear, another is awestruck by its beauty and power. We choose how we face the storm." —Journal of Kohlrabi Trust

Impact minus seven days

After the meeting, Flax asked Tamarind if he could hitch a ride on the Dark Matter Ventures jumpjet, and perhaps they'd get a chance to talk. They both needed to return to Nevada and Colorado to prepare their companies for the coming storm.

"I suppose you can't sabotage my jumpjet while you're on it," Tamarind said sarcastically.

Flax laughed and said, "Ok, I deserved that. I know it will take time to win back your respect and friendship. What I did to you was wrong and affected your whole life. I can never repay that or make it right. I can only hope that when you finish processing, we will still be friends. In the meantime, we need to work together to defeat Apollyon and minimize its effects, agreed?

Tamarind looked at him with steely eyes and flexed jaws. After an uncomfortable moment, he waved Flax toward the jumpjet. "How is DroneTech preparing for the storm?" Tamarind asked.

"Dronetech is expected to rebuild the global communication grid as soon as the peak of the storm has passed. We must keep going until that day. We've got portable generators inside Faraday cages constructed for the time when the overall grid is down. We can keep final assembly and check-out going throughout the storm and give the rest of the team a break for a few days. Once the threat has passed, all-hands-on-deck to ship and install drones around the world. How about you?"

"We'll move all critical electronics to a few locations that have been protected from EMPs, electrical surges, and X-rays. Then I'm going to send everyone home to watch the night sky. We are a space company, after all, and this is a spectacular cosmic event. Any chance you and Almond would like to come over and watch with Cali and me?"

Flax considered this for a moment and knew it would help heal their rift if he could come. "Would you be OK if just Almond came? I'm required to be available full-time until this communication grid is up, but she is not. I'd like to know she was safe and with a trusted friend."

* * *

Apollyon passed nearest to the Sun a few days later. Perihelion was 11:07:42 AM EST. As it passed through the corona of the Sun, it experienced temperatures nearing 1 million degrees Celsius. Such a large mass of metal moving through the Sun's geomagnetic field triggered an explosive interplanetary CME directed toward Earth.

The burst of protons was picked up minutes later by several of NASA's Sun-monitoring missions as well as space equipment from other agencies. Together they measured the intensity, velocity, and generated images of emissions in every band of the electromagnetic spectrum. Other tools created three-dimensional images, calculated mass, and estimated trajectories and effects.

President Jaspar had her military chiefs and Director Dr. John Lewis from NASA on hand to explain the information as it came in. Displays around the room showed satellite live images and data from each of the solar missions.

"John, explain what we see in a way we can understand it," the President said, calmly.

"The initial visible solar flare indicates the moment Apollyon triggered interaction with the Sun. An explosion near the Sun's surface has emitted an EMP that will likely damage some of our Sun-monitoring equipment in space. The protons from that event are now reaching Earth's magnetosphere and will charge our ionosphere and heat our atmosphere. This electrical activity in our ionosphere will affect long-distance radio signals. The heating will expand our atmosphere and add friction, causing the orbits of satellites to decay."

As if to punctuate his comments, several visual images became blurry static, their source affected by the radiation. President Jaspar asked, "What would this do to astronauts in space?"

General Sharon Ward of Space Command answered. "All countries have grounded their astronauts, fortunately. Had anyone been alive on the moon or in space, they would receive a deadly dose of radiation. Fortunately, the Earth's electromagnetic field will shield us from this."

Dr. Lewis nodded to confirm General Ward's answer, and then continued, "Over ten billion tons of magnetized plasma has burst forth from the surface of the Sun in a CME. This mass of plasma is traveling at millions of kilometers per hour, and the front edge will reach us in about twelve hours. A geomagnetic storm of historic scale will begin later today and continue with decreasing intensity for a few days."

Turning to General Breckinpaw, she asked, "Are we ready for this?"

"Yes, Ms. President, as ready as we can be. Local first responders continue to distribute Faraday bags and information sheets in every community. Power companies will take the electrical grid offline, disconnecting high voltage transformers, for at least the first six hours of the event.

We can't protect everything, but we will have military and all first responders active throughout the event."

Over the next thirty-six hours, the President and her team hardly left the White House Situation Room.

The energetic particles traveled in a shockwave toward the Earth while also delivering the initial EMP. These temporarily disabled deep space projects within a 15-million-kilometer radius of the Sun, destroying even hardened satellites designed and predicted to survive such a bombardment.

Despite all the warnings and preparations, there was extensive damage in every country in the world. New England and Quebec had power stations that caught fire, transmission cables overloaded, and the power grid severely impacted. Water pipes exploded in several high-rise apartment complexes in Vancouver, British Columbia, coupling electromagnetic energy straight into the metal pipes. In New York City, a skyscraper conducted so much electricity through its I-beam structure that cement was blown off the building's face, pummeling cars and buildings below. An oil storage facility in Yucatan, Mexico, exploded in flame as poorly grounded tanks ruptured and ignited their contents. Similar problems occurred globally though less than North America, which faced the full force of the pulse head-on.

Even with the precautions, some businesses and many households endured electrical fires and damaged electronic equipment, with televisions and computers destroyed.

With radio, cell phone, and internet systems down, communications to the Situation Room were temporarily disrupted, but as reports came in, the President and her team stayed informed. Everyone used battery-powered computing devices to collect updates on fires, injuries, deaths, downed power lines, vehicles on fire or disabled, buildings or infrastructure damaged, or general unrest. General Breckinpaw moved continuously around the table from display to display, providing updates for those in the room.

"Minor fire in Denton, Texas. Seven homes engulfed; four dead. Local firefighters have requested additional support from surrounding communities. Nationally, at least seventy-seven people dead from fires."

Moving to another station, he continued his discourse, "An electrical tower toppled in Atlanta, crushing a house and snapping all the power cables. The estimate is three days to reconnect those power lines once the storm has passed. Two high voltage transformers exploded in Olympia, Washington. Army Corps of Engineers is on-site with emergency backup transformers, and the region should suffer minimal downtime when the grid is re-enabled." The tireless General continued these updates, occasionally barking commands to support staff to get messages to his commanders.

Slowly, over the next 24 hours, the electromagnetic storm calmed down. Electrical grids restarted in much of the country, though regions in New England and parts of the Pacific Northwest would remain out for days.

The Drone CommNet was uploaded and began restoring connections within a few hours after the power grid was up. People were afraid, first responders and the military were extremely busy but able to keep control.

The first 24 hours after the EMP was chaotic, literally putting out fires all over the planet. As information began to come in from around the Earth and the effects lessened, it was encouraging that first response teams, typically nations' militaries, had slowly gotten things under control.

"Ms. President, I think you can take a rest now. Our crews have several days of emergency cleanup, and the billions in damages will take longer, but we are through the peak of it," General Breckinpaw looked fatigued but encouraged.

"Thank you, Corey. You've done a heroic job managing this. I'll leave the Situation Room in your control. Call me if there is a major development." It was the first time she had called the General by his first name, and he received it as a statement of trust, respect, and friendship. With that, she left the room for her quarters in the White House.

* * *

Half a country away, everything was quiet in the eastern Nevada town housing the Dark Matter Ventures headquarters. Tamarind had released his staff and advised them to stay up for the most epic aurora show they would likely ever see. He promised prizes for the best photos and gave them a printed card on how to photograph auroras. Almond, Cali, and Tamarind retired to his home, where he anxiously prepared dinner for them.

"What are you cooking?" Cali asked. They had grown more comfortable together, and she rested her hand on his shoulder as she bent forward to smell what was on the menu.

"A starter of Aurora Borealis Salad, flame-toasted Fireman bread, and End-of-the-World pasta, with shrimp and Parmesan cheese," Tamarind's eyes sparkled.

"That's the man I grew up with. The world could be on fire, and he'd be excited by the flames. Why no themed name for the cheese?" Almond asked playfully.

"It's cheese," Tamarind answered nonchalantly.

Almond walked over to Cali, hooked her arm, and steered her toward the couch. "Tamarind has told us a little about you, but I want to know everything. You must be pretty special to snag him." Almond looked directly into her eyes with an inviting smile on her face. Cali blushed but recovered quickly. They talked in hushed tones with occasional glances at their chef and muted laughter.

Although he couldn't quite hear them over the crackling sounds of the shrimp and mushrooms and the bubbling sounds of the pasta and sauce, he said, "OK, you two, no fair talking about me. I invited you over to meet each other and enjoy the spectacular light show I have arranged for you tonight." He deftly arranged their meals onto their plates, delivering them with a flourish to the ladies seated on the couch. He went back to the kitchen, grabbed his own, a bottle of red wine, and three wine glasses.

They were cut off from the tragedies evolving around the planet and engaged with each other's company. Almond told stories of Tamarind's awkward teenage years that had Cali laughing hysterically. He responded with adventure stories of Flax, Almond, and himself as they explored the island where they'd lived. They continued through the second and third glasses of wine.

Almond brought out a dessert she had procured for the occasion. "Dark Matter Café's Solar Flare Cake: a chocolate torte with spicy cayenne accents and red sugar sprinkles on top."

Cali looked surprised, "There is a bakery called Dark Matter Café in Loveland?"

Almond said, "Didn't Tamarind tell you? He is a one-third owner with Flax and me."

Cali could see the deep history and affection between them, and would have felt threatened if she wasn't so confident. She moved closer to Tamarind and put her hand on his leg, leaned into his face, and asked, "Is this true?"

"It was the only way I could get a decent cappuccino in Loveland," he said, "and they have the darkest chocolate cakes," He pointed toward the torte on the table. He snapped his fingers three times, and the lights in the room dimmed enough that they could barely see each other's faces outlined by the red lamps on the table. "Shall I tell you about this evening's light show?"

He directed their eyes upward through the skylight above the couch. Green and blue streams danced against the black sky with occasional red streaks. "The Vikings believed those formed a bridge to Valhalla, the dancing lights reflected off the shields of the Valkyrie. These were female warriors, like yourselves, who lived and died in battle." They smiled as he said they were warriors, urging him to continue.

"Aurora means the Roman goddess of the dawn. Borealis means northern, but tonight I have allowed the aurora to descend from the north to Nevada." He spoke dramatically in the dim light like a storyteller of old.

"Oh, tell us more, Odin," Almond said, sounding equally dramatic.

"When the plasma ions and electrons emitted from the Sun reach the Earth's magnetosphere, they interact with the atoms in our atmosphere. The green colors are oxygen, the blue colors nitrogen—the two most significant elements in our air."

"What causes red colors?" Almond asked.

"Higher energies in the plasma excite the red colors in the oxygen and nitrogen. Very rare to see red auroras, unheard of to see them this far south."

"Can they hurt us?" Cali asked.

"My home is not attached to the electrical, water, or sewer grid, so we will not be getting any EMP in here. I've designed this house to be a Faraday cage with Earth and lead lining to protect us from X-rays, protons, alpha, and gamma rays that could bombard us. We are safe here, but I propose we go up to the roof and lay on the grass. This way, my Valkyries." He grabbed some blankets and pillows and escorted them out the door and up onto the roof covered with grass guided by dim red flashlights. He laid down one blanket and the pillows and positioned himself between both women. Cali pulled his right arm around her and snuggled into his chest. Almond held on tightly to his other arm; the covers pulled up over the three of them.

They quietly watched the ribbons of color weave to and fro across the sky. Peaceful. Silent, amidst the beauty of the universe.

Amidst the magnificent display, Tamarind's skin tingled both from the air's electricity and the physical contact with the women on each side of him. To his left, the love of his life, his friend, that he had pined for, for so long. It felt so good to have her at his side. To his right, the woman he was growing to love. He was so proud of her, so pleased to be with her. The attraction to her was physical, mystical, intense. He also realized that for the first time in his life, his infatuation with this woman was more important to him than his affinity to Almond. He relaxed, and as the hours passed in wonder at the night sky, the conversation slowed, and the meal and wine had their way with him, drifting asleep in both of their arms in the warm desert air.

* * *

Flax's night was not as restful. The factory darkened from the downed electrical grid was in full three-shift production, and the team was exhausted but exhilarated. He'd asked the shift supervisors to put together work music suggested by their crews and had them vote on the best mix. Generators in Faraday cages supplied the electricity and lighting on the production line. The music kept beat. Food and energy drinks were available at stations. They couldn't do this forever, but they were feeling the end, the camaraderie, the unity of working for a great purpose.

* * *

President Jaspar returned to the Situation Room after a brief nap. Wall displays had returned to detail scenes and statistics from around the country and around the world. It would take weeks, months, maybe years to recover from this. She knew she did not have that long. Apollyon was coming. She needed to keep the US response team firmly focused on the next stage.

"General Breckinpaw. I know there is much left to do, but we must prepare. Transition the response from military to local first responders. Relieve your military crews so that they are rested for what comes next and go get some rest yourself." He saluted, thanked her, and left the room, a warrior wearied from battle.

Turning to General Ward, she said, "Sharon, we're ready for your team. Get them in place and contact me when you are ready." They'd received no information on what Apollyon had become after passing through perihelion. But they knew it was coming.

CHAPTER 32

Cataclysm

"Cataclysms have happened, are happening, will happen. There is no safe harbor. We must align with the destructive power of the cataclysm, steering its energy into positive outcomes and directions."
— *Journal of Kohlrabi Trust*

Impact minus four days

"Get me information, people. We can't attack an enemy we can't see!" Standing at the head of the conference table in the Security Briefings Room, President Jaspar was frustrated. All their technology and resources stood idle while they waited for data.

The President had ceded operational control of the Situation Room to General Breckinpaw as he managed the clean up after the solar event. She moved her base of operations to the Apollyon control center. General Ward called in from the Space Command center at Kennedy Space Port.

"Ms. President, it could be another twenty-four hours before we have definitive information."

President Jaspar responded, "Sharon, I'm not willing to wait that long." Then, more forcefully, "General Ward, launch your missiles along the last known trajectory of Apollyon. I want Apollyon destroyed as far away from Earth as possible, so we have time to react to any fallout. Get us information and operational control of those missiles so that we can redirect them if required." They both knew this was risky and that the missiles could miss if the trajectory had changed.

"Yes, Ms. President," said General Ward.

"Use your commlink to immediately reconvene a meeting when you have any data at all. President Jaspar out." With that, she terminated the link.

* * *

Tamarind awoke to the pulsed buzzing of his comm device, a signal he'd arranged with Paul Moncrief. They hoped Phosaster or LightStar would give them the first view of Apollyon and were not disappointed. About six hours after the President had terminated her meeting in DC, he received an image and compositional analysis from Phosaster. The picture he got back, however, was alarming. It showed three spherical objects, of equal mass, equally spaced about 4km apart, and all on the same trajectory toward Earth. Compositionally they were made of an unusual alloy of rare Earth metals on the surface. As far as he knew, this alloy mixture had never been researched. Tamarind analyzed the information in his control center and spent 10 or 15 minutes figuring out each sphere's speed and mass before organizing the data for concise presentation to the President. Minimal weight had been lost passing by the Sun, and each object looked identical. Using the secure comms link provided by the President, he reconvened the Apollyon response team immediately, without additional analysis.

The response team looked dumbfounded and puzzled by the images and data. General Ward and Dr. Lewis sat back in their chairs, hands or fists on their mouths, foreheads creased. No one said anything.

President Jaspar, however, was not confused. She knew this image conflicted with the simulation she'd seen previously. "Every analysis you have presented has shown that Apollyon would remain whole or fragment into two or more fragments traveling in different directions. Explain to me what we are looking at."

Still, no one spoke up. Director Taro Search spoke first. "This is confirmation that Apollyon is of alien construction. There is no conceivable way that any natural object could fragment into three equal spheres, uniformly spaced, traveling along the same trajectory."

"Seriously? Give me some other possibilities, people," she shouted at the room. Reluctantly, everyone else in the room agreed with Taro's conclusion.

Dr. John Lewis restated the conclusion. "Apollyon was engineered by someone, not from our planet."

"Now we have a confirmed alien attack, and presumably any competent scientist looking at this image will make the same conclusion as you have. Dr. Lewis, can you and Director Search glean as much information as you can about these aliens. Keep this on a need-to-know basis. I'm hoping to blow up these mini-Apollyons before they are detected. Come back to us with a revised action plan." Taro looked a little too excited, getting another glare from the President.

Dr. Lewis answered, "Yes, Ms. President."

Turning back to the virtual image of General Ward, the President asked, "We have five nukes in flight and three targets. The thousands of nuclear missiles controlled by various countries are designed for sub-orbital flight and are not useful, I understand? What is your plan B?" She knew they had not had time to alert their teams or do any analysis but still expected an immediate action plan.

General Ward went first. "We should redirect the warheads in flight for sequential attacks, two on the first object and two on the second object. Two should suffice to destroy the objects. If we set the impacts to be offset by just the right amount, we will get an additive impact wave. Coupled with the fifth missile, this impact wave may be enough to destroy or fragment the third object. We can then deal with any fallout with laser, missile, and kinetic weapons, as previously planned."

Dr. Lewis was scribbling on a notepad. "Ms. President, Sharon has proposed a credible plan which I'd like our teams to review. However, if we assume the aliens engineered Apollyon to split into three parts at Perihelion, we cannot be confident we can destroy the resulting spheres with our missiles. However, I do think we can divert them, no matter what their composition or construction. I propose we redirect the missiles for side-impact, diverting them away from their Earth trajectory, and reducing their velocity." Then turning to Tamarind, "Do you think Phosaster could assist with a beam aimed at the third object?"

Tamarind had also been considering a side-impact and had been scribbling calculations on his holodesk. "I believe so. Since Phosaster is rotating, I'll need to calculate the exact timing to fire the laser at the third object. I'll send you this timing, and we'll see if we can coordinate the missile and laser for maximum impact."

President Jaspar didn't understand the physics of the proposed attack or the implications of the alien science behind these spheres but clearly understood what they were trying to do. "Sharon, have you got any satellite communications or images yet?" she asked.

"No, Ms. President. We expect the first images within eighteen hours. However, they will all be in-line with the trajectory and appear as a single blurry object. We will have operational control of our missiles shortly. For our mission designations, I propose we refer to the three objects as Apollyon A, B, and C."

"Good. Talk of aliens is prohibited, and apparently, only us in this room will know that there are three objects instead of one. Let's keep it that way." President Jaspar looked around the virtual room until she got nods of agreement, then added, "We have one shot at destroying Apollyon; let's triple-check those calculations. If we are trying to divert, the farther out we detonate, the more time we'll have to redirect these objects away from Earth. We're wasting realtime, people!" With that, she ended the commlink.

Tamarind immediately put Athena to work, modeling the laser pulse's specifics from Phosaster to Apollyon C before separation from the asteroid. Phosaster was rotating, wobbling on its axis, and traveling in an elliptical solar orbit, making the analysis complex.

After the nuclear detonations, Paul could disengage the Phosaster laser from the asteroid and continue the laser assault on the fragments. When he had reviewed the trajectory and conclusions, he sent the data off to Dr. Lewis and Gen Ward.

Pleased with the contribution Phosaster could make to the response effort, he said aloud, "Well done, Athena!"

"Thank you, Tamarind," Athena said.

"I must stop talking to my AI assistant," he said. Athena did not answer.

CHAPTER 33

Apollyon's Puzzle

"Learned minds are trained to break complex problems into subsets that can be addressed by known methods and tools. Inventive minds see the puzzle, get lost in the mystery, and emerge with elegant solutions unforeseen." —Tamarind Chase

Impact minus 3.5 days

At NASA, Dr. Lewis pulled Taro Search into his office.

"Congratulations, Taro. You have been saying we aren't alone in the universe for years, and now there seems to be evidence to validate your theory." He smiled and then slowly tightened his mouth into a line. "Or, viewed another way, you have contacted an alien race, and now they are working to destroy our planet. Don't make our first contact our last contact. Put together some actionable information that can help the President save our planet."

Taro nodded, turned, and headed off. He was excited that his lifelong dream of alien contact had been achieved but horrified to think he might have initiated an attack on Earth. He didn't want to believe this was an act of aggression, but the evidence so far was to the contrary.

Immediately after the EMP, Dr. Lewis had directed NASA's remaining deep space missions to orient their sensors toward Apollyon. Using this data and the images from Tamarind, he began to dig in to get answers about the weapon that was hurtling toward Earth.

The first question was, how could one object split into three similar-sized spheres and continue with the same trajectory? He assembled NASA's propulsion experts, spaceship visionaries, and asteroid trackers, and put them in the cafeteria, the largest room in the building. From this larger group, he identified those who had security clearances to work on military projects and moved them into the Sagan conference room, which could hold about 24 people comfortably. There were 22 in the group.

"Ladies and gentlemen, what I'm going to share with you is top secret. Please put all your communication devices with internet access into this sealed pouch with your name on it." He grabbed them all and put them into a Faraday box near the door. This was standard procedure for military conversations, but Lewis had never seen the need for it at NASA until now. Once everyone had added their phones, wrist devices, pendants, and eyeglasses into the box, Dr. Lewis cleared his voice and began.

"No one is leaving this room until you've solved the puzzle of the century." Everyone at the table sat up and looked directly at him. "We have reason to believe that Apollyon is not a comet, but of alien construction."

As he spoke, Phosaster's image of Apollyon came up on the wall displays. "This image, recently provided by Dark Matter Ventures Phosaster capsule, shows Apollyon after perihelion. It has split into three spheres of approximately equal size, spaced four kilometers apart, shown on the same Earth trajectory as Apollyon before separation. Your job is to come up with a detailed explanation of how they accomplished this. Go. I'll return within an hour." Immediately, they all started talking as he left the room.

Dr. Lewis then proceeded to his office, stopping at his assistant's desk outside his office door. "Christine, could you please arrange for meals, drinks, and snacks delivered outside of the Sagan conference room for me to take in there within the hour? Also, contact Miles Madison and tell him to come to my office right away. Please notify the families of the staff on this list that we are in lockdown, working on an important issue, and that they won't be home tonight."

As soon as he settled into his desk, he sent a text to his wife. *I won't be home tonight, but don't worry*—as if that comment could keep her from feeling anxious.

Miles Madison came into his office, and instinctively closed the door. After years of working together on many projects, he and Lewis had developed a mutual respect. John thought of Miles as an unconstrained creative genius; he could work from various perspectives, a rare talent among scientists and engineers. Miles' title was Extra-Planetary Astrophysicist at NASA, and John gave him access to even clandestine missions. Dr. Lewis always treated him as a confidant and second-in-command, although his everyday responsibilities involved analyzing planets and objects outside the solar system. In his early 60s, Miles was a "lifer" at NASA, with a full brown and gray beard, balding, and thick, black, plastic-rimmed glasses. He wore his usual uniform of worn denim jeans, a white shirt, and leather sandals over black socks.

"Miles, Taro Search over at SETI has made the case that an alien race from Proxima Centauri launched Apollyon." Miles began to grin, assuming this was the setup for a joke but realized quickly that it was not.

"Do you want me to find holes in his data to show that he is wrong?" Miles asked, recognizing that the director might have reasons to be skeptical of a scientist's theories.

"No. I want you to get me everything we know about the planetoids in the Proxima Centauri solar system. Assume Taro is correct and project what these aliens might be like, what technology they could possess, and their purposes. And Miles," John continued, "keep this discussion top secret. At this moment, the world is focused on destroying Apollyon. If we succeed, we need to be better prepared for future encounters and understand what we can about this alien threat. Here is all the data we have so far," he said, handing him a data cube with Taro's original presentation, data on the trajectory, his assumptions about the acceleration and deceleration of Apollyon, and his thoughts on how the aliens became aware of us. He didn't give him Tamarind's picture of the three spheres or the chemical analysis of their surface just yet.

"I'm on it. I'll have a preliminary report as soon as I can," Miles said. As he walked away, he started thinking about what he could conclude with so little information.

Dr. John Lewis was an accomplished astrophysicist, but his leadership at NASA had nothing to do with his technical abilities. He was a shrewd politician, always outthinking and outmaneuvering those who would cut his funding or reallocate his research priorities. Putting NASA and SETI under Space Command might have made sense after the Space War. It made it challenging to justify the long-range research that SETI and NASA were known for without each project having a military objective.

It was essential to get this response to an alien attack right—it would determine the future not only of SETI and NASA but potentially the world. The military commanders above him would interpret this as a direct attack, which it indeed appeared to be, and would focus on damage minimization. As far as he could tell, he was the only senior director in the world thinking specifically about the aliens.

He did not want his team to reach a consensus too early, so he'd given Taro Search, Miles Madison, and the Apollyon Propulsion Team separate tasks. He now circled back to each group.

He began by delivering a cart of pizzas and drinks for the Apollyon Propulsion Team. As he deposited the pizzas on the conference table, their aroma overcame the distinct odor of sweat and anxiety. These were engineers and scientists working on a tight timeline, which for them seemed unnatural. Adding the global importance made it even more stressful. However, he found them all on task and working when he came in the room.

"Tell me how they did this," John asked, grabbing a piece of pizza to signal they could eat during the discussion.

Janice Tallon was the designated spokesperson for the Apollyon Propulsion Team. She was the most gregarious person in the room. Tall with curly, brown hair, she had broad shoulders and a lean physique from her years as a competitive swimmer at Stanford. Janice's undergraduate work was in aerodynamics and her dual master's degrees in astrophysics and mechanical engineering. As a NASA rocket engineer, she developed the new reusable V9 rocket deploying Space Command satellites into orbit.

"Dr. Lewis," she began, "we believe Apollyon had three separate propulsion systems of decreasing complexity. Constructed in space, it required a significant amount of energy, equipment, and technology beyond current human capabilities. The first propulsion stage was for targeting and accelerating Apollyon from the manufacturing base toward our solar system. We know the least about the first stage, but we suspect an electromagnetic accelerator, perhaps located on several planets or space, spread out over a long distance. Apollyon's construction likely includes highly conductive materials allowing acceleration by magnetic forces. Each push would accelerate it until it reached the incredible speeds necessary to cross light-years in a reasonable amount of time.

"Considering the distance required, electromagnetic forces, and scale of such a device, the electromagnetic accelerators would likely be anchored on multiple planets. They would have narrow launch windows such that the planets all aligned to give the electromagnetic push at the right time to Apollyon as it traveled by."

"I know that this wasn't our task, but the scale of this tells us a lot about this alien race. First, they are rich in metals. The quantity of certain elements in the artifact likely exceeds the amount of those metals ever mined on Earth. Second, they have a sophisticated space program that spans their entire solar system and perhaps beyond. Third, they have energy sources and space-based fabrication technologies on a massive scale. Forming Apollyon required an enormous amount of energy, and accelerating it required substantial infrastructure. Finally, they are accelerating an object from moving planets and hitting a target accurately at a great distance. Their computational capabilities were considerable, at least as good as ours. If the trajectory was off, even slightly at the 10th decimal place, Apollyon would have missed Earth completely."

"Thank you for that side note. We have others working on the technologies and capabilities of these aliens. What do you know about their stage two propulsion system?" Dr. Lewis returned to their primary task.

"The second stage decelerated this huge object before it entered our solar system. Essentially, a massive rocket with a single burn would accomplish this." Janice projected a sketch someone on the team had made, showing a small diameter cylindrical hole in the front of Apollyon that went all the way to the center core. "It is likely more complex than this, but upon ignition from a simple circuit, the rocket would fire in a single controlled burn. The deceleration would be enough to slow Apollyon to the velocity at which it entered our solar system."

She looked up at Dr. Lewis for any questions and then proceeded. "Stage three propulsion is the simplest and most ingenious in some ways. How do you separate a sphere into three separate spheres and keep them on the same trajectory? We think Apollyon was constructed from three separate pieces of solid metal assembled on a common shaft attached to the lead piece. The second and third are sphere-shaped donuts around a central shaft. They were likely held together by water or methane ice. As Apollyon approached the Sun, the ice melted explosively, separating the three parts. As the temperatures continued to climb, the metals were superheated until they were melted. Then the surface tension of the molten liquids caused them to be re-solidified as spheres. It is unlikely any technology, mechanisms, or controls were required, nor could have survived such close proximity to the Sun. In short, Apollyon intended to pass through Perihelion and absorb just the right amount of energy to convert into the three uniform spheres approaching us today."

Dr. Lewis nodded in approval and asked one follow-on question. "Are you sure there are not any control systems, explosives, or mechanisms inside of Apollyon now? Any more surprises waiting for us?"

Janice glanced around at the team and then back to John. "No, it is unlikely there are any remaining surprises from Apollyon. We have three large spheres approaching us at high velocity, and Newtonian physics governs everything that happens now."

"Thank you all for this preliminary summary. I'd like you to take this to the next level. Starting with three spheres and moving backward, design Apollyon. I want complete drawings, analysis of each of the three components, and each of the three propulsion systems. We have some additional information on the surface composition of the spheres that might aid your analysis. I want visual mockups of these before you leave this room. We've notified your families that you are working late tonight."

There was a moan from the team and a request. "We'll need our computing devices back?" Janice ventured.

"I'll have them delivered shortly," John left the room and closed the door behind him. He made a mental note to increase the fresh air exchange in that room.

Next up was Miles Madison. He walked to his office on the third floor, stepped inside, and closed the door. "Hi Miles, what can you tell me about the aliens' solar system?"

Miles, as expected, was ready. "Alpha Centauri is a three-star system and the nearest solar system to Earth. Proxima Centauri is the smallest star in the triad. It is a Red Dwarf star, about 4.25 light-years away, and has at least one planet in the habitable zone, Proxima b. Their Sun's proximity suggests water would be in a liquid form on this planet. Proxima b is 1.3 times the Earth's diameter with an orbit period of a little more than eleven days. There are likely several other planetoids in the system and mineable resources in asteroids. I suspect that the aliens—I shall refer to them as 'Proximans'—have come from this planet and have developed asteroid mining and fabrication technology spanning their solar system and perhaps out to other planets orbiting the other stars in the triad."

"What can you tell me about their technology?" John asked.

Miles continued. "We know they possess the technology to receive signals from Earth. We've been transmitting radio waves, microwaves, and laser light, plus a few other parts of the EM spectrum into space since the invention of the radio. It required significant technological development, on the entire SETI program's scale, to detect most of these signals. But the most likely explanation is that they used simple optical technologies to detect the laser pulses Taro Search has been sending out for the last several decades."

"This implies that they don't know much about us except that we are technologically developed with high-powered lasers searching for intelligent life. Taro's signals made no threat, stating we're here, advanced, and would like to communicate with them. It is hard to imagine their response would be to try to destroy us."

"They must also have significant astronomical capabilities. Apollyon not only navigated through our solar system, avoiding impacts with objects, but it used the gravitational attraction of each of the planets along the way and the energy of the Sun to achieve their final objective."

"Their ability to accelerate a large object and decelerate before entering our solar system tells us they have energy sources, fabrication capabilities, and metal mining spread across their solar system. These capabilities far exceed ours. However, they did not choose to reply to our laser signals with a laser message, which suggests they either don't have this technology or that simple communication did not meet their objectives."

"Finally, I'd like to suggest this might not be an attack; they don't intend to kill us. If that was the intent of the Proximans, why decelerate before entering our system? Why would a request to communicate result in a direct attack? If they are extreme xenophobes, why not just be silent? I think it is more reasonable that they assumed we have technology equivalent or superior to theirs and have developed the technology to move asteroid-sized objects around with significant accuracy. In that case, Apollyon might be a gift, or a show of wealth or force, or to test our response." Miles stopped here to address any questions that John might have.

"Interesting conclusions, Miles. It will be a tough sell to convince Space Command that this is not an attack. There is one new fact to share with you. Apollyon split after perihelion into three perfectly equal spheres on the same trajectory. Phosaster has done a material analysis of the surface. I've put together an Apollyon Propulsion Team, and they have some ideas on how Apollyon was constructed, split, and sent here. Rather than explain, could you join them in the Sagan Conference Room and share your conclusions with them? I think you will be able to add some practical nuances to what they have concluded so far."

"You've got it, John. Let me know if there is anything more I can do." With that, Miles headed off to join the Apollyon Propulsion Team, and John hurried to his final stop.

"Director Search," John began formally, as he walked into Taro's office. It was messy, cluttered with folders of various SETI projects and proposals, all shoved to the edge of his desk. NASA space photos and renderings of distant planets covered his walls. Taro's hair stuck up as if he'd stuck his fingers in his hair and then rested his head on his palm for a while. However, it was clear he hadn't been sleeping from the anxious dark circles around his eyes and coffee cups scattered around the room.

"Dr. Lewis," Taro exclaimed, optimistically. "I think the aliens might be amiable!" His hopeful expression suggested he was both relieved that he hadn't triggered aliens into destroying the world and that his life-long dream was coming to fruition.

"Taro, their current agenda appears to be a full-on assault, and we have our military and our bosses at Space Command in full defense mode.

Assuming they are successful in overcoming this attack, I'll need more than the fact that you think they are friendly. What have you got for me?"

Taro organized his thoughts and calmed down a little. "John, three things make me believe this isn't meant as an attack. First, the Proximans were responding to a message from us that was a friendly invitation to communicate. It is difficult to imagine why that would immediately cause them to want to kill us."

"Miles Madison would agree with you on that point," said Dr. Lewis. "What are the other two?"

"Second, the deceleration upon entering our solar system indicates a more peaceful intent. Apollyon was a more effective weapon at full velocity," Taro looked for approval, and John nodded for him to continue.

"Third, splitting into three equal parts further decreases the impact damage. I think the fact that there are three equal-sized globes of high value has a... spiritual significance."

"How so?" John asked.

"Consider that their planet has three Suns in their sky. On Earth, Sun-worship spanned many early cultures, from the Aztecs to the Egyptians. It is likely they also had some Sun-worship in their development, and three gods were a part of that. We've seen the spiritual significance of threes continue throughout cultures on Earth. Many religions include sacred threes—Christian Trinity, Hindu Trimurti, Tao's Three Pure Ones, and the Wiccan Triple Goddess, for instance."

"Scientists described discoveries in threes—three primary colors, three primes in alchemy, the three antidotes in Indian medicine. In sports, we assign special value to threes— triathlons, three-peats, and on and on, we even say, 'third time's the charm'!"

"We also say disasters come in threes," said John, sarcastically. "These are human examples; we are trying to understand aliens."

"I agree there is conjecture here. If you consider first contact scenarios throughout our planet's history, humankind naturally or symbolically chooses threes. The wise men brought three gifts to Jesus. Columbus sent three ships to the new world. The Dutch gave tools, beads, and musical instruments to the Native Americans on Manhattan Island. There are many other examples where first contact involved a gift, and often three gifts of significant value. Some Native American tribes would stage three feigned attacks on a peace envoy and only sign a treaty if the envoy proved themselves brave."

"I think what we are seeing is their cultural way of initiating communications. They learned enough about our solar system to navigate by the gravitational pull of our planets. They targeted Earth because we sent them welcome signals. It is reasonable that they see us as equals or perhaps as more advanced." Taro smiled to indicate his analysis was done.

"Not as conclusive as the President would like, but intriguing. Good work, Taro."

"Thank you, sir. Anything else I can do to help?"

"Miles and a team of propulsion engineers are meeting in the Sagan conference room. Please join them and work with them to concisely summarize our conclusions for the President."

Taro nodded, grabbed his notes, and headed off to join the team.

* * *

Dr. Lewis let them stew in that room for another 8 hours. He joined them when Miles indicated they were ready and found that the entire team had moved toward consensus.

The team had displayed concept sketches around the room about the design of Apollyon, with complete calculations of each of the propulsion engine stages. After Miles' initial explanation, Dr. Lewis had the team explain their math. Each of the propulsion stages seemed reasonable, even if they were on an unimaginable scale. At least to first order computations, their theoretical explanation of each method of propulsion seemed feasible.

They also had images from deep space telescopes and simulated images of the planet Proxima b, orbiting the star Proxima Centauri, the third star in the Alpha Centauri triple star system. Astronomers had considered the Alpha Centauri system to be a binary star, with two Earth Sun-like stars rotating together. Proxima Centauri was discovered much later, in the second decade of the 21st century, to be a part of this triple star system, but acted almost independently in many practical ways.

They had conceptual sketches of the electromagnetic accelerator that had jump-started Apollyon and technical calculations of the electromagnetic forces involved to achieve nearly half the speed of light. Critical to that propulsion method was the use of the lanthanide series elements on the surface. "We're not quite sure what those exotic alloys detected at the surface might be for, but we suspect they formed magnets used in the launch mechanism and might also become a protective coating to withstand impacts in space," Miles said.

The launch system the team described spanned the Proxima Centauri solar system. Rings many kilometers in diameter encircled with super-cooled conductors were aligned and spaced hundreds of kilometers apart in space along a line or arc, a kind of super rail gun. An electric current passed through each ring in sequence kicked Apollyon forward. After Apollyon had accelerated by a series of these magnets, it achieved the velocity required for the first stage of its journey.

Miles walked animatedly around the room, explaining each image, summarizing the conclusions, and occasionally one of the other engineers threw in a point they thought particularly important. Dr. Lewis allowed them to recount their findings to him without any comments or interruptions.

The cloistered group also came up with preliminary ideas about the manufacture of Apollyon: asteroid mining on an expansive scale, the fabrication facilities, and the type of equipment to build such a system. This part of the presentation was far more speculative than the Apollyon design and propulsion systems that were within their expertise.

Miles said, "We'll need a different set of experts in the room to consider the fabrication concepts in greater detail. However, the chemical analysis of the surface reveals the Proximans have researched alloys we've never considered on Earth, in part because we don't have significant quantities of some of the metals they've used."

"What more can you infer about the Proximans?" Dr. Lewis asked.

Taro began to lay out some of the constraints that would help the team understand the Proximans. "Since their planet orbits their Sun roughly every eleven days, they would experience all their seasons over that time. Growing food crops as on Earth would be impossible, so organic life must be limited. They must have liquid water, an atmosphere, and a magnetic field to shield the planet's surface from their Sun. Otherwise, life couldn't exist. The amount of UV radiation close to their Sun should break down their atmosphere much faster than on Earth by two to three orders of magnitude. Our models of the planet suggest that the atmosphere would have drained away by now due to stellar physics, so obviously, we are wrong about that. They exist, which tells us a lot."

"Additionally, Proxima Centauri is a red dwarf star, which is less stable than Earth's Sun. Although the three stars in the Centauri system would be visible, even during daylight hours, the planet would be in a twilight red glow. Solar flares would be frequent, further irradiating the surface. Proxima b is most likely 'tidally locked,' that is, it doesn't rotate as it orbits its Sun. This means one side is permanently hot, between fifteen and thirty degrees Celcius and the other in the dark, between minus fifteen and thirty degrees. Although the planet is in the theoretical 'habitable zone,' where water can be liquid on the surface, it would likely evaporate on the hot side and freeze on the cold side. Life would only really be possible in the band between these regions, which would be an environmentally turbulent region."

Taro summarized with some hypotheticals. "However, since we know that there is intelligence, we can assume there is or was life on the planet and that either the Proximans or the planet overcame these challenges. Maybe volcanoes on the hot side are constantly filling the atmosphere with smoke and dust and reducing the radiation on the surface. If C-class comets are regularly hitting the surface, they might restore water and the atmosphere. It could be that Proxima Centauri b has a Saturn-like ring that absorbs enough of the radiation to make the planet hospitable. If it is not tidally locked, perhaps the surface is more hospitable to plant and animal life. We don't have clear photos or probe data to give us better information, so what we know is based on a lot of calculations, assumptions, and observations. However, now we know there is intelligent life, so we need to revisit all previous Proxima b studies through this new lens."

Taro continued. "Proxima b is approximately one point three times the size of the Earth, so the gravity is proportionately stronger. Proximans must be more physically robust than humans. The environmental conditions imply a more limited food supply with less nutritional variety and a lack of abundance, so we suspect fewer Proximans than humans by an order of magnitude or more. The team agrees the Proximans are spiritual; they developed a culture where three is a symbolic number. While they certainly have significant fabrication capabilities, we don't know their evolutionary or development cycle, and we can't assume they are more advanced than us in everything. For example, if they have lasers, why not simply respond to us with a laser message analogous to the one we sent?" Taro finished his conclusions, raising more questions.

Director Lewis concluded, "There is much we don't know, and I'm sure we'll get funding to research much of this over the next decade. Thank you all for your work. Now go home to your families and don't come in tomorrow. Obviously, this is still completely confidential. I want you fresh and able to answer questions before we explain this to the President." As the teams left the room, he thought he might have to get the place fumigated or get the janitors to begin here tomorrow.

"Miles, Taro, another minute?" Dr. Lewis had one more question for them. They both looked physically exhausted but energized by the work they had been doing and were still interested in discussing it. "Let's walk to my office." John decided he couldn't spend any more time in that room.

When they were in his office, and the door was closed, he asked them the one question that had been burning in his mind. "Is there anything in your analysis that is actionable?"

Miles answered first. "No, I don't think so. I agree with Taro's analysis that the Proximans did not intend Apollyon as a weapon. However, from Earth's perspective, it certainly is. We've inferred a lot about the Proximans, but nothing helps us in the next few days. I do think any fragments that make landfall will give us a lot more information, and we should protect and collect them for further analysis."

Taro added, "We must deflect or destroy Apollyon, of course, but it would be unfortunate if we fail to see the opportunity of our first contact with an alien species. What is actionable at this point is to help our leadership see past this initial challenge to the potential relationship ahead, convince them to fund research to help us hone our answers, and learn from every fragment of Apollyon we collect."

Dr. Lewis nodded. His challenge now was to convince the people around the President's table to destroy the Proximans' gift but accept their invitation.

CHAPTER 34

Preparation

"Business leaders strategize, religious leaders hope, but true leaders prepare. Plan and hope for the best outcome but prepare for whatever may come." —Flax Venture

Impact minus three days

Flax got off the commlink with the President and realized there was nothing more the DroneTech team could do related to Apollyon, so he decided to check in with them on business matters. Mike Stapleton and Aislinn O'Malley were in a meeting with Jimmy and Telsun when he walked in. Aislinn immediately gave him a status update.

"Hi Flax," she began, "Mike's manufacturing team has completed the build of the last of the drones, and these will go online in the next few hours. We've coordinated with the President's Chief of Staff and now have secure communications to the world's GPS, media, banking, military, the internet, and other resources normally handled through satellite communications. The Drone commlink and Drone swarm software passed initial tests." Looking around the table, he could see the team were fully engaged with the single most significant work of their lives and were thriving in the middle of it. They knew about Apollyon, obviously, and the potential impending doom, but the work also energized them.

IMPACT

Pointing at Telsun, Flax said, "Your team has done an amazing job. If it weren't for the Swarm Team, our planet would have discovered Apollyon too late to do anything about it." Then he turned toward Mike and Aislinn and said, "And without DroneComms working through the myriad of challenges reestablishing global communications after the EMP, we would not be able to continue normal business operations on Earth and organize our response in space. Others are on the front lines working to neutralize Apollyon's threat, but they could not succeed without the people in this room. You are all heroes, and your stories will be told."

"As long as we can make it past next Tuesday," Telsun said, his dark humor always coming out in difficult times. Tuesday would be the day where the world would know if their efforts to save the planet had succeeded. "There should be another coolio light show anyway. Go out with a bang, so to speak?"

Aislinn and Mike looked stern and disapproving.

"Too soon," Aislinn said, shaking her head.

Flax just smiled, winked at them, tapped his hand twice on the door frame, and kept moving around the office. He made a point of checking in with each department, which was no small feat considering the size DroneTech had become. He left them all with words of hope and encouraged them to get home and enjoy the upcoming light show.

Almond met him when he returned to his office. "Flax, my love. Do we have a chance?"

"There has been an amazing global effort to pool resources to meet this threat. I think we have a good chance of surviving Apollyon," Flax said, hopefully. He didn't look worried. Flax the Unflappable.

"Can we go to the ocean this weekend? There isn't much we can do here, and if these are our last days, I'd like to spend them with you, in nature somewhere." He looked into her pleading eyes, considered that things were running smoothly here, and decided he should tell everyone to go home but be on standby until they knew more.

"I have just the spot in mind—a beautiful beach with sun, waves, and sand." Flax said with no resistance. He knew he would need to stay connected, but he wanted to be with her this weekend. "Can you pack up the things we'll need, and I'll zip things up here?" She smiled and walked with a graceful bounce out of the room.

"The biggest cataclysm on our planet since God created it, and somehow she is still at peace," Flax said to himself. Her faith was challenging, her spirit infectious, and he looked forward to a weekend away with her. He remembered the little place on the southern Oregon coast that they had stayed at on their honeymoon. Gold Beach. That is where he would take her.

* * *

President Jaspar paced the floor of the Oval Office. She was not at peace; she had the entire military preparing for war and the country locked down and preparing for impact.

Aliens. Cataclysm. Global destruction. How can any President be prepared for such things? She thought darkly to herself. *What more can we do? What am I missing?* She continued to pace, frustrated that she didn't have more information on which to act. Even though they were going to have a meeting the next morning, she decided to call each team leader.

"General Ward, Sharon, what is our status?"

"Everything is in place. The missiles remain on track and will reach their targets tomorrow. We're coordinating with Dark Matter Ventures to launch the kinetic weapons and direct Phosaster and LightStar's laser toward fragments."

"Have we restored comms to the missiles?"

"We've restored comms to the missiles and repositioned our satellite arrays. The hardened satellites remain in Apollyon's path to give us updated images and fragment trajectories after each explosion. We'll have clear images in the Apollyon response room in near real-time. We'll also be able to quickly disseminate target and trajectory information to Space Command and the targeting lasers and rockets."

"Thank you, Sharon, is there anything else we should be doing?" the President asked.

General Ward paused before answering. "Praying. I know I am."

Dr. John Lewis relayed their analysis of the Proximans and Apollyon concluding that nothing was actionable at this time. Then he added, "My team does not think Apollyon was sent to destroy us; it is more like a show of power to initiate a negotiation. We have a proposal for additional research and recommend recovering every fragment of Apollyon for further analysis of the Proximans."

The President was too unsettled to consider this thoroughly, thanked John for his team's analysis, and promised to review their proposal.

Finally, she contacted General Breckinpaw. "General, what is our status?"

"Ms. President," he began, formally, "The conflicts and disasters initiated by the EMP and CME are contained. National Guards and military personnel are positioned to secure strategically important assets and respond to any Apollyon debris hitting the ground. We're coordinating with local police, fire, and emergency responders to maintain peace and respond quickly to any crises. They will essentially be enforcing a house curfew for one hour before and after impact."

"Good. One more item. I'd like you to have your teams secure any Apollyon fragments that make it to Earth. We'll use these for further research on this weapon and on the aliens that sent it." This process of talking to each of her leaders had calmed her down, and she was feeling back in control again.

"Yes, Ms. President. We've got this." General Breckinpaw was nothing if not confident.

President Jaspar thought of calling Tamarind and Flax but decided it wasn't necessary. Fear of the future made it hard to relax or think clearly; she knew that she needed rest. She poured herself a brandy and retired to the White House residence. Tomorrow would be a big day.

CHAPTER 35

Impact

*"Many things outside us can impact us, but transformation comes when
we impact ourselves." —Journal of Kohlrabi Trust*

Impact minus two days

The coordinated heads of state simultaneously released a prepared
statement about the plan to destroy Apollyon. The world had been
distracted by the beauty and chaos following the EMP, but they had not
forgotten Apollyon. They knew another wonderous display in the skies was
coming with destruction in its wake.

The statement read: *At 12:17 pm Greenwich mean time, nuclear missiles launched from Earth will impact Apollyon. A shock wave from those
massive explosions will hit our upper atmosphere, but we expect no damage on Earth. The High-altitude Electromagnetic Pulse (HEMP) will create
aurora in the sky, like last week's solar EMP, temporarily affecting communications. It will take a few hours to confirm that Apollyon was destroyed as
expected; we will keep you posted as information is known. We encourage
you to stay with your loved ones and minimize travel until you receive the
all-clear notice.*

Media outlets had switched entirely from regular programming to
Apollyon-related coverage. Part of the pre-event coverage included the

times and place to best observe the "Apollyon fireworks show." Most people were planning to be outside during the event. The actual impact and explosion would be too far outside orbit for direct observation. The media displayed simulations of nuclear missiles flying into Apollyon and shattering it into small pieces. These pieces would fall like rain into the upper atmosphere creating a light show for much of the world. Of course, no one knew exactly what would happen, and the public was unaware three alien objects were heading toward the Earth. Because the three spheres were perfectly aligned, they appeared from Earth as a single sphere.

General Ward, Dr. Lewis, and General Breckinpaw were alone in the conference room with the President, and Tamarind Chase included virtually. All had their teams on stand-by and had triple-checked their calculations on the three objects now labeled Apollyon A, B, and C.

President Laura Jaspar asked, "Have we updated the missile trajectories?" While the others remained seated connected into the commlinks, she paced around the room, clenching her fists and rubbing her hands together at each turn.

"Yes, Ms. President, every few seconds," General Ward replied absently while sifting through data streams and incoming audio and video feeds.

The best images available were displayed around the Security Briefings Room, which became command central for the Apollyon assault. From the SWARMNET satellite images they had, the explosions would appear to be occurring on a single object and staggered by about 4 minutes. There just wasn't enough of a viewing angle, even from Earth orbit, to see all three. There would be a short white-out from the detonation, and then as the images came back online, they would complete an analysis of the effectiveness of each missile on Apollyon.

The French and Russian missiles hit Apollyon A within a few seconds of the predicted time. The impacts were offset slightly and at an angle to Apollyon A's trajectory. After all the discussions and simulations, modified with the information from Phosaster on the spheres' makeup and the two nukes' payload, this became the optimum plan. The first impact, the French missile, would generate a deep impact crater. The offset angle was both to deflect the sphere and to direct the pulse away from Earth. The Russian device would enter that crater and fracture Apollyon A with a massive second explosion, deflecting the resulting fragments at angles that would miss Earth.

The images bloomed to pure white with two bright peaks and then became static as the cameras received the EMP from the nuclear explosions. It took nearly 100 seconds for the images to calm down, showing that Apollyon A had fragmented, with large pieces moving off at different trajectories. After another thirty seconds, which felt like forever, the monitoring team reported to the Control Room. General Sharon Ward of Space Command announced, "Direct hit on Apollyon A, 95% of the mass has been shifted off course and will miss the Earth, and about 5% remained on trajectory." Fists clenched and pumped in the air or on the table.

"Make sure LightStar and our kinetic weapons team know the debris trajectories," President Jaspar said, stating the obvious. Everyone remained silent as the displays were updated to show debris trajectories. General Ward and Tamarind's team quickly allocated laser and space hardware to each fragment in the minutes before the second detonation. Those smaller impacts would occur closer to Earth over the next day.

The room was pregnant with expectation awaiting the second impact. The tension was unbearable though only 4 minutes had passed. Finally, another bloom appeared on the display, as the two American missiles hit Apollyon B. Like the first sphere, the simulations analyzed the effect of the initial detonation and the moderate payload of the two nukes. The impact angle was only slightly off Apollyon's trajectory, and the two impacts spaced farther apart, though still within seconds of each other.

Again, the displays bloomed white with two bright peaks, the first indication that the explosions had occurred, then static. Finally, the images cleared, showing Apollyon B fragmented with the bulk deflected off course in a misshapen piece, and this time, cheers went up around the room. "Direct hit," General Ward said, feeling the importance, as these two were American missiles, under her command. President Jaspar raised her arms to quiet them. "Status!"

"Ninety-nine percent of the mass fragmented and is no longer on a trajectory toward Earth. The trajectories on the remaining one percent passed along to the laser and kinetic weapons team." General Ward said, which was confirmed by Dr. John Lewis. Again, the displays updated, and each debris target switched from red to green as resources applied to destroy them.

Despite the success, they were running out of kinetic weapons. All the ground-based missiles, the rockets in the asteroid competition, the Earth mounted lasers from other nations, and the Light Star and Phosaster laser pulses had been assigned to incoming fragments, thousands of objects distributed across the planet. Nearly 3/4th of the kinetic weapons were allocated to the debris from the first two spheres.

"Two down, one to go," said the President, the tear forming in her eyes quickly wiped away. She could see the clenched fists around the room had changed to a more prayerful configuration.

The next four minutes seemed like hours. President Jaspar noticed she could hear her heartbeat pulsing in her ears. More than one person in the room had vocalized some variant of "C'mon!" A third flash appeared on the screen as the most powerful of the five missiles, the one built by Japan, struck the side of Apollyon C. A streak appeared from one edge just before the images bloomed. "That must be Phosaster," Tamarind said, watching from his remote comms. He had chosen to monitor from Dark Matter Ventures, where he could coordinate Project LightStar and Phosaster responses directly.

The room was quiet. Prayerful stances replaced with knuckle-biting and tensed face muscles. Finally, the image cleared, and they could all see a significant fragment veering off. However, the majority of the object continued straight toward Earth. The room was silent. President Jaspar said, "Analysis."

They had agreed that General Ward would leave the room to coordinate the debris response after hitting the third sphere, but she remained on comms in transit. This time, Dr. Lewis summarized the data; his voice wavered as he delivered the report. "A thirty-five percent fragment was split off and is on a trajectory to miss Earth, along with another four percent of the debris. Fifty-seven percent is heading toward Earth as a single piece, and another four percent as debris." There was a collective groan that went up around the room.

President Jaspar addressed the debris first. "Tamarind, Sharon, do you think LightStar and Phosaster and your remaining kinetic weapons can take out this smaller debris?"

They both answered, "Yes, Ms. President," They started assigning targets, but everyone was waiting for her to comment on the large mass still moving toward Earth.

"OK, then, you two may leave this meeting to focus on your task. Every deferred impact means lives; we are entrusting you with saving lives today." Laura Jaspar looked particularly presidential, maintaining composure in a difficult situation. General Ward and Tamarind Chase virtually left the meeting without hearing what she was going to do next.

* * *

Once disconnected from the secure communications, Tamarind contacted Cali, Stacy, and Scarecrow. "Guys," he said, "let me be the first to tell you we've mostly destroyed Apollyon. About five to six percent of the total mass is headed here as debris, and it will be up to LightStar and our kinetics weapons contest teams to take out the rest. I'll send the information now but wait for the President to announce the status before letting out the info. This is her announcement, not ours, so not a word until she speaks." He was silent about the large fragment heading toward Earth, not wanting them to be distracted from their immediate task.

"Paul, is the laser from Phosaster disengaged from the asteroid and ready for use?" Tamarind asked.

"Yes, it is fully online and ready to take debris coordinates. Fire at will!" The last line was out of character for Paul, but he had been working non-stop getting ready for this day, and the uncharacteristic geeky outburst made them all chuckle.

Cali, Stacy, and Paul were a bit giddy but knew they had to get their next tasks right. They micromanaged every detail, assigning tasks to different teams from the competition, and monitoring them to check on the process. Each projectile had a narrow launch window to achieve altitude and destroy the incoming objects. The next 48 hours were going to be a blizzard of details for them.

* * *

Back in the Situation Room, the President directed a question toward Dr. John Lewis. "John, where is this fragment going to land, and how bad will it be?"

He had been working feverishly on just that question using specialized simulation tools prepared for this day.

"Ms. President, the Apollyon C fragment will land in the Gulf of Mexico near the border with Mexico and Texas. The impact will cause an earthquake above nine on the Richter Scale, which will send a debris plume into the upper atmosphere, cause a mega-tsunami in both the Atlantic and Pacific oceans, and create an unprecedented impact shock. It will have disastrous effects over much of North America and in most of South America. Mexico will be leveled on impact, the tsunami will flood Central America, and the impact wave will destroy most of the USA and South America. Lesser effects, but still significant, will be felt around the world, and the debris will affect the weather for several years." The big man choked up, and tears filled his eyes, "I'm sorry, Ms. President."

"How could an impact down there affect so much of the Americas?" the President asked.

"The shock wave will trigger earthquakes along fault lines. The increased pressure may cause volcano eruptions in the magma of the core. The heat of the impact will vaporize and form sulfate aerosols in addition to the dust and particulates, which will be ejected kilometers into space. An air pressure shock wave powerful enough to liquefy organs will follow, accompanied by surface winds sufficient to destroy trees and buildings. Then the acid rain will fall, destroying whatever is left. All of these are likely, but we can't say with certainty what exactly will happen." Dr. Lewis spoke with a matter-of-fact tone, but his face filled with pain.

"Where is the safest place to be?"

"Probably Saudi Arabia or perhaps Australia, though nowhere on Earth is going to be pleasant for many years. The dust from the impact crater will change weather patterns for decades; global temperatures will drop, and eventually, UV radiation will increase. The impact won't become an extinction event, we have prevented that, but it will be close for the Americas."

"What is your recommended evacuation plan?" She asked, her mouth squeezed into a tight line, brows narrowed.

General Breckinpaw said, "Ms. President, based upon this impact location, we recommend transferring you and members of the government and their families to Raven Rock Mountain Complex facility in Pennsylvania. The structure holds three thousand people for thirty days in a safe nuclear facility requiring no outside connections. The E Seven Doomsday plane is ready for departure within minutes. There are nearly a billion people in the area directly affected, and no evacuation from the region is possible. I'm afraid any orderly evacuation would create end-of-the-world chaos we could not contain. However, we have secured humanity's existence and saved most of the people on the planet due to your strong and decisive leadership."

"We're not evacuating just yet, General. How long until everyone knows about this fragment?" the President asked.

Dr. Collier answered, "Probably twenty-four to thirty-six hours. A lot of cameras and telescopes are pointed in space currently. The debris will cloud the view temporarily, but they will be able to see it soon enough."

"Then let's use the next twenty-four hours to celebrate what has been accomplished today and prepare for the possible evacuation tomorrow. Except for those directly involved in the laser and kinetic weapon response, security, and peacekeeping—send your teams home, and if you can, spend your remaining time with your families. Let's give people a day of celebration and preparation."

She drafted a memo to the other Heads of State. *Apollyon has fragmented, and the majority will miss Earth. Kinetic and laser weapons will address debris fallout. Recommend no travel and stay in place until fallout is complete. Celebrate with your people!* Before returning to the White House residences, she went through the building, telling people to go home and celebrate with their families and view the momentous light show. She had often chosen to "misrepresent the truth" for the public's good, or so she told herself. This time it felt like giving a condemned prisoner their last meal.

* * *

Tamarind contacted Flax and told him, "There is a large Apollyon chunk headed toward Earth, and I don't know all the specifics, but it would likely decimate the Americas. It appears to be the end of everything we have created, and probably our lives."

"Where is the fragment going to land?" Flax asked.

"The President asked us to leave the room before we knew the trajectory and impact site. My estimation is on the Mexican side of our southern border, and it will destroy everything for thousands of kilometers with devastating side-effects for years to come."

Flax replied, "Tamarind, I believe in the sovereignty of God. I do not think He intends to destroy the Earth by an alien attack." He paused to let that comment sink in. "Take that new girlfriend of yours somewhere nice and rejoice that we saved many lives. ERIWA, my friend!"

"Flax, I…I don't want us to be anything but friends. I know you were just a kid when all that happened before, and I forgive you. ERIWA!" Tamarind's eyes welled with tears as the commlink ended. *Finish well*, he thought to himself.

He remembered that overwhelming grief after Kohlrabi's death, which he'd been unable to prevent. There must be something else he could do. He went back over the kinetic and laser weapons pointed at the incoming debris. Some of these would fall within the impact zone of the large fragment. This gave him an idea.

Contacting General Ward, he said, "Sharon, I know we are supposed to use the lasers to shoot falling debris. However, I think we should fire every single pulse at the remaining fragment. They won't destroy the Apollyon C fragment, but they will decrease its size before impact. It is the most significant way to save lives, I think." Tamarind pleaded with her for this change of direction.

General Ward considered his request and that it was different than what she had told the President. Not disobeying a direct order exactly, but making a command decision on an active battlefield. "I suppose shooting debris fragments will be irrelevant if this chunk destroys the whole region. The President told us to save lives. I agree. Set both lasers to fire non-stop at the Apollyon C fragment," They looked at each other meaningfully, nodded their heads, and broke the connection.

Tamarind personally oversaw the reprogramming of all Phosaster and LightStar's laser pulses at the Apollyon C fragment. While Stacy and Cali continued their monitoring of the kinetic weapons, Tamarind pulled

Paul Moncrief aside. He explained to him the confidential details about the Apollyon fragment he hadn't told him about earlier.

Paul raised his eyebrows, immediately understanding the significance of the request and assuring Tamarind he would stay with it until the last remaining piece entered the atmosphere.

Tamarind put his hand on Paul's shoulder and said, "You are a hero of the highest order, Paul. You are saving many lives today."

After the last launch of the rockets in the contest, Cali realized there was nothing left for her to do but wait and watch somewhere. Stacy and Paul stayed at the Dark Matter Ventures' makeshift control center to record the results of the kinetic and laser impacts and coordinate with General Ward to notify local first responders where chunks were going to make landfall.

Tamarind invited Cali to watch with him in his Phosaster control center. She said, "The whole world is celebrating outside and looking upward, and you want to celebrate underground?" However, her smile said yes.

He had a spectacular view on the screen, with images from LightStar, Phosaster, many of the world's satellites, and even one from the roof. Lasers went up from LightStar and Phosaster, ground rockets and satellites occasionally made dramatic impacts on chunks of debris. The whole world was celebrating a spectacular light show outdoors as objects hit the atmosphere, but in the Phosaster Control Center, they were seeing what was happening in real-time.

Cali snuggled in on the couch next to Tamarind, and they started kissing. After the past few days' activities and the intensity and exhaustion of the last 36 hours, cuddling by the fireworks was a welcome release. Kissing and fireworks have been working together since the Tang Dynasty. Tamarind relaxed, enjoying the peaceful moment, but of course, he hadn't told her everything.

Finally, he stopped kissing her and pulled back. "Cali, there is something I have to tell you." She was expecting something good, but looking in his eyes, she could see that it was not. "There is a big chunk of Apollyon still coming for us. We got most of it, but the remainder will cause the worst disaster in recorded history."

"Are we safe down here?" Cali asked, her eyes tearing up.

"No. We should survive the initial impact, but the fallout will overwhelm us here, I suspect. Right now, our lasers are fully focused on the chunk, lessening it by the minute, but there isn't enough time to get it all. I do have plenty of food and drink for a few days. I am glad you are here," Tamarind said with a smile.

Cali's face fell, her shoulders started shaking, and tears fell down her face. "After all we've accomplished, we're going to die?" Tamarind hugged her but had no answer. He didn't have the complete impact trajectory analysis but inferred from President Jaspar's steely response the impact would destroy much of the country.

They stayed like that for several minutes, hugging while she quietly sobbed. Finally, she looked up at Tamarind, wiped her eyes, and began kissing him more fervently.

Tamarind was almost wholly engaged in the intimate moment, but he couldn't help opening one eye to glance at the screen. The image showing the Phosaster asteroid bloomed suddenly, revealing a giant explosion. Tamarind relaxed his arms around Cali, pointed at the display, and jumped up from the couch.

"Did you see that?" His fists were clenched, and he began bouncing up and down on his toes anxiously.

Cali asked, "What was that?"

Tamarind watched as the data came in. "Could it be?"

"What?" said Cali, wiping her eyes. She could tell it was something good but had no idea what could happen on the Phosaster asteroid that could be relevant. The laser system had already separated and was flying independently.

"Athena, project the trajectory of the object fired from Phosaster. Overlay the trajectory of the Apollyon chunk." Tamarind put his hands on his head and said, "Oh my God!"

"What?!" repeated Cali, this time more loudly, while standing and clutching his arm.

"Phosaster somehow just fired all of our mined metals at the remaining Apollyon chunk. It looks like it just might hit it!"

He immediately activated his secure commlink to the President and response team and sent them the data link to watch it in real-time. The Apollyon response team was dispersed across different locations. The military leaders were on task, tracking fallen debris and coordinating the response with regional first responders and military personnel. President Jaspar was in the White House personal residence. Dr. Lewis was at NASA, General Breckinpaw was in the Security Briefings Room, General Ward was at Kennedy Space Port, and Flax was on the beach in Oregon.

"What are we looking at, Tamarind?" President Jaspar asked.

"The equipment remaining on the Phosaster asteroid used the mining shaft as a sort of a cannon and has fired a projectile of mined metals on a ballistic trajectory toward the fragment of Apollyon C," Tamarind announced excitedly.

"Tamarind, did you know Phosaster had this capability?" the President asked.

"Not really. I programmed Phosaster nearly ten years ago to provide maximum value to the people of Earth. We hadn't worked out yet how we were going to get the material off the asteroid."

"What is that projectile made of?" President Jaspar asked. "Is it enough to make a difference?"

Tamarind replied, "Phosaster has mined a tremendous amount of material, mostly heavy metals, worth hundreds of billions of dollars. Evidently, Phosaster configured the mined materials into a ball or cylinder or canister and used the hole drilled in the asteroid as a cannon or rail gun. It will take me some time to figure it out."

General Ward asked the next question. "What is the mass of the bullet? What is its velocity, and is it on target to hit Apollyon C?"

"The payload of that Phosaster projectile must be a significant fraction of the remaining mass of Apollyon C. Two lasers have been chipping away at that chunk all day too. The velocity of the projectile looks nearly as fast as Apollyon, and it appears to be on an intercept trajectory from the images we're looking at."

While the world watched the spectacular fireworks as debris from Apollyon A and B entered the atmosphere, the President's Apollyon Response Team viewed the transmitted images of the Phosaster bullet charging toward Apollyon C. At one point, all on the link could hear Dr. Lewis in his deep voice, "C'mon, C'mon..." as if he could coax them to connect.

Flax was sitting with Almond on a log at the beach, looking down at the images. Occasionally Almond would tug his arm and point up to a spectacular display in the sky.

When the Phosaster bullet finally hit the target, the impact caused a flash that overwhelmed the images much as the nuclear explosions had earlier. There were cheers across the commlink, from the military leaders, Flax and Almond, the President, and NASA.

"Status on Apollyon C," President Jaspar demanded amidst the enthusiasm.

"It appears that the entire mass has been deflected in one piece and will miss Earth completely," Dr. John Lewis reported. It was one of the first times anyone had seen him smile since Apollyon was discovered, and he was grinning from ear to ear and giggling like a schoolgirl with tears in his eyes. Cheers erupted even louder among those watching.

"It would appear, General Ward, that your prayers were answered," said the President.

"Ours too," said Flax and Almond simultaneously.

In Tamarind's bunker, there was also a celebration. Cali threw her arms around him and said, "You saved us." Tamarind's ears silenced to the cheers, and his eyes closed to more images amidst her loving embrace.

After the cheers quieted, the President said to the entire response team, "The world owes you a debt of gratitude for your remarkable work these past weeks. Let me be the first to give you my thanks!" Tamarind disconnected his commlink and turned off his displays to continue their private celebration with relief and joy as he had never felt in his life.

* * *

Because they broke the secure commlink and had turned off the images, Tamarind and Cali missed the last gift from Phosaster. At the point of impact, both the Apollyon fragment and the Phosaster projectile had veered off from their trajectories like billiard balls, each remaining in one piece. They all knew that the Apollyon fragment had missed the Earth, but the surprise was with the Phosaster projectile.

It had ricocheted off Apollyon into a perfect orbit around the Earth.

CHAPTER 36

Aftermath

"We just fought the first battle in a galactic war, but all our people experienced was the aftermath of our victory. —President Laura Jaspar

Impact plus one day

There was jubilation around the planet as the last pieces of Apollyon fell to the Earth.

There were also many tears. Because General Ward and Tamarind Chase diverted the laser power of LightStar and Phosaster at Apollyon, many fragments of significant size that could have been destroyed hit the Earth, mostly in North America. There were media accusations that the government mismanaged the destruction of debris, expressed with heart-breaking pictures of local damage. However, the President's Apollyon Response Team knew that their decision to redirect the lasers and the unexpected projectile from Phosaster had saved the Earth.

In Atlanta, a college dorm was struck by a 1-meter diameter fragment, which burrowed through the entire building before exploding from the impact, starting the whole dormitory complex on fire. Nineteen students were killed, and 37 were injured. General Breckinpaw's son Mark was among the dead. Despite the crushing personal loss, the General continued managing the ground response.

A debris cloud of gravel-sized particles crashed into a Key West marina filled with partygoers watching the fireworks from their boats, sinking 18 yachts, killing 52 people, and injuring 69 others.

In Dallas, a skyscraper was severely damaged, but first responders had evacuated the building quickly when the alert was received, with minimal injuries.

The Minneapolis airport was pelted by basketball-sized debris, destroying 15 planes, starting fires in the terminal, and damaging the runway. Thirty people were killed. Dr. Lewis' daughter worked at the airport, and it was nearly 18 hours before he learned she was alive in a local hospital ICU with serious injuries.

A 40-meter diameter chunk struck on a farm in northern Saskatchewan, leveling everything in a 500-km radius. It was a low-density area, and the death toll was still unknown days later.

Despite his loss, General Breckinpaw continued to manage the aftermath in the US. For several days, there was hardly an area of the country where sirens could not be heard. Forest fires in a dozen States burned out of control, with further evacuations requiring National Guard redeployments. Power outages rolled through New England when a regional power plant was damaged, later tied to an EMP from one of the detonations in space.

The death toll kept rising, with damage reports coming in from every region, from the Arctic Circle to the equator. South America was the least affected; the kinetic weapons successfully destroyed the debris headed in their direction.

But the sirens faded, the emergencies deftly managed, and things quieted down. By the end of the two-week emergency deployment, all fires were under control, security restored, and situations contained. It would be years before reconstruction would rebuild all that was damaged, but for now, the world returned to a stunned peace.

General Breckinpaw had more difficulty containing the treasure hunters wanting a piece of Apollyon. Fragments were not easy to recover, as some had burrowed tens of meters into the ground. He sent out announcements that all meteoroids would be tested for radioactivity and collected as a matter of National Security. The Apollyon chunks were not radioactive, and he took some heat for that call. All the pieces recovered were transferred to NASA's research center, which also housed SETI, and were analyzed by Dr. Lewis's and Taro Search's teams. Thousands of kilograms were recovered in chunks from a few centimeters to tens of meters in diameter. Each fragment's weight was surprising; the material density being much denser than iron meteorites recovered previously.

The satellites which maneuvered into the asteroid's path were destroyed in what was now called the Apollyon Attack.

The Dronetech team completed the setup of DroneNet within hours of the end of the fallout. Their preparation and rapid implementation of DroneNet lessened the impact of the satellite losses to the world. However, there would be a significant effect on the world's economy in the coming years, exceeded only by the Space War. Cheers went up around the office as the DroneNet links went online, operating at nearly 100%. Flax spent hours walking around, shaking every person's hand in the facility.

Dark Matters Ventures' Phosaster and LightStar's lasers were already working on cleaning up the new batch of space debris, which thankfully was less than anticipated.

* * *

With the immediate threat passed, the President called a special meeting to discuss the alien attack. She asked Taro Search, Miles Madison, General Breckinpaw, General Ward, and Dr. John Lewis to join her in the Situation Room. At the last minute, she also asked Tamarind Chase and Flax Venture to join them through their commlinks.

"Tell us your theories about these aliens, John," the President asked.

Dr. Lewis summarized the details NASA had gleaned so far regarding the alien planet and what they'd inferred about their technology.

Displaying images of their possible propulsion methods, he showed how they split Apollyon into three spheres traveling in the same direction. Animated simulations detailed the flight path, demonstrating each propulsion stage of Apollyon's flight from the Proxima Centauri system.

He proceeded to explain possible reasons for the attack and what the Proximans might do next. "Either they responded to the first TV signals from over a century ago, or, more likely, to Taro's message sent nearly twenty-one years ago." He finished with a startling conclusion. "My team believes that the Proximans did not intend Apollyon as an attack, but rather an invitation to communicate. Whether that is true or not, another action is probably many years in the future as they await our response."

President Jaspar was briefed on this information before the meeting, but most of the other people in the room were hearing it for the first time.

"Not an attack? It took the combined resources of our planet to defend ourselves, and many people died," General Breckinpaw spoke with indignation, and all in the room were aware of his personal loss in the tragedy.

General Ward was more circumspect. "You think this was just an introduction, like a first skirmish to test our mettle and bring us to the negotiating table?" She rubbed her chin like she was considering that with the grudging respect of a strategic military commander. "Interesting."

Taro Search couldn't help himself. "This was an amazing invitation. I think they intended Apollyon as three gifts and are inviting us to respond. Think of the potential, the opportunity, the technology. For the first time, we know we are not alone in the universe and that it is possible to travel interstellar distances and even engage in trade. We must learn all we can from Apollyon about the Proximans and respond appropriately. Our world will never be the same!"

President Jaspar wanted to act on this information immediately. "General Ward, Dr. Lewis, Director Search, I'd like you to put together a team for a top-secret interagency task force. It will be to conduct the research, analyze the fragments, develop the weapons, develop the space-ships, and prepare our response to these Proximans. Include everyone who knows about Apollyon's alien origins on the team and vet them for TS security clearance. That includes everyone in this room as advisors or direct contributors to this team."

"They will be back, and this time we'll be prepared," President Jaspar stated. Then directing her comment to Taro, Flax, and Tamarind, she said, "We're going to need to send a team from Earth to be our ambassadors. Where can we find a competent leader who will be acceptable to represent all the Earth's peoples? One of you Pan-Nationals, perhaps?" She didn't expect an immediate response, but the seed had been planted.

Her next comment was to Tamarind, "You'll have to give us the specs for that asteroid rail gun for when they come," and then added with a smile, "for a reasonable price, of course."

Tamarind smiled and nodded in affirmation. "Dark Matter Ventures does not make weapons, but we love playing space billiards." There was an uncomfortable laugh as the military personnel looked to the President for approval.

The formal meeting ended, but the room was abuzz with discussion on the information. Dr. Lewis, Miles Madison, and Taro Search were surrounded by the others, asking questions, drilling down on details, questioning assumptions.

As Tamarind watched remotely, he could see that Miles Madison was likely to be tapped to lead the research into the Proximans. He felt a swell of pride for Taro Search: he had done it. After decades of planning, his friend had made the first contact with an alien species, and it would change the world forever.

CHAPTER 37

Epilogue

"In the greatest battle of our time, Earth stood together. After the battle, we are still standing... together. Much was lost today, but if we continue working together, perhaps more has been gained."
— President Laura Jaspar, speech to the UN General Assembly

Impact plus three weeks

The DroneTech executive team, Flax Venture, Aislinn O'Malley, and Mike Stapleton, were all invited to the White House, along with the entire Swarm Team—Telsun, Jimmy, Cecilia, and Ardwana.

Dark Matter Ventures sent Tamarind, Stacy Norton, and Paul Moncrief, though indeed others could have been honored as well. Calisandra Spencer was the sole representative from Galactic Marketing. General Corey Breckinpaw from Joint Command and General Sharon Ward from Space Command were there in complete formal dress uniforms. Dr. John Lewis and Miles Madison came from NASA and Director Taro Search from SETI, the latter two looking uncomfortable in dark suits. They had not all met in person and weren't all read in completely, but each played a critical part in saving the planet.

The Yellow Oval Room was on the White House's second floor, which led out to the Balcony room that looked across the lawn toward the

Washington Monument. The room, part of the President's residence and used for small gatherings, had a crystal chandelier in the oval's center and decorated with Federal-style furniture. A podium with the Presidential seal was positioned on a raised platform at one end of the room. The event was being televised nationally, including the invited attendees gathered for the occasion on the White House lawn. Almond was present with the other spouses who were not directly involved in the Apollyon response but had had their own supporting roles to play.

President Jaspar greeted each of the honorees and then addressed the group, "Thank you all for coming. Without each of your brave and selfless efforts, we would not be here today. The planet united to defend ourselves from Apollyon, and you formed the front lines of that response. Today we acknowledge your courage, your competence, your creativity, and your heroism." She motioned first for General Breckinpaw and General Ward to step forward.

The President ceremoniously and personally pinned medals on their uniforms and made personal comments about their meritorious contributions to peace and stability during a global conflict. For General Breckinpaw, she noted, "You courageously stayed at your post even when informed that your son, Mark Breckinpaw, had been killed by one of the fragments. We have established the Mark Breckinpaw scholarship to honor him." His jaw clenched at this, but he remained at attention while she pinned the Medal of Honor on his chest.

She gave General Ward a special honor, the first-ever Space Command Medal of Honor. It was a rare historical moment, a female Commander in Chief granting a Medal of Honor to the first woman General of Space Command. She drew the moment out, acknowledging its significance. Together they posed with the other military awardees for a photograph.

"I'd like the DroneTech, Dark Matter Ventures, Galactic Marketing, NASA, and SETI civilians to step forward." It was a large group. President Jaspar beamed at them proudly.

Each of them stepped forward individually. The President stated their unique contribution to averting the crises, shook their hands, and gave each of them the Presidential Citizen Medal. She then posed for a photo before they left the podium. When she placed the medal on Taro Search, she winked at him knowingly.

She did not call Flax and Tamarind forward for this award.

Finally, the President asked the CEOs of DroneTech and Dark Matter Ventures to come out on the White House's balcony at the end of the room and have the others join them. There, before the media and a crowd of many thousands, with the awardees at her back, the President spoke.

"People of a united planet Earth. We have survived the greatest danger and the worst catastrophe to ever endanger our planet. We did not shrink in fear or squabble between ourselves as we have so many times before. In unity, the world's countries and greatest minds in science and industry worked together, and it was only through cooperation that we stand here today. If we could capture this moment and use this newly found wisdom and unity, we could solve any world problem and propel ourselves into a new generation benefitting from the fruitfulness of our world and the infinite majesty and mystery of space."

"Today, we celebrate these behind me, heroes all, whose brilliance, competence, and courage led us through this crisis. I would like to end by drawing attention to the singularly significant contributions of these two civilian leaders—Tamarind Chase and Flax Venture."

"It is my great honor to grant you the Presidential Medal of Freedom. It is the highest honor granted in this country to civilians. Mr. Venture and Mr. Chase, as Pan-Nationals, you chose to make the United States your home. Flax Venture, your Swarm Team, was the first to warn us of Apollyon, giving us the time to organize a response, and your DroneNet kept global communications operational during this crisis. Thank you on behalf of our country and the world." She placed the medal on a long red and white striped ribbon around his neck.

"Tamarind Chase, your LightStar and Phosaster missions provided us with critical information on Apollyon, and your work with our government enabled us to destroy Apollyon and the many fragments in time. Thank you on behalf of our country and the world." She placed the medal on a long red and white striped ribbon around his neck.

"These civilian leaders have made our world safe by their inventions, their leadership, and their heroic efforts in this crisis." President Jaspar ceremoniously gave each of them a long hug and held both of their hands. Bringing them forward to the balcony's edge, she raised her arms, holding theirs before the audience. The crowds cheered both on the White House lawn and in the crowds gathered in the National Mall as far as the Washington Monument. She allowed the moment to linger for an awkward amount of time until they both got embarrassed by the attention.

Then she turned back into the Yellow Oval Room with the rest of the awardees and said, "Let's have some champagne!" Everyone relaxed a little after the formal ceremony. Soon laughter and animated conversations filled the room. The President mingled, greeting people and making jokes or asking awkward personal questions like only the Commander in Chief could.

When she got to Jimmy and Cecilia, she noticed that they had their pinky fingers discreetly interlocked. "Are you two planning to get married?" she asked, inquisitively.

Jimmy blushed and said, "Yes, er, hopefully?" looking sheepishly at Cecilia.

"News to me," Cecilia said. Those around them laughed. Jimmy turned a brighter shade of red and looked down at his shoes.

"*Carpe diem,* Dr. Calhoun," the President said, patting him firmly on the shoulder.

When she circled to the team from Dark Matter Ventures, she walked up behind Tamarind while he was enthusiastically telling a story. He saw everyone was looking over his shoulder at the President and abruptly stopped talking. Then with a grin on her face, President Jaspar put a hand on Tamarind's shoulder and asked with feigned disapproval in her voice, "Tell me, Tamarind, how did that large object of asteroid-mined precious metals get into orbit around our planet without the necessary approvals?"

"Bank shot?" Tamarind said, shrugging his shoulders with an impish grin. All within earshot laughed. It was the first time they had felt the freedom to laugh in a long time.

The President pulled Tamarind aside and said, "Tamarind, I know your company sacrificed billions of dollars' worth of asteroids to the companies who supplied rockets to your contest, which helped to save our planet. A medal doesn't seem like enough, is there anything we can do to repay you?"

"There is something..." They turned away from the group and spoke quietly for several minutes, and then shook hands in agreement.

* * *

After the White House award ceremony, the small group of Pan-Nationals caught an international flight from DC to New Zealand, a helicopter flight to a neighboring island, and a boat to Hope Island in the Kermadec island group, and finally arrived at the PNLI. Flax, Almond, Tamarind, and Taro were provided accommodations in one of the little huts where they grew up. A special meeting was scheduled the next morning, where they were to be honored before the founders and teachers of the Institute.

Professor Lambardi, one of the founders and now Professor Emeritus, had asked to lead this special presentation. Hosted in the Founders' Board Room at the Institute, they took their seats at one end of the long conference table and admired the art and photos on the walls around the room, all about the school. As the Professor slowly stood, everyone in the room said, "ERIWA!"

"When we established the Institute, we challenged our students to aspire to five accomplishments in their lives, ERIWA. The first, Exploration, each completed here before they finished their studies at the Institute by discovering their life mission. Second, they had to become Relevant, achieving respect and significance in their chosen profession by accomplishing something useful and relevant to the world. Third, we encouraged them to make an Impact on their chosen global challenge. The last two achievements no students have yet been awarded, the Wisdom and Altruism awards.

Professor Lambardi first walked down the side of the table to Taro, who stood up. "Taro Search, you know I have questioned your search and your methods of reaching out to extra-terrestrials. While we don't know exactly what you have found, we infer from your Presidential Citizen Award that your work has recently become Relevant, a significant achievement. I suspect we will be giving you an Impact award soon?" Taro was honored by the recognition but flustered by the question, so he thanked him and sat down. He couldn't tell them anything about the aliens, but several of them congratulated him and looked at him with a knowing look.

"Flax and Almond, please stand together. Almond, you had the distinction of being the first of our students to achieve Impact recognition. Flax Venture, for your significant work at DroneTech, which has been Relevant for many years, the timely detection of Apollyon by your SWARMNET, and the rapid installation of the DroneNet that has kept the world connected, you have made an Impact. Congratulations!" Then with a nod to Almond, he said, "Perhaps this will restore some equality in your marriage?" Everyone laughed.

"Tamarind Chase, please stand. As you know, I've had misgivings about you. Your brilliance and boldness still seem to rule over your wisdom and humility, but perhaps you still have time to develop those, I think?" He paused to let that comment sink in. "Your work on LightStar and achieving your long-held dream of asteroid mining with Phosaster almost pale in comparison to your role in defending our planet from Apollyon. None of us have any doubt that you have achieved an Impact Award. In fact, you have very much put the 'I' in ERIWA," Again, everyone laughed at his little inside joke.

"Finally, I would like to announce one other Impact Award, posthumously. Dr. Kohlrabi Trust was respected by us all, a leader of phenomenal abilities and mathematical aptitude. His final words from Moonbase Verity helped the world, and each of you prepare for this day." They all nodded with the wisdom and fairness of that assessment.

"Flax and Tamarind, your Impact accomplishments and Kohlrabi's will be added to Almond's in the curriculum of all future PNLI graduates. They will learn and be challenged by your brilliant and bold choices, setting a high standard for others who strive to achieve an Impact Award. ERIWA!" Professor Lambardi said, and everyone in the room replied, "ERIWA!"

The founders came around and shook each of their hands, affirming them individually and asking about their work and accomplishments.

Since the founders had invested significantly in Phosaster, they came to Tamarind and asked for details. "How exactly did you get the cylinder of mined materials in orbit?" one of them asked, appreciatively.

"To be honest, I'm still trying to figure that out. Somehow I programmed Phosaster to be smarter than I am."

"That almost sounded like humility," said Professor Lambardi. "Almost."

"We still have much work to do to figure out how to get those materials from orbit to the Earth," Tamarind said seriously, summarizing the future actions of the Phosaster project to his investors.

"We look forward to your creative solution, Tamarind," Karl Oakley said, patting him on his back.

As the ceremony wound down, Professor Lambardi came to Flax, Almond, and Tamarind with three memory cubes in his hand. "To get you started on your Wisdom award, we decided to give you all the information that we have about you from the moment when you came to us. We believe that wisdom begins with understanding yourself. Please do not open it until you are ready to engage in the process fully. What you see inside might be shocking and disturbing to you. Before you leave, we'd also like you to each give talks to the students."

Tamarind made light of it as usual. "We save the world, and he still gives us homework." They all laughed.

They thanked the founders and teachers and walked together out the door, meandering down the palm-lined paths near the beach. The warm breeze blowing through the jungle, the sweet scent of the tropical flowers, and the moon reflecting off the gentle waves on the shore brought back so many positive memories of their time at PNLI, living on this island. For a while, they meandered along, silently lost in their thoughts.

Taro finally said, pointing up at the stars, "I think the course of my future is set. I have to be on the team studying the aliens."

"Taro Search, alien hunter," Flax joked.

"Are you guys excited to explore your histories?" Taro asked, the only one who didn't receive a memory cube about his past.

Flax answered, "I am. I've always wondered where I'm from. Perhaps I have relatives still alive. Wouldn't that be interesting?"

"I know who my family is, and all of them are right here. I think I already know what is in the memory cube, and I'm not excited about it, at least not for myself." Then Almond surprised them, "I'm glad you three finally caught up with me a bit with your awards tonight. However, I do have an announcement of my own that I don't expect any of you will ever achieve." When she had their full attention, she announced, "Flax and I are pregnant!"

After hugs and kisses all around, Tamarind said, "Congratulations, you two! Does that mean I'm going to be an uncle?"

Flax's announcement right after that was a bombshell. "I think I will take the President up on her offer to lead the team to Proxima b. I've done all I can at DroneTech and need a challenge of this magnitude."

Almond hit him on the chest, "What? I announce we're pregnant, and you say you are leaving the solar system? I don't think so, mister."

Tamarind could tell by looking at them both that the discussion was not over.

Almond faced Tamarind. "What is next for Tamarind Chase? The search for wisdom? Asteroid hunter? Husband, perhaps?" She spoke the last question slowly and with meaning and smiled as if expecting a confession.

"I don't think I'll look at my memory cube until after I get back," Tamarind said.

"From where?" Almond asked.

"I do have something to announce. I've negotiated with President Jaspar to lease me the rights to Moonbase Verity." He held up one thumb and used it to block out the moon with one eye closed. They all patted him on the back enthusiastically.

"I also have a confession," he added, and Almond and Flax looked at him excitedly, "I just hired your system engineer, Telsun, to go with me." They all laughed at this and then looked up with him at the moon's silvery light amidst the milky cloud of stars. "I've got a promise to keep to an old friend."

NOTES FROM THE AUTHOR ON THE SCIENCE AND TECHNOLOGY IN IMPACT.

• Near-Earth orbit is full of a significant amount of debris. Pieces larger than 10cm are tracked from Earth, and the International Space Station (ISS) occasionally gets hit by or must avoid space debris. NASA reports more than 500,000 fragments are monitored. Two satellites have collided, and one was destroyed by debris. Most have likely been hit but not destroyed.

• With the growth in commercial launches into space, the problem of space debris is projected to become much worse.

• Various techniques have been considered for destroying the debris, including a laser cannon fired from Earth.

• Tamarind's NetZero Shoebox home with no outside pipes or cables is nearing practical reality. As homes begin generating and storing their electricity, and appliances and materials become more energy-efficient, energy neutrality becomes possible. Thermionic energy conversion and waste conversion to recycle water and convert waste into energy are in development.

• The number of organizations and governments capable of launching objects into space is rapidly growing. Eleven countries and many dozens of companies are engaged in today's space race, developing propulsion systems, planning for asteroid mining, space tourism, transport, etc.

- Low Earth Orbit Satellites have been proposed to replace ground-based cables for internet connections. At the time of writing, several companies were competing to get tens of thousands of small satellites into orbit.

- The instantaneous connection of quantum entangled particles has been demonstrated. Such a link would be ultra-secure. Recent research has shown the exchange of information via quantum communications. Impact proposes using entanglement to verify the source of the signals, but not to transfer data.

- Thorium reactors are possible and have practical advantages for generating power in space.

- The Global Orphan Crisis is, unfortunately, very real. UNICEF has recorded that the number of children who have lost one or both parents exceeds 140 million globally and continues to grow in part due to the AIDS crisis in Africa. Global pandemics significantly increase the number of orphans when they occur.

- The anticipated shortage of rare Earth metals needed for the advanced technologies we use today is rapidly approaching. Our existing supplies of these metals are environmentally damaging to mine or are in countries that are not friendly trading partners.

- The estimated value on Earth of the materials in asteroids is significant. Various estimates of 1 km and 2 km objects are $200 billion to $20 trillion. For some, the rare Earth metals in a single asteroid would exceed all the material ever mined of that metal in Earth's history. The exact composition of asteroids is unknown, and the technology to survey, mine, and return the materials to Earth is in the early stages of development. At the time of writing, both NASA and Japan had just successfully touched down on a comet and will return with material collected from the surface.

- Drone swarms for entertainment have been demonstrated, including the 1000 drones in the opening games of the 2018 Olympics.

- Geodesic domes have one significant challenge to be practical. Most building materials are produced in high volume in flat sheets. Right triangles don't fully utilize the sheets, so some of the material is wasted. The second problem is that they are hard to design and build. Significant work has been done to simplify the problem.

- Electromagnetic stimulation of muscles has been used for medical purposes for decades. The potential to link VR headsets to EM suits has been proposed. It is conceivable that strength could be gained and skills developed while essentially playing a video game.

- There are a growing number of international space treaties covering war, nuclear power, colonization, and asteroid ownership and mining in space.

- While most comets travel at much slower speeds than Apollyon, the velocity proposed is not without precedent. The Great Comet of 1843 passed close to the Sun, traveled at 570 km/s, and survived perihelion. That comet had a period of 600-800 years, so it is conceivable that a new object in orbit could appear without previous detection.

- Proxima Centauri is the closest star to our own, and it has a planet, Proxima b, in the "habitable zone" in its distance from their Sun, and some have suggested oceans and atmosphere are possible on it. Several space missions have been proposed to explore it.

- The first TV signals that could have been detected from space were from the 1936 Olympics, and they would have traveled more than 100 light-years by the time of our story. However, since a radio signal decreases with the square of the distance from Earth, it could not be a very strong signal even at the closest planet. A powerful enough laser of an ideal frequency could reach another world and have enough intensity to be detected.

• Coronal Mass Ejections (CMEs) can have a significant impact if directed at Earth. Even glancing blows can cause high-frequency radio blackouts, damage satellites, and affect GPS navigation.

• The impact effects of an object hitting Earth has been extensively studied. An analytical tool for estimating the impact of an object hitting the Earth is available on the Perdue website.

• Mass drivers and rail guns are in the early stages of development for kinetic weapons and potentially for powering spacecraft to achieve velocities greater than currently possible with chemical rockets.

—